# Rough
# Winds

*Best Wishes*
*To John*

*Desmond Fitzgerald*

Desmond Fitzgerald

© Desmond Fitzgerald 2004
*Rough Winds*

ISBN 0-9548534-0-7


Published by
Dehra Press
2 Foxhill Avenue
Weetwood
Leeds
LS16 5PB

Design & production co-ordinated by:
The Better Book Company Ltd
Havant
Hampshire
PO9 2XH

Printed in England.

Cover design by MusicPrint, Chichester

# GLOSSARY

| | | |
|---|---|---|
| Ab khutam hogia | = | Now it is finished |
| Ayah | = | Children's nurse |
| Burra | = | Big |
| Chaukadar | = | Guard |
| Choli | = | Blouse |
| Chota hazri | = | Small, early breakfast |
| Dhobi | = | Washerman |
| Gharry | = | Horse-drawn carriage |
| Godown | = | Warehouse |
| Hakim | = | Indian doctor |
| Izzat | = | Honour, pride |
| Jai Ram | = | Hindu greeting |
| Jaziya | = | Head tax |
| Lathi | = | Stave |
| Mahout | = | Elephant driver |
| Memsahib | = | Adult European lady |
| Mufti | = | Civilian clothes |
| Nautch | = | Dance |
| Pice | = | Small coin, 1/100th of rupee |
| Pilau | = | Spiced rice dish |
| Punkah wallah | = | Servant used to work mechanical fan |
| Ram Ram | = | Hindu greeting |
| Sahiba | = | Name given to female European as mark of respect |
| Serai | = | Slang word for earthenware vessel |
| Sirdarji | = | High ranking army officer |
| Syce | = | Groom |
| Tamasha | = | Celebration |
| Tiffin | = | Lunch |
| Tonga | = | Two-wheeled carriage |

# THE FAIRBROTHER FAMILY

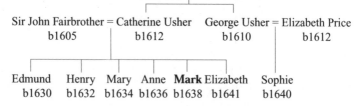

Sir John Fairbrother = Catherine Usher    George Usher = Elizabeth Price
b1605          b1612           b1610         b1612

| Edmund | Henry | Mary | Anne | **Mark** | Elizabeth | Sophie |
|--------|-------|------|------|----------|-----------|--------|
| b1630 | b1632 | b1634 | b1636 | b1638 | b1641 | b1640 |

# THE TRENT FAMILY

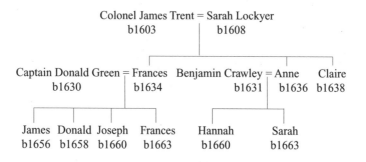

Colonel James Trent = Sarah Lockyer
b1603        b1608

Captain Donald Green = Frances    Benjamin Crawley = Anne    Claire
b1630          b1634           b1631    b1636   b1638

| James | Donald | Joseph | Frances | Hannah | Sarah |
|-------|--------|--------|---------|--------|-------|
| b1656 | b1658 | b1660 | b1663 | b1660 | b1663 |

Roland Lockyer (Cousin of Sarah Lockyer) b 1625

**Ruth Parker** (Ward of Colonel James Trent) b 1644

# 1

## MAY 1658

Ruth felt a slight feeling of alarm as she glanced at the six-foot gap in the privet hedge. She did not recognise the tall, rather thin, young man who was standing there about twenty feet away. He looked about nineteen or twenty years of age and wore the brown leather breeches usually worn by soldiers. The rest of his clothes were rather more elaborate than those of the people she knew. When Ruth saw that the expression on his face was not particularly friendly, she blushed and lowered her eyes. After a moment's hesitation, Ruth began to walk slowly along the path through the small, enclosed, formal garden back to the house. As she skirted round the fountain in the centre of the garden, the stranger took a step forward towards her. He removed his wide-brimmed hat by way of greeting, showing a head of long, dark, curly hair.

'This is the family's private garden,' he told her. 'Do you live here?'

'Yes, sir.'

'One of Colonel Trent's daughters, young mistress?'

'I live with his family.'

Ruth thought his face softened a little at her answer. He would be quite handsome if only his hair was shorter.

'I didn't question your being here.' The stranger bowed slightly and smiled for the first time. 'May I detain you for a little longer.' He waited for an answer but none came. 'I have heard nothing but Dutch, German and Swedish voices for the past three years.' His cheeks reddened and he looked at his feet. 'The sound of the voice of an English lass. Well. I…I… It refreshes the spirit.'

Ruth did not know how to reply. She had been studying hard that morning and had decided to get half an hour's fresh air before resuming her studies. The gardens were at their best on this perfect May afternoon, making her feel relaxed until she met this stranger.

'Your pardon, sir,' Ruth said. 'I must go back to the house to resume my work.' She knew the stable clock would soon be striking, signalling that her half hour's rest was at an end. Ruth could see the young man clench his fists.

'This upside-down world is a curious place.' He bit his lower lip for two or three seconds. 'Now a gentleman may not talk to a kitchen maid. I won't detain you against your will. I'm sure you have plenty to do elsewhere.'

Ruth flushed. How dare he take it for granted that she was one of the servants? She was tall for her fourteen years and drew herself up to her full height. The stranger's abrupt dismissal annoyed her. She tossed her waist-length, fair, curly hair back and looked at him with cold, clear, blue eyes.

'Do you live near here?' she asked.

'My mother lives nearby.'

'Then you ought to know I am Ruth Parker, Colonel Trent's ward.'

'My apologies, Mistress. I didn't know.'

Ruth felt herself becoming a little irritated. She turned to face him squarely. 'Perhaps your mother does live nearby but what right have you to be in the family's private garden?'

There was a long pause before the young man replied. Ruth was surprised to see a wistful expression cross his face. 'You ask about my right. I used to live here. I am Mark Fairbrother.'

'Are you the son of the widow who lives in the steward's lodge?'

'Yes. Her youngest son.'

Ruth remembered hearing that the previous owner of Aireton Hall had been killed fighting for Charles I while his eldest son had died of wounds after the battle of Worcester. She had been told that the two surviving boys followed the King's son into exile.

'I am sorry you had to leave your home, Master Fairbrother,' Ruth said softly. 'I have lived here with the Trent family for six years but I was only a child when I came.'

'Why should you be sorry?' Mark shrugged his shoulders. 'My family were on the opposite side to your guardian during the rebellion.' Ruth was beginning to feel her previous irritation turn to annoyance. There were thousands of former royalists in the same position as Mark Fairbrother. Surely he knew her own father had been killed while serving with the parliamentary army. Why should she feel guilty because she was living in his old home?

'I must go back,' she replied. 'Shall I tell Mistress Trent you are coming to the house, Master Fairbrother?'

He smiled wryly. 'Don't think that's wise.'

'Then why are you here?'

'In God's name,' Mark replied sharply, 'may not a man visit his mother's house and look at his old home?'

Mark took a step or two forward and Ruth became suddenly aware of how close he was to her. 'Sorry. I shouldn't have taken you to task,' he continued quietly. 'It's not your fault I've a touch of melancholy. After a year's campaigning with the Swedish army, fighting against the Danes, one gets a little tetchy at times.'

'Are you home for good now?' Ruth asked.

Mark gave a short laugh but there was no amusement in it. 'Not with Old Nod as England's Lord Protector. Anyway, I've a commission in the Swedish Army. This peace with Denmark won't last long and then I'll be back on full pay again.' Ruth felt a tinge of regret at the thought of the danger likely to face this man she had known for so short a time.

'Why not stay in England?' she asked. 'I've heard my father speak of indemnities for supporters of Charles Stuart. If your family pays the fine for any harm done to the Commonwealth, cannot the lands be restored to them?'

'I've no money. Even if I had, brother Henry wouldn't let me pay the fine. What would you have me do in the meantime?

Become a tenant farmer? How would I pay the rent?'

Mark's grey eyes suddenly filled with anger. For a moment, Ruth thought he would shout at her. The clock over the stables struck two, breaking the tension. Mark turned away and started to move off.

'John Milton wrote "Peace hath her victories no less renowned than war",' Ruth called after him.

Mark stopped. He turned round slowly and moved towards her, a surprised look on his face. This vanished quickly, to be replaced by a cool stare.

'So you can read?' he asked. 'And poetry as well?'

'The same tutor who instructed Colonel Trent's daughters teaches me Latin, to read the Bible and my catechism, and allows me also to read English poems.'

'I couldn't go to University,' Mark told her. He studied her closely. 'Do you think one of your Commonwealth grandees will marry you?' he asked. 'One of those Puritans who did so well as army contractors during the rebellion?' Ruth began to cry. She started to move towards the steps which led up to the terrace at the back of the house. This seemed to annoy Mark even more. He moved quickly to the gap in the hedge and stood in her way. His eyes were bright with the hatred he had suppressed all his young life.

'You and I are birds of a feather,' Mark said. 'You may have been brought up as a Puritan gentlewoman but you have no family, no money, no dowry, no land and no title. My family's been dispossessed of our money and our land so that I'm now no more a gentleman than you're a lady. That's why I serve Charles the Tenth of Sweden. Perhaps I can win with my sword the position in life which you, your adopted family and your Commonwealth have taken from me.'

He brushed passed her abruptly and was gone before she could answer. Ruth sobbed and ran quickly up the steps and into the door at the rear of Aireton Hall.

\* \* \* \* \*

There was a knock on the door of Ruth's room and she hurried across to open it. The small, grey-haired woman she had regarded as her mother during the past nine years stood there. Sarah Trent looked anxiously at Ruth, then at her daughter Claire and back at Ruth again. She told them her husband was sending for Mark Fairbrother and had expressed the hope that an hour or two in the village stocks would improve his manners.

'I hope he is not too hard on him,' Ruth said. 'He's very young. He had to leave his own country and home when he was a boy and be in danger in a foreign land.'

'Don't feel sorry for Master Fairbrother,' Claire told her. 'You're too young to understand. Let me tell you, if people like him ever regain power in England, they'll bring their Papist ideas back from Europe with them. We won't be allowed to worship Lord Jesus Christ in our own way.'

'You shouldn't upset Ruth, Claire,' her mother said. 'Do you feel like going to see Father now, Ruth?'

'Yes, of course, Mother.' Ruth kissed her foster-mother on the cheek and smiled. 'I was just a silly girl to cry.'

Ruth went through the bedroom door and walked slowly down the staircase. The room which Colonel Trent used as his office was on the first floor, at the end of the long gallery. She and her foster-sisters had always been told to stay outside the room because Colonel Trent kept dispatches from the Major-General, who was his superior officer, in there. The State papers which the colonel sometimes received were also locked in his room.

Ruth's feelings as she approached the door of the long gallery were a mixture of curiosity and trepidation. She glanced at the walls of the gallery as she walked through. There were portraits of Fairbrothers who had lived during the previous hundred and fifty years, painted by Italian masters. The most recent one was of Sir John, Mark's father, painted by the young Dutchman, Peter Lely, just before the outbreak of the civil war. Ruth wondered what the Fairbrothers' ancestors would think of her. She slowed down the nearer she approached Colonel Trent's office and was a little surprised to find the door already ajar. It was obvious that her foster-father was expecting her. Ruth peered round the door. Colonel Trent was sitting at his writing cabinet studying some papers. He had removed the helmet and breastplate which he always wore on official business and had hung his sword on a hook on the wall. His bright red soldier's tunic contrasted sharply with the close-cropped, iron-grey hair on his head and his grey moustache. Ruth thought he looked tired and a wave of affection swept over her for this kindly, elderly man who had taken the place of her father. Colonel Trent stood up and said, 'Come in, Ruth.'

He moved round and held out a chair for her to sit on. Ruth noticed that he limped slightly as he went back to his seat. This was caused by an old wound playing him up and was always a sign of his being tired. She became aware that the scar over his left eye was a dull red. This was another memento of some long-forgotten battle and always became red when her foster-father was angry. 'Your mother tells me Mark Fairbrother's home from the wars and that he insulted you.'

'He was angry, Father.'

'Why not tell me what happened?'

Ruth described the incident in which she had been involved. On going through it again she realised that she no longer felt angry with the young man. Her anger had been replaced by pity. This charitable feeling was not felt or shared by Colonel Trent. He bristled as she came to the end of her story.

'Young puppy,' he barked. 'He'd no cause to be offensive to you or be in the grounds without permission. I've a good mind to have him whipped or put him in the stocks.'

'Oh! No, Father. Not on my account.'

'Perhaps you're right Ruth. But this young cavalier will get the dressing down he deserves.'

Ruth breathed out slowly as Colonel Trent continued.

'I don't want to make a public spectacle of him. There are still a few unconverted royalists in the district who might make a demonstration if I put him in the stocks. I've never used my troops or the local militia to maintain order and don't want to start now.' Colonel Trent thought carefully for a few seconds. 'I'll send Captain Benton to Lady Catherine's place, ordering this fine fellow to come to see me at ten o'clock tomorrow morning. You stay in the house as well, Ruth.'

\* \* \* \* \*

The next morning saw Ruth sitting on a chair halfway down the long gallery. She heard the clock over the stables strike ten o'clock and simultaneously Mark came through the door, escorted by Captain Benton, Colonel Trent's adjutant. Ruth noticed that Mark was wearing a large, white, lace collar and was dressed in brightly coloured clothes, similar to those worn by supporters of the old king. They were such a contrast to the simple, plain clothes worn by Ruth and all the people she knew. Captain Benton was wearing the helmet and breastplate which he always wore when accompanying Colonel Trent on his duties in the garrison and surrounding areas.

Ruth rose from her chair when the two men approached. Captain Benton saluted her and said, 'Good day, Mistress Ruth.'

Mark bowed slightly as she replied, 'Good day, gentlemen.' When she caught his eyes she thought he looked like a lamb being led to the slaughter. Ruth sat down again as Mark and the adjutant stopped outside the colonel's office. Captain Benton knocked on the door and the two men went inside.

Ruth let her eyes roam idly over the pictures in the gallery for a minute or two. She had always thought the Fairbrothers looked a stern, forbidding lot. Her eyes rested at last on a picture of Adam and Eve in the Garden of Eden. The two figures were shown as completely naked and in a state of complete innocence, before the temptation of the serpent. It seemed a curious choice to hang there. A few other paintings of religious subjects were also on the walls but all the other pictures in the long gallery were severe, humourless, family portraits. She had been told that Sir John Fairbrother, Mark's father, brought the Adam and Eve back to Aireton Hall as a young man, following a visit to Europe. Ruth wondered what Sir John had been like as a man. Her train of thought was interrupted by the sound of footsteps. Ruth turned and saw Claire coming towards her. She put her fingers to her lips and her foster-sister slowed down. When Claire stopped she asked Ruth to help with her crochet, telling her that she had spoiled the pattern and would have to unpick the thread. Ruth was an excellent needlewoman. She was often asked to help Claire out and had never had the heart to refuse before today.

'Father told me to stay,' Ruth told her. 'I can't come now.'

'Don't be silly. He said stay in the house. He didn't say sit here, rooted to the spot like a some young oak tree.'

Reluctantly, Ruth allowed herself to be persuaded. Within a minute or so the two girls were laughing together in the drawing room. All thoughts of Mark Fairbrother and his family were temporarily banished.

\* \* \* \* \*

When Captain Benton and Mark stopped outside Colonel Trent's office the adjutant's sharp knock on the door was answered by a crisp, 'Come in.' The colonel's adjutant opened the door and saluted as he stepped inside. Mark followed him a second or two later.

'Thank you, Captain Benton. Please sit down,' Colonel Trent ordered, giving Mark no more than a cursory glance. Mark looked round for another chair only to find there were just two chairs in the room. He did not realise that the colonel had given orders for all but two of the chairs to be removed, with instructions that they should be replaced later that day. Captain Benton appeared completely at ease while Colonel Trent finished reading some papers. Mark felt somewhat at a disadvantage in front of these men who had taken over his home. He was determined, however, to restrain himself and remained perfectly still. Colonel Trent looked up at last. 'You were in the grounds of Aireton Hall yesterday afternoon. Walking in the private garden. Did you ask permission? From Captain Benton or my wife?'

'I didn't think I needed permission. I'm here on a very short visit to my mother. In ten days' time I'll be on my way to Hull.'

'To take service again under Charles the Tenth of Sweden, I presume.'

'Yes, colonel.'

'The last news we had of the Swedish army's campaign in Denmark, they had plundered their way right across Jutland. Just like the army of Charles Stuart. Moving like locusts through the English countryside. An army of marauders, paying nothing for their food and lodging.'

'I can't be held responsible for that, colonel. And the right to walk through the grounds of the house where I was born seems a small favour for a gentleman to ask.'

'A gentleman does not need to mend his manners. Especially in the presence of a lady.'

'I apologise, sir. I didn't know Ruth Parker lived in Aireton Hall.'

'That's no excuse!' Colonel Trent barked. 'If you were a gentleman, you would always treat a lady with courtesy, be she milkmaid or marchioness.'

'I can only say I was moved by emotion, seeing my old home on my return from abroad. I felt tears in my eyes as I saw this strange girl in the private garden where my sister, my brothers and I used to play in happier times. No offence was meant. I didn't realise Mistress Parker was under your protection.'

'Ruth has been brought up as a daughter of mine, as your mother will tell you,' Colonel Trent snapped angrily. 'She has lived with my family since her mother died of typhoid, soon after her father was killed at the battle of Preston. Ruth's father saved my life at the battle of Naseby. Every day I live is a debt of honour to her I can never repay. You offend her and you offend me. And I'll have you out of my district quicker than you can say 'Charles Stuart'. Ruth is not one of your Swedish or German trollops in the Swedish army's baggage train.'

Mark stook rigidly. His voice was trembling as he replied. 'I'm no harlot chaser, sir. I laid not a finger on your foster-daughter. Nor do I intend to harm her in any way. My feeling now is of remorse. Please accept my apologies.'

'The only restitution which will satisfy me is to hear that you've apologised to Ruth herself. Be in the gallery outside at eleven o'clock.' Colonel Trent nodded an unspoken command to Captain Benton. 'I will see Ruth is there then to accept your apologies,' the colonel continued. 'Remember I'll be in this office at the same time.'

'I have no thoughts in my mind except to apologise to your foster-daughter. You have my word on it.' Mark paused briefly. 'As an officer, if not as a gentleman.'

The ghost of a smile crossed the adjutant's face but Colonel Trent's features became almost stone-like. 'You say you leave for Hull in ten days time. Keep out of trouble while you're here. Go now but be back at eleven o'clock.' Mark turned and walked towards the door. As he did so, Captain Benton leaned forward to murmur in his colonel's ear.

'Just one moment, Master Fairbrother,' Colonel Trent called out. Mark paused and turned to face the two army officers looking at him from the other side of the room.

'That sword you're wearing. The only people allowed to carry arms in this district are army officers, dragoons in my regiment when they're on duty and gentlemen who have been given permission by the justices of the peace. I'm responsible for order round here. What you do after ten days is your concern but don't wear a sword while you're in my district.'

Mark bit his lip in frustration. Was there to be no end to his humiliation? 'I'll do as you ask,' he said quietly. 'You won't see me wearing it again.'

'Good. Go now. Be back here at eleven.'

Mark walked through the door and retraced his steps. He smiled wryly as he looked at his family portraits. His eyes were moist as he paused for a few seconds in front of the portrait of his father but his mouth hardened into a thin fine line. Was it for nothing that his father and eldest brother had died? So that a parvenu like Colonel Trent could live as the lord of the manor? The Trent family lived in comfort in his old home while his mother and sister were in comparative poverty and forced to live in the steward's lodge.

Mark wondered if his elder brother Henry would ever be able to return to England. Could Henry ever claim his baronetcy and the property which was entailed to him? Mark shrugged his shoulders and tried to put the thought out of his mind. Henry was mean-spirited, unlike his father and much-loved eldest brother Edmund, both of whom had been generous natured and popular with the tenants on the estate. Even in the unlikely event of England ever becoming a kingdom again, Mark did not place much reliance on Henry providing him with sufficient income to support a gentleman's establishment.

He was brought back to the present by the sound of Colonel Trent's door opening and Captain Benton's footsteps coming towards him. He hurried away.

\* \* \* \* \*

Mark had always been taught to be punctual at all times. Ten minutes to eleven saw him being admitted to the back of the house by Digby Foster, the steward. Digby had been in service with the Fairbrother family since 1640. Henry Fairbrother's refusal to pay the fine levied by the Parliamentary Commissioners had led to the family's expulsion from Aireton Hall. Digby Foster moved out from his lodge at the same time and asked Mark's mother and sister to stay as long as they liked. No amount of argument prevented his moving to rooms in the village. He had lost his wife a few years earlier and refused to accept that he would be any worse off in rooms rather than the lodge.

'It's good to see you again, sir,' he said. He gave Mark a searching look. 'I would say you've grown five inches since you were here last.'

Mark laughed. 'Let's hope I don't grow another five inches in the next six years or I won't be able to get in and out of the house.' His mood changed as he realised the implications of what he had said. 'How do the Trents treat you, Digby?' he asked.

'Well enough, Master Mark. They're fair minded. They know I do what I can for Lady Fairbrother.'

'And Ruth Parker. How does she treat you?'

Digby Foster looked quizzically at Mark. He let his eyes rest on the small posy in Mark's hand and hesitated before replying. 'You know she's an orphan, don't you sir? When she first came here she was a shy, timid girl. Wouldn't say 'boo' to a goose. She doesn't give herself airs and graces, though she's been brought up as the colonel's daughter. Not like Frances and Anne, Colonel Trent's two eldest daughters. They were a flighty pair. Both married now, of course.'

'Yes. But does Ruth Parker treat you well?' Mark asked impatiently.

'Well enough, considering I am a servant and she's one of the daughters of the house, even though her father was only a tenant farmer. She'll grow up into a handsome woman one day. No money, of course. She's pious, though. I'm sure she'll make a good wife for some grocer or preacher,' he said, with emphasis on the last word.

Mark chuckled. 'I do believe you're jealous, Digby.'

'Not for myself, sir. Only thinking of her sleeping in the old nursery, the room which should be your sister's by rights.'

Mark shrugged his shoulders. 'Fortunes of war.'

'Yes. Apart from that I've no complaints. She's always polite to me.'

'Good. Give my compliments to Mistress Ruth. Say I'm going to the long gallery.'

'Almost like old times, Master Mark.'

'Not quite, Digby. But ask her to spare a minute or two of her time.'

\* \* \* \* \*

The chimes of the stable clock struck eleven as Mark sat down on the chair halfway along the wall of the gallery. He felt a brief pang of regret as he looked up and down again at the family portraits. Mark found it a little surprising that Colonel Trent had not ordered their removal. Henry had told him of friends whose possessions were sold to commute the fines imposed on them by Parliament. Colonel Trent might be an old bear but perhaps he had one or two redeeming features.

A few seconds went by before Mark suddenly realised he was sitting on the same chair which Ruth had occupied an hour before. His cheeks flamed, he leapt from the chair and sat down again on an adjacent one.

'God in Heaven!' he whispered as he asked what was wrong with himself. His brother Henry had always regarded him with a certain amount of amusement, describing Mark as naïve and gauche. Henry was very successful with women, while Mark was singularly unsuccessful. If Henry had been in his position yesterday afternoon, he would have handled everything with much more finesse. Just as he wished Ruth would hurry up, she came through the door at the end of the long gallery. Mark stood up from his chair. Ruth blushed slightly as she felt his eyes on her and he looked quickly away. She continued walking towards him and stopped when they were about five feet apart. Mark bowed slightly. Neither of them spoke for a few seconds. The hostility which they had felt on the previous day was now replaced by an uneasy awkwardness. Ruth noticed that Mark had changed his clothes since the interview with her foster-father. He was now much more soberly dressed. She smiled slightly. The thought flashed through her mind that he might be taken for the son of a respectable tradesman instead of a wild cavalier. Her smile broke the ice and Mark suddenly produced a small posy of lily-of-the-valley flowers from behind his back.

'For you,' he said.

'Thank you, Master Fairbrother.'

Mark seemed at a loss to know how to continue.

'Why don't we sit down?' Ruth asked.

If they did that, she thought, she would no longer need to look directly at him. She placed the posy on her lap and Mark sat beside her. Out of the corner of her eyes, Ruth could see the knuckles of his hands going white as he clenched them. His voice trembled slightly as he spoke.

'Saint Matthew tells us that Jesus Christ said "I bring not peace but a sword." I'm not as good as Our Lord. I bring not a sword but flowers, hoping for peace between us.'

Ruth was startled to hear him quote scripture and stared at the floor as she hesitated to reply. When she turned his way, he was looking at her intently. 'I notice you no longer wear a sword,' Ruth told him. 'You look much better without it. Remember Our Saviour also said "Blessed are the peacemakers for they shall be called the children of God".'

'That's why I hope for peace between us. Please accept my apologies.' Ruth could feel Mark's body leaning towards her. She moved away very slightly and turned her head so that her eyes rested on the door of Colonel Trent's office. It was as though she willed him to come out and rescue her from Mark's close presence. Mark sensed that she felt threatened. He moved back slightly and scraped his chair along the floor.

'I intended to apologise for the way I spoke to you yesterday. Even if Colonel Trent hadn't sent for me, I'd have come.'

Mark stared at her earnestly. A flicker of a smile crossed Ruth's face. She guessed her foster-father had given this presumptuous stranger a verbal lashing. Her smile seemed to ease the tension. Mark's voice steadied as he went on, speaking more slowly.

'I do regret my disturbance of your peace in this way. If we'd met under different circumstances...' His voice trailed off.

'I will tell my father you called to see me, Master Fairbrother.'

'That's not necessary,' Mark replied. 'He's enough of a judge of character to know I keep my word.'

Ruth made no reply and he felt the need to check himself becoming impatient.

'Let me have the consolation of leaving here without ill will. Even if our families can't be friends. Please say you'll accept my apologies.'

Ruth turned her face so that she was looking Mark squarely in the eyes.

'Very well. I accept,' she replied. Ruth was surprised to see the relief on his face. She continued to look into his questioning, grey eyes and thought to herself that he really had been sincere. 'I must return to my sister. I promised to help her with some needlework.'

Mark sprang out of his chair at this dismissal and stood back slightly. Ruth glanced briefly in his direction and then stood up herself. The posy of flowers fell to the floor between them. The movements of Mark's left hand and Ruth's right hand were simultaneous. The two hands reached the lilies-of-the-valley at the same time as Ruth felt his shoulder brush hers. She felt a sensation at the contact which was both strange and disturbing. Ruth released the flowers into Mark's hand and stood up slowly. Mark rose a second or two later. She was startled to see he was biting his lower lip and both his cheeks were red. He had suddenly remembered that the posy had been in the middle of Ruth's lap.

'I...I...I'm sorry,' he stammered. 'I can't get ... get things right as I mean to. When I'm with you, I mean.'

He stood still, holding the posy in his left hand.

Ruth smiled. 'I had forgotten about the flowers. I did not mean to reject your peace overtures so precipitately.'

A look of relief crossed his face and he held the flowers out towards her. Ruth thought how like a vulnerable schoolboy he looked. She wondered what sort of life he had led in the past six years of wandering around Europe. Her right hand moved slowly forward to take the flowers from him. Just before her hand reached his left hand, he quickly moved the posy to his right hand. His left hand held her wrist while he gave her the flowers with his other hand.

'We don't want them to fall again,' he said in a husky voice, clasping both his hands round her hand and the posy.

Ruth looked up into his grey eyes, still aware of the warmth of his hands. Their eyes met and Mark looked away, releasing his grip at the same time.

'No. We don't,' she replied. 'I must put them in a vase. With some water. And some rosemary twigs. For remembrance.'

'May I come with you? I'd like to see them safe now they're out of my hands.'

'If you wish, Master Fairbrother.'

'Please call me Mark.' He hesitated for a moment and then asked eagerly. 'May I call you Ruth?'

'That is what my friends call me.'

'Then that's what I'll call you, Ruth.'

She was at a loss to know how to answer. It was less than twenty four hours since they had first met and the circumstances had hardly been auspicious. Ruth deferred an answer by turning towards the door at the end of the gallery and walking towards it. Mark quickly reached her side and they walked in silence past the portraits on the walls. Ruth heard the door of her foster-father's office open from behind her back. It remained open as the two of them walked through the door at the opposite end of the gallery.

\* \* \* \* \*

While the Trent family were seated at the breakfast table next morning, Digby Foster handed the Colonel a letter from

Mark. He told Colonel Trent that it concerned his whole family and then left the room.

At the mention of the Fairbrother name, Ruth's heart had seemed to skip a beat. Even Claire paused in her eating. There was silence in the room as Colonel Trent broke the wax seal on the letter. Ruth looked at her foster-father and noticed the scar over his left eye gradually turn to a dull red as the seconds ticked by. This was always a bad sign. Half a minute elapsed before Colonel Trent reached the end of the letter. He placed it carefully on the table and looked across at his wife, who was wearing an anxious look on her face.

'Well. I'll say this for young Fairbrother, Sarah. He's got gall.' The three women in the room were tense with expectation, waiting for the colonel to elaborate on his comment. 'He's asked if Claire,' … there was a second's pause, 'and Ruth, can visit his mother and sister. It seems he also wants my permission to walk round the grounds.'

'Would it do any harm to let him stroll round the gardens?' Sarah Trent asked. 'He's here for such a short time and this is his old home.'

'I don't like it. The Fairbrothers were well thought of in this area. I wouldn't want his visible presence to be a rallying point for miscreants in the district.'

'You're right, James. The risk is too great.'

Colonel Trent picked up the letter and rose from the table. He looked down and then slipped the letter behind the belt around his tunic. The ebullient Claire could restrain herself no longer.

'I feel sorry for Elizabeth Fairbrother. She's got that limp through breaking her hip. You remember she fell down the icy steps at the rear of this house. In January. Just after we arrived. Then she had a bad attack of smallpox two years ago. She never goes anywhere and nobody visits her these days.'

'Quiet, Claire,' her mother ordered. 'You heard what your father said.'

---

'Yes, mother. But it still seems unfair we can't be friends. Just because Sir John chose the wrong side in the civil war.'

'You're growing up fast, Claire,' her father said. 'I tend to forget you were only twelve years old when the young Charles Stuart lost the battle of Worcester. And the Fairbrother girl was only ten years old at the time. Perhaps I shouldn't regard the younger generation as irreconcilable.' Colonel Trent turned and looked at his foster-daughter. 'What do you think, Ruth?' The statement made by Mark yesterday that their families could not be friends flashed through her mind. Yet he had called her by name when she had told him her friends called her Ruth. Claire smiled across the table in encouragement as Ruth hesitated.

'I don't know, Father. Perhaps if Claire has set her heart on going.'

'It's too strong to say I've set my heart on it. I feel sorry for Elizabeth Fairbrother,' Claire said. 'And, to a lesser extent, her mother also.'

Ruth had always found it difficult to refuse any of Claire's wishes. 'Yes, Father, I will go with Claire. It must wait until tomorrow morning. I have exercises to prepare for my tutor this afternoon.'

'I'm glad to see you take your studies seriously, Ruth,' Colonel Trent replied. 'I'll write out a reply and give it to Master Foster. Just to say you two will call on Lady Catherine and her daughter in the steward's lodge. I won't have Mark Fairbrother prowling around these grounds on his own.'

\* \* \* \* \*

Ruth's mood on the morning after Mark's letter had been received did not match the bright, warm, sunny, May weather. She began to regret her agreement to accompany Claire to the steward's lodge, almost as though she was afraid that today would mark the end of her childhood. The two girls walked down the steps at the back of the house and then linked arms to go through the small, formal garden. They soon reached the gap in the privet hedge, leading to the private garden, where

Mark had been standing when Ruth first saw him. Neither girl spoke as they skirted the fountain. Ruth was conscious that it was only three days since their first meeting and yet it seemed much longer. She was still silent as they walked through the gap in the privet hedge at the opposite side of the garden and went into the much larger South Garden. Claire sensed the thoughts going through Ruth's mind and determined to find an innocuous topic of conversation.

'I love the month of May,' Claire said. 'Look at all these flowers here.' Ruth nodded as they paused for a moment to admire the lilies growing at the edge of the garden and then moved through another gap in the hedge into the Rose Garden.

'Aren't these rosebuds marvellous?' Claire asked. She released Ruth's arm and bent down to smell the flowers on one of the bushes. 'What was it Will Shakespeare wrote in one of his sonnets? The one that Master Phillips made us memorise. Something about the darling buds of May. That's what we are Ruth.' She giggled and squeezed Ruth's hand. 'The darling buds of May.'

Ruth tried to remember the sonnet. She puckered her brow as she searched her memory. The lines came back to her at last. 'You didn't complete it,' she said to Claire. 'That's not all. The lines go "Rough winds do shake the darling buds of May. And Summer's lease hath all too short a date". I think the poet meant to say that even when we are young something can always come along to make us unhappy.'

'My, my, you are serious, Sister.' She slipped her arm round Ruth's waist. 'You'll have to be a little more frivolous when we talk to Lady Catherine or she won't ask us back again.'

They walked in silence for a few seconds. As they turned right at the end of the garden, they saw the wall around the steward's lodge. Claire removed her arm from Ruth's waist.

'Nearly there,' she said, taking Ruth's arm instead. 'I wonder what they'll think of us?'

'I wonder if Mark Fairbrother had to persuade them to invite us,' Ruth mused. It was with a certain amount of trepidation that she watched Claire knock on the door of the cottage where the Fairbrothers lived. After a few seconds the door was opened by a young girl who lived in the nearby village of Blackmoor. The girl stood back and said, 'Come in, ladies.' It was obvious that she recognised them and that they were expected. She seemed a little in awe of these representatives of the Trent family as she closed the front door behind them.

'Wait 'ere a moment, ladies,' the girl said. 'I'll tell 'er ladyship you're 'ere.' She disappeared down a narrow passage.

A few moments later Mark came towards them. Ruth noticed that he wore the same sober clothes he had been wearing at their second meeting. He bowed to both of them in turn, smiling ironically as he said, 'Welcome to my home.'

'Are you alone?' Claire enquired. 'Your letter asked us to meet your mother and your sister.'

'They're in the living room.' He glanced quickly at Ruth. 'Thank you both for coming.'

Claire and Ruth followed him down the same narrow passage which the girl had used a minute before. He paused as they came to a door on the left hand side. Turning the handle of the door and pushing it open, he said, 'This is the living room.'

Mark stood back and motioned Claire and Ruth to walk through the narrow doorway and past him into the room. Claire moved forward at once. Ruth hesitated, as if unsure of the next step. She could feel her heart quickening as she moved past him into the doorway of the room. She took another step forward as Mark closed the door behind him. The living room was small and sparsely furnished. It brought back dim memories to Ruth of the living room in her parents' home in which she had lived so many years ago. Mark moved quickly past her and stood beside a grey-haired woman in her late forties, seated in a high backed chair. Ruth guessed this must be Catherine Fairbrother. Her eyes wandered between Mark and his mother. They had the same grey eyes, high cheekbones and firm, dimpled chin. It was clear that Lady Fairbrother must have been very good-looking when she was younger. Her clothes were made of fine cloth but were well worn. They were in the fashion which had been popular before the establishment of the Commonwealth. As Claire was being introduced to Lady Fairbrother, Ruth noticed a young woman seated a little way apart from where Mark was standing. Although smallpox was a common enough disease, Ruth shuddered internally when she saw how the girl's face had been disfigured. She realised at once that this must be Mark's sister Elizabeth. Confirmation soon came when Mark introduced his sister to Claire and then went on to say, 'Let me finish the introductions. Mother, this lady is Ruth Parker.'

'Good day, Mistress Parker.' Mark's mother gave Ruth a long, searching look. 'You are younger than I expected. You are Colonel Trent's ward, are you not?'

Ruth lowered her eyes and made a slight curtsy in the older woman's direction. 'Yes, Lady Catherine.'

Mark hurried across to the corner of the room. He picked up a small chair in each hand and enquired rather wistfully, 'Would you like to sit down?' Mark placed one chair to Claire's left and the other behind Ruth, holding the back of it as Ruth sat down. Claire glanced at the chair by her side and followed suit. Mark remained standing behind Ruth.

'I think you'd better sit down as well, Elizabeth,' Lady Fairbrother said, looking in her daughter's direction. 'You'll have to make allowances for my son, Mistress Trent,' she continued frostily. 'He's no ladies' man. Wandering round Europe for the past six years. Mixing with all manner of ruffians. It's no upbringing for a gentleman. If the times had been different he'd have gone to University like his father. Now he's a soldier.'

'Needs must,' commented Mark quietly.

His mother disregarded this observation. 'My middle son Henry is much more polished. He's been with King Charles's court during the past six years.'

'Has your brother been with you in Sweden?' Claire asked mischievously.

'No, no. I've been in Sweden. Not my brother.' He searched for words and continued in an embarrassed tone. 'Henry's been in France and Germany and lately he's been in Holland.'

'You're not going to talk about politics, are you, Mark?' Elizabeth asked. Lady Fairbrother sat unsmiling, outwardly unaware of the controversial nature of her original comments. Ruth could sense the tension which had been created and was sure Mark's mother could sense it too. She felt sorry for Mark, out-numbered four to one by the women in the room. Ruth looked across at Claire in a beseeching way. Claire smiled back at her before turning to Mark's mother.

'Are you a good needlewoman, Lady Catherine?' she asked. 'I'm always asking Ruth for help?'

'Fair enough, I suppose. Needlework was part of my education as a young girl.'

'May I see some of the work which you and your daughter have done? It might help me to improve my own poor efforts.'

'If you think it will assist you, Mistress Trent. Elizabeth, go and fetch the patterns you have been working on.'

As Elizabeth Fairbrother stood up again, Ruth noticed how short she seemed. The limp was very pronounced as she went out of the door. Ruth thought she looked older than her seventeen years of age. There were a few seconds of uneasy silence after Elizabeth left the room. This was broken at last by Claire asking if she could talk about the well-stocked herb garden round the lodge. Lady Catherine explained that she used the herbs for cooking and also grew some of them as medicines for Elizabeth. When Claire asked her to prescribe some herbs which would stop over-eating, Lady Fairbrother looked at Claire's plump, young body and smiled for the first time since the visitors had entered the room. Ruth thought it gave her a much more sympathetic look. At that moment Elizabeth returned, carrying several hooked needles, pieces of cloth and a variety of coloured threads. Elizabeth handed the needlework to her mother while Claire picked up her own small chair and sat beside Lady Fairbrother. Mark moved quickly and took Elizabeth's chair out of her hands as she was obviously having difficulty in trying to pull it across.

'Let me do that for you,' he said.

'Thank you, Mark,' his sister replied gratefully.

Within a short space of time the two older girls were intent on watching the nimble fingers of Elizabeth's mother. Mark moved to Ruth's side and bent down to within an inch of her left ear. She could feel the warmth of his breath on her lobe as he whispered, 'We seem to be superfluous here.'

Ruth was almost afraid to move but turned slowly and gave him a slight smile. 'Could Ruth and I walk in the gardens for a few minutes?' Mark asked his mother as he straightened up.

Both Claire and Elizabeth stared at Ruth in surprise. Lady Fairbrother looked up sharply. Ruth could feel three pairs of probing eyes on her. She flushed and turned away.

'If Mistress Parker wishes to walk,' Lady Fairbrother answered carefully. 'It is usual to ask a lady's permission first, Mark.'

'I would like you to come,' Mark said as his sister suppressed a giggle. 'I mean if you will allow me to escort you,' he continued hurriedly.

'Yes, Mark,' Ruth replied firmly and smiled up at him. She rose and stretched herself to her full height. Ruth could feel Mark shiver slightly as she placed her right hand in the curve of Mark's left arm. She was conscious of his mother's eyes boring into her.

'Thank you, Ruth,' Mark said. They started to walk out of the room together. From the corner of her eye Ruth could see the frozen expression on Lady Fairbrother's face.

\* \* \* \* \*

# 2

Claire and Ruth called at the steward's lodge every morning during the following week. Although Lady Fairbrother's welcome was polite it was far from friendly. Ruth sensed that Mark's mother was growing more resentful towards her as each day passed. Elizabeth seemed oblivious to this and her smile became broader on each visit. Claire and Elizabeth tended to spend more and more time with each other. Mark had one or two twinges of regret when he felt he was neglecting his mother and sister but somehow he and Ruth found themselves excluded from their gossip. Fortunately, the weather that May was perfect. Within a day of her first visit to the lodge, Ruth had sought her foster-mother's permission to walk with Mark in the grounds of Aireton Hall. This had been freely given, bearing in mind that Colonel Trent did not want Mark to walk round the gardens alone. They came back each day to the fast developing buds in the Rose Garden. They admired the rhododendron bushes, which were a mass of colour in the Rhododendron Walk. Ruth was aware that she did not feel the same awkwardness with Mark as she had felt in the presence of Captain Benton or any of the young ensigns in her father's regiment. She sensed that Mark was equally at ease with her and was no longer tense in her presence. They spent a great deal of their time together going backwards and forwards along the long Elm Walk and the slightly shorter Sycamore Walk. From time to time they came across estate servants who touched their caps to Ruth but gave the two of them curious glances. The grooms and gardeners appeared to ignore Mark. It was obvious that they knew he was the younger brother of the exiled royalist who owned Aireton Hall. They probably thought it strange that he should be found in the company of Ruth, even if she was only a foster-daughter. This did not worry Ruth. She was content just to walk with him and listen to his tales of the places he had visited in his travels. During the past six years Ruth had not been more than two or three miles from Aireton Hall, except four times when she had visited the farm of Benjamin Crawley, husband of her foster-sister Anne. His farm was at Great Hampendown, eight miles away. Ruth was fascinated by Mark's descriptions of the great cathedrals in Paris, Cologne and Chartres. She listened intently to his descriptions of the medieval cities of Bruges and Ghent and the great trading city of Antwerp. When he described the dark, northern forests of Sweden, she recollected with regret that he would be returning soon to rejoin the Swedish army.

Six days after her first call on Lady Fairbrother, Ruth obtained Colonel Trent's permission for Mark to visit the estate farm. She regretted it afterwards as it brought a recurrence of Mark's old awkwardness and lack of self-confidence. After inspecting the piggeries and poultry houses, they decided to visit the cowsheds. The animals were being led from their byres out on to the pasture when they arrived. Ruth and Mark stood back to let them pass. One of the milkmaids who was following the herd ignored Ruth but curtsied to Mark saying, 'Thank you, sir,' at the same time. He blushed and seemed at a loss for a reply. The girl tossed her head in the air, grinned and walked on.

Ruth put her hand into his and squeezed it. They walked across the yard to the laundry room. The two girls inside looked at Ruth in a disinterested way as she came through the door. Their interest quickened as Mark followed her. The two laundry maids began to giggle and the nearer of the two told Mark she would wash his clothes for him if he took them off. He stammered out a non-committal reply and backed out of the door. Ruth followed with as much dignity as she could muster. She put her hand on his arm and was surprised to find he was trembling.

Ruth felt angry on his behalf. She blamed herself for his embarrassment. The servants would not have dared to behave like that if her mother had been there. Even Claire, small as she was, would have stood no nonsense. As for Mark's mother,

Ruth thought wistfully, she would have frozen them into silence and immobility with a single glance. She felt so inadequate as they walked slowly back across the yard. After they had gone about twenty paces, Mark stopped suddenly and put his hands on Ruth's shoulders. She was surprised to see his eyes were moist and felt guilty for suggesting a visit to the estate farm. 'Why are you the only girl I feel at ease with, Ruth?' She made no reply. He looked at her intently. 'Why am I so awkward with everyone but you?' Ruth could feel him trembling as he spoke. 'Why can't I be more like brother Henry?'

'We are as God made us,' Ruth answered quickly.

'Yes. But why am I different from other men?'

'I think we should go back to the house. You will feel better in a little while.'

Mark released his hands from Ruth's shoulders and they walked back, side by side, in silence to the steward's lodge. When they were about fifty yards from the house, Digby Foster came out of the door and paused to look carefully at them for a few seconds. They were about twenty yards away when he nodded quietly to them and hurried off in the direction of Aireton Hall.

\* \* \* \* \*

The day after this incident was a Sunday. The Trent family drove in their carriage to the church at Blackmoor in time for the morning service. Ruth followed her foster-mother and Claire out of the carriage and was helped down by Colonel Trent. Ruth raised her eyes when she reached the ground and was surprised to see Mark and Elizabeth standing about ten feet to the left of the church door. Elizabeth was resting on a walking stick in her left hand with her right hand on her brother's shoulder at the same time.

Ruth had never seen Mark's mother or sister at any of the church services before. Claire told her some time ago that Lady Fairbrother ceased to attend when penalties for not worshipping in a church had been withdrawn. Before that time, Lady Fairbrother was a vocal opponent of the prohibition of the use of the Anglican Book of Common Prayer. Her hostility to the Commonwealth had increased when the incumbent vicar had been expelled from the parish, for allegedly holding royalist views, and his place taken by an independent preacher.

Elizabeth gave the two girls a broad smile as they approached the church door. A second later, Mark raised his hat to them. Colonel Trent gave a brief nod in recognition but continued to escort the ladies of his family into church. They took their usual places in the pew reserved for them at the front of the congregation. Mark and his sister followed the Trents through the door and took their places in the pews at the back of the church which were reserved for strangers. After a few seconds of silent prayer, Mark's eyes searched to find where Ruth and her adopted family were sitting. A slight feeling of resentment welled up in his heart as he saw they were sitting in the Fairbrother family pew. The seat which used to belong to his father, and afterwards to Edmund, was now occupied by Colonel Trent. The colonel's wife was sitting in the place where his mother formerly sat. Claire was in the place which belonged to Elizabeth. His resentment changed to a mixture of pleasure and slight guilt as he saw that Ruth was sitting at the far end of his family pew. He had occupied the same seat at the left end of the pew until he and his mother stopped going to the parish church when he was just thirteen years old, a year younger than Ruth at the present time. Mark wondered if a son of his would ever sit in the place now taken by this orphan girl he had met just eight days before.

As he looked round the church, he saw that the altar had been replaced by a plain wooden table. An icon of Jesus Christ, which a crusader had brought back from the East three centuries before, had been removed. A Byzantine painting of the Virgin Mary, placed in the church during the reign of Henry VII, was also missing. There were no flowers in the church and no banners hung from the walls. The lectern, on which the Bible used to be placed, was missing. All the walls of the church had been whitewashed. Mark glanced upwards and was shocked to see that the beautiful medieval ceiling, with its painted blue sky, and the sun, moon and stars painted in gold leaf, had also been whitewashed. What a sacrilegious crowd these puritans were, he thought. At least the stained glass windows were in place and the carved stone pulpit and font had been left untouched. In so many parishes these had been smashed to pieces by puritan iconoclasts. Perhaps Colonel Trent had a degree of sensitivity after all, in preserving the structure of the church intact. The service which followed contained no set form or liturgy. It was very different from those which he had attended during his stay in Holland, supervised by exiled priests of the Church of England.

Ruth could feel Mark looking at her from the rear of the church from time to time during the service. She found she could not give the full attention she usually gave to the preacher's words. While she normally followed his sermon closely, today her mind wandered. For the first time in her experience, she found the sermon long-winded and tautological. At the end of the service the congregation remained quietly in their pews while the minister went through the door into the churchyard outside. Colonel Trent rose, moved into the aisle and then stepped back to allow the ladies of his family to precede him. As Ruth's eyes wandered over the back of the church, she saw with a look of surprise that Mark and Elizabeth were already going through the door into the churchyard. It was customary for the worshippers to allow Colonel Trent and his family to leave the church first, as a mark of respect to the local representatives of the Commonwealth. She shook her head slightly and smiled, thinking Mark seemed unable to keep out of trouble.

The minister was talking earnestly to Elizabeth when the Trents left the church. Mark was standing about a yard from his sister, looking somewhat detached. On seeing the colonel's family, the minister expressed the wish to Elizabeth that he would see her again and then moved over to pay his respects to the military governor of the district. Mark moved across to take his sister's arm as the minister exchanged compliments with the colonel and his wife. The rest of the congregation was now leaving the church and the minister took his leave of the Trents so that he could mingle with the other parishioners.

Colonel Trent's carriage was standing at the gate of the churchyard just a few yards from the church door. The ladies of the Trent family moved across to it escorted by the colonel. He helped his wife up the steps and then moved back so that he could assist Claire in the same way.

'Why can't we take Elizabeth Fairbrother back with us?' Claire asked impulsively. Her father stood still, trying to find the right words to reply. 'It must have been a great effort to walk to church with that limp of hers,' Claire continued.

'There won't be room for five of us,' Colonel Trent answered. 'Still less for six if that brother of hers is invited as well.'

'Ruth will walk back with her brother, won't you Ruth?' Claire asked.

"I... I... yes ... I..."

Ruth's mind was a mixture of confused emotions. Fortunately, her foster-father interrupted her at that point. 'I have a better idea,' he said. 'You three return with Elizabeth Fairbrother. I'll walk back with her brother. I want a few words with that young man.'

It was obvious from the rather stern expression on his face that this was the end of the discussion. Neither Claire nor Ruth made any comment as he started to walk towards Mark and his sister. Ruth looked across to the two of them. They seemed isolated and apart from the rest of the family groups who were talking animatedly in the churchyard. Mark smiled slightly as he saw Ruth looking in his direction. She turned away as Colonel Trent began talking to the two Fairbrothers. When Ruth looked round again she saw her foster-father walking slowly towards the carriage with Elizabeth holding his arm.

Her eyes sought Mark. He had not moved from the spot where he and his sister had stood. There was no smile on his face now as he half turned to watch a few soldiers in the Commonwealth army leave the church.

Elizabeth smiled warmly as she approached the carriage. Claire took her hand and said, 'I'm glad you're coming with us.'

Any further pleasantries were postponed by Colonel Trent. His manner was almost brusque as he told Ruth and Claire they would be going back with their mother. He opened the carriage door wider and said to his wife, 'I'll tell the coachman to stop at the steward's lodge. I should be back in the Hall in about fifteen minutes' time.'

Colonel Trent moved from the doorway. He helped Elizabeth up the steps and then placed his hand under the right elbows of Claire and Ruth as they each took their turn to get into the carriage. The coachman folded up the steps, took his place on the box and, at a signal from the colonel, began the journey back to Aireton Hall.

Mark had not been pleased when Colonel Trent told him his sister would travel back in the Trent's family carriage. He detected the influence of Claire and Ruth in this decision. While he appreciated their thoughtfulness, he felt that, as a matter of courtesy, he should have been consulted first. After all, he had escorted Elizabeth to church and was responsible for seeing her back. The colonel's approach was in the best parade ground manner and left Mark no choice but to allow his sister to go back with the ladies of the Trent family. They stood together as the carriage moved away and Mark noticed Ruth's face at the side window, her eyes turned in his direction. She was still looking at him as the carriage disappeared from view round the first curve in the road. Mark was sure Colonel Trent had seen Ruth gazing at him and waited for some comment. The colonel seemed in no hurry to say anything or make a move, however. Several parishioners shot curious glances at the sight of their military governor and the scion of the district's leading royalist family standing together. Most of the worshippers had started to drift away before Colonel Trent told Mark he would accompany him to the steward's lodge. The few people left by this time stepped aside to allow the two men to proceed without hindrance. Mark could hear one or two whispers as they passed but the colonel's only response was to return the salutes of a small group of soldiers standing in a corner of the churchyard.

Colonel Trent did not resume the conversation until they were in open country. Slightly to Mark's surprise, his manner softened. He asked about the places which Mark had visited in the past six years and the sights he had seen. No questions were asked about his brother Henry or about the court of the exiled Prince of Wales. The conversation then moved to the recent war between Sweden and Denmark. Colonel Trent enquired about the weapons which the Swedish army used and the tactics they employed. Mark replied that he was returning to Sweden because he was certain war would break out again soon, after the colonel had asked why he was going back.

'There's nothing here to change your mind then?' Colonel Trent continued. 'Perhaps I could recommend you for an ensign's commission in our army?'

Mark laughed. 'That would be the wheel turning full circle. Thank you for the offer, colonel, but the answer must be 'No'. The pay in the Swedish army, when I get it, is better than I can earn here. The only choice for a younger son like me is to marry an heiress or make a fortune abroad.'

'Does Ruth know your views?'

Mark flushed. He had to exercise control to prevent himself from stammering. 'She knows I'll be returning to Sweden.'

'I'm very fond of Ruth,' Colonel Trent said softly.

'I know you are, sir,' Mark replied.

For a few seconds neither of them spoke.

'Let me ask you to consider this carefully. Think before you answer. You've an uncle who is prepared to pay your family's fine, haven't you?' Colonel Trent asked.

'You are well informed, sir.'

'His name is George Usher, is it not? With a large estate near York. And he's Lady Catherine's brother.'

'As I said before, Colonel, you're well informed.'

'If you serve two years in my regiment, your family's fines can be substantially reduced. At the end of that time, if you paid the fines left, those imposed on your brother, the commissioners could be persuaded to transfer Aireton Hall into your name.'

'But the property is entailed to my brother. It's a family trust. Our land must pass down in the direct male line.'

'Listen to me, Mark. It's nearly ten years since Parliament executed the king. It's not far short of that time since the House of Lords was abolished. When Parliament can take these actions, do you think the Parliamentary Commissioners would allow a long forgotten deed to stop justice being done? The only thing which has stopped Aireton Hall being sold to pay the penalties imposed on your family is because I have chosen to use it as my headquarters. I must tell you candidly that the actions of your brother in roaming round Europe, in company with that vagrant, the former Prince of Wales, do not make my efforts to stop the sale of your home any easier. How can your brother think of serving a man who led an army of Scotsmen against the people of England?'

Mark was too stunned to reply.

'Think carefully, Mark,' the colonel continued. 'Aireton Hall is forfeited to the Commonwealth for a penalty of a quarter of its value. Join us for two years and you'll be able to compound the penalty for a tenth of the value of the land.'

'My loyalty to my brother would stop me. Only he can take such action.'

The two men were now within sight of the steward's lodge. Colonel Trent hesitated as if uncertain how to continue. He stopped and looked Mark straight in the eye. 'Many people believe a good soldier should have no commitments. They think a married soldier's only half a soldier, while a soldier in love is no soldier at all. What do you think, lad?'

Mark could feel his cheeks burning again. He wished this sensation would cease. He was anxious to get the discussion over as soon as possible. 'Do you mind if we go on?' he asked.

'No. If that's your wish.'

They started to walk together towards the steward's lodge. Mark noticed that Colonel Trent's limp was slightly more pronounced than when he had started the walk back from church. Their silence was broken after a few seconds by the colonel. 'You haven't given me your opinion. About a soldier and his commitments I mean.'

'I think a man who goes off to war is likely to suffer less than a woman he leaves behind.' Mark carried on speaking in a slow, deliberate voice. He wanted to give greater emphasis to his reply. 'I have no commitments here. Nor do I regard the house my mother occupies as my home.'

'I see.'

The two men walked on in silence until they came to the steward's lodge. When they stopped, Colonel Trent said, 'Think about all I've said, Mark. I'm not a wealthy man or I would have bought the estate myself. I leave the army in just over three years' time and then the Hall will have to be sold to pay your family's fines.'

Mark thought his heart would stop. While he had no prospects himself, he had lived in hope that Henry would be able to return to Aireton Hall one day. He raised his hat and bowed slightly. 'Thank you for your company, Colonel Trent.'

'Good luck, Mark. God go with you wherever you travel.'

Mark turned on his heels and went through the door. Colonel Trent sighed as he watched him go.

\* \* \* \* \*

When the Fairbrothers were seated at their breakfast table on the following morning, Elizabeth told her mother that Claire and Ruth had been asked to come early that day. Lady Fairbrother made no comment. Instead she turned to Mark and said, 'You seem to have seen a great deal of the colonel's ward in the past week.'

'That's not fair, mother,' Elizabeth interjected. 'Ruth and Claire come over to see us all.'

'Don't be a fool, Elizabeth. I'm not blind, even if you are. I've seen the way this girl looks at your brother.'

'That's unkind, Mother,' Mark said quietly.

'Perhaps so,' Lady Fairbrother replied. 'Did you and Colonel Trent talk about her yesterday?'

'Only briefly. We talked about other things. Military tactics. Military weapons. My travels.'

'There must have been more said than that.'

'Well, Colonel Trent offered me a commission in his regiment. I turned it down.'

'I knew it!' Lady Fairbrother exclaimed in an exasperated voice. 'They want to keep you near that orphan girl. She's no money. No rank.'

'Ruth's still very young,' Mark said softly.

'Your family's history goes back over three hundred years. You should be proud of your heritage.' His mother's voice became loud and high pitched. 'This girl has no background! She's nobody. Compare her to your cousin Sophie. Uncle George would provide a handsome dowry for his only daughter. Don't you see that? If you chose to marry her, you need not return to Sweden.'

'Claire's lucky,' Elizabeth interrupted. 'I wish Ruth was my sister. Even if she is a nobody.'

'Don't be ridiculous,' her mother answered. 'She'd have to be my daughter for you to be her sister.'

Elizabeth began to cry at this point.

'Go to your room, if you can't control yourself,' Lady Fairbrother told her.

Mark gave an exasperated look across at his mother and helped his sister to her feet. He knew her room was on the ground floor, next to the living room. 'Can you manage, Elizabeth?' Mark asked, 'Or shall I help you?'

His sister shook her head and choked back her sobs. 'I can manage. Ruth will be here soon. I'll go to my room until then.'

*Rough Winds*

Mark was sorry his mother had mentioned her niece Sophie. He had stayed with his uncle for two days during his journey back from Sweden and had regretted it ever since. Before that, he had only seen Sophie as a child. His cousin was now plain as well as a spoilt adolescent. She was frivolous and immature compared to Ruth, even though Ruth was four years younger. But he must put all thoughts of Ruth out of his mind for the present. He waited until Elizabeth shut her door and then asked his mother, 'Why don't we sit and talk this over calmly?'

'I'm sorry I lost my temper and upset Elizabeth,' Lady Fairbrother replied. 'It's just that I'm concerned about what is going to happen to you.'

'Colonel Trent shares your concern. Unless I serve this Commonwealth, I will have no status in England and no money to live on. I must go abroad again.' Mark gave a wry smile. 'Ruth's family history goes back to Eve. She's a good looking girl. Even though she's only fourteen now. I'm glad she has Colonel Trent's protection.'

His mother looked at him intently as a wistful expression crossed his face. 'I know, Mark. I saw the way you looked at each other the first time she came here to see me.'

'If circumstances were different for both of us ...' Mark began, leaving the unspoken question in the air. 'But I'm not stupid, Mother. I know what must be done for all our sakes.'

Lady Fairbrother gave a sigh of relief. 'Yes, son. For you and all your family. Will you call on Uncle George during your way back to Hull?'

'No, Mother. Not this time.'

# 3

Ruth and Claire arrived at the steward's lodge just under an hour later. Lady Fairbrother greeted them politely enough but both she and Mark seemed rather subdued. The two girls expressed concern when they were told that Elizabeth was unwell. Eventually Claire persuaded Lady Fairbrother to take her to Elizabeth's room. When Ruth tried to follow the other two women down the passage, Mark grasped her arm to detain her. She turned towards Mark with an anxious look on her face to ask if she could go in to see his sister as well. Ruth blushed slightly when he told her that his sister would be surprised to see them apart. Her anxiety lessened as she heard the murmur of conversation from Elizabeth's room, followed by the sound of laughter.

Eventually, Mark was able to convince Ruth that his mother and Claire would be adequate company for his sister. Elizabeth had been just a little upset and would soon get over it with Claire to talk to. He grasped Ruth's hands in his own, smiled, told her they would only be in the way if they stayed, and suggested walking round the estate that day.

The next half-hour or so passed quickly. They re-explored all the places through which they had walked in the past few days, such as the Rose, vegetable and herb gardens, and the Rhododendron, Sycamore and Elm walks. Ruth carefully avoided the estate farm. Mark seemed very light-hearted and his cheerfulness was contagious. He was a mine of information about the countries he had visited, telling her about Holland, where the people wore wooden clogs, there were windmills everywhere and they had to build dykes to keep out the sea. She was fascinated by his stories of the theatres and opera houses he had visited in France, listening closely as he told her of the troupes of extempore players known as the Commedia del Arte. Ruth laughed at his stories of the extravagance of the clothes worn by the wealthy people in

France, so different from those worn by the people among whom she had been brought up. The weather gradually became windier as their walk progressed. It began to cloud over as they went into the South Garden.

'We'd better hurry back to my mother's house before it begins to rain,' Mark said anxiously. They turned in that direction but heavy spots began to fall before they had gone twenty yards. 'Look, Ruth. You go back to the Hall. I'll see you as far as the formal garden.'

They walked quickly from the South Garden into the private garden. The rain became much heavier as they moved towards the gap in the privet hedge where they had first met.

'Come on! Run for it!' Ruth shouted, starting to run towards the house.

'But I can't go into the Hall,' Mark called after her in a half-hearted voice. Ruth stopped and looked round. He looked so dejected standing on his own, she laughed out loud. She went back quickly and took his hand.

'I am not staying here to see you soaked,' Ruth said, tugging at his arm. The two of them ran towards the house, charging up the steps hand in hand, laughing at the same time. Both of them were giggling as they went through the door, shaking themselves like young puppies and with the rain still dripping from their hats.

The door of Digby Foster's pantry was ajar and he came out as he heard the noise. After glancing first at Mark, then at Ruth, he turned in the direction of the kitchen and called, 'Mary.'

The servant girl hurried from the kitchen, lifted her hand to her mouth in surprise when she saw Mark and Ruth standing together, and gazed at Mark as if transfixed. Ruth smiled inwardly. He was certainly handsome. It was probably the first time the servant had seen Mark at close range.

Mary was ordered to bring two pieces of cloth which she handed to Digby, who handed them in turn to Ruth and Mark. She remained staring at Mark until the steward reprimanded her and ordered her back to the kitchen.

After they finished drying themselves, Digby told Mark that Colonel Trent was out but he suggested Mark might pay his respects to the colonel's wife who was in the drawing room. The steward said, 'Follow me, sir,' when Mark agreed that he would be glad to see Ruth's mother.

Ruth felt a vague sense of irritation. After all, Aireton Hall was her home. She felt no need to put on a show for anyone's benefit when Mark stood back to allow Ruth to precede him as they followed the steward into the drawing room.

Sarah Trent looked up in alarm as the steward announced them. She stared hard at Ruth, then at Mark and back to Ruth again. They both remained standing as she asked where Claire was. She looked relieved when Ruth told her that Claire was still with the Fairbrothers while she had brought Mark in to shelter from the rain.

Mark studied Ruth's foster-mother while Digby Foster was leaving the room. It was the first chance he had been given to look at her closely. She was a short, grey-haired woman of about fifty years of age. She had a kind, gentle look on her face and, like her daughter Claire, was a little on the plump side. Mark apologised for inconveniencing her and said he would take his leave now that he had escorted Ruth home.

'I can't allow you to go until the rain eases off,' Sarah Trent told him. 'But an old woman like me is not much good for company. Why don't the two of you walk in the long gallery? My daughters sometimes go there when the rain stops them exercising in the gardens.'

Mark shot a quick glance at Ruth who smiled back. He turned to her foster-mother and raised his eyebrows momentarily as he asked, 'Colonel Trent?'

The face of the colonel's wife broke into a broad smile. 'My husband and Captain Benton are visiting some troops at Great Hampendown. They're not expected back before this afternoon.'

Mark laughed. 'That should allow me time to explain to Ruth that all my forbears weren't quite the dragons they look.

I will leave, of course, as soon as the rain stops. May I take my leave of you when I go, Madam?'

'Yes, of course you may.'

Mark opened the door for Ruth and they went up the stairs side by side. Ruth noticed two of the young servant girls giving appreciative looks in Mark's direction but he seemed oblivious of their attention. They were not alone even when they reached the long gallery. Three other servant girls came into the gallery, one after another, on some pretext and gave them curious glances before leaving again. Ruth wondered if she should report them to her foster-mother, smiled inwardly and decided against it. Fortunately, the gallery was long enough to ensure that their conversation was private.

Mark identified all his ancestors in turn as well as describing the landscapes and pictures of religious subjects which also hung on the walls. The Fairbrothers had been substantial landowners for the past two centuries. Their wealth had increased, however, when Mark's great-great-grandfather acquired considerable properties on the dissolution of the monasteries in the reign of Henry VIII. He showed her a portrait of his grandfather, the first baronet, and told Ruth the title had been acquired fifty years before when his grandfather lent a large sum of money to James I.

'My family's been lucky, I suppose. We've always had the knack of choosing the winning side. Until now, that is.' Mark said.

Ruth was unable to think of a suitable reply. They paused for a long time in front of the portrait of Mark's father, Sir John Fairbrother. Neither Mark nor Ruth spoke until they walked quietly to a picture which hung nearby. It showed a group of four children. There were two older boys, a boy of around three and a babe in arms. The baby was being held by the eldest boy who looked about eleven.

'Part of my family,' Mark told her. 'I had two other sisters who died before I was born. Mary was just over a year old, while Anne died after a few weeks.'

'I am very sorry,' Ruth replied before lapsing into silence. Words seemed inadequate. She took Mark's hand in hers and continued looking at the group. Ruth thought the features of the eldest boy looked familiar. Was it Mark? she wondered. Could it be him?

Mark sensed the thoughts going through her mind.

'Painted over sixteen years ago. Just before the start of the civil war.' He pointed to the lad holding the baby. 'My eldest brother Edmund. He was only twenty-one when he died of wounds after the battle of Worcester. The baby is my sister Elizabeth. I'm the little boy. The other one is Henry.'

'You are very like Edmund.'

Mark looked hard at the painting. 'I suppose I am. Although he was always my mother's favourite.' There was just a trace of bitterness in his voice. 'I'm not like Edmund in that respect.'

He moved away abruptly, almost as though he wished to change the subject. They stood together before a picture of St. Jerome, painted by an Italian master who visited England in the time of Mark's grandfather, and then the two of them moved towards the part of the wall where the painting of Adam and Eve was hanging. Mark seemed slightly embarrassed at seeing the naked figures in Ruth's presence. He shuffled past it uneasily, without saying anything. Ruth paused briefly to look at the picture but Mark gave it no more than a glance. He walked slowly towards the window. After he had told her it was no longer raining, Ruth replied that they would be able to walk back to the lodge together and she would return with Claire. They went back to the drawing room so that Mark could take his leave of Sarah Trent. 'I have come back to thank you for your kindness,' he told her. 'My mother and sister are grateful you permitted your daughters to visit them.' He glanced at Ruth. 'I am glad you allowed me to walk in the grounds.'

'I'm pleased our families are friends now, Master Fairbrother.'

'And to bid you goodbye,' Mark continued.

She looked at him sharply.

'I may not see you again before I leave,' was his hurried answer to her unspoken question.

Sarah Trent stood up. 'I'll come to the terrace with you,' she told him. The three of them made their way to the door which opened on to the terrace at the back of the house. She held out her right hand and said, 'God go with you. God keep you. Wherever you travel.'

Ruth muttered a whispered Amen. She thought Mark's eyes looked exceptionally bright. It seemed as though he was trying to hide his emotion when he bent down to kiss her foster-mother's hand instead of shaking it, as she had expected. He turned quickly away and started to walk down the steps.

'Don't forget me.' Ruth called out as she hurried after him. 'I'm coming as well. It is not going to be that easy to lose me.'

He stopped and waited until she was alongside him. 'I'm sorry. Forgive me.' Ruth laughed and took his arm as her foster-mother watched from the terrace above.

'You cannot go on like this forever, Mark. Making excuses to me all the time.'

Their light-hearted mood of the early part of the day seemed to have disappeared with the sunshine. The weather was now blustery and overcast while Mark's mood was very subdued on the way back to the steward's lodge. He appeared upset after seeing the pictures of his father and brothers. Mark told her he was only four years old when his father went off to join the king's army and only six years of age when Sir John was killed in action.

Ruth squeezed his arm, 'I am sure he was a fine man.'

'Just a plain country gentleman,' Mark replied. 'Not a courtier like my grandfather or my brother Henry.'

'Why did he buy that painting of Adam and Eve?'

'He brought it back from Europe. Just before he and mother were married. He gave it to her after they were wed. I think it was a symbol for him of an island of peace in a changing world.'

'What a lovely thought,' Ruth replied.

'Edmund told me that even then father could see that the differences between the king and Parliament were becoming irreconcilable. He realised that the old aristocracy would have to adapt to make way for the new men who had done well under Elizabeth.'

'I am afraid I do not understand politics but I wish I had known him.' Ruth gave a shy, sideways look at Mark and recited.

> *'When Adam delved and Eve span,*
> *Who was then the gentleman?'*

'The times may be changing, Ruth, but they haven't changed that fast. My father didn't even believe in absolute monarchy. He and my brother fought for the king because they didn't want these levellers and diggers taking our land from us. They believed we should be able to pass our family's property on to future generations. They thought men ought to be free to worship God in their own way.'

Ruth took her hand from Mark's arm. She held his hand in hers. 'I am so sorry. I didn't mean to upset you by reciting that rhyme. We think differently because of the war.' She gave his hand a squeeze. 'And because your father and my father were on opposite sides. But we can still be friends.'

'Yes, of course we can still be friends.'

He took Ruth's right hand in his own and placed it once more on his left arm. They walked in silence for the rest of the journey to the steward's lodge. Mark stopped when they were about ten yards from the front door. Ruth could feel his arm trembling as he stopped beside her.

'Please don't go in yet,' he begged. 'I'll send Claire out to you.'

He took both her hands in his and looked at her as though she would melt in front of his eyes.

'You're not going to kiss my hand as you did with mother, are you?'

---

'No, I'm not,' Mark answered in a husky voice, a little above a whisper. He seemed unsure of what to do next. Suddenly he squeezed her hands, lifted his hands to her shoulders, bent his head down towards her and kissed her lightly on the lips. After two or three seconds he released her, turned quickly and went into the house.

Ruth's cheeks were burning. She stood rooted to the spot, unable to move. It would be unthinkable to follow him now. But what was she to do? How should she behave when she saw him tomorrow? Ought she to visit the Fairbrothers on the following day? What should she tell Claire, if she decided not to come? All these thoughts raced through her mind and she turned so that her face would not be visible from the lodge.

She heard Claire's cheerful voice from behind her saying, 'Come on, slowcoach. Where have you been all morning?' Ruth turned and Claire's expression changed. 'My. You do look flushed. What happened to you?'

'Mark kissed me,' Ruth blurted out.

'Kissed you!' Claire exclaimed. 'I didn't think he had it in him.'

'Well, only lightly. And just for a second or two.'

Claire took her arm and started to lead her gently away.

'Tell me about it, Ruth. On our way back.'

Ruth recounted the events of the morning while Claire listened in silence.

'What do you think mother will say?' Ruth asked as the girls came near the house. 'And Lady Catherine?'

'I wouldn't worry, Ruth. Mother's pretty shrewd. She won't be surprised if you ask me. She's seen the two of you together this morning. So has Mark's mother.'

'But it was so unexpected.'

Claire gave a slow chuckle. 'To you maybe. But I saw the way he looked at you. And I told mother.' She sighed. 'He's a handsome young man. If you hadn't been my sister. Ah, well.'

\* \* \* \* \*

A few hours later the Trent family were about to take supper in the dining room. After the food had been distributed on to the plates, Digby Foster motioned the other servants to leave. He then told Colonel Trent that Lady Fairbrother had asked him to say that her younger son Mark was staying at the Blackmoor Inn overnight. 'He stabled a horse there when he arrived home, sir,' Digby continued. 'It seems he wants to make sure it's fit for the return journey. He proposes to leave for Hull tomorrow morning. Master Fairbrother is making an early start, sir.'

Ruth felt her lungs constricting and she inhaled sharply.

'Steady, Ruth,' Claire said to her in a sotto voce voice.

'Why the change in plans, Digby?' Colonel Trent asked.

'Master Fairbrother thought it best to leave a day or two early, sir. In that way there's less chance of his missing the ship to Sweden.'

Ruth started to sob quietly.

'Leave us, Digby!' the colonel ordered.

'Yes, sir.'

'I should've had the overdressed young popinjay whipped when he first arrived,' Colonel Trent exclaimed as Digby Foster closed the door on leaving. Ruth's sobbing became more pronounced. Her foster-mother left her chair to place her hands on Ruth's shoulders.

'I knew this would happen,' the colonel went on angrily. 'I gave the young puppy every chance and he goes without a word. Without so much as a "By your leave." I ought to send two of the guard to the inn. Get them to bring him back here. On his knees, if necessary. That's the right position for all royalists.'

'Not now,' Sarah Trent said to her husband. 'Ruth is too upset.'

Ruth rose from her chair and was enfolded in her foster-mother's arms.

'It makes me angry,' Colonel Trent spluttered. 'The young fool could've made something of a life. But he's thrown it all away. Gone off on some wild goose chase. On a mistaken sense of family honour. Much good will it do him now.'

'Please be quiet, James,' his wife pleaded.

Colonel Trent looked across at the sight of Ruth being comforted by her mother. She was already two inches taller than his wife. His ward would be a striking looking girl when she was Claire's age, he thought wryly. Why was that idiot Mark Fairbrother not prepared to wait a couple of years?

'You'll cry now,' he heard himself saying. 'Cry as much as you like, Ruth. But in a year or two, you'll laugh at this. In four or five years' time, you'll have forgotten Mark Fairbrother. The only time we're likely to hear of him is if we get news he's been killed in some skirmish in a far-off place or he's married a foreign bride.'

Ruth tore herself free from her foster-mother's arms and ran crying to her room.

# 4

## MAY 1660

There had been an air of tension at Aireton Hall throughout the morning, ever since the mud-stained dispatch rider had arrived just after dawn. Ruth had not seen her foster-father after that time but noticed a succession of visitors coming in and out of the house. She recognised two of the local magistrates as well as Colonel Trent's company commanders. The bustle of activity around the stables destroyed her concentration and she gave up trying to read, contenting herself with looking out of her room instead. She loved the sight of the gardens at this time of the year, with the blossom on the trees and flowers in full bloom. They had looked like this when Mark left just over two years ago, she remembered. Ruth opened her door in response to a sharp knock and found Digby Foster outside. He told her that the colonel wished to see her in the drawing room. She hurried downstairs, thinking it must be important for her foster-father to send for her when he was so busy. There had been rumours of royalist plots ever since Richard Cromwell had resigned. Could this be another scare? Up to now, none of the plots had involved their locality but the latest news from London had been worrying and confused.

When Ruth went into the drawing room, she noticed how grave her foster-parents looked. Colonel Trent's hair was now almost white and he had aged a great deal recently. Years of hard campaigning, followed by the administration of a difficult district, had left their mark. Ruth thought how tired and dejected he looked.

'I would like you to go to the steward's lodge and bring your sister back, Ruth,' the colonel said.

'Yes, Father. What's the trouble?'

'Charles Stuart landed in Dover four days ago after the fleet brought him back from Holland. He's on his way to London now.'

Ruth's hand went to her mouth.

'If only Oliver Cromwell had nominated John Lambert as his successor instead of 'Tumbledown Dick', none of this would have happened,' Colonel Trent continued.

'Careful, James,' his wife said quietly.

'All my work wasted.'

Ruth felt a wave of pity for the elderly man who had been like a father to her most of her life. She went up to him and hugged him. 'You still have your family, Father.'

'Thank you, Ruth. Now go off to fetch your sister. I've to go round to give the news to the troops in my garrison. General Monck's given instructions for the army to maintain order until King Charles decides what to do next.' He looked at Ruth with a fresh eye. The top of her head was already on a level with his cheekbones. Over the past two years, she had developed a quiet, serious manner which, combined with a fast maturing body, made her seem older than her sixteen years. She was old enough to understand, he thought. 'General Monck wants the army to stay in being because he doesn't want any settling of old scores. Any private revenge. The King, on the other hand, may decide he can't afford a standing army and there'll be plenty of people round here who'll agree with him.'

'Yes, Father. I see that.'

'I'll no longer be responsible for the administration of this area. My regiment could be disbanded. We'll almost certainly have to leave Aireton Hall. It may not happen for a few weeks yet. I'll move back to my farm near Colchester. Will you mind that, Ruth?'

'Of course not. I was born on a farm. Why should I mind?' Colonel Trent remained silent while Ruth kissed him gently on the cheek. 'I will give the news to Claire as I bring her back here, Father.'

'Thank you, Ruth,' he replied.

She went across to where Sarah Trent was sitting. Ruth squeezed her foster-mother's right shoulder and bent down to kiss her left cheek. She could see tears in the older woman's eyes. Ruth was near to tears herself as she muttered, 'I must go now,' and hurried through the door.

Memories of the past came flooding back as she walked through the gardens. Although just over two years had passed since Mark's abrupt departure, time had not softened the hurt she had felt at the time. Claire had continued to visit Elizabeth daily but it was almost a fortnight after Mark left before Ruth could bring herself to go to the steward's lodge again. Elizabeth seemed friendly enough but her mother, while polite, had been cool towards Ruth. During their visits Claire and Elizabeth gravitated together, leaving Ruth alone with Lady Fairbrother for long periods. As a result Ruth accompanied Claire less and less. After the death of Oliver Cromwell in September of that year, Lady Fairbrother's manner had become almost distant, as though she was expecting the immediate restoration of Charles Stuart to the throne, together with the return to England of her two sons. Claire did not appear to notice and continued to visit Elizabeth whenever the weather allowed but Ruth no longer sought the company of Lady Fairbrother and her daughter. It was over eighteen months since she had last seen them and she wondered about the reception she would receive now.

When the servant girl ushered her into the small living room of the lodge, Elizabeth smiled warmly but her mother gave Ruth a long, hard look. Lady Fairbrother's eyes ran over Ruth's well-formed body from head to toe and back again, as if she was examining a prize heifer.

'You've grown, girl, since I last saw you.'

Ruth was aware of the older woman's appraising eyes and blushed slightly. 'Yes, Lady Catherine.'

'Why are you here?'

'Our father has asked me to escort Claire back home. Father wants to tell her the news. About Charles Stuart landing at Dover. Now that Parliament has proclaimed him king.'

'No!' Claire interjected.

Lady Fairbrother ignored the interruption. 'Colonel Trent is well informed. I had a letter from Holland yesterday. My son, Sir Henry, wrote that he is accompanying King Charles back to England.'

'Then we will take our leave, Lady Catherine,' Ruth said.

Lady Fairbrother appeared not to have heard this remark. She looked through Ruth and turned to address Claire. 'Please tell Colonel Trent I will call to see him at the Hall the day after tomorrow, Claire.'

Ruth felt anger swelling up inside her. She quickly interjected. 'I will ask my father to send Digby Foster to you. Our steward will tell you when it will be convenient for you to call, madam.'

'Have a care, Mistress Parker. You are not mistress of Aireton Hall, nor ever likely to be. Within a few days, I will decide who comes to Aireton Hall, who leaves and who stays.'

'Why can't we all be friends?' Elizabeth pleaded.

In Ruth's eyes, her body looked more ungainly then before and her face seemed even more puckered. She looked much older than a girl approaching twenty.

'If that is what you wish, Elizabeth,' her mother replied. 'So long as we all remember the station in life to which God has called us.'

Lady Fairbrother looked hard at Ruth and the eyes of the two women locked. The impasse was broken by Claire.

'Come on, Ruth. Father wants us home.' Claire kissed Elizabeth on the cheek and said, 'Goodbye for now. I'll see you again soon.'

'Until tomorrow then,' Elizabeth responded eagerly.

Ruth moved towards Elizabeth but stopped in mid-stride as she heard a voice saying, 'We Fairbrothers are not usually a kissing family.' Surely Mark's mother was not still harbouring resentment about her son's abrupt leaving two years ago. Ruth felt her face go white with anger.

Her voice was icy as she answered, 'So I have seen, madam. Now and also in the past. Good day, Elizabeth.' She made a slight nod towards Lady Fairbrother, saying, 'Goodbye, madam.'

Claire said, 'Good day, Lady Catherine,' and followed her out.

* * * * *

Two days later Lady Fairbrother and Elizabeth drove up to Aireton Hall in the carriage which Colonel Trent sent to pick them up. Ruth felt she could not face the Fairbrothers again and went upstairs to the long gallery, leaving her foster-parents and Claire to meet them. She heard the chimes of the stable clock strike eleven as she gazed idly out of the window, looking over the sunlit grounds.

Ruth wandered up and down for a few minutes examining the paintings on the wall and wondered how long it would be before she left her home for the last time. She sat in a chair and found herself looking at a picture of Mark's father, hanging on the opposite wall. When Sir John was sixteen years old, he probably thought nothing in his world could ever change. She reflected on how secure her own world had seemed such a short time ago.

The chimes of the clock on the stables struck the quarter after the hour as the door at the end of the gallery opened. Ruth looked in that direction to see Lady Fairbrother come in, followed by Digby Foster.

'Leave us, Master Foster,' Lady Fairbrother said as she saw Ruth sitting down.

'Yes, your ladyship,' he replied, bowing low in a manner which had not been seen before.

'Do you mind if I join you, Ruth?' Lady Fairbrother asked as she approached.

'Not at all, Lady Catherine.' She rose from her chair. 'Aireton Hall will soon be yours.'

'Let's walk together then. If you don't mind keeping an old woman company for a while.'

Ruth thought her companion seemed in a remarkably good humour. She was surprised when Lady Fairbrother asked her to hold her arm as they started to walk side by side.

'You know, Ruth. You and I are very much alike,' the older woman said suddenly. Ruth was too startled to reply. 'The only one who stands up to me is Henry. He's the only one with spirit like yours. As for Elizabeth ...' Her voice trailed off and she shrugged suddenly. She gave Ruth a long, searching look and, in a peremptory voice, commanded, 'Turn round, girl.'

Ruth was too taken by surprise to disobey. She turned her back, wondering what was going to happen next. Lady Fairbrother stepped behind her and quickly placed her hands under Ruth's arms. She could feel the older woman's hands running down her sides, caressing her waist, moving quickly down the outside of her thighs and then feeling her buttocks. Ruth felt herself being quickly spun round. Lady Fairbrother rested her hands on the girl's breasts for two or three seconds and then placed them on Ruth's shoulders. She chuckled, took a hand off one shoulder and held Ruth under the chin.

'No need to blush like that, girl. You're a strong, well-made woman. Not like my Elizabeth or like my niece Sophie Usher.'

'No one has ever spoken to me like that,' Ruth muttered.

'Then it's time someone did.' Lady Fairbrother's tone became more serious. 'I was married when I was your age, Ruth. Had my eldest son when I was eighteen.' The two women walked in silence for a few paces. 'What are you going to do with your life, Ruth?'

'I've never thought about it.'

'You're sure you've never thought about it?' Lady Fairbrother stopped suddenly and looked deep into Ruth's eyes. 'Not even when Mark was here?'

'Not like that,' was Ruth's shy reply.

'And you never think about it now? Would you think about it if Mark came back with Sir Henry?' Ruth lowered her eyes away from the other woman's searching eyes. 'Life would have been so much easier for you, Ruth, if you had been the daughter of a gentleman. If you had money of your own.'

'I have my family.'

'The Trents,' Lady Fairbrother snorted. 'Much good they'll be for you now King Charles is back in England.'

'Where they go, I go.'

'I like your spirit, girl.' Lady Catherine continued cheerfully. 'We don't have to talk about it now. I've told your foster-parents they can stay for as long as Sir Henry allows. He's in London at present and will be here in seven days' time. Come and show me your room. I haven't been here for eight years. You're in the old nursery, aren't you?'

'That's right, Lady Catherine.'

The two women went up to the next floor together, arm in arm. Ruth felt sad at the implications of Lady Fairbrother's words. After eight years she would have to leave her room and go elsewhere. She could hardly remember her parents' home and had never seen the farm owned by Colonel Trent. Lady Fairbrother released Ruth's arm when they reached the bedroom. She moved round the room, showed a keen interest in the way Ruth had arranged the furniture, the ornaments and vases of flowers, and examined the books kept on the bedside table.

'I can tell this is how you like it. The room doesn't look much like the old nursery now.' Lady Fairbrother sighed. 'With Henry not yet married, it won't be needed as a nursery. As for Elizabeth, she won't want to climb two flights of stairs to get to her room. No, I think it will always be your room until a young Fairbrother occupies it.'

Ruth looked at the older woman and was surprised to see her eyes were moist. It suddenly dawned on her that, for all Lady Fairbrother's intolerance and stubborn pride, she was a lonely woman, fast approaching old age If only her husband had not been killed in the war. If Edmund had not died of wounds, he would be married by now. If only Elizabeth was not crippled and scarred. If Mary and Anne had not died in infancy, they would also be married. Under normal circumstances, Lady Fairbrother might be in her own home now, together with her husband and surrounded by half a dozen grandchildren. It had been a cruel time in which to be born and the repercussions of the war were not yet over. If Mark... yes, if only Mark had not gone away.

Ruth reached out and took Mark's mother's hand. Lady Fairbrother became aware of the curious way in which Ruth was observing her. She turned her head to look out of the window but did not remove her hand from Ruth's.

'I always admired the view from here,' she said. 'It's the best view in the house. The grounds look so peaceful from this angle.' She turned back to Ruth. 'We'd better go downstairs to rejoin Elizabeth and your family.'

They were descending the stairs arm in arm when Lady Fairbrother saw one of the servant girls. 'Tell Master Foster I'll be in the drawing room, girl,' she commanded.

The servant curtsied, replied, 'Yes, Lady Fairbrother,' and scurried away. Ruth smiled inwardly. It did not take very long to change the established order, she thought. Elizabeth, Claire and Sarah Trent were already seated as they entered the drawing room.

'My husband sends his apologies,' Sarah Trent began. 'He was called away on urgent military business while you were upstairs.'

'My compliments to Colonel Trent,' Lady Fairbrother replied. 'I would have returned earlier had Ruth not detained me.'

Sarah Trent gave a warm smile. 'She's grown up to be a credit to us all. I'm very proud of both my daughters.' There was no reply to this statement and she hesitated for a short while before continuing. 'As I'm sure you are of your own daughter, Lady Catherine.'

'Yes.' Lady Fairbrother turned to look at Ruth. 'A credit to you and your husband.'

The exchange of pleasantries was brought to an abrupt end by Digby Foster's entrance. He announced that the carriage was at the entrance to the Hall. The two older women stood up and shook hands while Claire and Elizabeth embraced and kissed each other on the cheek. Ruth went round to assist Elizabeth and took her right arm while Lady Fairbrother took her left arm. The trio moved slowly along the hallway, through the door and on to the front terrace. Ruth was surprised to find that Digby Foster had already mustered a small group of servants. They stood at the foot of the steps where the carriage was waiting. Half a dozen soldiers of Colonel Trent's regiment were standing outside their small guardhouse about a hundred yards away but made no attempt to move closer. It was obvious that the news of the visit had travelled fast. As the three of them reached the end of their journey down the steps, the coachman made a low, deferential bow and opened the door of the carriage. Taking their cue from him, the knot of assembled grooms and gardeners bowed awkwardly. The servant girls curtsied with varying degrees of proficiency. Ruth met Digby Foster's eyes as he finished his bow. The wicked thought crossed her mind that he would have the servants practising before the new master arrived.

Ruth and the coachman helped Elizabeth into the carriage. She squeezed Elizabeth's hand as she did so and then stood back to watch Elizabeth's mother mount the first step. Lady Fairbrother paused and half turned as if expecting Ruth to curtsy to her. Although the Commonwealth might be dead, its spirit lived on in Ruth. She would not publicly curtsy to anyone. Ruth reached out her right hand to take hold of Lady Fairbrother's hand and raised herself up on to her tiptoes. As she did so, she brushed her lips across the other woman's cheek. A look of surprise which flickered across Lady Fairbrother's face was quickly suppressed. Ruth heard a slight buzz of noise from the group of servants behind. This was quickly stilled as Lady Fairbrother looked down and said, 'You *have* grown up since the last time I saw you, Ruth.'

She turned to go into the carriage as Ruth replied, 'Yes, Lady Fairbrother.'

# 5

## JUNE 1660

Although Claire visited Elizabeth daily after the Fairbrother's visit, Ruth thought it best not to accompany her. She preferred to help her foster-mother begin the packing in preparation for leaving Aireton Hall. By the end of that week, the small troop of soldiers who mounted guard had returned to their unit and the guardhouse was already being dismantled. Ruth detected a subtle change in the attitude of the servants towards her. They were still polite but seemed to have become slightly more wary and distant than before. Claire still remained as cheerful as ever but Ruth felt her foster-parents were worried and abstracted. No doubt they were anxious to know what their future would be under the newly restored monarchy. Six days after Lady Fairbrother's visit Claire returned home in a high state of excitement to say that Sir Henry would arrive the following day. He was going to call on his mother first and then the two of them would come over to Aireton Hall. Colonel Trent gave orders for one of the grooms to ride over to the steward's lodge early in the morning. The groom was to wait there until Sir Henry arrived and then ride back to the Hall so that the carriage could be sent for Lady Fairbrother and her son. Colonel Trent specifically asked Claire and Ruth to be present to meet Sir Henry on his arrival.

Both girls found it hard to concentrate the following morning. Claire tried to engage Ruth in conversation but Ruth was disinclined to talk. The events of the last few days had revived the memories of Mark which she had pushed to the back of her mind during the past two years. She wondered if Sir Henry would be like his brother and if Mark had returned to England with King Charles's court.

The groom rode up at last and instructions were given to the coachman to take the carriage on the short journey to and from the steward's lodge. Sarah Trent joined the two girls in the drawing room to be followed shortly afterwards by her husband. After what seemed an interminable time, they heard the sound of a carriage on the drive. This was followed almost at once by a knock on the door and then by Digby Foster opening it to announce Sir Henry's imminent arrival. Colonel Trent stood aside to allow the three ladies to leave and was followed in his turn by the steward. As Ruth accompanied the family to the front terrace, she was surprised to see all the household servants ranged on one side of the steps, with the grooms and gardeners standing on the other side. The coachman had already assisted Lady Fairbrother from the carriage. Digby Foster took up a position at the top of the stairs, a few yards from the family group. It was almost as though he had already distanced himself from the Trents and those who served them.

Sir Henry appeared in the doorway of the carriage and, at a signal from the steward, the servant girls curtsied and the men bowed. It was a more polished performance than the display of the previous week. Sir Henry dismounted from the carriage, waved his hand in the direction of the servants and then began to climb the steps, followed by Lady Fairbrother two or three paces behind. When he reached the top, Colonel Trent stepped forward, extended his hand and greeted him formally. There was the briefest of handshakes. Sir Henry looked across in the direction of the steward who made a low bow for the second time.

'Very glad to see you back, Sir Henry,' Digby Foster said.

'Glad to be back, Foster. Won't be staying long this time.' Sir Henry turned his head to look at the groups of servants and other workers clustered at the base of the steps. 'You still steward here, Foster?' he asked.

'Yes, Sir Henry.'

'Then get these people back to work,' he snapped.

Digby Foster move his hands apart. The servants began to disperse slowly and reluctantly. Ruth had been studying Sir Henry closely while this interchange took place. He had the same dark hair as his brother Mark and the same grey eyes but was about two inches shorter. He was overweight for his height and looked older than his twenty-eight years. There were deep, cynical lines about his face. She wondered if his eight years of voluntary exile had been spent in dissipation. To her eyes, he appeared extravagantly dressed with his wide lace collar and cuffs, brocade coat and waistcoat, together with voluminous silk breeches. He was carrying a black gold-topped cane and wearing a court rapier. Sir Henry was not quite how she expected Mark's brother to look. He walked past the Trent ladies without pausing to be introduced and Digby Foster hurried to open the front door for him. Lady Fairbrother followed in his wake, with Claire and her mother close behind. Ruth took Colonel Trent's arm as the two of them brought up the rear. Sir Henry and his mother were already seated by the time Ruth arrived in the drawing room.

Colonel Trent waited until the ladies of his family were seated and then sat in his own chair.

'My wife, Sir Henry,' he said. 'And these two girls are my daughters. Your mother and my family are already acquainted.'

Sir Henry looked first at Claire and then at Ruth in a slightly puzzled way. 'Any other members of your family?' he asked.

'I'm lucky enough to have two more daughters.'

Sir Henry still appeared dissatisfied. 'Two other daughters, y'say?' Sarah Trent intervened to confirm that there were four daughters in the Trent family and to say that she had asked the steward to bring wine for the gentlemen and four cups of chocolate for the ladies.

'While we wait for Foster,' Sir Henry began. 'I'll give you news from London. I return there tomorrow. Anxious to finish as much work as I can today. First thing is about Aireton Hall. Fines imposed by rebels were never paid. Because you, Colonel, used the Hall as your headquarters, land couldn't be sold to pay fines. Means title is still in name of brother Edmund. As estate is entailed, I'm fully entitled to take possession. Is that clear?'

---

'I've always understood that to be the position,' Colonel Trent answered in as mild a manner as he could muster.

'I'm not a hard man.' Sir Henry's face broke into a smile and he looked at Ruth. 'Understand from Mother your family's been quite kind to sister Elizabeth.'

'Claire is the girl to thank there,' Sarah Trent interrupted.

Sir Henry ignored this intervention. 'Be in London another month or so. Don't need Aireton Hall myself till then.'

His flow of speech was stopped by the arrival of Digby Foster and one of the servant girls. They placed the wine, glasses and cups of chocolate on the table.

'Is there anything else you need?' the steward asked.

'No, Foster. Not now,' Sir Henry answered impatiently. He waited until the servants left and then asked, 'Where was I?'

'Saying you wouldn't need Aireton Hall for some time,' Colonel Trent replied.

'Right. Mother asked me to let you stay. Another three weeks. Because of your kindness to Elizabeth, you understand.'

'We are indebted to you, Lady Catherine,' the colonel said gallantly. 'But what if your youngest son returns before then?'

'He won't be returning,' she answered, looking straight at Ruth.

A sudden fear swept through Ruth. Surely this could not mean that Mark was dead? As Lady Fairbrother continued to look at her, Ruth thought she detected a brief expression of compassion on Mark's mother's face.

'Fact is,' Sir Henry interrupted, 'Mark's off to the Indies. Got a passage on a Dutch ship. On his way to join army of the Great Mogul. European mercenaries are well paid in India.'

Ruth fought to contain her emotions. If only Mark had taken her foster-father's advice, he would not now be sailing off to danger in a far-away land. Sarah Trent looked across anxiously at Ruth and hurriedly changed the subject. 'You would like your mother and sister to move in when we leave in three weeks' time then, Sir Henry?' she asked.

'Yes. Leave you ladies and Foster to arrange details. As for you, colonel. News at court is that most of parliamentary army will be disbanded. Your regiment's to go. Your General Monck'll send written orders soon. He's Duke of Albemarle now. Got the Garter as well. He'll tell you to take your troops to Newmarket. Royalist officer'll take over. He'll choose enough trustworthy noncommissioned officers and men to form a company of king's army. Rest of you'll be discharged.'

Colonel Trent made no reply. Ruth thought he looked old and frail suddenly.

'Cheer up, Colonel. You can go home quietly. Only the regicides are going to hang,' Sir Henry said with spurious cheerfulness. 'For the moment.' He paused for two or three seconds to give a hint of menace to the last phrase. 'Anyway, I've to return to London. The king doesn't know where to turn for advice. Since the Parliamentary commissioners dissolved, the country's run itself. King Charles needs to employ all sorts of parliament men to keep government going. Got to go back to give him support. He came to rely on me when we were together in Holland. Don't get much thanks for it though.' He grinned almost to the point of leering. 'Tell you the truth. Charles is an ungrateful devil. Expects everything from his friends and gives nothing in return. But you roundheads wouldn't tell on me, would you?'

'Then why go back to Charles Stuart?' Ruth demanded. 'Why not stay in Aireton Hall?'

'It's the company he keeps I like,' Sir Henry replied, looking hard at Ruth. 'Especially the ladies, young Mistress Trent.'

'I don't think the ladies wish to discuss politics, Henry,' Lady Fairbrother interjected before Ruth could answer.

Sarah Trent rose from her chair. 'With your leave, Lady Catherine. And yours, Sir Henry. My daughters and I will withdraw.'

'I too, if I may,' Colonel Trent added. 'I will send Master Foster to you. He will give you every assistance. In the meantime, I have military duties to attend to. Please let me take my leave of you tomorrow before you return to London, Sir Henry.'

\* \* \* \* \*

The following day was bright and sunny. It was a typical day in early June with a few white clouds moving slowly in an otherwise clear, blue sky. A little breeze stopped the temperature being more than pleasantly warm. Claire had decided not to visit Elizabeth until after Sir Henry left for London but Ruth was in no mood to keep her foster-sister company. Nor did Ruth feel like sewing or reading that morning. She offered to help Sarah Trent with packing but was told there was no hurry now that Sir Henry had given the family three weeks grace. Ruth found herself wandering around the house. The events of the past few days had been difficult to comprehend. If only Mark had acted on Colonel Trent's advice, he would be master of Aireton Hall now. She felt resentment that her world, with the world of thousands like her, could be turned upside down because a thirty year old former Prince of Wales returned to England from his exile in Holland.

Ruth decided she would take a stroll around those beloved gardens she knew so well. They were at their best this time of year. She always felt sad when the blossoms became full blown during the hot summer days, only to die at the approach of autumn. Finally, she found herself by the ornamental ponds at the left side of the house. Ruth walked slowly round, looking at the fish swimming beneath the water lily plants. At last she sat on a stone bench at the side of one of the pools. The sunlight was bright and Ruth closed her eyes so that she could concentrate on listening to the sound of the birds singing in the trees around.

She must have dozed off because the next thing she was aware of was the sound of a man's voice asking, 'Mistress Ruth?'

Her eyes opened and she saw Sir Henry in front of her. She rose quickly.

'Don't get up for me,' he said, taking his place on the bench beside her as she sat down again. 'Foster told me I might find you here.'

Ruth was at a loss to know how to reply. Her brain was still a little drowsy.

'You're Mistress Ruth, aren't you?'

'Yes, Sir Henry.'

'Mistress Ruth Trent?'

'No. My name is Ruth Parker.'

'Indeed.' Sir Henry turned towards her, his eyes resting on her firm, well formed breasts. 'Ruth Parker, ay?' She found his intent look uncomfortable. 'And you're the colonel's ward?' His voice was clipped and harsh, so unlike the soft, gentle speech of Mark, which Ruth remembered.

'He has been like a father to me,' she answered. 'Why do you ask? Of what concern is it to you, sir?'

He chuckled. 'Like brother Mark said you'd be. And as I saw yesterday. Girl with spirit. Fine looking woman, too.'

Ruth began to rise from the bench, 'Your pardon, sir.' She felt his hand on her shoulder as he pushed her down again.

'Sit down, girl. I've something to say to you.' Sir Henry ruminated for a few seconds and then continued. 'Could never see why Mark lived like a monk. Didn't seem to be interested in other women. Now I understand.'

'Please say what it is you wish to tell me, so that we can bring this meeting to a close,' she replied with as much dignity as was possible in the circumstances.

'Just so. Always get carried away at sight of pretty filly. Fact is, Mother wanted me to talk to you before I go back to London.'

'Your mother? She knows where I am. Lady Catherine saw me a few days before you came.'

'Not so simple, Ruth. Concerns where you're going to live. Involves my sister too. I'm master here now and Mother felt I ought to speak to you. Even though I'm returning to London this afternoon.'

'I am sorry. I do not understand how this concerns me and Elizabeth.'

'I'll explain. Mother's not getting any younger. You must have noticed. As for my sister. Her body's like a sack of potatoes. Face like a plate of oatmeal. No chance of her ever getting a man.' He gave an admiring glance at Ruth. 'Not like some I know.'

Ruth squirmed uncomfortably. 'Elizabeth's a very sweet natured woman. I'm sure she'd be a loving wife, if she was given the chance. If she had a large enough dowry.'

'Pigs might fly. No good looking to me.'

'Couldn't your Uncle, Master Usher, help out?'

'Not Uncle George. Been sending money to support Mother for the past eight years. Also sent funds to me and Mark while we've been abroad. Must have drained the old devil dry. Between you and me, hopes either Mark or I'll marry Sophie. His daughter, a plain, little thing but she'll get a good dowry. He's a widower. Sophie's his only child and will get his land when he dies.'

'But why was your brother penniless, Sir Henry. Why did he have to return to Sweden and then go to India?'

'Devilish expensive staying with the king. Always needed money. Had to use Mark's share as well. That's why he joined the Swedish Army and is in India now. Fact is, king couldn't wander round Europe like a beggar.'

The full enormity of Sir Henry's remarks struck Ruth like a blow. 'And you let your own brother face danger and sail far away. Just... Just so that you... you and that reprobate Charles Stuart could squander your brother's money. Have you no principles?'

'Steady, girl. Mark thought it his duty and a privilege to help. I had to have money of my own. The king couldn't see me in rags.'

Ruth rose from the bench. This time she was too quick for Sir Henry to push her down. He stood up and they faced each other, Ruth's eyes blazing with anger. She was furious not only with Sir Henry but also with Mark for allowing himself to be used in that way. 'Good day, sir. You and I have nothing to say to each other.'

Sir Henry did not seem perturbed. He smiled ingratiatingly. 'Look, Ruth. Hear me out. Can't go back to Mother before I say what she asked me to tell you.' Ruth made no reply. She looked at him unflinchingly. 'Forgot myself, Ruth. Got to talk about you and Elizabeth.' There was a brief pause. 'In the name of Christ, sit down, Ruth. Can't talk to a pretty girl standing up, dammit.' His tone became more placatory. 'Come on. Sit down, please.'

Ruth sat down reluctantly on the stone bench and Sir Henry sat down to her right.

'That's better,' he continued. 'Fact is, Mother and Elizabeth going to be pretty lonely soon. Elizabeth doesn't go out much but she's pretty friendly with your sister.' He waited for a response but none came.

'And my sister quite likes you, Ruth. Anyway, Mother wants Claire to stay on at Aireton Hall. Be like a sister to Elizabeth.'

'Then you must seek her father's permission.'

'Not necessary,' he snapped back. 'She's twenty two. Own mistress now. Fact is, Mother wants you to stay as a companion for Elizabeth and herself. What d'you say, Ruth.'

'Lady Catherine must know I could not take a decision like that without seeking my father's advice.'

'Don't be a fool, girl. What can an old couple like the Trents do for a fine looking woman like you now?'

'I don't understand.'

Sir Henry leaned towards her and lowered his voice. 'Won't spend all my time in London, you know. Be back here half a dozen times a year.' He rested his right hand on her knee and slipped his arm round her waist. 'Look at those dowdy clothes you're wearing. Don't you want fine clothes, expensive perfumes, rich jewels. I could be your *bel ami,* as the French say.'

Ruth sprang to her feet. Her cheeks were scarlet but her voice was as cold as ice. 'You, Henry Fairbrother are the most despicable, most contemptible man I have ever met. You are not fit to be called a gentleman. I hope I never see you again.'

She turned her back on him without waiting for a reply, and started to run towards the house.

\* \* \* \* \*

Claire came out of the drawing room as Ruth hurried through the entrance of Aireton Hall. She took one look at Ruth's flushed face and heaving breasts and asked what was wrong.

'Henry Fairbrother,' Ruth answered breathlessly. 'I hate that family!' When the sound of the conversation brought her foster-mother into the hall as well, Sarah Trent looked at Ruth anxiously and enquired what had happened. Ruth looked round her quickly, as if expecting the servants to appear at any moment and then suggested they went into the drawing room. Her foster-mother and Claire were both a fraction over five feet tall, while Ruth was already five inches taller than either of them, but they each took one of her arms as they walked together into the drawing room. Ruth sat down, with the other women hovering nearby and peering enquiringly at her.

'What's happened between you and Sir Henry?' Sarah Trent asked.

'He insulted me. Asked me to be his paramour.'

'No,' Claire said, looking shocked.

'He told me his mother wanted Claire and I to live here and keep them company. Those Fairbrothers are in it together.'

'Why are you so sure that Sir Henry ...?' her foster-mother asked tentatively.

'Because he asked me. And because he held me,' Ruth replied almost brutally.

'I blame myself,' Sarah Trent said as she started to cry. 'We should have moved as soon as we knew Charles Stuart was back.'

'Don't cry, Mother. There's no need. I've grown up in the past two years. I'm a woman now, not a silly girl. He knows exactly what I think of him.'

'I'm sorry, Ruth,' her foster-mother replied. 'You're growing up so fast. I forget you're not a child.'

'Don't worry, Mother. That Fairbrother man leaves for London this afternoon. God willing, none of us will ever see him again.'

'I'll have to tell your father, of course, Ruth. He'll know what to do.'

'I won't mind. Can I go now to splash some cold water on my face?' The others looked anxiously as she left to climb the two flights of stairs to her room.

\* \* \* \* \*

A few minutes later Ruth returned downstairs and Digby Foster came to say that Colonel Trent wished to see her in his office. As she walked along the long gallery, towards the door at the far end, Ruth wondered how many more times she would come through here before she left Aireton Hall for good. Colonel Trent rose as she entered his office. His face was grim. He helped her to a chair and then sat down himself.

'Fairbrother's a blackguard,' he said, looking at her closely. 'No lasting effects, I hope?'

'No, Father. I'm a harder character than I was two years ago.' Ruth gave a wan smile. 'The people of England didn't fight a long and bitter war just to have the likes of the Fairbrothers doing as they please with us.'

Colonel Trent's face clouded over as he recollected all the battles in which he had fought. 'If I wasn't in uniform I'd call him out.'

'Please, Father. Not on my account. Fairbrother knows my opinion of him.'

'As you wish, Ruth. However, I propose to visit one of my company commanders. If Fairbrother has the gall to take his leave of me, I shall be elsewhere. I suggest you, your mother and sister are unavailable if he comes back here.' Colonel Trent rose from his chair. At the same time, Ruth hurried forward, kissed him and held him tightly. There were tears in his eyes as he released her.

*     *     *     *     *

At two o'clock that afternoon, Sir Henry rode up to Aireton Hall to be met by Digby Foster. When he asked if he could take his leave of Colonel Trent, he was told that the colonel had been called away unexpectedly to Great Hampendown. Sir Henry then asked to see the ladies of the house. He was told they were indisposed.

*     *     *     *     *

Colonel Trent was out early next morning and the three ladies of his family were just finishing breakfast when Digby Foster announced the arrival of Lady Fairbrother and Elizabeth. Sarah Trent asked her steward to show the two visitors into the drawing room and to tell them that she would be with them in a minute or so. Elizabeth and Claire greeted each other warmly when the Trent ladies joined the Fairbrothers. By contrast, the greetings between Lady Fairbrother on one hand and Sarah Trent and Ruth on the other hand were so formal as to be barely polite. After these exchanges were over, Lady Fairbrother sat bolt upright in her chair.

'I'll come straight to the point, Mistress Trent,' she said sternly. 'My son told me none of your family had the courtesy to take leave of him yesterday. I accept Colonel Trent might be called away urgently but why did you, your daughter and your ward not receive Henry?'

'We were all unwell, Lady Catherine,' Sarah Trent stammered. 'Digby Foster gave our regrets to your son.'

'I know very well what Master Foster told Sir Henry.' Lady Fairbrother replied in a voice tinged with menace.

'In that case, madam,' Ruth said. 'Since you have heard the news from our steward as well as your son, there's no need to question my mother.'

'Indeed, Mistress Parker? And which precise ailment laid you low yesterday afternoon?'

'Shall I say an attack of the vapours. Brought on by boorish behaviour,' Ruth snapped back. 'Your son Mark did not take his leave of us two years ago. Should we feel obliged to your other son?'

'Please, Mother,' Elizabeth said. 'Why can't we all be friends?'

'Be quiet, Elizabeth,' Lady Fairbrother shouted at her. Elizabeth started to cry, making her mother more exasperated. 'Why can't we discuss this like ladies?' Lady Fairbrother looked hard at Ruth. 'Do we need to talk in the presence of the younger generation, Mistress Trent?'

Claire and Elizabeth got up. Claire put her arm round the other girl's shoulder. 'You come along with me, Elizabeth. I'll take you to my sitting room.'

Elizabeth nodded and the two girls put their arms round each other's waists as they left the room.

Lady Fairbrother continued to stare at Ruth. 'Are you not joining them?'

'I prefer to stay here.' Ruth turned to look at Sarah Trent. 'Unless you wish me to go, Mother.'

'You don't have to leave,' her foster-mother replied. 'You can stay if you want to.'

Lady Fairbrother looked sourly at Ruth and then turned her head away. 'I would have preferred to speak to you privately, Mistress Trent. Your ward should remember she's in my house now.'

'So your son reminded me yesterday morning, madam,' Ruth said sharply.

'Please, Lady Catherine,' Sarah Trent pleaded. 'May we all come to the point?'

'Quite so, Mistress Trent. I wished to find out why my son was turned away from his own home?'

'I am sorry to cause ill-feeling but Ruth was very upset following an encounter with Sir Henry.'

'How was this?'

'I am best able to answer,' Ruth interrupted. 'Your son, madam, insulted me. To be frank, he asked me to be … to act in an illicit way.' Ruth began to blush.

'You refused him?'

'Of course. How else would you expect me to behave?'

'Henry's a hot-headed fool. He's been so used to the favours of these foreign women, he can't recognise an honest woman when he sees one.'

'Ruth is pure gold,' Sarah Trent interposed gently. 'Not like your counterfeit coin.'

'Or like your loose cavalier ladies,' Ruth added.

'Watch your tongue, Ruth!' Lady Fairbrother exclaimed. 'Sir Henry's actions do not excuse yours. His proposal to you did not have my approval.'

'But that's not all,' Ruth continued angrily. 'He said you wished Claire and me to live at Aireton Hall. Did you not consider that I am under my father's protection? Do you not think my father should have been asked?'

'Perhaps so,' Lady Fairbrother replied. 'But Sir Henry is the master now. He and I decide who lives in Aireton Hall, who stays and who goes.'

'It need not have been so.'

'Pray why not, Mistress Parker?'

'Why not indeed, madam?' Ruth enquired angrily. 'If Mark had joined my father's regiment, instead of going back to Sweden, your family's fines could have been reduced to a small sum. If that nominal amount had been paid by his uncle, Master Usher, the Commissioners would have transferred the land to Mark. He would be the master of Aireton Hall now.'

'I see.' Lady Fairbrother's tone was frosty. 'Quite a plot. What went wrong then?'

'Mark would not agree. He has too much sense of honour.'

'Quite so. That's what I would have expected from Mark.'

'And why do you expect the precious Fairbrother honour to be more exalted than mine?'

'You're making things difficult, Ruth.'

'I think not, Lady Catherine. It's your son Henry who is making life difficult. Not for me but for your other son. Henry told me that Mark's share of the money sent to them by their uncle had been used to keep Charles Stuart and Henry in fancy clothes. And spent on fast women, no doubt. It verges on a swindle.'

'Mark was always soft-hearted. He almost certainly considered it his duty.'

'And because of that Mark is now far away while Henry is in favour at the court of that man Charles Stuart.'

'Take care, Ruth,' Sarah Trent warned her. 'England is a kingdom again.'

'I congratulate you on your perspicacity, Madam,' Lady Fairbrother said tartly. 'I only wish your ward shared your good sense.'

Ruth raised her head again. 'You asked me why I did not receive your son yesterday afternoon.' Her eyes were blazing with rage. 'Should you still care to know, I can tell you that he is a vile seducer, a disgusting libertine, a venal swindler and a coward. If I were a man, I would have killed him.'

Both the older women looked startled at this outburst. Lady Fairbrother was the first to recover her speech 'You're quite a firebrand, Mistress Parker. Whatever Sir Henry's faults may be, he is still my son. He is now the legal owner of Aireton Hall, so stop dreaming of my other son Mark.'

'Just so, Lady Catherine. He has given us three weeks in which to leave and leave in that time we will. Please tell him if he returns before his three weeks is up, I do not wish to see him. And as you cannot condemn Henry Fairbrother because he is your son, you are not welcome here. I have no wish to see you or either of your sons ever again. None of the Fairbrothers or their precious Hall. Therefore, I wish you goodbye, Lady Catherine.'

Ruth went to the door and held it open. For a moment, she thought she detected a look of regret on the older woman's face but it was replaced at once by a haughty stare.

'Goodbye, Ruth,' Lady Catherine replied.

Ruth went across to comfort her foster-mother who was quietly weeping.

# 6

## APRIL 1663

The passengers on the 'Falcon' spent a tedious few hours, waiting until a place had been found for their ship at the quayside. The heat in the harbour was almost over-powering during the day and Claire spent the whole time lying down on her bunk in the small cabin which she shared with Ruth and with Maria Ferrara. The ship finally docked in the late afternoon and by that time the slight breeze made the heat a little more endurable. Ruth did not wish to be confined to the cabin all day long and had accompanied Maria up on the deck. She was fascinated by the sight of so many merchant ships congregated together. There must have been nearly a hundred vessels of all different nationalities. As well as the ships of English, Dutch, Portuguese and other European nations, there were many Arab dhows and even a few Chinese junks. The dhows had brightly coloured triangular shaped sails and flew giant streamers of crimson silk, making the junks look clumsy and almost dowdy by contrast. Once their ship reached the harbour of Swally, Ruth had been eager to get ashore, away from the vessel which had been their home for three months but Claire seemed strangely indifferent. Ruth was worried about the change in her foster-sister's mood during the twelve weeks' voyage from London. The ship had only touched land once during the long sea trip. That had been when they called at Oporto to unload some English woollen cloth and to take on water and a cargo of Portuguese wines. A few Portuguese passengers, bound for India, also embarked at the same time. Maria Ferrara was one of that group. Because of the very limited accommodation, passengers were put three to a cabin and the middle-aged Portuguese lady had come into theirs at Oporto. Claire was strangely resentful of the time which Ruth and Maria spent together and disliked the invasion of her privacy. Her appetite had gone and she was frequently sick. Ruth put this down to seasickness and the unappetising nature of shipboard food. Once they were back on dry land, Ruth felt that Claire would soon be restored to her normal good humour and robust health. Ruth was forced to admit it was a worry to her that Claire had lost ten or eleven pounds of weight during the voyage.

It was now evening and the three women stood together on the quayside waiting to pass through the Mogul Emperor's customs house. They seemed a curiously assorted group. Ruth's face had been tanned to a light brown through the long weeks in the tropic sun, making her blue eyes and long, fair, curly hair seem even paler by comparison. She was about six inches taller than the other two women and there was just a hint of plumpness about her, no doubt caused by the inactivity of the past few weeks. Maria Ferrara was a short, plump, middle-aged woman. She had the swarthy face and dark brown eyes typical of the Portuguese. Her shiny, black hair was already streaked with silver grey. Claire's complexion was sallow to the point of pastiness, accentuating the darkness of her hair. The recent loss of weight meant that her clothes hung loosely round her and the skin on her face had lost its customary elasticity. Claire seemed almost to have shrunk into herself and Ruth, who was standing erect, appeared to tower over her. The other twenty-one passengers had also disembarked and were waiting to go into the customs house. There must have been several dozen porters arguing and jostling with each other to carry the Europeans' luggage. Fifteen of them clustered round the three women to gesticulate and offer their services. Ruth was glad she had asked Maria to start teaching her Marathi while they were on the voyage together. At least she could understand some of the words the porters used. Maria spoke rapidly to the porters and they moved back a few feet, talking among themselves in a more subdued tone. Ruth was able to follow the sense of Maria's instructions to the porters and Claire, who had not made any effort to learn the language, asked her to translate. During the voyage Ruth felt that their roles of elder sister and younger sister were becoming reversed. She was the one who cared for Claire during her illness and who had persuaded the purser to give them as much privacy as was possible on a crowded ship. It seemed strange to her that she was the one who had befriended the good natured Maria Ferrara, even though she was only eighteen at the start of the voyage and Maria was thirty years older.

Their hand luggage was brought to them at last by two members of the crew and placed at the feet of the three ladies. Ruth and Maria tipped the two sailors and this was a signal for the fifteen porters to push forward. The Portuguese lady called out in a loud voice that she wished to engage three porters at a fee of two pice each. Considerable dismay greeted this statement. Expressions of lamentation which would have done justice to a funeral procession greeted Maria's fresh offer to engage six porters at one pice each. Ruth saw that some of the other passengers had struck bargains with their porters and were already moving into the customs house. 'Why don't we employ nine porters at one pice each?' she asked. 'We only have nine pieces of hand luggage between us. If we don't hurry we'll be here until dark.'

'Yes, my dear,' Maria replied. 'That is the offer I was going to make as a last resort.' She quickly chose the nine porters nearest to her and dismissed the rest, who went off in search of other passengers. The porters picked up the baggage and went trotting off towards the long shed of the customs house, with the three women walking behind. The heat inside the customs house struck Ruth like an oven. Maria gave a small gold coin to an official at the entrance. He directed the porters to take places behind a stout Arab merchant, whose baggage was being meticulously examined, and motioned the three women to follow them. There were two Africans, carrying long whips, who stood at the side of the customs officials checking the Arab's baggage. As the porters engaged by Maria put the luggage down, the Africans playfully whipped the ground by the porters' feet.

Ruth saw there were hundreds of people of all nationalities waiting for their baggage to be examined. The customs house was filled with a babel of noise as travellers sought to attract the attention of officials. Maybe the passing of the gold coin had helped to speed their passage through the customs check. The official in front of them was dressed in a silk robe and wore a large turban with a jewel just above his forehead. He wore three heavy rings on each of his hands. After the examination of the Arab's baggage finished, Maria stepped forward and greeted the customs official. He nodded and then looked in the direction of the two young women. Maria replied in a language which Ruth did not understand but the customs officer indicated that all the bags must come forward together. An assistant moved at a leisurely pace towards them and opened every piece of luggage. The examination itself was laborious. The contents of each bag were emptied out and checked in detail. Ruth began to feel acute embarrassment as all her clothes were examined, including underwear which she had not had time to wash before disembarking. 'Don't worry, Ruth,' Maria whispered. 'It is always like this. You did not understand what I said because I spoke in Court Urdu.'

It was over at last, leaving the three women to repack their bags so that the porters could carry them out. The evening air seemed quite cool as they left the customs house. A large group of people were waiting a few yards away and Ruth wondered if Roland Lockyer, her foster-mother's cousin, would be there to meet them. She glanced round quickly but could not see him. At that moment a grey-bearded gentleman of about fifty years of age stepped out of the crowd to embrace Maria. After kissing each other, they began talking rapidly together until Maria laughingly indicated Ruth and Claire standing with the group of porters. She then introduced her husband Fernando to the two girls.

'One attends you, Senhora Trent?' he asked.

'Yes. We're going to Roland Lockyer's house,' Claire replied.

'Senhor Lockyer. Him I know. His bungalow is in Surat. He may not know your ship is here.'

Claire gave a cry of alarm.

'Do not worry, ladies,' Fernando continued. 'My house is your home tonight. I send message to Senhor Lockyer in morning.'

'We do not know how to thank you, Senhor Ferrara,' Ruth told him.

'Do not think about it. But, please hurry. It will be dark soon. Follow me.' He gave a quick command to the porters who picked up the hand baggage. The little party was soon surrounded by a shouting crowd. Although Claire became alarmed, neither of the Ferraras showed the least concern. As far as Ruth could understand, the milling crowd consisted of drivers of little two-wheeled carriages drawn up about a hundred yards away. The horses between the shafts looked very thin and hung their heads to the ground.

Fernando walked resolutely on, followed by the porters and the ladies of his party. There was a continual exchange of banter between the drivers of the carriages and the porters carried on, it seemed to Ruth, at a screaming pitch. The noise died down at last as the drivers became convinced they would not be hired. A short way past the row of horse-drawn carriages, Ruth noticed a large cart drawn by two white bullocks. Much to her surprise, she found that her host was making towards it. He stopped beside it and gave a command to the porters who loaded the luggage. They were paid off but not before another discussion took place about their pay. Fernando observed Ruth looking suspiciously at the bullock cart and smiled.

'You young ladies will find it slower but more comfortable than those tongas,' he said, waving his hands in the direction of the horse-drawn vehicles. On closer inspection, Ruth saw that their cart was upholstered in silk with a good supply of cushions available for the passengers. Fernando helped them into the cart and took his place beside the Indian driver. They travelled no faster than walking pace along a road shaded with trees. It was fast becoming dark but their host said there was no need to be alarmed as his house was only a mile from the quayside. After about a quarter of an hour the cart pulled off the road on to a little track and stopped in front of a large, one-storied, flat-roofed house. Fernando clapped his hands and three servants appeared carrying oil lamps. The lamps were placed on the ground and the servants put the palms of both hands together and raised them to the level of their mouths in greeting. Ruth turned to pick up her baggage only to be stopped by her host. He said that the servants would bring it to his guests' room. Fernando then helped them down from the cart and they followed the Ferraras through an archway into a small courtyard, which was surrounded by a series of rooms.

Ruth looked up to see that the centre of the roof was open to a cloudless, starlit sky. The group stood together in the small courtyard as Maria clapped her hands. This time a young, slender Indian girl appeared, carrying a lamp. Their hostess gave an order to the servant girl who began to move to a small opening in the wall, opposite the archway through which the Europeans had entered.

'Follow her,' Maria said. 'She will show you your room.'

The English girls followed the servant through the opening and found themselves in another courtyard. It was slightly smaller than the main courtyard and open to the sky in the same way. The servant led them to a room at the side. An oil lamp had been placed in the room already and was shedding its soft light on the walls. Although the day had been almost unbearably hot, the temperature in the room, with its thick walls and roof, was not unpleasant. The air was heavy with the smell of flowering plants. Crucifixes were nailed to the wall over the two small beds. When the servant began to speak in a mixture of Portuguese and her native tongue, Ruth waved her arms up and down and tried answering in the Marathi phrases which Maria had taught her on the voyage. The girl responded by bowing and going out.

Ruth thought how elegant the servant's long gown looked. Although she could not judge the girl's appearance in the limited light given by two oil lamps, she felt that the servant moved with remarkable grace. The pattern of her thought was broken by Claire saying, 'I'm beginning to wonder if I made a mistake in coming here.'

'You'll feel better when you get to Roland's house,' Ruth replied.

'I would never have come without you,' Claire continued. 'Promise you'll never leave me, Ruth.'

'Cheer up, Claire. You know we will always be together.'

Maria came in at that moment, closely followed by the servant.

'I am sorry, Ruth. Sorry, Claire,' Maria said. 'I should not have left you. Pushpa will help you with your toilet. Supper will be ready in ten minutes.' She spoke rapidly to the servant in Marathi. Pushpa busied herself with pouring water and attar of roses into two bowls.

'Thank you for your kindness, Maria. I don't know what Claire and I would have done without you,' Ruth said.

'I could not leave two young women, who do not know this country, alone at dusk on that quayside, could I? Now let Pushpa help you get ready.'

'Do not trouble to stay, Maria,' Ruth replied. 'Claire and I can manage. The next ten minutes passed quickly, enlivened by the non-verbal gestures used by Claire to communicate, combined with the good humoured way in which Ruth and Pushpa tried to talk to each other in Marathi. It had been a long day but Ruth was mentally and physically refreshed when Pushpa led them back into the main courtyard. They followed her through a small room and on to a verandah at the side of the bungalow.

The Ferraras were already seated at a small table and once their hosts had seen Ruth and Claire, Pushpa moved silently away. That girl's back is so straight when she walks, Ruth thought, she might almost be gliding. Fernando rose as the two girls approached the table. 'I thought it best to have supper here,' he began. 'It is always hot this month of year. End of next month, monsoon comes. Very heavy rain but once monsoon over, air is fresher.'

Two bearers came in at that point, carrying dishes of food which they placed on a side table. Ruth noticed that they were both dressed alike with a flat, red turban, a yellow jacket and a white cotton skirt reaching to their knees. They were dark-skinned, short but sturdily built and each had a large, black moustache.

The bearers moved silently and quickly to serve the food and needed no word of command. After they had gone back into the bungalow, Fernando, as if in answer to Ruth's unspoken enquiry said, 'Marathas. They are very honest. You treat them well, they are faithful. Our servants come from a village near Poona. About a hundred and fifty miles from here. That is why we speak Marathi when in house. When I go to port I talk to imperial officials in Urdu. Many other people in Surat speak Gujerati.'

'I wondered,' Ruth answered. 'I didn't understand when Maria spoke a different language in the customs house.'

'India is a land of many tongues. You cannot learn all of them. But the people will love you for ever if you speak to them in the language they learned at the knee of their mother.'

'You are a poet, Senhor,' Ruth laughed. 'But we have more immediate problems than learning to converse with your servants.'

'Forgive me, Senhora. I forget you are alone in a strange land. Leave things in my own good hands. I see to everything. I am shipping agent in port. That is why I live so close to Swally. I also good friends with agents of your East India Company. When the luggage is unloaded from the 'Falcon' tomorrow it will be put in East Indian warehouse. If you give me authority, I bring it to you.' He beamed at Ruth. 'It is least I can do for a friend of my wife. If you like, I also get local money for you at Exchange Office. It is near Imperial Customs House.'

'What about Roland Lockyer?' Claire asked.

'Ah, yes. Senhor Lockyer.' He turned to Ruth. 'Are you a relative of him?'

Claire intervened quickly. 'He is my mother's cousin. Ruth and I were brought up together.'

'Claire is to marry Master Lockyer,' Ruth said.

For a fleeting moment she thought she detected a look of incredulity pass over Fernando's face but it was quickly suppressed. He glanced at his wife, who nodded briefly.

'Forgive these questions, ladies. I have to know what kind of message to send to Senhor Lockyer. Tomorrow I send servant to say his future wife here.' He hesitated before turning to Ruth. 'And you, Senhora Ruth. Does Senhor Lockyer know you here?'

'He knows I am accompanying my sister,' she replied.

'And how old are you?' he asked quietly.

'I am just nineteen. I had my birthday a few days ago.'

Ruth was surprised to see Maria grasp her husband's hand. There were tears in her eyes as she did so. Fernando's tone was serious as he continued. 'India is a beautiful country but it is a very cruel country. Many Europeans do not live more than three or four years after they come here. Only the very strong survive. It is even harder for European children. Maria and I had three sons and a daughter but they are all buried here. Their bones lying under an alien sky.'

Nobody spoke for a few seconds. Fernando looked intently at Claire before speaking again. 'Believe me. In the name of Holy Mary, Mother of God. What I say is true. Unless you cannot live without Senhor Lockyer, go back now. The 'Falcon' does not leave for England until three days' time. Senhora Claire, are you certain you wish to marry Senhor Lockyer?'

'I gave my word.'

Fernando turned to Ruth. 'How long you stay in India, Senhora?'

'I made a promise to Claire and our mother that I would never leave her,' Ruth replied.

'Maria, these ladies are welcome to stay as long as they wish.' His wife nodded.

'I ask Senhor Lockyer to call at my house,' Fernando

continued. 'If you wish, you leave with luggage and go with him. If you want to stay, my house is yours.'

Maria looked softly at Ruth and said, 'You know, Ruth, you are the same age as my daughter would have been.'

Ruth rose from her chair and kissed Senhora Ferrara. As if to break the spell, Fernando rang a little bell and the two bearers came in to start clearing the dishes away. The small party moved back into the bungalow and their host suggested they sat in the courtyard to take advantage of the cooler night air. Claire asked to be excused on the grounds of tiredness but Maria only agreed that Claire should retire to the guest room on the understanding that Pushpa would wait there until Ruth came to bed.

'That girl is only fifteen,' Maria said, 'but very sensible. Women grow up very fast in this country.'

In spite of Ruth's protests, she was over-ruled and Pushpa was summoned to escort Claire to bed. The remaining trio settled down and Fernando pulled a clay pipe from his pocket. After filling it with tobacco, he lit a taper from one of the oil lamps and proceeded to light the pipe. He paused reflectively and then turned to Ruth.

'You did not finish telling me how you and your sister came to India.'

'How well do you know Roland Lockyer?' Ruth asked.

'I know him as a factor for East India Company. He and I work together sometimes. The English or Dutch may have a cargo of tobacco or cotton or sugar. If they have no ship of their own, they come to me. I find a ship for them.'

'What do you think of him?'

'Please, Senhora. He is man who is future husband of your sister Claire. What must I say to you?'

'Very well, Fernando. I will start from the beginning.'

Ruth began by saying how she had first met Roland Lockyer over six years earlier. Although she was fascinated by his stories about India, she had found herself, even as a young girl, vaguely repelled by this short, fat man with a high-pitched voice, who had looked much older than his real age. He was a cousin of her foster-mother and left for India after serving in the king's army. Thoughts of him had been put out of her mind by the change in her family's fortunes at the restoration of Charles II.

She explained how the Trents were compelled to leave the large country house which had been their home for the previous eight years. Ruth then went on to say how she had accompanied her foster-mother and Claire on the long, wearying journey from West Yorkshire to Suffolk, while Colonel Trent had gone with his regiment to Newmarket.

When they arrived at the Trent family farm, they found that it had been allowed to run down by her foster-father's brother. A great deal of work needed to be done to put it back into good heart. It was some weeks later before Colonel Trent was able to join them after his discharge, with several months' arrears of pay still owed to him. The financial problems were aggravated because her foster-father had made generous payments to all the house servants and estate workers before leaving Aireton Hall for good.

The following winter had been a hard one for them. Although Ruth helped in the house and on the farm as much as possible, it had not been enough. Colonel Trent was out in all weathers, working from dawn to dusk. Things improved in the following summer but in the middle of October he contracted pneumonia. Although he had appeared to rally at the end of November, he died, a worn-out old man, in the first week in December.

'I am sorry, Ruth. Please forgive me,' Fernando said. 'I do not wish to bring back painful memories to you.'

'He gave his life to the Commonwealth,' Ruth replied laconically. 'He had no will to live after the king returned.'

'Do you wish to continue?' Fernando asked gently.

'Yes. After all, I owe you an explanation for my presence here.'

Ruth went on to say that Roland Lockyer returned to England for a visit eighteen months previously. He stayed on the farm for three weeks in October. Ruth had found him physically unattractive. He had lost most of his hair and now covered his head with a large, powdered perriwig. Roland Lockyer seemed even flabbier, compared with his previous visit. Although he expended a great deal of effort in trying to flirt with Ruth, he proposed marriage to Claire just before he was due to return to India. When Claire declined on the gounds of her father's severe illness, he told Claire she need only write to him, to say she had changed her mind, and they could be married as soon as she reached India. After Colonel Trent died, the family could not keep the farm going. A lot of money had been spent on stock and new agricultural equipment and these had to be sold at a loss. In addition, the land did not fetch the price expected. So much land was previously sold by the Parliamentary Commissioners to pay the fines levied on royalist families that all land prices were depressed. When the Trent family paid off the debts owed to seed merchants and other creditors, there was not a lot of money left.

Ruth paused for a few seconds to collect her thoughts. This time Fernando did not prompt her. Both he and his wife waited patiently for Ruth to continue.

'Claire and I moved to London at the beginning of last year. We stayed with Frances, Claire's eldest sister. It was not a success. Her husband used to be a captain in father's regiment and is now a merchant in London. They live in a house in Cheapside. The trouble is they have three children in the family and Frances was expecting a fourth at the time. Mother would have been alright on her own as the devoted grandmother. Claire and I were just in the way. After six weeks, the three of us moved out and went into lodgings. Claire began to worry. With our money dwindling, she kept asking, 'What's going to happen to us?' Anyway, she decided to write to Roland Lockyer to see if his offer still stood. Claire's nearly twenty five years old and no beauty. So she took the letter to the office of the

East India Company in London and asked them to forward it. Six months later she received a reply and here we are.'

'But you are not marrying Senhor Lockyer!' Fernando exclaimed.

'I know. Mother was upset at the thought of Claire going. She kept asking if Claire was sure. In the end, Mother only agreed if I would go with Claire. She gave her some jewelry and a small dowry and has gone back to live with Frances. I promised Mother I would stay with Claire as long as she needed me.'

'Master Lockyer has a bad reputation among women,' Maria said. 'Let us hope marriage will change him.'

'He also drinks heavily and is said to take opium,' Fernando added.

'I have also found him a difficult man to like,' Ruth replied. 'I suspect Mother had considerable doubts about him. But Claire's mind is closed. She is determined to marry Roland Lockyer.'

'Speak to her as a sister, Ruth,' Maria said. 'If all she wishes is to be a bride, there are a dozen young men in the English factory who would be happy to be husband of Claire.'

'Do not forget, Ruth. My house is yours. As long as you wish,' Fernando added.

'Thank you. Both of you. I must go to bed now.'

Fernando stood up as Maria said, 'Follow me, Ruth.'

She followed Maria across the courtyard, watching the pool of light formed by the lamp which Maria carried. They went through the small opening and Ruth saw a dim light showing in the room which she had left just before supper. As they approached, Pushpa appeared at the entrance. At a brief word from Maria, she placed her hands together, raised them to her chin and glided away. Ruth looked across at the bed where Claire was lying and saw she was already asleep.

'You will be safe here,' Maria told her. 'May Holy Mary and all the angels watch over you.'

* * * *

Pushpa was standing nearby when Ruth awoke next morning. A tray containing two cups of brownish liquid and a hand of bananas had been placed on the table between the two beds. Designs in coloured chalk had been drawn around the edge of the tray. Pushpa held her hands together and raised them in the same greeting which Ruth had seen the previous day. Through the window and the open doorway Ruth could see the courtyard filled with bright sunshine. Claire stirred in the bed alongside and then rubbed her eyes sleepily before sitting up.

'Did you sleep well?' Ruth asked.

'Yes. I was tired out. And you?'

'Well enough.'

Ruth did not say her own night had been restless, disturbed by thinking about the talk with their hosts, after Claire had gone to bed.

'What's the time?' Claire asked sleepily as Maria came into the room.

'Good morning,' Maria answered. 'Just after five o'clock.'

'What?' Claire sat bolt upright. Her voice betrayed incredulity.

'At this time of the year, it is necessary to rise early,' Maria replied gently. 'It becomes very hot in the day and it is difficult to go out then.'

Ruth took a sip of her tea. 'We used to drink chocolate at home,' she said. 'Tea was always very scarce and expensive.'

Maria laughed. 'Tea grows in India. We drink it all the time. You cannot drink much wine during the day in hot weather or you become ill. When it is hot, tea is very refreshing.' She gave Ruth a significant look. 'I am sure you two sisters have very much to talk about. I leave you now and see you both at breakfast time.'

\* \* \* \* \*

An hour later Ruth and Claire were sitting outside in the main courtyard. It was already sultry and they were finding their European clothes heavy and uncomfortable. Claire appeared lethargic but at last roused herself sufficiently to ask Ruth about the subjects which had been discussed last night after she went to bed.

Ruth started by talking about the heat and how the weather would change soon when the monsoon came. Then she spoke about her wish to master the language of the people of the country. Finally, she mentioned that she had explained to their host why the two of them had come to India.

Ruth's tone became serious. 'Are you sure you want to marry Roland? We can always go back.'

'I'm nearly twenty five,' Claire answered wearily. 'What can I do if I go back? How will I live if I return to England? I'd be a laughing stock. And, of course, I gave my word.'

'Maria tells me he has a bad reputation with women.'

'I never expected a single man of thirty eight to be a saint. Once we're married, things will change.'

'Fernando says Roland drinks heavily.'

'Perhaps he's lonely,' Claire countered. 'If he's not alone so much, he will drink less.'

'Fernando suspects him of taking opium.'

'That may be just his imagination,' Claire replied stiffly. 'There are always tongues ready to wag.'

'Yes, but do you love him?'

'I'm going to marry him. Isn't that enough?'

'I could not marry a man I did not love,' Ruth answered.

'You've youth on your side now. You've beauty too.' There was a touch of bitterness in Claire's voice. 'But the years slide away. Like water running through the fingers. And beauty fades. Fading like the buds in May. Blooming for just a few hot summer days before the petals start to fall.' She sighed. 'Can't you see why I'm marrying Roland? He's the only man who has ever asked me.' Ruth was silent. In her present mood, Claire was impervious to rational argument. Perhaps her foster-sister might change her mind when she saw Roland Lockyer again. If he was really as debauched as the Ferraras said he must have greatly changed in the past eighteen months.

\* \* \* \* \*

Fernando's jaw tightened as he read the message brought in by his bearer. He had just finished breakfast in the company of his wife and his two guests. The three women looked at him intently as they waited to hear the reply from Roland Lockyer.

'I sent syce with message before dawn. Tell Senhor Lockyer his bride and her sister wait at my home.' His tone became almost contemptuous. 'Now he writes I must bring you to him. He does not say he is ill.'

'Do you wish my husband to take you there?' Maria asked, looking directly at Claire.

'Yes, of course.'

Maria glanced at Ruth, who nodded quickly. Fernando rose from the table and picked up the reply from Roland Lockyer.

'I go to make arrangements, ladies. Please excuse me.'

'My husband will take his own horse and ride with you,' Maria told them after Fernando left the room. 'You two will ride in a gharry.'

'A gharry? What's that?' Ruth asked.

'A horse-drawn carriage. It is faster than a bullock cart and bigger and more comfortable than those tongas you saw yesterday. Your heavy luggage will come by bullock cart later today. The syce who will be with you in the gharry is Des Raj, Pushpa's husband.'

'How long will it take to get to Surat?' Ruth enquired.

'Less than an hour. I often go there. If you are ready, I will send Pushpa to collect your bags and see they are loaded on the gharry.'

'How can we ever thank you and your husband?' Ruth asked.

'By promising to ask for help if you ever need it. Both of you.' She embraced the two girls and hurried out.

\* \* \* \* \*

The journey from the Ferrara's house to Surat passed pleasantly enough as Fernando rode alongside the horse-drawn carriage and chatted to the girls. The road along which they were travelling was lined with trees and they could see several vehicles moving in the same direction along the road. On four successive occasions, European horsemen rode in the direction of the port of Swally, greeted Fernando warmly and glanced curiously at the two English ladies. They also passed a number of carts loaded with produce, drawn by a single bullock and moving in the direction of Surat.

Fernando entertained them by pointing out the mango groves at the side of the road and the fields where tobacco and sugar cane were being grown. The houses at the edge of the city were of the same one-storied flat-roofed variety as the Ferrara's house. Alongside and between these large houses were small huts with mud walls and straw roofs. Fernando explained that these were quarters for the servants of the rich merchants. Many of the large houses had private gardens and some had pools. Because of the dry weather, the gardens were looking somewhat parched and the level of water in the pools was low. Wild begonia could be seen on the walls surrounding some of the houses. Ruth noticed that very few of the windows were glazed. Most of the windows just had wooden bars across them with wooden shutters outside.

They drove past a large open space where a market was being held. To Ruth's unaccustomed eyes, the impression was of an overwhelming mass of colour, both of the produce on display and the clothes worn by the people. The clothes of the few Europeans she had seen seemed dowdy by comparison. A little further on, they drove past a large, well-kept, enclosed garden with three or four pools inside.

'That is a public park,' Fernando called out. 'Europeans often go there after Mass on Sundays.'

'It looks very pleasant,' Ruth replied.

'Yes. And it is also near house of Senhor Lockyer.'

They drove in silence for another minute or so and then turned off the main road on to a small track, leading to a house surrounded by trees. There was a small verandah at the front of the building. Des Raj called out as they drove up and a small, wiry man came from a hut in the compound at the side of the house. Fernando dismounted, handed the reins of his horse to the syce and helped Ruth and Claire down from the gharry. Des Raj called out again and a bearer appeared from inside the house. There was a brief exchange of conversation between Fernando and the bearer. The servant bowed to the two girls and led them into the courtyard, followed by Fernando. Unlike the Ferrara's house, there was only one courtyard. A small verandah had been built all round the courtyard on the inside of the house, with rooms leading off it. Another servant was summoned and brought three chairs for the guests.

Roland Lockyer appeared half a minute later. He was not a prepossessing sight. The hair on his head had receded even further in the year and a half since Ruth had seen him last. By contrast, his greying moustache and side whiskers seemed longer and more unkempt than before. In spite of this, his chin looked unshaven. Ruth was trying hard not to be prejudiced but she thought he should have been wearing something other than a loose-fitting dressing gown, considering that she and Claire had been up for four hours. Roland Lockyer seemed even flabbier than she remembered him and he looked ten years older than his thirty-eight years.

He seemed to sense her unspoken thoughts because he turned to her and said. 'Sorry about not coming to meet you yesterday. Couldn't come to Master Ferrara's house this morning. I've been overworked for days. Had to get shipments out before monsoon breaks. Up half the night last night, y'know.' He paused but none of his visitors responded. 'Anyway, glad you're both here now.' He moved across and kissed Claire on the cheek. As he went towards Ruth, she held out her hand to him and reminded him that he had not thanked Fernando. 'No. Damned stupid of me,' he answered. 'I'm obliged to you, Master Ferrara. And, of course, to your wife. Glad you could take care of these charming girls.'

'It was our pleasure, Senhor Lockyer. You are a fortunate man.'

'Yes, I shall be the envy of Surat,' Roland beamed. 'A staid bachelor like me. Two young ladies in my household.'

'Senhor Lockyer, may I speak frankly?' Fernando hesitated for a moment or two as if waiting for a reply but none came. 'As you say, you are a bachelor. How many servants have you?'

'Five: a bearer, cook, syce, washerman and sweeper. Isn't that enough?'

'Please do not misunderstand me, Senhor. Are they not all men?'

'The sweeper and washerman have wives here. The women live with them in the servants' quarters. You don't expect me to have women fussing round the place, do you?'

'Forgive me. I do not wish to interfere, Senhor Lockyer. Might it not be fitting for your future wife and her sister to have a woman servant. One they can share?'

'Servants are damned expensive these days. They expect to be paid seven or eight rupees a month. Food and quarters as well,' Roland answered ungraciously.

'Perhaps you have place for other servant?' Fernando asked, with a slight edge to his voice. 'The mother of personal servant of my wife looks for position. She is widow of farmer who had land in Western Ghats to South-East of Bombay. After husband died she worked as ayah. She looked after small child of English lady in Surat. English family now gone back home. Sushi has been living at my home. With daughter and daughter's husband.'

Roland Lockyer looked unconvinced. 'Any references?' he asked.

'She has letter from English mistress. It speaks highly of her. Sushi knows some English. She could help your wife and her sister learn local language. She is very pious woman, even if she is not Christian. Sushi would be duenna for these two young ladies. Please let me make wedding gift to your bride. I will pay her wages for first year Sushi with you.'

'Very well, Fernando. I suppose you're right. Lot of old gossips round here. Nothing better to do than think about what a man does with his time.'

'We settle that then. I send her with rest of baggage for these ladies. She be here this afternoon.' Fernando turned to the two girls and bowed. 'I am always at your service, Senhoras.'

Ruth held out her hand and said, 'Thank you for everything, Fernando.'

He raised it to his lips and replied, 'Enchanted, Ruth.' As he kissed Claire's hand in turn, he told her, 'You will always be in my thoughts, Senhora Claire.' Fernando held his hand out to Roland who slowly lifted himself out of his chair.

'Good of you to come,' Roland muttered, shaking hands.

Fernando replied that he had already taken enough of Roland's time and walked out of the courtyard with Ruth following him. Although she had only known Fernando a short time, he seemed to be the last link with her previous life. He looked a little surprised to find Ruth standing alongside him but made no comment. The gharry had already gone and Fernando called across to the servants' quarters. The heat of the day was becoming fiercer than when they arrived and the syce had taken the horse into the shade of the stables behind the servants' huts. The syce led Fernando's horse round for him to mount while Ruth watched in the shade of the verandah. He turned as he rode away and called out, 'Holy Mary protect you, Ruth.'

\* \* \* \* \*

Roland and Claire were sitting in silence on the verandah when Ruth returned. They seemed awkward and ill at ease with each other. Ruth excused herself by saying that she would ask the bearer to show her to her room so that she could unpack the bags she had brought with her and get her Bible and other books out.

'Don't go for books much myself.' Roland rose and stretched himself. 'Let Chand Narain unpack your stuff. Give the lazy devil something to do. Got to get off to work now. You girls amuse yourselves until I get back.'

Claire looked discomfited but made no comment. After Roland had gone, she turned to Ruth. 'It's bound to be strange at first. For both Roland and me.'

'You know what Fernando said last night and Maria said this morning.' Ruth felt herself getting impatient. It was unfair of Claire to expect constant reassurance. 'We can always go back to them.'

'No. I don't want that. I want to be Roland's wife. You won't leave me, will you, Ruth?'

'You remember what I promised Mother. That I would stay with you as long as you needed me.' Ruth smiled. 'Cheer up. There will be plenty to do when our heavy luggage arrives. I don't want you moping around all day.'

\* \* \* \* \*

After Roland left, Chand Narain came to show the girls their rooms. He was a sturdy, bronze-skinned man of about thirty years of age. He wore a flat, orange coloured turban on his head. There was a white loin cloth tied round his waist, over which he wore a yellow jacket. His legs were bare from the knees downwards. When Ruth answered him in the Marathi which Maria had taught her, his face broke into a smile as he led them across the courtyard. The rooms they were to occupy were next to each other and on the opposite side of the courtyard to Roland's room. Chand Narain had already unpacked the belongings which were brought with them that morning. He had carefully placed Ruth's small pile of books on the table alongside her bed. Ruth quickly glanced at them to make sure none of them were missing. As well as copies of Virgil, Horace and a small volume of Milton's poems, there was her copy of the Bible. It had been given by her father to his bride on their wedding day, more than twenty-one years before. Ruth turned to the fly leaf, as she had done so many times before, to read the dedication. 'To my love, knowing you will be with me always.' Short though her parents' life together had been, they must have been happy. Now they were united once more.

It was so different with Claire. Who would want to spend eternity with Roland Lockyer? She shuddered at the thought. Her mind was recalled to the present by Chand Narain asking if there was anything the memsahibs wanted. Ruth turned to Claire and suggested they explored the house and gardens, getting to know the servants at the same time. After Claire lethargically agreed to allow the bearer to show them round, Chand Narain took them through the eight rooms, four on each side of the courtyard. As he walked with the two girls, Chand Narain talked about his own life, saying that he was married, with a family who lived in the hills about ninety miles South East of Surat. There were two daughters and three sons in the family. Chand Narain said he owned a small farm which was sufficient for his family's needs. It was being managed by his father at present. He explained that the reason he had become a bearer was to save enough money to pay for his daughters' weddings and dowries. They were ten years old and eight years old respectively and would be married soon. It was considered a dishonour for a father not to provide a festival for the whole village when a daughter was married. The father was also expected to give a handsome dowry to the bridegroom's family. Chand Narain explained that only by working away from home could he find the money for his two daughters' weddings and dowries. Many men in his village had been in debt for the rest of their lives after their daughters' weddings. He looked diffidently at Ruth. 'You marry soon, memsahib? Like your sister?'

'I have no parents,' Ruth answered in a slightly brusque manner. 'Nor dowry either.'

'So sorry, memsahib. Perhaps one of English merchants in Surat marry you.'

'May we see the outside of the house?' Ruth asked, a little abruptly. As they followed Chand Narain out on to the verandah at the front of the house, Claire held Ruth's hand and said, 'You'll always have me, Ruth.'

They followed the bearer round to the side of the house. He pointed out the stairs leading to the flat roof and seemed surprised when Ruth asked if she could go up. Claire reluctantly agreed to climb the stairs with them.

'Lockyer Sahib sometimes come here in evening,' Chand Narain told them when they reached the roof. 'He come here after day is hot.'

Ruth and Claire made no comment but continued to look at the fields of sugar cane on two sides of the house. The bearer thought carefully for a few seconds and then added, 'In my village women go to own place. Men go to their place. English ladies and gentlemen different.'

'Yes,' Ruth replied. She did not elaborate on her answer.

Chand Narain remained silent for four or five seconds before saying diffidently, 'I help you with my language. I will be honoured if you help me speak proper English.' He looked straight at Ruth.

'Of course, Chand,' she answered. 'I will be glad to. When our baggage has arrived and been sorted out, we will have more leisure time.'

Claire walked across the roof and looked down at the buildings alongside. 'What are these?' she asked.

Chand Narain moved beside her. 'Those huts for servants. Dev Singh, the cook, sleeps in one. Ram Kopal, the syce, sleep in hut near stables. Stables in row of buildings behind. Bhadre, our dhobi, and Swamy, sweeper, live down there.' He waved his hands in the general direction of the stables.

'May we see the other servants?' Ruth asked.

'If you wish, memsahib. Lockyer Sahib always ask me to deal with servants.'

'Yes, Chand. But we would like to see them. A woman servant will be coming here this afternoon to look after my sister and myself. You will not expect us to call you, will you, every time we want to see her?' Ruth asked.

'As memsahib wishes.'

For a second or two, a look of disapproval crossed his face. If his skin were a different colour, Ruth thought, he and Digby Foster could be brothers. Why did she think of Digby Foster, now of all times? The two girls followed Chand Narain down the steps and round to the opposite side of the house. When they were a few yards from the huts, the bearer stopped. He clapped his hands and a plump man appeared from one of the huts. The man was wearing a white loin cloth and, over the top of this, a garment which appeared to be one of Roland Lockyer's cast-off shirts. He raised his hands to his chin but said nothing. 'Pev Singh, your cook,' said Chand Narain.

A moment or two later, the small, wiry man they had seen earlier came from the back of the stables and was introduced as Ram Kopal, the syce. He was quickly followed by two men dressed only in loincloths. They stared curiously at the two girls as they raised their hands in the conventional way. Chand Narain nodded in the direction of the washerman and said, 'Bhadre, dhobi.' Without even glancing at the other man, Chand Narain said, 'Swamy, sweeper.' Ruth asked the bearer to tell the others how glad she and Claire were to be with them. Much to her surprise, Chand Narain addressed the remainder of the servants for about a minute. Although she could pick out a word here or there, the bearer was speaking too quickly for her to understand much of the sense of the remainder. When he had finished he turned to Claire and asked her in English, 'Is it permitted for servants to go now, Trent Sabiba?'

She nodded as though she was only half aware of what was happening and replied, 'Yes. Yes.'

'May we see their wives?' Ruth asked.

'Wives, memsahib?' Chand replied. He looked startled.

'Yes,' she answered. 'Master Lockyer told us that the sweeper and the washerman have wives.'

'I tell husbands,' he said doubtfully.

He issued a few words of command so rapidly that Ruth was unable to understand anything he said. The two servants looked almost as startled as the bearer had done and then hurried away. A minute later they returned, followed by their respective wives. They were each dressed in a cotton sari such as Pushpa had worn. Unlike Pushpa, they had pulled the top part of their gowns over their heads in the form of a cowl so that their faces could not be seen. The two wives stood in a deferential manner behind their husbands, looking firmly at the ground. Ruth moved past Bhadre to where his wife was standing. The woman bent her head even lower and placed her hands on the ground to each side of Ruth's shoes. Ruth reached down quickly, grasped the other woman's hands in hers and pulled her upright. As she did so, Ruth spoke the greeting which Maria had taught her, 'Ram. Ram.'

The woman looked up quickly. Her startled expression was replaced by one of pleasure. 'Ram. Ram, memsahib.'

Ruth released her hands and moved across to the sweeper's wife. The woman bent her head but Ruth forestalled any lowering of hands to the ground by quickly seizing the other woman's fingers. She seemed almost reluctant to allow Ruth to touch her hands but responded to Ruth's greeting with a beaming smile. Chand Narain coughed discreetly. There was a slight frown of disapproval on his face as Ruth turned to walk back. He barked a quick command at which the servants and their wives scurried away. Chand Narain led the way back to the verandah in silence. When they reached the courtyard, he turned to Claire and said, 'Please let me know if you wish anything, memsahib,' and then hurried away.

\* \* \* \* \*

Ruth was alone on the verandah, reading her Bible, at around two in the afternoon. She heard the sound of a bullock cart drawing up in front of the house. It was driven by Des Raj, Fernando's syce, who was accompanied by a grey-haired woman who looked like an older edition of Pushpa. The cart also contained their heavy baggage which had been stored in the hold of the 'Falcon'.

'I am Sushi, memsahib,' the woman said gravely as she climbed down from the cart and moved elegantly towards Ruth. She was wearing a green silk blouse, covered by a long, blue, cotton sari. Her feet moved so silently underneath the long gown it was almost as though she glided. Ruth was glad to see that there was to be no repetition of the morning's incident when the dhobi's wife had touched the ground by her feet. It was clear that she had worked for an English family as Fernando had explained. The eyes, which looked at Ruth from the delicate bone structure of the servant's face, were both frank and tender, while Sushi's erect posture gave her an imposing presence.

Ruth rose from her chair. 'I am Ruth, Sushi,' she said.

At that moment Chand Narain came from one of the huts and eyed the other servant suspiciously.

'This is Sushi, Chand. She will look after my sister and me.' The two servants greeted each other in the conventional manner.

'Lockyer Sahib is aware, memsahib?' Chand Narain asked.

'Yes, of course.'

Chand Narain spoke rapidly to Sushi. It was too fast for Ruth to understand more than a phrase or two and she was glad when Sushi replied in halting English.

'I come from house of Ferrara Sahib. Daughter Pushpa take care of his memsahib.' She waved her arm in the direction of the bullock cart. 'Des Raj daughter's husband. He take care of sahib's horses. Now I care for Trent ladies. Before this I good nurse of Robinson child in house of Robinson family.'

Chand Narain replied in English. 'You come now. I show you other memsahib. Then I show you where you live.'

'Can you get someone to help Des Raj with the luggage?' Ruth asked.

'Yes, memsahib. First you come with me to your sister. Then I call Ram Kopal and Swamy to help with luggage.'

Sushi and Des Raj bade quiet farewells to each other and Sushi followed Ruth and Chand Narain into the house. They went into Claire's room to find her lying on the bed, looking pale and frightened.

'What's wrong?' Ruth asked anxiously. She sat on the side of Claire's bed and held her hand. Claire seemed lethargic and made no attempt to lift herself up or answer Ruth's question. 'I've brought Sushi here. She is going to look after us. And the rest of our baggage has come as well.'

After three or four seconds pause, Sushi moved closer. She looked down at Claire and asked, 'You are Trent Memsahib?'

'That's right. I'm sorry, I felt sick and worn out.'

'Does memsahib need hakim?' Sushi asked.

'A physician,' Ruth explained.

Claire gave a wintry smile. 'No. I'll be alright now you and Ruth are here. You'll look after me.'

Ruth looked at Chand Narain hovering in the doorway. 'Show Sushi where she will be staying, Chand. And arrange for the baggage to be brought to my room, please.'

'Yes, memsahib.'

After Chand Narain spoke rapidly to Sushi in local dialect, she answered him in English and turned to Claire, a look of concern showing on her face.

'I go now. You be alright with sister, memsahib?' Sushi asked.

'Yes,' Claire replied. 'Ruth will take care of me.'

The two servants left with Sushi showing greater reluctance to go than Chand Narain.

'When did you start feeling unwell?' Ruth asked her.

'After the midday meal. I started getting pains in my stomach and I felt sick.'

'I wonder if it was something you ate. Although you didn't eat much. How do you feel now?'

'A little better, thanks.' Claire squeezed Ruth's hand. 'I'm glad you're back with me.'

'We have Sushi as well now,' Ruth answered. 'We must concentrate on your marriage in three weeks' time.'

# 7

It was well after dark before Roland Lockyer returned, accompanied by another man. Ruth heard the noise of the pair of horses being ridden up to the house, the shouting as they were led away, and then the loud cries as Roland came on to the verandah, accompanied by his friend. The level of noise fell as the two men went into Roland's room on the opposite side of the courtyard. A few minutes later, Chand Narain knocked at the door of Claire's room to say that dinner was ready.

'Do you feel up to it?' Ruth asked.

'Yes.' Claire smiled wanly. 'I can't disappoint Roland the first evening I'm in his house.' She rose from the bed, put her shoes on, and then washed her face and hands.

'Let me comb and brush your hair,' Ruth said.

'All right but please be quick. I mustn't keep Roland waiting.'

Ruth smiled, 'That's a woman's privilege.'

At last the two girls were ready to leave and they went through the door into the dark courtyard. Roland Lockyer and his friend were seated at a table in the corner of the verandah. There was a lamp on the table which was already laid for a meal.

'Come here, Claire m'dear,' Roland called out in a slurred voice. 'You as well, Ruth.'

The girls walked across to the table and the two men rose to greet them. Roland had placed the palms of both hands on the table as if for support. 'Want you to meet Jake Firman. Good friend of mine.' He grinned somewhat vacuously. 'Stout fella, Jake. One of the best.'

Ruth studied the other man closely. He looked about forty years of age. She could not see the colour of his hair because his head was covered with a white-powdered perriwig. Jake was slightly taller than Roland but was just as fleshy. His skin was dried to the colour and texture of parchment after long years in the tropic sun. There were hard lines round his mouth and his eyes were surrounded by crow's feet. When neither girl replied, Roland lifted a hand from the table, waved it in the general direction of Claire and said, 'This lady's Claire. Lady I'm gonna marry.'

Jake stepped forward, seized Claire's hand, and kissed it.

'Delighted to meet you, madam.' He turned to Roland. 'You're a lucky dog, you dark horse. And who's the other lady?'

'Other lady?' Roland appeared momentarily puzzled. 'That's Claire's sister, Ruth.'

Jake looked speculatively from Ruth to Claire and back again. He raised Ruth's hand to his lips and said, 'Enchanted.' Even in the open air she could detect the smell of brandy as he lowered his head. 'Sister, you say?' Jake asked, looking at the two girls again.

'Not real sisters,' Roland replied. 'Been brought up together.'

'I feel Ruth is as much my sister as Frances or Anne,' Claire told him.

'Pardon, Claire. You don't mind me calling you Claire, do you?' Jake smiled broadly at her. 'But who are Frances and Anne?'

'Frances is my eldest sister. She's married and has a house in London. Anne's my middle sister. She and her husband have a farm near where my father was garrison commander. Ruth's been my constant companion for the past ten years and just like a sister to me.'

'I'm obliged, Claire.' Jake turned to Ruth and smiled wolfishly. 'So you'll be a sister-in-law to Roland, eh? After he's married your sister, eh, Ruth?'

'I promised Claire's mother, sir, I would stay with Claire as long as she needed me,' Ruth replied in a quiet voice.

'C'mon, everybody,' Roland shouted. 'We're wasting time. Let's all sit down. Where's that Chand Narain?'

The bearer came out of the shadows as the Europeans sat down.

'Here, sahib,' he said. 'What are your wishes?'

'Let's have our dinner. And a bottle of wine. Bring two bottles.'

The dinner which followed was not a social success. Both of the men drank to excess and Roland's speech became almost incoherent towards the end of the meal. Claire ate little and had to be coaxed by Ruth to eat any food at all. Neither of the men enquired about the voyage from England nor did they ask the girls about their first impressions of the East. Claire lapsed into silence as the meal progressed and Ruth found herself becoming the centre of the men's attention, particularly that of Jake Firman.

He told her he was employed as an agent for the Sultan of Bejapour. Jake arranged to buy goods for the Sultan from the traders in Surat and Goa. He was not only well paid by the Sultan but received substantial commissions from the traders as well.

'Apart from the East India Company,' he said, slapping Roland on the back. 'That's right, isn't it, Roland?'

His host gave a muttered reply.

'Becoming more dangerous now,' Jake continued. 'This rebel Shivaji makes life hard for us all. Got that pack of half-naked tribesmen behind him. Don't know why the Emperor's army can't finish him off once and for all.'

'Surely we are not in any danger here?' Ruth asked.

'Not if you have a man with you,' Jake replied, beaming at her.

Ruth stood up. 'I think Claire and I will leave you gentlemen to your port.'

'Port? Port?' Roland asked. 'What's matter with brandy?'

'It's time to go,' Ruth said to her foster-sister. 'With your leave, gentlemen.'

Claire rose slowly, took Ruth's left arm, and the girls walked away.

\* \* \* \* \*

Claire decided to lie down once she reached her room. 'Don't leave me, Ruth,' she pleaded. 'I know I'm silly but I don't want to be on my own yet.'

'Of course I will stay with you,' Ruth replied.

They remained silent for a couple of minutes listening to the men's laughter becoming less restrained. During a brief quiet period Ruth heard a tentative knock on the door. She opened it to find Sushi carrying an oil lamp. The servant came in and peered anxiously at Claire on the bed.

'Are both memsahibs well?' Sushi asked.

'I'm tired,' Claire answered. 'It's bound to take time to adjust.' Sushi placed her lamp alongside the one already on the side table.

'I get water for wash,' she said. 'And night clothes. Get you ready for bed, memsahib. I stay with you until you sleep.'

Ruth watched the servant prepare Claire for the night. Sushi was as gentle and patient as if she was handling a child. At last Claire was ready but, in spite of Sushi's offer, she refused to let her stay. Ruth sat quietly in the chair after the servant left, watching Claire doze and listening to the laughter outside. She must have dozed herself and was suddenly woken up by the sound of a horse being ridden away amid shouted farewells. Ruth got up from the chair but was stopped in her tracks as Claire stirred, saying, 'Don't leave me, Ruth.'

'I'll not leave you.' Ruth moved to the bed and placed her hand on Claire's forehead. 'Rest now, sister.'

When Claire's breathing became regular, Ruth went back to the chair and closed her eyes. The first streaks of daylight could be seen through the wooden bars of the window when Ruth woke up. Claire awoke an hour later as Sushi came in with tea and fruit for the two girls.

'Please forgive me,' Claire said, holding Ruth's hand. 'I'll be all right when I get used to things.'

'There's nothing to forgive. You will feel better with some food inside you.' Ruth stood up and stretched, forced her shoulders together, arched her back and grinned. 'I feel better for a night's rest.'

\* \* \* \* \*

Roland rose from his chair as the girls approached the breakfast table. He looked tired but was fully dressed and greeted them politely. It was obvious to Ruth that he was making an effort to create a more favourable impression than he had given on the previous day. He told them he was meeting the Anglican chaplain that day to confirm the arrangements for the wedding in just under three weeks' time.

'You won't mind an Anglican priest marrying you, will you, Claire?' Roland turned to Ruth and smiled. 'You'll be maid of honour, Ruth. You don't mind taking part in an Anglican service, do you? Even if your parents were Puritans and Colonel and Mistress Trent were Independents.'

'So long as you and Claire are married in the sight of Almighty God, the searcher of all our hearts, I'll be perfectly happy whether a Justice of the Peace or the Archbishop of York performs the ceremony.'

'Spoken like a true Puritan,' Roland said jocularly, patting Ruth's hand. 'You girls brought all your wedding finery with you?'

'Yes, Roland. Mother made my wedding dress and Ruth made her bridesmaid's gown.'

'Good. When I get back here this evening we'll have to go through the wedding list.'

Claire looked startled. 'I don't know anyone here.'

'No need to worry, my dear. Must invite Sir George Oxindon, President of our company. And his wife Lady Alice. She'll be glad to see you. Not many ladies here. Ask rest of company factors as well. Two of them married to English ladies. One of them married a woman from Dutch factory in Surat. I know two or three officers in King's troops in Bombay. Ask them as well.'

'Who will give me away?' Claire asked anxiously.

'Blessed if I know. Perhaps I'll ask Sir George.'

'Why not Fernando Ferrara?' Ruth enquired.

'Wonder if he'd do it? He's a papist, of course. But I'll ask him anyway. What do you think, Claire?'

'I would feel safe with him. Yes, please ask him, Roland.'

'I'll go to his office today. Leave it to me.'

'Would you like Maria as a matron of honour, Claire?' Ruth asked.

'I hadn't thought about it. What's your opinion, Roland?'

'Damned if I know,' he replied. 'I'll ask Fernando what he thinks.'

'I wonder if Maria would let us stay overnight on the day before the wedding?' Ruth asked him.

'Why's that? What difference does it make?'

'It is supposed to be unlucky for a bridegroom to see his bride on her wedding day before she arrives at the church.'

'Lot of superstitious nonsense,' Roland commented. 'We'll see what Fernando says about that.'

'Please humour Claire,' Ruth said. 'A woman only gets married once in her lifetime.'

'Alright m'dear,' Roland replied. 'We'll all look forward to it. I'll ask Fernando.'

The remainder of the meal passed pleasantly enough with the three of them discussing the rest of the wedding arrangements. As far as Ruth was concerned, the only jarring note was struck when Roland announced that Jake Firman would be his best man. After breakfast was over, Roland took his leave. He apologised for the fact that he would be out all day but said that Chand Narain would look after them. If the girls wanted to go out before it became too hot, Ram Kopal could drive them with Chand Narain providing an additional escort.

'May we take Sushi with us?' Ruth asked.

'Yes, of course,' Roland replied. 'I'd forgotten about her.'

He kissed Claire lightly on the cheek before he left the house. Perhaps I have been wrong about him, Ruth thought to herself. Rather to Ruth's surprise, Claire did not take up Roland's offer for them to use his carriage to explore the area around. The discussion at breakfast time seemed to have tired her and she seemed disinclined to do anything other than sit on the verandah inside the courtyard. She even seemed reluctant to talk and Ruth sat beside her reading her Bible. An hour or so before lunch Chand Narain asked Ruth if she was ready for the language lesson they had arranged. Claire seemed disinclined to let her go until Ruth sent for Sushi and asked her to sit with Claire. Chand went with Ruth to the verandah at the front of the house. The first part of the lesson was spent in Chand trying to teach Marathi to Ruth. Their roles were reversed in the second part of the lesson with Ruth trying to teach Chand grammatical English, amid considerable hesitation and giggling. It was hard work and neither of them noticed the passage of time. They were interrupted by Dev Singh appearing in front of them to say that lunch was ready and the food would be spoilt.

\* \* \* \* \*

The following few days seemed to go by very quickly. Although Claire's appetite improved she did not regain any of the weight which she lost during the voyage from England. Because of this, Claire's wedding dress hung loosely around her when she tried it on. Ruth spent a long time altering all Claire's dresses so that they fitted more easily. By contrast, her own bridesmaid's dress was a little on the tight side even though her flesh was firming up now that she was more active. She still managed to get two or three hours of teaching each day with Sushi and Chand Narain. Both of them complimented her on being a quick learner with a good ear for the local accent.

Roland Lockyer seemed more attentive to Claire now that his wedding was imminent. He was always present at breakfast and the evening meal and only drank in moderation. Ruth began to think she had been wrong about him after all. Even Claire responded to the new regime. She seemed more alert and quite prepared to go out in the carriage with Ruth and the three servants in order to explore the district.

During one of these expeditions through the town, their carriage was brought to a standstill, just before a crossroads, by a large number of bullock carts and pedestrians blocking the way. From some distance off, they heard the sound of kettle drums and trumpets. The sound gradually came closer and Ruth was surprised to see that a large procession was approaching, led by an elephant. This elephant was covered by a richly embroidered red silk cloth and ridden by a mahout who was equally richly dressed. The kettle drummers and trumpeters followed immediately behind, directly in front of a large column of foot soldiers. Ruth estimated that there must be around three hundred of these infantrymen. They were wearing multi-coloured turbans, yellow jackets and white breeches. The officers carried swords but the remainder were armed with spears. Ruth could just see a figure reclining in a covered litter to the rear of these foot guards. He was closely followed by two elephants arrayed with clothes decorated with gold and silver thread. Behind the elephants were about twenty-five men carrying banners and they, in turn, were followed by a troop of cavalrymen, riding Arab horses. There was a short gap in the procession before a company of around two hundred infantrymen came along the road. They were escorting another covered litter which, in its turn, was followed by a troop of cavalrymen.

'Who are these people?' Ruth asked.

'First procession for Governor of Surat. He goes to Hall of Justice,' Chand replied.

'Who is in the second procession?'

'Chief Judge in second procession. Also to Hall of Justice today. He preside in court.'

'And do they always have as many soldiers with them?' Ruth enquired. 'Yes, memsahib. Surat important town. Governor important man. Mohammedan people come here from all over India. Just before start of pilgrimage to Mecca. Emperor Aurangzeb keep nearly two thousand soldiers here.

'That's rather a lot,' Ruth said.

'Governor is high official,' Chand replied non-committally. 'Representative of Mogul Emperor.'

'Yes. But why does he need so many troops?' Ruth persisted. 'Is it because of this rebel Shivaji that Master Firman spoke about?'

Chand Narain and Sushi exchanged significant glances. Ram Kopal turned his head to glance at Ruth and Claire and then turned quickly away.

The crowd was now beginning to disperse and the traffic slowly moved forward again. After they had travelled about fifty yards Sushi suddenly turned to Ruth. 'The Emperor says that Shivaji is bad man. Sultan of Bejapour also say he is bandit. But on Shivaji's land Hindus do not feel like slaves in their own country.'

'Quiet, Sushi,' Chand ordered.

Even Ram Kopal responded by whipping the horses into a trot as he heard Sushi raise her voice.

'You know I speak true,' Sushi continued. 'When Mohammedans went into country of Shivaji they burnt the houses, destroyed the crops, pulled down our temples. They urinated on statues of Shiva and Krishna, slaughtered sacred cows, and put bodies of cows on our altars.'

Chand Narain looked round wildly to see if anybody was listening. Sushi was sitting bolt upright in the carriage, her eyes bright with anger.

Ruth bent forward and took Sushi's hands in hers.

'I'm sorry, Sushi. I didn't mean to upset you. Please forgive me. I know so little of your country. War is always a cruel business.'

Sushi sounded surprised by Ruth's remarks.

'You have wars in England, too, memsahib?'

'Yes, Sushi. My father died in war,' Ruth replied. She looked wistfully across at Claire before continuing. 'And the good don't always triumph in the end.'

'Oh, Ruth. Don't always think about the past,' Claire said impatiently. 'Don't forget Roland served with Prince Rupert.

And King Charles has been on the throne for over three years now. Come on, let's go back home.'

\* \* \* \* \*

Roland Lockyer was in a very good humour when he arrived back that evening. He had bought a pearl necklace for Claire which he insisted on placing round her neck and told her she must wear it the following day also.

'Of course I'll wear it, Roland,' she said. 'But why do you ask?'

'We're off to see the President tomorrow. You must look your best. And you too, Ruth. Sir George said that Lady Alice wants to see you both.'

'Will there be other ladies present?' Claire asked.

'I expect so. Englishwomen abroad stick together. And that Dutchwoman Jacoba. Married to Master Streynsham. They'll want to gossip. Hear the news from England.'

'I hope they won't be too disappointed,' Claire said. 'Ruth and I are only farmers' daughters.'

'They're only merchants' wives.'

Ruth laughed. 'Don't say it like that, Roland. Claire will be a merchant's wife after she's married.'

'She'll be my wife,' Roland replied. 'That's what matters.'

Claire smiled warmly. Ruth looked at her and wondered if everything would turn out well after all. There had been so much disappointment in Claire's life. It was time for a change.

\* \* \* \* \*

Sushi woke them a little early the following morning. She wanted to ensure that everything was perfect for their meeting with the President and his wife. The baths took longer than usual and Claire was dressed with greater care. Breakfast was to be taken a little earlier that day as they were due to meet Sir George Oxindon at half past eight. Because of this, Sushi asked Ruth to agree to postpone that morning's lesson.

Roland was exquisitely dressed when he joined the two girls at the breakfast table. His head was covered by a large, white perriwig. His breeches were of pure silk and trimmed with ribbons in the manner which Ruth had seen among the royalists who had returned from Europe with King Charles. The long row of buttons on his doublet were of pure silver. He wore heavy-heeled, square-toed shoes which were surmounted by silver buckles. After breakfast was over, he called for Chand Narain who helped him put on a shoulder belt to which he attached a court rapier. The bearer also handed him a very wide-brimmed hat with a large osprey feather in the silk hatband.

Their journey to the factory of the East India Company was slow but uneventful. It was obviously too early for the Governor's procession. On arrival at the factory, Roland asked for three chairs to be brought out on to the verandah so that they could see the daily procession of the President from his house to the factory. After a lapse of two or three minutes, they heard the sound of trumpets coming from the road along which they had travelled.

Although the procession was tiny in comparison with that of the Mogul Governor, it was still impressive. A rider, mounted on a large, white, Arab horse, led the way. He was followed by four trumpeters, who in their turn, were followed by three mace bearers. A standard bearer came immediately after the mace bearers. He was carrying a silver halberd to which was attached a silk flag bearing the cross of St. George. Behind him came four men carrying a palanquin in which Sir George was sitting. A servant walked on each side of the palanquin, fanning the President with large fans made out of ostrich feathers. Four men carrying spears walked behind the palanquin and they in turn were followed by a group of people who wished to present petitions to the President.

When the procession arrived in front of the factory, the palanquin was placed on the ground to allow Sir George to get out. He then went up the carpeted steps, preceded by the mace bearers. The spear carriers followed and formed a guard outside the door to prevent anyone else following the President.

An Indian clerk came out to collect the documents which the petitioners were presenting. Roland Lockyer spoke to him when this operation was over. The clerk looked speculatively in the direction of Ruth and Claire and then beckoned all three of them to follow him. The spear carriers allowed them through and they followed the clerk into an ante-room.

After they had waited a minute or so a bearer came along to show them into the President's private drawing room. Ruth saw there were two European ladies there as well as the President. Sir George rose from his chair as Roland and his party entered.

'Good day, Master Lockyer,' he said, 'Good day, ladies.

'Good day, Sir George,' Roland replied. 'May I present Mistress Trent?'

Sir George bowed slightly. 'Mistress Trent. Allow me to present you to my wife Lady Alice.'

'I am delighted to meet your ladyship,' Claire answered.

She was then introduced to Jacoba Streynsham. When Ruth's turn came for her to be introduced to Sir George Oxindon he told her there was no formality in his private apartments because they were a very small community.

'And far fewer ladies than gentlemen,' Lady Oxindon said before Ruth could reply. Ruth began to feel a little self-conscious. The other women were dressed in brightly coloured silk clothes and both of them wore heavy jewelry. Ruth was dressed in a plain-coloured bodice and skirt, with a gorget pinned round her neck. Even Claire was wearing an embroidered lace collar with her bodice as well as the pearl necklace which Roland had given her. In addition, she was wearing a gold bracelet on her right wrist as well as a jewelled ring on each hand. These three items of jewelry were part of the collection which her mother had presented to her before Claire and Ruth left for India. Lady Oxindon looked from one to the other of the girls.

'Which of these two ladies is marrying you, Master Lockyer?' she asked.

'Mistress Trent, your ladyship,' he replied.

'My felicitations, Mistress Trent,' Lady Oxindon said. 'That's rather formal. May I use your Christian names? You are going to join our little band here, after all.'

'Yes, of course, your ladyship. My name is Claire and my sister is Ruth.'

'And what will we do with you, Ruth? There are no single ladies here. But I'm sure with your long hair, the colour of ripe corn, you'll soon have some young Englishman falling head over heels in love with you.'

Before Ruth could reply Roland intervened.

'We'd better warn our friends Ruth is a Puritan.' he said jocularly.

'I can see that from her clothes, Master Lockyer,' Lady Oxindon replied.

'I mean she doesn't agree with people wenching and drinking. Not like all the fellers in Surat. Your ladies' husbands excepted, of course.'

'Zat ees quite right too,' Jacoba Streynsham interrupted. 'Peter thinks too many of our men here behave badly. When Dutchman comes to Indies, ee nearly always marry first.'

'Ladies,' Sir George interjected, 'Master Lockyer has brought his wife-to-be here so that you can meet her. We are not here to discuss Claire's sister or the morals of the young men who work in Surat. You come over here and talk to me, Ruth. And you Master Lockyer, you and Claire go and chat to Lady Alice and Mistress Streynsham. Tell them about the arrangements for your wedding.'

Ruth had no wish to discuss her romantic prospects and was grateful for Sir George Oxindon's intervention. She went and sat on a chair in the corner and he came over to join her. There was a buzz of animated conversation from the far side of the room as Lady Oxindon and Jacoba Streynsham were engaged in discussion with Claire and Roland.

'You mustn't mind them, my dear,' Sir George said, when he settled down alongside Ruth. 'They have so little chance to mix with women of our nationality.'

'Why don't they mix with the women who live here?' Ruth asked. Sir George looked puzzled.

'The natives, you mean, Ruth? Well. I don't know. Very few of the natives speak English, I suppose. As for my wife, she's been here six years but I don't suppose she knows more than a dozen words of the local dialect. Her servants speak English. I have to speak a bit of Urdu myself when I talk to Mogul officials but I can't say I've learnt much of the local language. My babus, the Indian clerks, speak to me in English.'

'I started to learn Marathi on the ship coming from England.' 'Did you, by Heaven?' Sir George exclaimed.

'Yes. Senhora Ferrara taught me.'

'I know the Ferraras. Good people, even if they are Portuguese. Get quite a lot of help from Fernando Ferrara from time to time.'

'Maria started lessons with me on the voyage out. Now I'm getting lessons every day from Roland's bearer and from the personal servant who looks after me and Claire.'

Sir George looked quite hard at Ruth. 'You are taking this seriously.' he said. 'Most of my factors don't know more than a hundred words of the local dialects, Gujerati and Marathi.'

'I want to find out all I can about the country. Find out about what the East India Company does. Get to know the people.' Ruth replied earnestly.

'Where are you going to start?' Sir George asked.

'May I start with you telling me about the trade of your company? When I stayed in London with Claire's sister Frances, her husband Donald said that the East India Company was a drain on England. He said it's because you export gold and silver to India.'

'You know, you're the first lady who's ever asked me a question like that. Most of them think only of ruffs and cloaks and fine jewels.'

'I'm sorry, Sir George.'

'Don't apologise, Ruth. I'll be glad to talk. Where shall I begin? The company buys copper ware and porcelain from China, gold and ivory from Sumatra and cowrie shells from Siam. Some of these goods we sell in India but most of them we send on to England. We also buy tea from China and spices from Java to re-export to England. Do you follow me so far, Ruth?'

'Yes. That's quite clear, Sir George.'

'Our agents also buy up tea, brass ware and sugar in India. These goods are shipped to England together with calico, silks, and indigo. All these items are goods which people at home need and are prepared to pay for. Our ships bring out woollen cloth from home which we sell in Northern India during the cold weather. We also arrange for our ships to carry wine from Portugal to India.'

'But why did Claire's brother-in-law say you were a drain on the country?'

'We don't sell as much woollen cloth as we would like to,' Sir George replied. 'If we export more to England than we import from home, the company has to send out gold bullion to pay for the balance.'

'I see.'

'But what Claire's relative overlooked, Ruth, was that if we don't export the goods from here, people in England would buy their spices from the Dutch, their tea from the Portuguese, and their silks from the French. The gold would go to these other countries instead of to India. It's impossible for England's trade with every individual country to exactly balance on a country to country basis. That's why the East India Company doesn't try to make the trade between India and England exactly balance, especially when the round trip takes six months. But we're better traders than most people. That's why we have the richest factory in Surat. It's the finest emporium in the East.'

'Is that why people are worried about this rebel Shivaji?' Ruth asked.

'Shivaji. Shivaji. Who's been telling you about Shivaji?' Sir George asked.

'Master Firman,' she replied, not disclosing her discussion with the servants.

'I know him,' Sir George said, a trifle guardedly. 'Agent for the Sultan of Bejapour. What's he said about Shivaji?'

'Something about life becoming more dangerous for us all because of Shivaji.'

'He may be prejudiced. Bejapour and Shivaji were at war for three years. Ended last year. But the directors of the East India Company have no great love for Shivaji, either. He has taken four of our factors hostage. Asking for a ransom, which we won't pay, of course. Damned fools of factors at Rajapour sold some guns to the Sultan of Bejapour. I've always said we ought to keep out of these quarrels. What made things worse was that these idiots of factors thought they would accompany the guns to Panhala, flying the English flag.'

'When were the factors taken hostage, Sir George?'

'It's a long story, Ruth. Shivaji was forced to retreat by the Sultan's army and soon afterwards, at the end of 1660, he attacked Rajapur, burnt the company's warehouses there and carried off the four factors. It's an impasse, I'm afraid. Shivaji claims compensation for our breach of neutrality and we claim compensation for his destruction of our property and continued imprisonment of our four factors.'

'What will happen now?' Ruth asked.

'I'm blessed if I know, Ruth. It's a question of izzat, as the Indians say. Each side is looking for a way out but neither side wants to be seen making the first concession. Some new element will have to be introduced before we get an agreement. You know, I've a sneaking sympathy for Shivaji. Both his father and grandfather were loyal soldiers of the Sultan of Bejapour. But because Shivaji is a devout Hindu, he's treated as a second class citizen. Bejapour is a vassal state of the Mogul Empire and we now have that bigot Aurangzeb as Emperor.'

'Sorry, Sir George. Where does the Emperor come in?'

'Since Aurangzeb's been Emperor he's become intolerant. Music of any sort is outlawed. Drinking of wine is illegal. He's destroyed famous Hindu temples at Muttra, Benares and other holy places, and built mosques on their sites. Aurangzeb has destroyed libraries, burning ancient Sanskrit books and he's closed Hindu schools. Worst of all, he's revived the jaziya, which is an invidious poll-tax levied on all non-mohammedans. It's not to be wondered at that Hindus from miles around have flocked to Shivaji's banner.'

Sir George paused for a moment and studied Ruth carefully. 'I don't see young ladies very often but I must apologise for being bad company.'

'Please continue, Sir George. I want to learn as much as I can about this country. That's why I'm learning Marathi as well.'

The pair of them made a striking contrast. Ruth was in plain, almost sombre, fustian clothes, without any jewelry on her person and with her fair hair completely free, leaning forward and listening attentively to Sir George. He wore a high perriwig on his head and a heavily ornamented orange-coloured silk tunic, tied around his waist with a purple sash. Lace-frilled shirt cuffs were showing below the sleeves of the tunic and silk ribbons were tied round Sir George's forearms. Over his right shoulder he wore a large, blue sash. The earnest look on his face was completely different to the bored expression which Ruth had seen when Sir George was sitting in the palanquin. He reflected for a short time before continuing. 'This is a beautiful country but you mustn't get starry-eyed about it, my dear. It's also a very cruel country.'

'That's what Fernando Ferrara told me as well,' Ruth replied.

'Sensible advice. Take Emperor Aurangzeb for example. He's no real right to the throne. When his father fell ill, the eldest son Prince Dara acted as Regent. Aurangzeb wouldn't accept this. Marched on the capital saying that the second son

Prince Murad should be Regent. Shah Jahan, the father, suddenly recovered and ordered his sons to return to their duties. The younger sons refused to obey and a war of succession began. Of all wars, civil wars are the most cruel.'

Ruth nodded and lowered her head.

'Anyway, the outcome was that Shah Jahan was defeated. He and his daughter Jehanara were imprisoned in the fort at Agra and Prince Dara was executed by order of Aurangzeb. Just before his execution he asked if he could see a Catholic priest as he wanted to be converted to Christianity. This was refused but he went to his death saying, "Mohammed has killed me but the Son of God and Mary will give life to me".'

'That's a very sad story,' Ruth said.

'But it's not the end,' Sir George went on. 'Aurangzeb also executed his older brother Prince Murad, his younger brother Prince Shuja and poisoned Prince Dara's son, Sulaiman. As a final humiliation, Aurangzeb decided to possess Princess Ranadil, Prince Dara's widow. He summoned her to the royal harem. When she received this command, she picked up a dagger, stabbed herself repeatedly in the face and said to Aurangzeb's messenger, "Tell your master the beauty he desires no longer exists".'

Ruth could feel her eyes becoming moist.

'That was a very brave thing to do,' she said.

'Yes,' Sir George answered. 'I doubt if any man would have had the courage to do it, and few European women would have been so brave in defence of their honour.' They were interrupted by an official who came into the room and bowed to the President. At a signal from Sir George the official came forward and reminded him that the agent for the Sultan of Golcanda was in an ante-room, waiting for an audience.

'Tell him I'll see him in two or three minutes,' Sir George answered. He turned to Ruth and gave her a broad smile as the official left the room. 'It's been a great pleasure talking to you. A girl with an interest in things apart from clothes and gossip. I must ask Master Lockyer to bring you again. We don't want him and his friends to monopolise you. Next time I see you, I must tell you about Shivaji and his father.'

He rose from his chair. Ruth followed suit and they walked across to the group in the far side of the room so that Sir George could take his leave of the ladies. When he came to bid farewell to Roland he said, 'Clever girl, your future sister-in-law, Master Lockyer. Brains as well as beauty. We'll have to make sure you let her see more of us and the rest of our community. Once you and your charming bride are married, of course.'

'As you wish, Sir George,' Roland replied.

'Our tutor always said that Ruth was the best student of the girls in our family. She can read and write Latin as well as she can read and write English. Ruth also studied mathematics with our tutor.'

Sir George laughed. 'Now, now, Mistress Trent. You'll be making your sister blush. Your pardon, ladies. I really must leave now.'

He bowed to each of them in turn and then left the room.

'Come and sit next to me, Ruth.' Lady Oxindon called out. 'You're a lucky girl.' She continued as Ruth sat down. 'When I was a child, we were only taught needlework, our catechism and a little music.'

'Yes, your ladyship,' Ruth answered. 'I am grateful to my family.'

'Don't you be too clever,' Jacoba said. 'Zees men. Zey don't like brainy vomen.'

'That's unfair, madam,' Roland protested. 'It's because most clever women have faces like pickled walnuts. But Ruth is different.'

'Certainly my husband was impressed,' Lady Oxindon remarked drily. Roland got up from his seat.

'May my party be permitted to withdraw?' he asked. 'The heat of the day will soon become oppressive for these ladies.'

'Of course, Master Lockyer,' Lady Oxindon replied. 'But please return with your bride and Mistress Parker after you are married.'

\* \* \* \* \*

On the ride back to the bungalow, Ruth's mind kept coming back to her talk with Sir George. It was difficult to reconcile the cruelties of which he had spoken with the sights she observed from Roland's carriage. There were heavy banyan trees each side of the road, covered with red berries. Every time a parrot landed on a tree she heard the noise of falling berries pattering on the ground. Rows of great, green-headed palm trees lined the banks of the River Tapti which ran parallel to the road along which they were travelling. Rich flowers grew in the gardens of the merchants, most of which were shaded by large trees. Ruth could no longer contain her impatience about the last comment which Sir George had made when the two of them were in conversation.

'What does Sir George know about Shivaji and his father, Roland?' she asked.

'Shivaji?' Roland replied guardedly. 'Who's been talking about him?'

'Jake Firman mentioned him to me and I asked Sir George to tell me what he knew.'

'Did you, by Jove? The man's a brigand. Holding four of our men prisoner. Won't release them unless the company pays a ransom.'

'Yes, Roland. I know that.' Ruth's voice was tinged with impatience. 'But he told me that he would tell me about Shivaji's father next time we met.'

'Damned if I know what Sir George means. Unless it's the same story Jake told me four or five years ago.'

'What was that, Roland?' Ruth asked.

'Well, it happened when Shivaji was twenty-one. Few years ago now. He gathered together a band of cut-throats and they raided a caravan. Trouble was, it wasn't just a trading caravan. It was a special caravan. Going to Bejapour. Carrying a year's taxes from the city of Kalyan. Young fool followed it up by capturing the palace in Kalyan itself. As you can imagine, the Sultan of Bejapour was furious. Sent a message demanding an explanation from Shivaji. Commanded him to go to Bejapour in person. Then the Sultan remembered that Shahaji, Shivaji's father, was one of his own officers. So he arrested Shahaji, chained him to a wall, and bricked him up alive, one brick a day.'

'Oh, no!' Claire exclaimed in horror.

'That's not the end of the story,' Roland continued. 'The Sultan persuaded Shahaji to write to his son, telling him what was happening. At last only one row of bricks was left to be put in place. Once that was laid, all light and air would be shut out and Shahaji would die. By slow suffocation. Shivaji was only kept from going to die in his father's place by the impassioned pleas of his wife Sabai and his mother Jijabsi.'

'What happened then?' Ruth asked. 'Did the father die?'

'No,' Roland replied. 'This rebel Shivaji is as cunning as a fox. He sent a messenger on a fast horse to Prince Murad, who was Viceroy of Central India. Shivaji asked to become a subject of the Great Mogul. He put his troops and his land at the disposal of the Emperor Shah Jahan. Prince Murad wrote to Shivaji accepting his offer. He also wrote to the Sultan of Bejapour and to Shahaji telling them that a place had been found for Shivaji's father at the Imperial court. The Sultan had to order Shahaji's release. Shivaji, of course, didn't keep his side of the bargain. He still led his band of tribesmen in the hills, and the forts which he had captured from the Sultan were kept under his control.'

'Was Prince Murad the same prince who was executed by Emperor Aurangzeb?' Ruth asked him.

'That's the one,' Roland said. 'They're a grim bunch, these Moguls. Mind you, the people in Bejapour are no better. When the war with Shivaji started again four years ago, Afzul Khan, the commander of the Sultan's army, ordered all the sixty-four women in his harem to be drowned. Like unwanted kittens.'

'What! Drowned?' Claire exclaimed.

'It seems he didn't want any of them to submit to the embraces of a stranger if he was killed. Sixty-three of them died uncomplaining. One of them ran away. She was hunted down and killed. Jake told me that there are sixty-three graves laid close together in rows, while the one who ran away is buried in a separate plot as a mark of dishonour.'

'What happened to Afzul Khan?' Ruth asked.

'He laid the land waste,' Roland replied. 'Crops burnt, shrines defiled, idols defaced and Hindu temples destroyed. Then he offered to meet Shivaji under a flag of truce. When they met, Afzul Khan and his party tried to trick Shivaji and capture him. In the ensuing fight, Afzul Khan was killed.'

'I can't really say I'm sorry!' Ruth exclaimed.

'Don't be so bloodthirsty, Ruth,' he said. 'What these people do is none of our business. You can't judge them by European standards.'

'I agree with Ruth,' Claire said. 'Think of those unfortunate women. Sixty-three of them drowned and the other one hunted down and killed like a wild animal.'

'You've no need to worry, Claire,' Roland replied as his carriage drew up in front of his bungalow. He smiled slowly. 'I won't have you drowned if I go on a journey.'

\* \* \* \* \*

The next ten days passed very quickly. Ruth still found time to take her language lessons daily and became proficient in the native tongue. She and Sushi arranged for every item of Claire's clothing to be washed by the dhobi Bhadre and his wife. Ruth was also busy making alterations to most of the clothes so that they would fit Claire.

On three of the following days Sushi had accompanied the two girls on a visit to the local market. The two young women were the centre of attention with Ruth's long, fair, curly hair, falling down from under the rim of her wide hat, being a particular source of interest. The traders were especially pleased when Ruth spoke to them in their own language. Each day they went to the market two or three traders shyly presented single flowers to Ruth. Sushi always smiled at this and helped to place the flowers either in the band around Ruth's hat or pinned in her hair above her ears.

One of the duty visits they made during this time was when Roland took Claire and Ruth to meet Thomas Robertson and his wife. During the visit the girls were also introduced to Luke Farmerdale and his wife. Thomas and Luke were factors with the East India Company and spent almost the whole time discussing business with Roland. The two wives were pleasant enough but only seemed interested in asking Claire and Ruth about the latest fashions and gossip in England. Ruth sensed she was a disappointment to them, particularly when she started questioning the women about the customs of the people of the country.

Ruth was happier after a visit which they made to the bungalow of Peter and Jacoba Streynsham. Jacoba was the Dutchwoman who had met them on their visit to Sir George Oxindon. Peter Streynsham was English and Sir George's deputy. They seemed a strangely ill-matched couple. Peter was well-proportioned and handsome. He was above medium height, had brown, curly hair and was around thirty years old. Jacoba was short and plump. She had plain features and Ruth estimated she was about six years older than her husband. Jacoba must have guessed what Ruth was thinking. She slapped her on the wrist and laughed.

'Don't you vorry, my dear. You come to Indes. You soon get husband.'

'I hope Ruth is as lucky as I am,' Peter interrupted.

'Ho, ho,' Jacoba laughed again. 'You know I get all best part of zat bargain. A handsome, good-natured, young husband. All girls in England vild about you.'

Peter smiled. 'Go on, Jacoba. I must have been meant for you.'

'You know vot dis man do?' Jacoba asked, turning to Claire and Ruth. 'I sailed to Indes to marry Dutchman. In Dutch factory in Surat. Unlucky for me, he die of cholera while I on boat. Ten veeks before I get here. Peter meet me just after I arrive. He sweep me off my feet. Marry me six veeks after I come.'

'That was five years ago,' Peter said. 'And you still talk Double Dutch.' He went across to his wife, held her hand, and kissed her on the forehead. It was obvious to Ruth, from the look which passed between them that they were still very much in love.

'How long have you been in this country, Master Streynsham?' Ruth asked.

'Eight years, Mistress Ruth,' he replied.

'I'm trying to learn the language. Do you think the people here will laugh at me?'

'Good gracious, no!' Peter exclaimed. 'They respect any European who can speak to them in their own tongue. It shows sympathy for the native people. The Imperial officials are inclined to be arrogant and a few of them are corrupt. The country people, however, are polite, charitable and gentle. They will give you every help if you want to talk to them.'

'You sound as though you like them very much.' Ruth said.

'I do, I do,' Peter replied. 'They have a lot of character. They're very devout, even if most of them are Hindus. Only wish the missionaries would leave them alone.'

'You can't mean that, Master Streynsham!' Ruth exclaimed.

'Indeed I can. Some Jesuits converted a few people in Bombay. I call them 'Rice Christians'. What the Jesuits didn't know was that their converts had no land and no food to eat. They professed the name of Christ because the alternative was starving to death.'

Ruth was quite shocked. 'That's a terrible thing to say.' she told him.

'We should be the last people to deny the right of others to worship God in their own way,' he said seriously. 'Our civil war ought to have taught us that. It's no wonder the natives get confused. We all had to be Presbyterians at Surat during the time of the Commonwealth. Now we must all be Anglicans. Up to two years ago, everybody in Bombay had to be Catholics. Since King Charles has married a Portuguese princess, with Bombay as part of her dowry, they must all profess to be Anglicans. Just to make things worse, I had a storekeeper here a year ago. Said the light of the Holy Spirit had moved him to preach. Went down to the native markets, causing disturbances among the traders. Sir George was on a journey to Agra at the time and left me in charge. So I put the storekeeper in jail. After four days, he came to a soberer understanding. Said the Holy Spirit had left him. He wasn't the stuff martyrs are made of.'

'Oh, Peter, stop it,' Jacoba cried. 'You vill make zeez young English ladies believe you a hard man.'

She smiled at her husband and then at the two girls. 'He's so kind, really.'

'Peter's got a way with the natives,' Roland interrupted. 'Damned if I know how he does it. I don't seem to be able to make them understand somehow. They seem a bit stupid to me.'

Peter gave a little sigh as though he had heard this view expressed many times in the past.

'Remember, Roland,' he said, a little wearily, 'most of them can't speak English. With those who can, most of these have a vocabulary in English which is about as large as many of our factors have in Gujerati or Marathi. That is, not very big.'

'They ought to try harder,' was Roland's ambiguous reply.

'We should all try harder,' Peter answered. 'They are the many. We are the few. To understand these people we have to try to think like them.'

\* \* \* \* \*

'Funny chap, Peter Streynsham,' Roland said while they were driving back to the bungalow. 'Got some odd ideas how to treat the natives.'

'Do you think so, Roland?' Ruth asked.

'Can't understand why Sir George made him his deputy.' Roland grumbled. 'Plenty of better candidates around. All this stuff about not teaching them Christianity. Letting them wallow in superstitious nonsense.'

'Isn't that why there's this rebellion now. With Shivaji, I mean. Because the Hindus believe that the Moguls will try to suppress them and their faith.'

'Don't mention that Shivaji to me. Feller's nothing but a bandit. Shouldn't be surprised if Master Streynsham don't secretly sympathize with him, being such a lover of natives.'

Ruth thought the conversation was getting on dangerous ground. She decided to change the subject.

'Have the Streynshams any children?' she asked.

'Not now,' he replied. 'They had a girl four years ago but she died before she was a year old. Had another girl two years ago but she didn't last three months. First one died of cholera. Second one died of dysentery.'

'Oh, what a shame,' Claire said. 'They seem such a devoted couple, too.'

'I suppose so,' Roland replied half-heartedly. 'Although I could never see what he saw in her. She's dumpy and plain and was no longer young when they married.'

He seemed unaware of how tactless this remark was. It could easily be applied to Claire. Ruth looked sideways at her foster-sister sitting beside her. Claire had lowered her head and was staring at the floor of the carriage. Ruth slowly extended her hand toward Claire's. As their hands touched, she took Claire's hands in her own.

# 8

Just after five o'clock in the afternoon five days later, Fernando's bullock cart arrived to collect Claire's wedding dress, Ruth's bridesmaid's gown and their other clothes. Sushi came to tell the girls that the cart was in front of the bungalow and Ruth went outside to greet Pushpa and Des Raj in the way she had been taught. She pressed the palms of her hands together, raised them to her chin and said, 'Ram, Ram, Pushpa,' and 'Ram, Ram, Des Raj.' They responded in the same way and after enquiring about each other's well-being, Pushpa asked to be excused, saying that she would have to assist her mother. 'Shall I get my sister so that we can travel back with you, Des Raj?' Ruth asked.

'No. No, memsahib.' He looked slightly shocked. 'Your sister is a bride. She will come to bungalow of Ferrara Sahib in the sahib's carriage. The servants of our house decorated it specially for Trent Memsahib.'

'That's very good of them and you. And very thoughtful, too,' Ruth replied. 'When do you think Master Ferrara will arrive here?'

'Soon, memsahib. Carriage will travel faster than bullock cart.' Ruth excused herself and went off in search of Sushi and her daughter. She found them in Claire's room, carefully packing the clothes into chests which Sushi had brought into the bungalow. The servants were chattering together as she entered but stopped when they saw her.

'Please go on, Sushi,' Ruth said. 'You don't see your daughter very often.' Pushpa was looking at the floor with downcast eyes while Sushi was looking a little embarrassed.

'What's wrong, Sushi?' Ruth asked.

'Pushpa and I only talking together, memsahib.' She hesitated before continuing. 'We wonder when you marry like your sister.'

Ruth laughed. 'There's no need to look so downcast. That's in the hands of fate. My blessings on both of you.'

The two servants looked relieved and finished packing Claire's clothes. When they completed this task, Sushi asked if she and Pushpa could go into Ruth's room to collect her clothes.

'Of course,' Ruth replied. She turned to her foster-sister. 'Do you mind if I go with them, Claire?' she asked.

'No. That's all right,' Claire replied listlessly.

After the three of them reached the other room Sushi hesitated for a moment or two and then said, 'Pushpa thinks Trent Memsahib not well and not happy. She thinks she not like a bride.'

Pushpa looked away as Ruth glanced in her direction. 'I expect my sister is a little tired now,' Ruth said. 'She will be all right once she's married.'

'We hope so, memsahib.' Sushi answered.

After a second or two Pushpa spoke. It was obviously a great effort for her. 'When I marry, memsahib, I very happy. I only see my husband once before I marry but I still very glad. Like all Hindu girls we long to marry and get good husband like Des Raj. Is it not so with English ladies?'

'Englishwomen usually see their husbands more than once before they marry,' Ruth answered non-committally. 'Most of them choose their husbands. Sometimes their families choose them, especially if landed estates are involved. A few English ladies, like Queen Elizabeth, never marry.'

'Forgive me,' Pushpa went on. 'Trent Memsahib knew Lockyer Sahib when she was young girl. He is friend of family. She has been with him now three weeks. If I was like that with future husband my body would be bursting with longing for him. My heart would overflow with love and gladness and rise singing like a bird in morning.'

Ruth could sense that the conversation was becoming dangerous.

'Your husband is a lucky man to have such a loving wife. Now let us get my clothes packed or Senhor Ferrara will be here before Claire and I are ready. Shall I get Ram Kopal to help you lift those chests on to the bullock cart?' she asked.

'No, memsahib. Pushpa and I will manage.' Sushi replied. 'If not, Des Raj will help us.'

* * * * *

The Ferrara household was alive with activity from four o'clock next morning. Even though it was still not light, Ruth awoke to the sounds of noise from the servants' quarters and the stables. They were boiling fresh water for the ladies of the house to bathe, while Des Raj and other servants from the houses around were decorating the carriage and each horse's harness with fresh flowers for the journey to the English chapel. Ruth could already smell the heavy perfume in the cool night air. It reminded her of the journey from Roland's bungalow to the Ferrara's home yesterday evening. Claire had decided she did not want to travel in the carriage without Ruth. She insisted that Ruth must wait to travel with her, rather than letting Ruth travel in the bullock cart. Fernando had ridden ahead on his own horse with the two girls coming behind in his carriage. Before they left, all Roland's servants and their wives came to see them off. The whole of the carriage was covered with garlands of flowers, and passers-by called out blessings on the two girl passengers as the vehicle went from Roland's bungalow to the outskirts of Surat and on to the Swally road. After they reached the Ferrara's bungalow, Claire seemed pale and listless. She excused herself after the evening meal and went to lie down in the room which she and Ruth were to share. Claire would not hear of Ruth being unsociable, in spite of the Ferraras expressing concern about her lassitude. Ruth was only persuaded to stay with Maria and Fernando when Sushi volunteered to sit with Claire until Ruth came to bed.

The evening passed pleasantly enough. Ruth was glad of their company as she had found that there were few opportunities for social life in Surat. She mentioned the visits which she and Claire had made to Sir George and Lady Oxindon, Peter and Jacoba Streynsham, the Robertsons and the Farmerdales. The only Europeans she had seen, apart from these few, had been some men friends who had come to visit Roland and whom she did not care for.

'Once Claire is married, you come on visits to us more often, Ruth,' Maria said. 'On your own if you wish. Or bring Sushi with you. She always loves to see her daughter and Des Raj.'

'Thank you, Maria,' Ruth answered. 'That would be kind of you. I don't want Claire and Roland to feel I'm always in the way.'

Fernando and Maria exchanged glances but made no direct reply.

'Claire must not keep relying on you,' Maria said. 'You are fine looking girl. Only unmarried woman from Europe among so many men. I do not think it is long before servants decorate carriage for you, too.'

Ruth laughed. 'I haven't seen anyone here I like. It could be a long time to wait.'

'I bring one of Fernando's friends for you to meet then,' Maria countered. 'Handsome young Portuguese from Braga.'

Ruth thought the subject was getting too personal and decided to make a switch. 'Pushpa tells me she only saw Des Raj once before they married. And they seem happy enough.'

'Quite right,' Fernando replied. 'It is very rare for marriages among native people not to be arranged. They want to make family alliances. Sometimes to join land together. Mostly to get good dowry from family of bride.' Ruth reflected that if she was an Indian girl her case would be hopeless.

'Chand Narain, who is Roland Lockyer's bearer, told me he is working as a bearer and saving hard in order to pay for his daughters' weddings. And they are only eight and ten years old,' she said.

'I am sure he is,' Fernando replied. 'Just because marriages are arranged when girls are young does not mean they will not be successful.'

'I could only marry a man for love,' Ruth answered. 'And I'm old enough to make up my own mind. Not like Pushpa or Chand Narain's daughters.'

'Indian ladies do not always marry when they are young girls. How old are you, Ruth?' Fernando asked.

'I'm just nineteen now. My birthday was a few weeks ago.'

'Same age as my daughter would have been.' Maria murmured softly. Fernando allowed a few seconds to elapse before continuing.

'I made a journey from Swally to Agra, the Imperial capital, five years ago,' he said. 'Business to transact with Imperial officials. While I was there I saw Taj Bibi Ka Rauza. Moguls call it Taj Mahal. After Mumtaz Mahal. It is a giant monument. Made of white marble and delicate beyond words. I saw it from opposite bank of River Jumna. Built by Emperor Shahjahan in memory of his dead Empress.'

'The same Shahjahan who was deposed and imprisoned by his son?' Ruth asked.

'Yes,' Fernando answered. 'Before he became Emperor he was Prince Kurram. He was told a marriage was arranged for him with Arjumand Bano. For political reasons. Bride was a niece of his father's wife, Empress Nurjahan. And daughter of one of his father's ministers.'

'You are losing me,' Ruth interrupted gently.

'I am sorry, Ruth,' he replied. 'Arjumand Bano was given title of Mumtaz Mahal after she was married. I think she was nearly twenty before she married. Very old for Indian lady. No man good enough until she was told to marry Prince Kurram. The one who became Emperor Shahjahan. They were devoted to each other. Never apart for a single day in all the years of married life. Mumtaz went everywhere with her husband. Even on military campaigns with him. Shahjahan wanted to give up the throne after his wife died.'

'That's a beautiful story,' Ruth said softly.

'Mumtaz Mahal was famous for her understanding of how the poor lived. For her education. Above all, for her beauty. Shah Jahan employed around twenty thousand workmen to build the monument to his wife. It took over seventeen years from start to finish. He has asked to be buried at her side when he dies.'

Nobody said anything for several seconds. The silence was broken at last by Fernando. 'You see, Ruth,' he said. 'You might have nearly a year to wait before your prince comes along.'

'It seems very strange to me,' she replied. 'A family which can be so cruel to each other and yet show such single-minded devotion.'

'You must not judge them like us,' Fernando answered. 'This country can be a very harsh place to live. In few days time, monsoon will come. Rain, rain, rain for days on end. Sometimes if too much, floods come. Houses swept away, crops destroyed, cattle drowned. Often rains come so suddenly that peasants crossing wadis are caught by torrent of water, swept away and drowned. Every few years, the monsoon fails. No rain falls that season. Crops dry up and people have little to eat. Sometimes, if monsoon fails two years running, there is great famine. Many people die.'

'Do not be so gloomy, Fernando,' Maria interrupted. 'Ruth's sister is to be married tomorrow. We should all be happy for Claire.'

'I'm grateful to your husband, Maria,' Ruth said, smiling across at her. 'If I can understand this country better, then I'll adapt more easily.'

'Understanding is one thing, Ruth,' Fernando said. 'But if you love anything too deeply, your heart may be broken.'

Ruth looked from Maria to Fernando and then back again. 'Does that apply to the two of you?' she enquired gently. Their only answer was soft laughter.

'I think I must go to bed. I've already kept you up too late.'

Maria rose, handed Ruth a small oil lamp and said, 'Holy Mary and all the angels watch over you, Ruth.'

'Thank you, Maria. Thank you and good night to both of you,' Ruth said. As she opened the door of the bedroom which she was to share with her foster-sister, Sushi rose from her chair and placed a finger on her lips. Ruth looked across to Claire's bed and saw she was already asleep.

All these thoughts raced through her mind the following morning while she waited for Claire to stir. She could see through the window that it was now getting quite light outside. In a few minutes time, the courtyard would be filled with bright sunshine. So unlike the May dawns she used to see when working on her foster-father's farm. Instead of the long, slow sunrise of an English midsummer, there was only a gap of a few minutes between the black darkness of an Indian night and the garish brightness of an Indian day.

Sushi came softly into the room and looked at Claire's sleeping figure. Ruth sat up in bed, smiled and put a finger to her lips. Sushi then placed the palms of her hands together in greeting and stood waiting. Ruth rose from the bed quietly, took Sushi by the arm and led her from the room. When they were outside she asked the servant quietly how long it would be before Claire needed to be roused.

'Soon, memsahib. All servants in house very busy but very happy. Want to see Trent Memsahib. I help bathe young bride. Dress her. She do nothing for herself today.'

'All right, Sushi,' Ruth answered. 'You come back in ten minutes time. I promise you Claire will be awake by then.'

She went back into the bedroom and looked at the sleeping form of her foster-sister. Ruth sat in the chair and did not move for a minute or two. Claire looked so untroubled in her sleep. It seemed almost an intrusion to have to wake her. Ruth bent low over her foster-sister. The courtyard outside was now bright with the sunlight pouring through the open space in the flat roof.

'Claire. Time to wake up. Claire,' Ruth whispered softly.

The other girl stirred.

'Sushi will be here soon,' Ruth said in a slightly louder voice. 'To get you ready for your wedding.'

Claire's eyes opened and for a brief moment Ruth thought she detected the wild-eyed look of a hunted animal.

'Ruth. Ruth. It is you, isn't it?' Claire asked.

'Of course, darling.' She bent across and kissed her foster-sister on the forehead. 'Sushi will be here soon. She'll look after you.'

Claire grasped her hand.

'Can't you stay with me, Ruth? You promised you'd always be with me.'

'I know that,' Ruth answered in a slightly irritated way. 'But I do have to get myself ready. And I'll have to leave you behind when Maria and I ride to the chapel together.'

'Oh, Ruth. Can't you come with me?'

'Listen, darling,' she felt it was almost like talking to a child. 'Sushi will stay in the house with you. I'm sure her daughter Pushpa will help as well. Fernando will be here all the time. And when you go to the chapel he'll ride with you.'

Claire leant across and clung to her foster-sister.

'I'm afraid, Ruth. What am I to do?'

For a few seconds the two girls embraced and then Ruth put her hands on Claire's shoulders to push her away slightly. She looked at her foster-sister's white face and searched into Claire's frightened eyes.

'The only women I have seen marry are Frances and Anne,' she replied. 'And they seemed cheerful enough. As for myself, I could never marry a man if I didn't go to him joyfully. Pushpa told me a bride should go to her man with her heart singing and her body filled with longing for her husband. Do you think that's right?'

'But I can't feel like you or Pushpa do, Ruth. It's not like that with me.'

'Then answer me carefully, Claire.' Ruth spoke slowly and deliberately. 'Do you still want to go through with it? We're in

Fernando's house now. We need never go back to Roland if you decide against it.'

'I like Roland well enough.'

'Do you love him?' Ruth persisted in her questioning. 'Do you really want to spend the rest of your life with him? Do you feel you can't live without him? Can you think of spending eternity with him?'

Claire was saved from having to reply by a knock on the door.

'Come in,' Ruth called out.

Sushi entered carrying a large tray. Apart from the usual cups of tea, it was laden with fruit and sweetmeats. Flowers were heaped around the edges of the tray.

'Chota hazri for the bride,' Sushi said as she placed the tray down. Claire was too moved to reply.

'Come back in a minute or two, Sushi,' Ruth said. 'Then you can help my sister with her bath.'

'Yes, memsahib,' Sushi replied as she left the room.

'How can I not go through with it?' Claire asked, pointing to the tray. 'How can I disappoint everyone? All those guests. All those presents they've given. Roland's pearl necklace. And Fernando paying Sushi's wages.'

'Listen to me, Claire.' Ruth spoke urgently. 'We haven't much time. If you're not sure that you can marry Roland, let's go away together. Fernando will arrange something. I'm certain he and Maria will understand. The presents can be sent back. Messages can be sent to the guests.'

Claire hesitated. Although it was only a few seconds, it seemed an interminable time to Ruth. She was constantly on edge waiting for Sushi to return. Just when Ruth was about to rephrase the questions Claire straightened her shoulders. 'I'll go through with it,' she decided.

Ruth made no comment except to pick up a cup of tea and offer it to Claire. She lifted up her own cup, took a sip of tea, placed it down again, and started unpeeling a banana.

'Have some fruit, Claire,' she said. 'It's going to be a long time before breakfast.'

'You do think I'm doing the right thing, don't you?' Claire asked plaintively.

'If you want to marry Roland and you think it's the right thing for you, there's nothing more to be said. Except to give you my blessings. I'll pray for you,' Ruth replied.

Sushi opened the door quietly at that point and peered round. 'May I enter?' she asked.

'Yes, please come in,' Ruth replied. She heaved an inward sigh of relief. The responsibility for Claire would now pass to her husband, assisted by Sushi. The last four months with Claire, three of them on the outward voyage and one of them in India, had taken their toll on Ruth's reserves of mental energy. In a way, she was glad that the problem would soon be out of her hands. She only hoped that her worst forebodings about Roland Lockyer would not come true and she could get back to feeling less jaded and short-tempered. Ruth slipped a gown over her shoulders and went on to the verandah to be greeted by Pushpa. Screens had already been put up around two tubs which were a third full of warm water.

'You wait here a little,' Pushpa said. 'Wife and daughter of dhobi bring more water soon for you and Trent Memsahib.'

'Thank you, Pushpa. We seem to be causing you a lot of work.'

The servant girl beamed. 'I very happy for you both. Not every day is there wedding in house of Ferrara Sahib. Servants from all houses around come to help make this a special day.'

# 9

Somehow, now that Ruth had shed her responsibility for Claire, she felt herself becoming a mere spectator in the day's events, instead of a participant. She felt disinclined to talk when she and Claire were bathing and the only way to avoid becoming impatient with her foster-sister was to give monosyllabic replies to her demands for reassurance. Ruth was glad when Sushi hurried Claire away and left her to her own devices. After drying her body, she put her dressing gown on and sat down on a chair. Maria had told her on the previous evening that they would take an early breakfast but there was still time to spare before she needed to dress. Ruth picked up her Bible, which she had left there on the previous evening. She turned to the Old Testament book named after her namesake but found she was unable to concentrate. Sushi's voice could be heard from the next room. The door had been left ajar and Ruth could hear her talking first to Claire, then to Pushpa. There was a clatter from the servants' quarters and the stables, where Fernando's carriage was being decorated. She put her Bible down and started to pace up and down. Two or three minutes later Pushpa came on to the verandah to ask if Ruth needed help.

'No thank you, Pushpa,' Ruth replied. 'My sister is the one who needs help.' As she watched the girl leave, Ruth thought her comment was apt in more ways than one. She had promised she would pray for her and went down on her knees, put her hands together, and shut her eyes. A few minutes later, Maria came along wearing the gold-coloured, matron of honour's silk gown, which she was going to wear at the service. Ruth opened her eyes to see Maria crossing herself. She rose from her knees and Maria apologised for disturbing her while she was at prayer but said breakfast would be ready in a few minutes.

'Thank you, Maria. I'll be ready soon. But don't stay. Look after Claire. She's the one who needs help.'

Maria gave a half-hearted smile. 'I think you not need any help when you marry, Ruth.'

'Not if I marry the right man.'

Maria's smile became broader. 'I go now. Help your sister.'

The conversation from the bedroom became slightly more animated when Maria joined the three who were already inside. The noise from the servants' quarters seemed to have increased and was now interspersed with bursts of singing. Ruth had found this type of song strange when she first arrived in India but was now becoming more accustomed to it. Around three minutes later, Claire came out on to the verandah. She was dressed in her white wedding gown and stood for a moment with Maria and Sushi on either side, while Pushpa stood in the doorway to their room.

'You'll be a lovely bride, Claire,' Ruth said. 'I've been praying for you. And for Roland.'

'Thank you for everything,' her foster-sister answered.

'Come on, Ruth. Time for that when wedding over.' Maria said. She spoke quickly to Pushpa in Portuguese and then turned to Ruth again. 'You get dressed now, Ruth. We must not miss our breakfast.'

As the two of them went into the room together, Ruth asked Pushpa what had been said.

'She tell me I look after Parker Memsahib this morning. Make sure you ready to go when Ferrara Memsahib leave in carriage.'

'I'll be ready,' Ruth laughed. 'She sounds just like Mother.'

\* \* \* \* \*

Fernando joined his wife and the two girls in the main courtyard. Over breakfast, he told them one of his neighbours was lending him a horse and carriage which Maria and Ruth would ride in. The neighbour's groom would be their coachman with one of Fernando's bearers sitting alongside. Fernando was to accompany Claire in his own carriage, driven by Des Raj. Sushi, Pushpa and one or two other servants were to follow in Fernando's bullock cart, driven by a syce employed by another neighbour. After the service was over, Ram Kopal was to take Roland and Claire to Roland's bungalow for the wedding reception. Fernando, Maria, Ruth and Jake Firman would follow in the second carriage. The servants were to follow in the bullock cart so that Sushi could look after Claire and Ruth.

A slight mental shiver went through Ruth's mind at the mention of the name of Jake Firman. She quickly suppressed it. There was no need to worry either Claire or the Ferraras with her own unreasonable fears. Claire had enough problems of her own as it was. Ruth excused herself and went out on to the front verandah. The three vehicles were already lined up outside the bungalow with their drivers standing alongside. She recognised Des Raj, Pushpa's young husband and smiled at the brightly coloured clothes which he and the other drivers were wearing for the occasion. The harnesses of the horses and bullocks, as well as the carriages and cart, were decorated with fresh, heavily perfumed flowers. Des Raj bowed slightly to Ruth as he saw her come to the front of the bungalow.

She walked across to the vehicles in order to examine the decorations more closely. The flowers had been skilfully woven together in a pattern of bright colours. Even in the brilliant morning sunshine, the effect on the eyes was almost overwhelming. In spite of the vehicles being in the open air, the perfumes from the flowers were heavy and, to Ruth's unaccustomed nostrils, slightly sickly. The three syces stood together silently, waiting for Ruth to say something.

'You have all worked very hard,' she told them. 'Thank you.'

They beamed with pleasure and Des Raj replied diffidently, 'We very happy for Trent Memsahib. Wedding good tamasha for us.' He hesitated before going on. 'Ferrara Memsahib she tell us when you marry. We all make burra tamasha for Parker Memsahib.'

The other two drivers looked expectantly at Ruth as she wondered how to answer. She was saved from the need to reply by the sight of Pushpa standing in the archway to the main courtyard.

'I must go now. Your wife is waiting for me. My blessings on all of you.' She turned to return to the bungalow.

As Ruth came through the archway, Pushpa said, 'Very sorry, memsahib. Ferrara Memsahib ready to leave in few minutes. Help you now.

'Of course,' Ruth replied. 'I was just seeing how hard your husband and his friends had worked.'

When she returned to the bedroom she found Maria and Sushi putting the finishing touches to Claire's appearance. Ruth noticed that Claire was wearing the pearl necklace given to her by Roland over her bridal gown, with one of her mother's jewelled rings on her right hand and her mother's gold bracelet on the right wrist. Her left hand was completely bare of jewelry, no doubt to emphasise the importance of the wedding ring which she would receive from Roland. Pushpa handed Ruth her bouquet and hat as Maria stood back to admire Claire's appearance.

'I leave you now,' Maria said. 'I send my husband to you. And Sushi will look after you.' She turned to Sushi. 'You take good care of bride. You give her flowers. Make sure her veil is right.'

'I take special care, memsahib. I see her into carriage with Ferrara Sahib. Then Pushpa and I change into special clothes to see Lockyer Memsahib after she married.'

'Good,' Maria replied. 'You come with me now, Ruth.'

Claire looked across to where Ruth was standing near the door. She looked so vulnerable and unsure that Ruth handed her bouquet and hat back to Pushpa and went across to kiss her foster-sister. Claire clung to her, pressing her forehead against Ruth's shoulder and saying, 'I do love you so. I'll always be a sister to you.'

'You'll spoil your headdress,' Ruth answered. 'Come on now. We mustn't keep all your guests waiting.'

Claire released her reluctantly and Pushpa handed the bouquet and hat back to Ruth. Maria walked quickly to the door, paused momentarily to look at Ruth and then went out. Ruth turned back to look at Claire again, before going through the door. Her foster-sister had become a woman who was so different from the happy, care-free, ebullient girl Ruth knew in her childhood. It was difficult to remember she was one and the same person. Ruth went quickly into the courtyard to find Fernando standing there.

'Everything goes well?' he asked her.

'She's almost ready. Look after her for me.'

'Of course,' Fernando replied earnestly. 'I look after Claire as if she my daughter. I know she very precious to you.'

Maria came out of the Ferrara's bedroom carrying her bouquet and wearing her hat. As if on cue, one of Fernando's bearers appeared in the archway to the courtyard.

Maria laughed. 'It is, as you say, uncanny. How do these servants know when we ready, Ruth?'

Ruth merely shrugged her shoulders in an abstracted fashion and turned to Fernando. 'Thank you for all your kindness.'

He took Ruth's hand and kissed it. 'We can always do more for each other. May the Good Lord watch over you.'

\* \* \* \* \*

Ruth was glad when she and Maria arrived in front of the English chapel. Both of them had been quiet on the journey from the Ferrara's bungalow, almost as though they were filled with foreboding about Claire's future. The road was dry and dusty and, although it was still only eight in the morning, the temperature was already uncomfortably warm. Once the bearer had assisted her from the carriage, Ruth moved to the front of the chapel, where she could be shaded from the sun.

In addition to a group of inquisitive onlookers standing on the opposite side of the small square, several English people were standing under the brightly coloured canopy which had been put in front of the chapel. Ruth introduced Maria to Peter and Jacoba Streynsham, the Robertsons, and the Farmerdales. Ruth noticed the elaborate clothes which the women were wearing, making the dresses which she and Maria wore look comparatively simple. They all had very large feathers in their wide-brimmed hats and wore heavy jewelry on top of their gowns of silk brocade. The men were almost as gorgeously dressed with their high boots, silk breeches, and doublets with heavy buttons and slashed sleeves. When the normal courtesies had been exchanged Peter Streynsham led the others inside, after reminding them the President and his wife were expected at any time. Ruth peered into the door of the chapel to see about twenty or so of Roland's men friends sitting behind him and Jake Firman, on the right-hand side of the small chapel. Nobody was seated in the left-hand side pews and, as she watched Peter leading the others up the aisle, she saw him indicating places three or four rows behind the left-hand front pew. She moved outside again to rejoin Maria as she heard the noise of drums and trumpets. A procession of two drummers and four trumpeters was followed by two mace bearers and a standard bearer. Immediately behind them were two palanquins, each carried by four men and the whole procession was followed by four men carrying spears and a rider on a white charger. Four servants walked alongside the palanquins, keeping the occupants cool with the help of large fans. The procession halted in front of the chapel to allow Sir George and Lady Oxindon to get down. Ruth curtsied to them as they approached the door of the chapel.

Sir George smiled at her. 'You're looking very handsome, Ruth. You'll quite outshine the bride.'

'Good day, Sir George,' she replied. 'Good day, Lady Alice. May I present my friend Maria Ferrara. She's Claire's matron of honour.'

'Good to see you, Senhora,' Sir George answered. 'I know your husband well.'

'Good day, Sir George. Good day, Lady Alice,' Maria said.
'Now we've been introduced, Senhora,' Lady Oxindon replied.
'We must see more of you.'

'I live in Swally, Lady Alice.'

'That's not far, Senhora. We will ask you to join us when our little group meet next time.'

'We must take our place, my dear,' Sir George interrupted. 'We don't want to be outside the chapel when Claire arrives. There'll be time to chat when we're at Master Lockyer's.'

Lady Oxindon took his arm and they walked through the porch together. A little time later Master Boland came out with his prayer book in hand. He greeted Ruth and Maria and then stood quietly composed under the canopy. The next five minutes seemed interminable. Just when Ruth was beginning to think that Claire must have changed her mind, the carriage driven by Des Raj appeared and drew up in front of the chapel. The crowd of curious bystanders moved forward and Sir George's attendants formed a barrier to give Claire and Fernando room. Master Boland greeted them and said everything was ready. He asked Fernando to give him a few seconds start and then to lead Claire into the chapel. Ruth squeezed Claire's hand before she and Maria took up their places two or three paces behind the bride. At Fernando's signal they went through the door and walked slowly up the aisle. As Claire came level with her bridegroom, Ruth and Maria took their places on the left-hand front pew.

When she tried to recall the ceremony afterwards, Ruth found it difficult to remember any of the details. It was as though the upheaval of leaving England, the anxiety she had felt over Claire's health on the voyage and the emotional trauma of the last month had disorientated her. She felt detached from the proceedings. When Jake Firman kissed first Claire and then her, after she had signed as a witness, she felt curiously remote, almost as though it was happening to somebody else. Jake took her arm and they followed Roland and Claire out of the chapel. The Ferraras moved behind the bride and groom and the little procession went down the aisle again and through the door. The escort for Sir George had been drawn up on either side of the entrance and they presented arms as Claire and Roland left the chapel. Jake smiled at Ruth and spoke some words of encouragement to her. She was only half aware of what he said and made no reply. Jake placed his right hand over Ruth's hand as she held his left arm. Well-wishers crowded round Roland and Claire offering their congratulations and Ruth was temporarily forgotten in the excitement.

Sushi and Pushpa had reached the front of the crowd by now. They each placed a garland of flowers around Claire's neck. Chand Narain was close by them and he placed a garland around the neck of his master. Although Claire accepted them graciously enough, Roland was obviously irritated by the gesture. Ruth could see him fingering at the garland, almost as though he wanted to take it off. Claire said something which Ruth did not catch but was near enough to hear Roland say 'Alright. Suppose I'd better wear it until we get back home.' Chand Narain tried to hide his feelings but was obviously disappointed. Roland's reaction had confirmed Ruth's opinion that he was no gentleman. Further embarrassment was avoided by their carriage drawing up and there were cheers and shouts of encouragement as the bridal pair got in. More whoops and cheers could be heard as the carriage drove off, with Chand Narain sitting alongside Ram Kopal. As the crowd began to thin out, Sushi and her daughter came towards Ruth and Jake. Sushi greeted them politely but looked a little severely at Jake's hand holding Ruth's. The expression on the servant's face recalled Ruth to the present and she lifted Jake's hand, withdrawing her own from his arm at the same time. Pushpa and Sushi were in fine, brightly coloured silk saris. They had obviously dressed for the occasion.

'Very sorry, sahib,' Sushi began, 'I come to tell Parker Memsahib all clothes and holy book in bullock cart. We bring now to house of Lockyer Sahib.'

'Thank you, Sushi,' Ruth replied. 'And thank you too, Pushpa.'

'Holy book?' Jake enquired, looking puzzled, 'What's she talking about, Ruth?'

'My Bible,' Ruth answered. 'I took it with me to Senhor Ferrara's bungalow.'

'Don't know any other women who care to read the Bible. Can't say I do much reading myself.'

The need to reply was avoided by Des Raj bringing Fernando's carriage to the front of the chapel. Maria moved across to Ruth and Jake and asked, 'Are you two ready? You come in carriage with Fernando and me.'

'We'll come at once, Maria,' Ruth replied.

Maria allowed Ruth to get into their carriage first and then took her seat by Ruth's side. The journey from the chapel to Roland's bungalow was mercifully short. Ruth was disinclined to chat and left Fernando and Jake to carry on a desultory conversation. The carriage finally drew up outside the bungalow and Ram Kopal appeared from the side of the servants' quarters to hold the horse's head. Ruth had never seen him dressed in such startling colours before. He was wearing white silk breeches, which might have previously belonged to Roland, a thigh-length green cloak, tied with a red silk girdle, and a large orange turban. When Ruth alighted from the carriage he bowed to her and said, 'I am very happy for Lockyer Sahib and your sister, memsahib.'

'Thank you, Ram,' Ruth replied.

Chand Narain met the party at the entrance to the bungalow. In addition to his normal dress of orange turban, yellow jacket and white loin cloth, he was wearing a large, green, silk sash over his left shoulder. He bowed gravely and offered his felicitations to Ruth.

'Thank you, Chand,' she answered. 'You look after these two gentlemen now. I'll take Senhora Ferrara to my room so that we can wash.'

When Ruth led Maria across the courtyard she saw that tables had already been laid for their guests. On side tables around the verandah there were bottles of wine, bowls of fruit, and cold dishes which Dev Singh, the cook, had already prepared. She guessed that the servants from their neighbours' establishments were helping with all the arrangements for the wedding meal.

Ruth took Maria into her bedroom and was surprised to find Claire already there. Claire was lying on Ruth's bed and got up slowly as the other two women entered.

'Are you unwell?' Maria asked anxiously. 'You look a little pale.'

'I'm tired, that's all. I was up early and it's very warm.'

'You ought to be ready to meet your guests, Mistress Lockyer,' Ruth told her breezily. 'You can't leave Roland to do it alone. They'll be here any minute now.'

'I know, Ruth. I'm going.'

Ruth embraced Claire. 'Many congratulations, sister.'

'I wish our mother could have been here.'

'I know,' Ruth answered cheerfully. 'That's why she sent me instead. Go off now or we'll have Roland battering the door down.'

After Claire had left, Ruth turned to Maria and said, 'I know I shouldn't say it but I'm worried about my sister.'

'You the one I worry about.' Maria replied earnestly. 'Claire is wife of Roland now. She marry him for better or worse as Father Boland says. He responsible for her now. But you just sister of wife. Why should he care for you?'

Ruth made no reply. It was the same unspoken question which had gone through her mind repeatedly ever since she and Claire landed in India. So long as relations between Roland and Claire were good, Ruth was likely to be tolerated. Once there was any friction, expecially if she took Claire's side, her position was likely to become intolerable. Ruth realised that her undefined status made her vulnerable but she had no intention of being rushed into a hasty marriage, snatching at the hope of security. Maria looked at her searchingly. 'I very fond of you. And my husband also very concerned. You promise you come to see us if you need help. You do nothing silly before you see us first.'

Ruth smiled. 'You mean I can do something silly after I've seen you.'

'You naughty girl, Ruth. You know what I mean.'

Ruth took the older woman's hand. 'I'm sorry Maria. I'm very fond of you. And Fernando too. I'll come to you for advice whenever I need it. And don't forget, there's also your husband's young friend from Braga.'

\* \* \* \* \*

Just after Ruth and Maria had finished washing, Sushi knocked at the door.

'I just come in bullock cart,' she told Maria. 'Is it permitted for Pushpa to stay, memsahib? She help other ladies who come. Pushpa look after them in Lockyer Memsahib's old room.'

'Of course, Sushi,' Maria answered. 'She stay now. Come with Senhor Ferrara when we go back with Pushpa's husband.'

'I tell her take good care of other ladies, memsahib.'

'Have you spoken to my sister, Sushi?' Ruth asked.

'She not need old room. She married lady now.'

'Nevertheless, Sushi, you must ask her.' Ruth replied. 'She is the mistress now. There are jewels in that room. Ask her if she wishes to move them to Master Lockyer's room.'

'I ask her. I go now, memsahib. Take good care of mistress and her jewels.'

After Sushi left the room, Maria said, 'You have to watch that one, Ruth. She make all your plans. Run your life for you.'

Ruth laughed. 'She's a good sort. I know she means well.'

\* \* \* \* \*

The reception and meal which followed were not particularly enjoyable as far as Ruth was concerned. She was the only single girl among the six ladies present.

By comparison, there were more than twenty men guests, of whom over three-quarters were unattached males. Her Puritan upbringing had not taught her how to cope with the compliments paid by a dozen or so ardent, would-be Lotharios. Ruth's discomfort was increased by being placed between Roland and Jake during the meal. Both of them tried to persuade her to drink wine but she preferred to drink sherbet instead. When the toast of 'The King' was proposed, Jake reached quickly for an empty glass, filled it with wine and placed it in front of Ruth. Although she stood with the rest of the guests, Ruth did not pick up the glass to join in the toast.

'You don't drink His Majesty's health, Ruth,' Jake commented.

'No, sir.'

'Why not, Ruth?'

'My father died fighting against the army of the Stuarts. My foster-father wore himself out in the service of the Commonwealth. I am sure the present head of the house of Stuart has no need of my good wishes.'

'Lucky you're in India, Ruth,' Jake replied. 'Talk like that in England would get you in a gaol as a dissenter.'

The need for a reply was avoided by Peter Streynsham proposing a toast to the bride and groom, which Roland answered with a rather rambling speech. When Fernando rose to answer on Claire's behalf as father of the bride, he made a short, carefully phrased reply which was politely applauded. Jake replied with the toast to 'The matron of honour and the maid of honour'. Ruth blushed with embarrassment as Jake looked at her throughout his reply, lauding her beauty, charm and wit. There was prolonged applause and a little cheering as he sat down. Ruth was relieved when Lady Oxindon led the women guests out on to the front verandah, to enable the men to finish their port and brandy. A few minutes later Sir George Oxindon joined them.

'You'll have to forgive their exuberance, Mistress Lockyer. It's not every day we have a wedding in Surat,' he said. 'In any event, they're not all East India men.'

'I know, Sir George,' Claire replied. 'There are three officers from the King's troops, who have sailed here from

Bombay, and Roland invited four other guests who are not factors of yours. Then there's Jake Firman. He's Roland's friend.'

'Ah, yes. Jake Firman,' Lady Oxindon said. She looked at Ruth. 'I hope you won't think too badly of my husband's young men. It may seem to you they're like a pack of hounds, Ruth, but they're not always like that.'

Ruth laughed. 'I know how the fox must feel.'

'They're better in ones and twos. You'll have to visit me soon and I will ask two or three of our young factors at the same time.'

Roland came out of the courtyard at that point to say the servants had cleared the tables away and to ask the ladies to rejoin the rest of the guests. Ruth took Claire's arm and they walked together through the archway into the courtyard. A ragged cheer went up as the two young women appeared.

\* \* \* \* \*

By the end of the afternoon Ruth was exhausted. Sir George and Lady Oxindon had left at about one o'clock and the other married couples, apart from the Ferraras, left shortly afterwards. Fernando and Maria said goodbye to Claire and Roland and then Ruth walked out with the Ferraras to the front of the bungalow where their carriage and bullock cart were waiting. While Sushi said goodbye to her daughter and son-in-law, Maria asked Ruth if she would like to come back with her for a few days.

'No, Maria. I can't go now. I gave my word to Claire's mother that I wouldn't leave her.'

Maria hugged her and kissed her on both cheeks. Fernando took Ruth's hand and said to her, 'I am always at your command. If you need me, let me know.'

'Thank you, Fernando.' she replied

He kissed her hand, took his wife's arm and turning back to Ruth, said, 'Angels protect you, Ruth.'

She watched them drive away and was reluctant to go back into the courtyard after they had left. The guests seemed to become rowdier after the married couples had gone and the level of noise rose. Although the afternoon was hot and humid, Roland kept plying his guests with wine and brandy. Ruth was never alone with less than three or four of the men at a time but found it difficult to remember all their names. The three army officers told her they would be staying at a government guest house during the next few days and hoped to call on Roland during that time. Most of the other guests were employees of the East India Company and all expressed the wish to see more of Ruth now her sister was married. Ruth excused herself about six o'clock and went to her room. She had a headache by that time and the unabated shouting and singing from the guests only made it worse. Ruth was glad when Sushi brought in a serai containing cool water so that she could wash her face, neck, and hands. A few minutes later Sushi brought in some tea and looked at Ruth with concern.

'English sahibs very noisy.' she said. 'You be better when you get some sleep.'

'Yes, Sushi. It has been a long day.'

The words were hardly out of her mouth before there was the sound of a crash outside, as though a table had been pushed over. The less inebriated members of the party must have decided that it was time to go because she could hear shouts for their horses to be brought from the stables. When Ruth looked through her window she could see it was nearly dark. She remembered the long twilight of an English summer's day and contrasted it with the rapidity of change from a bright Indian day to a black Indian night.

'I go now, memsahib,' Sushi told her. 'You call me if you want me.'

The noise gradually died away in the half an hour after the servant left, until the only sound Ruth could hear was the quiet movement of the bearers in the courtyard. It was still quite warm and humid in her room and she decided to sit on the front verandah. The courtyard was deserted apart from Chand Narain and two of the neighbours' bearers clearing up the debris from the day's festivities. Roland and Claire were nowhere to be seen. The air was fresher outside the bungalow and a slight breeze made it seem cooler than it had been in the courtyard. Ruth moved to the far left of the verandah, which was about twenty yards from the servants' quarters. She could see the dim lights from the huts and heard the slight noise made as the servants cooked their evening meals. Her thoughts reverted to Claire. She hoped that Roland would make a good husband for her sister and reminded herself to pray for them that night. From somewhere in the near distance she could hear the sound of a drum beating and slightly discordant singing coming from a Hindu temple. Ruth suddenly became aware of being watched by a man standing three or four yards away in the darkness. She stood up and as he took a step towards her, she heard Jake say, 'Don't get up, m'dear. It's Jake. Come to keep you company.'

He swayed slightly and, even in the perfumed night air, she could smell brandy. 'I thought all the guests had left, sir.'

'Ah,' Jake replied. 'I'm special friend of your brother Roland. He asked me to stay. Keep you company.'

'He did not consult me. With your leave, sir, I will return inside.'

Jake swayed towards her so that he was standing immediately in her path. 'Give me a proper kiss m'dear. I only pecked you on the cheek in the chapel.'

'You forget yourself.' Ruth said icily. 'I have no wish to be kissed by a man old enough to be my father. If I'd wanted kissing, there were a dozen men here today I would rather kiss than you, sir.'

'But they're not here,' he answered. 'And I'm old friend of Roland. Friend of the family now.'

He grabbed her left wrist with his right hand and placed his left hand on her right breast. Ruth pushed his left hand away and turned her head as he leant forward to kiss her.

'You are despicable,' she hissed. 'No gentleman would behave like you. Let my wrist go!'

He released her reluctantly and said sheepishly, 'Just a little bit of fun. No need to get upset, Ruth.'

'Stand back, Master Firman! I am going inside.'

Jake shuffled back and Ruth took a step forward. As she did so, he grabbed her round the waist. This time she was ready for him and slapped him hard across the face. He momentarily released his grip and then tightened it again. 'Wenches don't play the puritan with their friends,' he said.

'Sushi,' Ruth shouted at the top of her voice. She stamped hard on the toes of Jake's left foot at the same time.

'You damned vixen! You frigid bitch!' he exclaimed. 'You'll pay for that.' She brought the heel of her shoe down on Jake's foot again and felt him release his grip. For a second neither of them moved and then Ruth turned and ran towards the servants' quarters. Before she had gone ten yards, Ruth saw Sushi hurrying towards her and ran sobbing into her arms.

'What is trouble, memsahib?' Sushi asked.

'Let me stay with you tonight, please,' Ruth sobbed.

'I do not understand.'

'I want to be with you tonight.'

'In servants' quarters, memsahib?' Sushi enquired in a surprised tone.

'Yes. Just let me stay with you.'

'That would not be fitting. You sister of Lockyer Memsahib. You stay in Lockyer Sahib's bungalow.'

'You don't understand, Sushi, I'm afraid.' When the servant made no reply, Ruth's plea became desperate. 'It's Master Firman. He's staying here as well.'

Sushi comforted her and replied, 'You wait here, memsahib. I bring tea and food for us to your room in bungalow. I stay with you until Firman Sahib go.'

Ruth kissed her cheek, 'Thank you, Sushi. Thank you. Thank you.' The servant seemed embarrassed but took her arm and lead Ruth to just outside the door of her room in the servants' quarters. 'I be ready in just a minute, memsahib. Then we go to bungalow.'

A very short time later Sushi reappeared carrying a tray with tea and food on it.

'I stay with you, memsahib. We go now.'

There was no sign of Jake as the two of them walked together into the courtyard. The neighbours' bearers had also gone and only Chand Narain remained. 'Evening meal ready soon,' he said to Ruth as she hurried to the door of her room.

'Thank you, Chand,' Ruth replied. 'But I will stay in my bedroom this evening.'

When she went into her room she saw that a lamp had already been brought in. She lay down on the bed and then got up again quickly.

'Oh, Sushi, I hadn't thought. There's only one bed here. You must use this.'

'I will watch over you from chair, memsahib. No one will harm you while I am here.' Ruth started to cry again.

'You have this tea. You feel better.' Sushi pushed a cup into Ruth's hands and the sobbing stopped. 'When you finished, you have food. Very simple. Millet, rice and peas.'

'I just want to lie down,' Ruth replied. 'Don't worry about me. You have your own meal.'

Although Sushi looked very doubtfully at Ruth, she did not try to prevent her stretching out on the bed. Ruth felt her eyes grow heavier and heavier and within two or three minutes she was asleep.

\* \* \* \* \*

When Ruth awoke the following morning, bright sunshine was streaming through the window. Sushi rose from the chair as Ruth opened her eyes.

'You safe here, memsahib,' the servant said. 'Chand Narain in courtyard. He has been to Lockyer Sahib's room. I go now. Get chota hazri. We wait for Lockyer Sahib and Firman Sahib to go. Then you have bath and proper breakfast.'

'Thank you, Sushi,' Ruth replied. 'I'll be all right now.'

After the servant returned and Ruth had eaten her light meal, they started the normal daily language lesson, but Ruth found it very hard to concentrate. The next two hours dragged by. She was not only concerned about the continued presence of Jake in the bungalow but wondered how Claire was feeling after the excitements of the previous day. At last she heard the sound of a pair of horses being ridden away. Sushi told Ruth she would get screens for the two young women and then ask Bhadre to prepare hot water for their baths. When Sushi had gone, Ruth left her room and walked across the courtyard to Roland's room. Claire was still in her night clothes and sitting dejectedly in a chair. As Ruth walked through the door, Claire looked up. Her eyes looked hollow and dull, with deep shadows beneath them.

'Are you unwell?' Ruth asked.

'I've made a terrible mistake,' she answered listlessly. Ruth made no reply. She guessed what this mistake had been. 'Never marry a man you don't love,' Claire continued. 'Promise me that, Ruth. You can't imagine the unspeakable horror of being forced to know, to submit to, a man you don't love.'

Ruth stood behind the chair where Claire was sitting and rested her arms on her foster-sister's shoulders. 'I'm very sorry,' she said, bending her head down and kissing Claire lightly on the cheek. Ruth moved slightly to one side and was surprised to find that there were no tears in Claire's eyes. It was as though all emotion had been drained out of her.

'You were right, sister,' Claire said. 'You were right. About marriage, I mean. Promise me you'll never make the mistake I made. Please promise me, Ruth. That you won't be forced to marry. It must mean everything to both of you.'

'I promise,' Ruth whispered gently in the other girl's ear. Sushi knocked gently on the door and asked if she could come in. When Ruth went across to open it a look of alarm crossed Sushi's face as she saw Claire. 'Shall I send Ram Kopal to fetch physician, memsahib?' she said.

'No, thank you,' Claire replied. 'You help me bathe and dress. I'll be all right.'

The hours seemed to drag throughout that day and Ruth felt a sense of anticlimax after the wedding. She would have liked to go out but Claire was disinclined to stir from her chair. Ruth found it hard to concentrate on her usual noontime language lesson with Chand. The air was hot, heavy, and sticky and she was worried when Claire ate nothing during their midday meal. After Ruth confided her anxiety to Sushi, the servant replied, 'Memsahib not well. She should see physician. Perhaps she be better when monsoon comes in few days time.'

Claire had a general aura of lassitude about her and after a few minutes desultory conversation with Ruth after their meal, she decided to lie down.

Sushi insisted on going to sit with her. Concerned though she was about her foster-sister, Ruth was glad to have some time to herself. She took her books on to the verandah but still found it hard to concentrate. Her mind kept reverting to Maria's invitation. Would she have felt easier if she had accepted the Ferraras' hospitality? At least she would have been spared Jake Firman's behaviour of the previous evening. She quickly brushed the thought aside. While Claire was unwell, there was no possibility of leaving her alone. Ruth knew she must honour the promise made to Claire's mother, whatever her own inclination.

* * * * *

Roland was in a foul mood when he returned just before dark, shouting loudly for Ram Kopal as he rode up. Ruth rose from her chair at the same time as he dismounted from his horse.

'Dammit all,' Roland bellowed as the syce hurried toward him, 'you been asleep all day?'

Ram Kopal took the reins without replying and led the horse towards the stables. Roland turned and walked towards the bungalow.

'Good evening, Roland,' Ruth called.

'Want to see you,' he answered brusquely, continuing on his way.

Ruth sighed inwardly and followed him through the archway. As he entered the courtyard he yelled, 'Chand Narain, give me a brandy.'

Ruth caught him up when he paused momentarily.

'You wished to see me, Roland,' she said mildly.

'Damned displeased with you,' he replied.

'I fail to see why, Roland.'

'You fail to see. When my oldest friend, who was going to stay here for three days, leaves in a huff after one night.'

'I might have supposed you would be displeased with Master Firman rather than with your sister-in-law.'

'Sister-in-law,' he snorted. 'You're no sister-in-law of mine.'

Ruth could feel her cheeks becoming warm and flushed. The annoyance she felt could not be seen because of the rapidly fading light. Chand Narain appeared at that point with a glass of brandy which Roland drained at a gulp.

'Bring me another,' he ordered his bearer. 'And be quick about it. You took your time with the last one.'

'I will see you at dinner, Roland,' Ruth said, as soon as Chand Narain was out of earshot.

'You'll see me now. I want to know why Jake left in such a hurry.'

'Surely you asked Master Firman?'

'He said you insulted him. Called for help from a servant woman when all he wanted was to give you just a little kiss.'

'His conduct was inexcusable.'

'Don't be such a God almighty Puritan, Ruth. In the name of Christ, what's wrong with a bit of harmless fun?'

'I found his behaviour gross and offensive.'

'Next time he comes under my roof, you remember your manners. You be pleasant to him.'

Her need to reply was avoided by Chand Narain bringing Roland the second glass of brandy. After Chand Narain had

*Rough Winds*

left the courtyard Ruth started to move toward the door of her room. She paused after a couple of paces and said, 'I have no wish to see Jake Firman again, Roland. I will leave you now so that you can greet your wife.'

Ruth turned without waiting for a reply and went into her room.

# 10

## JUNE 1663

The monsoon broke a fortnight later. Outbursts of distant thunder heralded the fierce winds, which in their turn were followed by hard, grey rods of rain beating against the baked ground as though the sky was trying to cause the earth a mortal hurt. Torrents of rain continued to pour down from the dark, grey clouds and the dry, parched earth soaked the moisture up like a sponge. The breathless, dusty heat which tore at the lungs was replaced by cooler, humid air as the cloudbursts continued. Rain dripped from the trees around the bungalow, lying in pools on the ground. During the temporary respites from the torrential rain, the hot sun beat down on the dark, wet earth and the heavy, steamy smell of growing vegetation replaced the parched, furnace-like air of the days before the monsoon broke.

Ruth's brief outings away from Claire stopped with the start of the monsoon. After two or three days' heavy rain Roland said he could not ride during the rainy season and needed the carriage for his journeys between the bungalow, the port and the English factory. Even if Ruth had been prepared to brave the heavy rain, movement outside the bungalow was impossible. Both the track leading from the road and the ground adjacent to the bungalow were more than ankle-deep in soft mud.

The symptoms of Claire's illness became more pronounced with the change in the weather. Ruth had hoped that her foster-sister's shortness of breath would cease when the weather became cooler but Claire was finding it more and more difficult to breathe. Claire's skin was losing its normal elasticity as her loss of appetite caused her to lose weight. When Ruth suggested to Roland that a physician should be called to examine his wife, he replied that Claire would be better once she settled down to a normal married life. Ruth was increasingly worried over the next few days, with Claire's complexion becoming increasingly pallid and her skin becoming drier and more parchment-like as it lost its elasticity.

Shortly after breakfast on one morning towards the end of June, Claire complained that her stomach was painful and felt distended. Roland had already left in his carriage and Claire was reluctant to send for help in his absence. When Claire went back to bed to lie down, Ruth took a long, searching look at her foster-sister. Claire's eyes were hollow and dull. Her hair was lank and lacklustre and Claire seemed unutterably weary.

'I'm going to send for a physician,' Ruth told her in a decisive tone.

'Please don't. You'll only upset my husband.' Claire started to cry. 'Please wait till Roland comes back.'

'As you wish.' Ruth sighed. 'I did promise mother I would look after you.'

'You've been a wonderful sister,' Claire sobbed. 'But I'm a married woman now. Just sit with me while I rest.'

She lay down and closed her eyes. Ruth sat in the chair and studied the motionless form of her sister. Claire's appearance had deteriorated fast since they had left England together. She now looked much older than the twenty-five years of her age and Ruth was beginning to regret ever agreeing to accompany her to India. Claire lay motionless for several minutes until she suddenly sat up in bed and began to retch. Ruth hurried across to pick up the large washbasin and then moved quickly to her foster-sister's side. Claire retched three or four more times after Ruth reached the bedside and then started to vomit into the basin which Ruth held in one hand, while supporting her foster-sister's forehead with the other hand.

'Relax. I'm here with you. Don't strain or force anything,' Ruth told her, trying to speak in a soothing voice. She felt far from confident of her ability to decide what was best for her foster-sister.

At last, Claire began to breathe heavily and lay back on her pillow in an exhausted state. Ruth put the basin on the floor and noticed that the vomit was streaked with blood. She walked towards the door but stopped when Claire called out wildly, 'Please don't go. Don't leave me, Ruth.'

'I won't leave you, sister. I just want to call Chand Narain.'

She went to the door and called the bearer's name. A few seconds later he came hurrying towards Ruth and she stood aside so that he could see into the room. The bearer looked quickly from Claire to the basin on the floor.

'I call sweeper Swamy, memsahib,' he said.

'Thank you, Chand. And ask Sushi to come here as well.'

'I call both,' he replied as he went out.

Ruth sat quietly in the chair until Sushi hurried in, followed by the sweeper. Sushi glanced first at the blood-stained vomit in the wash basin and then at the still form of Claire lying on the bed. She felt Claire's forehead.

'I go. Get surgeon sahib from English factory.'

Claire opened her eyes. 'Please don't do that, Sushi. Wait till my husband returns.'

'You not well lady, memsahib. If you want me to stay I take good care of you.' She turned to the sweeper and spoke to him in Marathi. He picked the washbasin up quickly and went out.

'I stay here, memsahib.' Sushi looked at Ruth. 'Young memsahib bring surgeon.'

'Don't go, Ruth,' Claire pleaded. 'Stay here with me, please.'

'Sushi is capable of looking after you, Claire. She's an experienced ayah. It's better if I bring the physician.'

Claire started to cry. 'I'm so alone without you,' she sobbed.

While Ruth hesitated, Sushi lifted her mistress gently and held her as though she was a child. She turned her head and said to Ruth, 'You go quickly, memsahib. You bring back surgeon sahib.'

Ruth paused by the door.

'You go now,' Sushi told her firmly. 'I take care of sister.'

When Ruth explained her wishes to Ram Kopal, he let her ride one of Roland's horses and insisted on accompanying her on another horse. The heavy rainfall and the thick mud on the roads prevented them travelling at more than a brisk trot.

The physician had already left on a call before they arrived at the English factory but Ruth left a message with Luke Farmerdale, asking the physician to come as a matter of urgency. In spite of Luke's entreaties, Ruth refused to delay her return to Claire's bedside.

She was soaked to the skin as she hurried along the verandah after arriving back at the bungalow. Sushi appeared at the door of Claire's room and put her fingers to her lips as Ruth hurried towards her.

'Lockyer Memsahib sleeping,' she told Ruth quietly. 'I help you change your clothes now.'

'No. You stay here. I can change my own clothes.'

Ruth peered into the doorway. Claire was still fast asleep and appeared to be breathing more easily than when Ruth had left.

'When will surgeon sahib come?' Sushi asked.

'Soon, I hope. Thank you for taking care of my sister.'

\* \* \* \* \*

The physician drove up in his carriage towards the end of the morning. When he entered the courtyard he apologised to Ruth for the delay in arriving, due to taking longer over a patient in Swally than he had expected. Ruth remembered him slightly as one of the guests at Claire's wedding. He was a thin, elderly man who wore glasses. There was a small, grey beard on his chin and his head was covered by a white wig.

'May I get you some refreshment, Master Moxon?' Ruth asked him.

'No, thank you, Mistress Parker. I want to concentrate on the patient. How is Mistress Lockyer?'

He remained impassive as Ruth told him of her worries

about Claire during the past four months. There was a momentary flicker of concern when he heard Ruth mention that Claire had vomited blood.

'Will you stay with me, please, while I examine your sister?'

'Of course, Master Moxon.'

'May I question your sister's maid as well?'

'Yes. You'll find her English is quite good.'

Sushi got up from the chair as the physician entered the room with Ruth. 'Please stay,' Master Moxon said to her. 'I would like to talk to you.' He went across to Claire's bedside, took her hand and smiled.

'Do you remember me, Mistress Lockyer? I was a guest at your wedding. You were a lovely bride. We'll have to see if we can make you as lovely again.' Claire just smiled feebly. Nobody spoke as he looked at his fob watch and took Claire's pulse. He felt her forehead and then turned to Sushi saying, 'Get this dress off. I want to examine Mistress Lockyer.'

'Yes, sahib.'

Sushi sat her mistress up in bed and skilfully unfastened Claire's gown. 'Let me help, Sushi,' Ruth said.

'You hold your sister. I take dress off, memsahib.'

Ruth swung Claire's legs round so that her foster-sister's feet were touching the floor. She placed her hands in Claire's armpits and raised her slightly.

'I'm sorry I'm such a trouble,' Claire said in a feeble voice. 'You're no trouble,' Ruth replied. 'We'll have you better in no time.'

She eased Claire off the bed slightly, while Sushi quickly removed the dress. As she was lowering Claire back on the bed, she heard the physician's voice behind her.

'That corset will have to come off,' he said.

Sushi unfastened the corset and slipped it off as Ruth lifted Claire off the bed and then gently lowered her down again. Claire's breathing was becoming more erratic now. Master Moxon placed his left hand at the top of Claire's rib cage between her shoulder and chest. He tapped at it with the fingers of his right hand. He repeated the procedure on the opposite rib cage and then asked Claire to sit up. Sushi hurried forward to support Claire as the physician tapped Claire's back in the same way.

'You can let your mistress lie down now.' He reflected for three or four moments and then felt the loose skin at the top of Claire's arms, between her elbows and shoulders. 'I'm going to feel your stomach, Mistress Lockyer. Please tell me if it hurts.'

Master Moxon began with gentle pressure at scattered points in the abdomen. Claire made no sound until he pushed firmly at her left side, just below the ribs. She gave an involuntary groan and he lifted his hand.

'Tell me if this hurts,' he said, pressing in a similar way into Claire's right side.

'No, Master Moxon. I don't mind that.'

He moved his hand quickly across to the left side again and Claire let out a cry of pain.

'You must rest, Mistress Lockyer. I will return tomorrow morning with my colleague. The surgeon at the French factory. Monsieur Le Fanu. Please ask your husband to wait for us. Would you stay with your sister, Mistress Parker? I wish to speak to your servant.'

'Yes, of course, Master Moxon.'

After Sushi and the physician left, Claire's dull, hollow eyes stared out of her ivory-coloured face.

'What do you think is wrong with me, Ruth?' she asked.

'I don't know. And I'm not sure the physician knows either. That's why he wants a second opinion from Monsieur Le Fanu.'

'I hope Roland won't be cross, Ruth. About you sending for the physician, I mean.'

'I had to send for him. You're ill, Claire.'

'I've been a big disappointment to him as a wife. I've tried to love him, without success. It will be more difficult now I'm ill.'

'Then we must concentrate on getting you better.'

Although Ruth's tone was outwardly cheerful, inwardly she was filled with foreboding as to what the future would bring. Sushi looked grave as she returned.

'Surgeon sahib want to see you, memsahib,' she told Ruth.

Master Moxon was waiting on the verandah as Ruth left Claire's room and they walked through the archway together, on to the outside verandah at the front of the bungalow. The monsoon rains were still falling, almost as though the angels of Heaven itself were shedding their tears.

'I want you to make sure Master Lockyer is here tomorrow morning,' the physician began. 'It's important that I talk to him when I bring Monsieur Le Fanu.'

'Yes, Master Moxon. But what's wrong with my sister?'

'I would prefer to get another opinion from my colleague before discussing my diagnosis. If I am wrong, I will worry you unnecessarily. If I'm right, etiquette demands I tell your sister's husband first. I have some medicine with me in my carriage. I want your assurance that you will give the stated dose, and only the stated dose, once every four hours.'

'Of course, Master Moxon. I'll do all I can to help my sister recover.

The physician looked over the top of his spectacles at Ruth. 'How old are you, my dear?'

'Nineteen.'

'Are you planning to marry?'

'I haven't met any man in Surat I care enough about for me to marry him.'

'Don't wait too long, Mistress Parker.'

'I don't follow you, sir. What has the possibility of any future marriage to do with my sister's present illness?'

'Let me ask you a hypothetical question, my dear. What do you think your position will be in this household if anything happens to your sister?' A sudden chill crossed Ruth's heart. Surely the question could only mean that Master Moxon was trying to hint, in an oblique way, that Claire's illness might be terminal. Ruth was unable to find words to reply. She knew how tenuous her hold was on Roland's affection, and how vulnerable she would be to gossiping tongues if she shared Roland's bungalow with only the servants for company. She quickly dismissed these thoughts from her mind. The most important future task was looking after Claire.

'You don't think much of my sister's chances, do you, Master Moxon?'

'With any illness, my dear, there's always an element of risk. We physicians are not magicians. Perhaps in centuries to come medicine will be able to banish disease from the earth, but our present knowledge is little further advanced than that of the ancient Greeks. I hear you're a good Christian, Mistress Parker.'

'I try to follow the teachings of our Saviour. I don't always succeed.'

'Then you will know that this short life of ours is but a prologue to our life to come. I made a visit to Delhi when I was a younger man. While I was there, I saw the great mosque at Fatehpur-Sikri, built by the Emperor Akbar the Great. On the gateway of the mosque the builders had carved the inscription, 'Jesus, on whom be peace, said "This world is a bridge. Pass over it but do not build your dwelling here".'

He hesitated for a couple of seconds before going on. 'I think I have already said more than enough, my dear. I suggest you ask Master Boland to see your sister sometime.' He smiled. 'Just a precaution, Mistress Parker.'

Ruth shook his hand and said, 'Thank you for coming.'

'I haven't quite finished. There's still the matter of the medicine. Wait here a moment.'

He went to his carriage and came back about half a minute later with a small bottle of medicine.

'Give a small spoonful of this in water every four hours. It's most important you do it regularly and don't exceed that dose.'

'I'll do all you ask, Master Moxon.'

* * * * *

Roland was not pleased when he returned that evening to find that Ruth had called the physician in his absence. He was even less pleased when she told him that Master Moxon would return the following morning, accompanied by a Frenchman. His displeasure mounted when Ruth told him that Claire would need to take the medicine every four hours.

'In the name of Christ,' he asked. 'What got into you Ruth? My sleep to be disturbed at midnight and four in the morning. Waiting here for Master Moxon and his French friend. Don't you know I have business to attend to?'

'You also have a wife, Roland. And your wife is ill.'

'Yes, I've a wife. Don't you think I know. A wife who gets sick every time I touch her or come near her.' He looked at Ruth speculatively. She could feel her cheeks burning and was glad that the twilight was quickly turning into darkness.

'Most women aren't like that, are they, Ruth?'

'Your wife's sickness is a matter for Master Moxon to comment on tomorrow morning,' she answered coldly. 'I doubt if he will tell you that Claire is with child.'

'Devil take me, I didn't think of that.'

'Neither, I am sure, did Master Moxon. I suggest you see Claire now. She has been most anxious to be reassured all day.'

'Don't let's quarrel, Ruth,' he said weakly. 'It's just I'm the one who ought to make the decisions.'

'That's why Master Moxon wishes to see you tomorrow morning.'

She waited outside the door as Roland went into the bedroom to see Claire. When Sushi came out as Roland entered, Ruth told her that she would go to bed immediately the evening meal was over. She asked Sushi to wake her at midnight so that she could administer the medicine and told the servant she would wait up until four in the morning to administer another dose.

'It is not fitting, memsahib,' Sushi replied.

'Not fitting?' Ruth asked in a surprised tone.

'You not married lady. I am widow. It is not proper for you to go into bedroom of Lockyer Sahib. Indian ladies not go into rooms of men. Only nautch girls do.'

'But my sister must have medicine, Sushi.'

'I give Lockyer Memsahib medicine at night. You give in day. I sleep when sahib not here.'

'She's my sister, Sushi. I must be responsible for her.'

'She also my memsahib. We take care together. Your sister very sick. I think she be sick for long time. I be glad when other surgeon see her.'

Ruth felt the same sudden chill that she experienced when Master Moxon had spoken.

'You don't think my sister will get better, do you, Sushi?'

A few seconds of uneasy silence passed before the servant answered. 'I not lie to you, memsahib. I not know. When surgeon sahib come again he speak truth.'

Ruth could feel her eyes filling with tears. Claire's failing appetite, her loss of weight, her lassitude over the past three months, and now the pain and vomiting of blood, all seemed to confirm Ruth's worst fears. If Claire died, she would be alone in a strange land, far from home. The tears began trickling down her cheeks and she started to dry her eyes with a handkerchief. She became aware of Sushi looking at her intently and compassionately.

'Tomorrow I pray for your sister in temple, memsahib.'

'Oh, Sushi. Pray that she will stay with me.'

Ruth burst into tears and Sushi took hold of her hands, saying quietly, 'I will pray, memsahib, but it is in hands of gods. Some have life like flowers. When monsoon comes they come alive for a short time until hot sun dries up earth. Then they die. Other people live like jacaranda tree or palm tree. Perhaps your sister like beautiful flower.'

\* \* \* \* \*

Ruth found it difficult to sleep that night. She was already awake when Sushi brought her chota hazri to her at five in the morning.

'You should be sleeping now, you know, Sushi. Have you been up all night?'

'I get Dev Singh, our cook, to wake me an hour ago. He always up early in morning.'

'You must sleep during the day. How is my sister this morning?'

'She sleep now. Lockyer Sahib sleeping also.' Sushi permitted herself a slight smile. 'I think he not pleased when I wake memsahib with medicine.'

'You did well, Sushi. But you must get some sleep during the day. I won't trouble you or Chand Narain to give me my lessons while my sister is ill.'

'Oh, no, memsahib,' Sushi cried in sudden alarm. 'I and Chand Narain we very pleased to help you learn our language. All servants very proud when you speak to them in Marathi. Sometimes they not understand Lockyer Sahib when he speaks English.' She lowered her voice and her tone became confidential. 'They not happy to talk Urdu.'

'Very well, Sushi. I promise. When I have finished my bath, we'll start our lesson. After it's over, I will eat breakfast. But I must see my sister as soon as she wakes.'

Chand Narain had taken Ruth's breakfast away before Roland appeared about two hours later. He looked tired, haggard, and hollow-eyed. Apart from a pair of slippers and thin cotton trousers, his only garment was a silk robe tied loosely at the waist.

'How did you sleep, Roland?'

'You might well ask. God, I don't want another night like that. With your servant creeping in at all hours.'

'She was only obeying Master Moxon's instructions. He'll be here soon with Monsieur Le Fanu. You can talk to him yourself.'

'Sooner we get Claire up and about the better. Stop all this nonsense. When weather's better, take her into Surat.' He glanced balefully at Ruth. 'Get her someone else to talk to apart from you and that native woman.'

'Please excuse me, Roland,' Ruth said, standing up. 'I must go to see Claire now.' She was fuming as she went into the bedroom belonging to Roland and Claire. How could Roland be so callous? She looked across at her foster-sister and saw Claire was still sleeping. Ruth checked the time with her watch and saw there was another hour to go before the next dose of medicine. She sat down in the chair near the door and prepared to wait.

Roland came in half an hour later. He was now fully dressed but Ruth smelt the aroma of brandy as he entered the room. Ruth rose quietly and went to meet him.

'How is she now?' he asked.

'Still resting,' she replied in a whisper. 'You wait for the physicians, Roland. I'll sit here with her.'

'I'll get your servant to come in. She does little enough work as it is.'

'Please leave her, Roland. Sushi can keep an eye on Claire later today.'

'Very well,' he replied half-heartedly. 'I'll wait outside.'

\* \* \* \* \*

The two physicians arrived just under two hours later. Ruth was introduced to Monsieur Le Fanu and then went outside into the courtyard, leaving them alone with Claire and Roland. Sushi was standing on the verandah outside Ruth's room at the opposite side of the courtyard. She looked anxious as Ruth walked slowly towards her. Ruth smiled weakly when she reached the door of her room but for a few seconds neither woman spoke. Sushi glanced towards the closed door of Claire's room and then said, 'You wait here, memsahib. I bring you tea.' She went inside Ruth's bedroom, brought out a small cane chair and placed it on the verandah beside her mistress. 'You rest now. You have plenty time to work later.'

'Thank you, Sushi,' Ruth replied. She sat down and lowered her head. Her thoughts were a mixture of anxiety on her sister's behalf, combined with feelings of weariness and helplessness. She became aware that Sushi was standing in front of her. As Ruth looked up she could see the look of concern on the servant's face. The eyes of the two women met and Ruth sensed the sympathy which Sushi had for her in her present plight. She felt a wave of affection for the grey-haired, thin-faced, erect Indian woman who had been with her for the past few weeks. Ruth smiled at Sushi and was rewarded with a warm, loving smile in return.

She always remembered that moment. The look exchanged between them was no longer between mistress and servant, Christian and Hindu, Englishwoman and Indian, but that of an older woman comforting a younger sister by giving her love when she needed it most. Ruth stood up, embraced Sushi and kissed her on the cheek but the spell was broken. Sushi pushed her gently away.

'Other servants see. I get tea now, memsahib.'

'I don't care.' Ruth kissed her. 'Thank you for being so kind.'

She held the older woman's hands. Sushi tried to speak sternly but her eyes were bright and smiling. 'You naughty girl.'

It was almost as though she was speaking to a child. Ruth remembered she had been an ayah to an English family before going to the Ferraras.

'You let me go now,' Sushi continued. 'Or I be cross with you.' Ruth laughed and released her hands.

'I like you when you laugh,' Sushi said. 'I not happy when you not happy.' She pushed Ruth gently on the shoulders. 'You sit now. I go make tea.' Sushi was a little wary when she returned with the tea a few minutes later. It seemed almost as though she was concerned that the worry which she and Ruth shared for Claire's future, had tempted both of them to break the normal rules of conduct between servant and mistress. In the Maratha village from which she came, outward demonstrations of affection through physical contact were uncommon. While she had been an ayah for the Robinson family, the Robinson's young daughter Rachel had kissed and cuddled her from time to time, but neither Robinson Memsahib nor Ferrara Memsahib had ever demonstrated any emotion towards her, nor she towards them. The young English mistress, who looked so vulnerable staring towards the door of her sister's room, was the only foreigner who had ever touched her feelings in that way.

Ruth seemed abstracted when the tray was placed on the small table beside her chair. Sushi was relieved when Ruth did no more than thank her politely, allowing her to withdraw without further conversation. The next few minutes dragged by and Ruth let her tea grow cold waiting for Master Moxon and Monsieur Le Fanu to leave Claire's room. The morning was becoming humid and sultry without any breeze to disturb the leaves of the trees around the bungalow. Even the sounds from the servants' quarters had died away, as though they were waiting for news of their mistress.

Ruth rose from her chair as the physicians came through the door of her sister's room. She crossed the courtyard towards them but Master Moxon waved her away, saying, 'Later, Mistress Parker.'

Ruth watched them leave the bungalow, conversing in low tones. A moment or two later, Roland appeared and stood in the doorway of his room, looking at her. She went across, checked to see Claire lying with her eyes shut and asked Roland, 'What did they say?'

'Nothing. Master Moxon'll come back and talk to me when he's finished with the Frenchman.'

Ruth thought how old Roland had become suddenly. His head was lowered and his shoulders rounded almost to a stoop. Ruth hoped for everybody's sake that the physicians would be able to cure Claire of whatever illness troubled her. She and Roland stood side by side on the verandah without speaking, waiting for Master Moxon to return. A minute or so later the physician came through the archway, halted, and motioned the two of them towards him. He looked grave. 'Monsieur Le Fanu and I have both made the same diagnosis,' he began. 'We think Mistress Lockyer has a tumour in the stomach. It is likely to grow quickly until it fills the stomach and causes pressure on the lungs.'

'What does that mean, Master Moxon?' Ruth asked anxiously. 'And how can it be cured?'

'I'm afraid it means your sister will probably die in eight to ten weeks' time. You ask about cures. They are not possible in the present state of the art of medicine. Even if I attempted to cut the tumour out, the shock would almost certainly kill Mistress Lockyer, no matter how much belladonna I administered. There is still no guarantee that the tumour would not recur after surgery. I can control the pain by giving her morphine but, apart from that, she is in your good hands. And the hands of God. See she is kept comfortable. Ask Master Boland to call. There is no need to tell her the illness is terminal unless she presses for an answer. You must use your discretion.'

Ruth could feel her eyes fill with tears but she was determined to control her feelings. 'Will you see her maid before you go, Master Moxon?' she asked. 'The two of us will take it in turns to nurse her and to administer the morphine.'

'Yes, of course.' The physician looked at Ruth with a new respect. 'I will call every other day for the present. Later on I will call everyday.' He turned to Roland. 'Must keep an eye on you and your sister-in-law as well as Mistress Lockyer. It will be a trying time for everyone. And you'll all need my help.'

# 11

## JULY – SEPTEMBER 1663

The next four weeks dragged by as though each day was a week and each night lasted a thousand hours. Soon after the second visit made by the physician, Roland decided he did not wish to be woken up at night when Claire took her medicine and moved into Claire's old bedroom, next door to Ruth. Claire's complexion was becoming increasingly pallid and her body more skeleton-like. She was now eating and drinking very little and, because of muscular weakness, Ruth and Sushi had to lift her in and out of bed. Her mind started wandering and she refused to have a lamp in her room. During the day she insisted on the windows of her room being shuttered. Ruth's patience began to wear thin when Claire refused to be left alone with Sushi because she said the servants were trying to poison her. Claire's bodily temperature was subject to violent fluctuations. Sometimes, Ruth was obliged to pile blankets on top of her foster-sister's shivering form. At other times, Claire would not allow herself to be covered even by a sheet.

Ruth now spent every night watching over Claire. She dozed on and off during the day, snatching irregular meals where she could. Ruth's complexion was becoming pale and her clothes began to hang on her as she lost weight almost as quickly as Claire. Several times towards the end of the month, Ruth became aware of Master Moxon looking at her anxiously during his visits. In answer to his questions, she always replied that she felt a little tired. If he had probed further, Master Moxon would have realised that Ruth was under an emotional strain of a different nature.

Roland had recommenced heavy drinking almost as soon as Claire became ill. Three weeks after the visit by the two physicians he arrived home one evening accompanied by two nautch girls. When Ruth tried to reprimand him for bringing them to the bungalow, he leered at her and said he would send them away if she took her foster-sister's place. Ruth felt sick with disgust. She turned from him and went back into Claire's room, where Sushi was sitting in the dark. It was obvious that Sushi was aware of the presence of the nautch girls and the altercation between her mistress and Roland. She stood up as Ruth came in, walked towards her, and enfolded her mistress in her arms. Ruth laid her head on the older woman's shoulder and wept quietly and in despair.

A week after this incident Roland arrived in the evening, accompanied not only by two nautch girls but also by Jake Firman. Ruth had no reserves of mental stamina left for another scene with Roland and stayed quietly in the room with Claire, listening to her fighting for breath. Ruth held her foster-sister's hand and spoke words of comfort to her but there was no reply. Claire seldom talked these days. It was as though the ever-increasing doses of morphine which Master Moxon prescribed were making her more and more remote.

Shortly before eight o'clock, Sushi came in with a beaker of water. She measured out the required dose of medicine and handed it to Ruth. The two of them raised Claire up to a sitting position. Ruth held the beaker to Claire's mouth and encouraged her to drink the liquid. After the last drop had gone down, they lowered Claire to the bed and she closed her eyes, breathing heavily at the same time, as though worn out by the effort.

'I stay with memsahib now,' Sushi whispered. 'You go and rest.'

'Where can I go?' Ruth asked her bitterly, listening to the music and laughter in the courtyard outside.

Sushi made no reply. After a few seconds' pause, Ruth said, 'I need some fresh air. I haven't been out all day. I will be on the roof. Call me if you need me.'

'Of course, memsahib.'

The night air smelt cool and fresh after the stuffiness of the sick room. She moved round the verandah, carefully avoiding looking at the group in the opposite corner of the courtyard, went through the archway, and up the stairs at the side of the bungalow. The sky was clear and bright with a thousand stars. A new moon was shining, giving a pale light to the earth below. During the previous fortnight, the monsoon showers had become lighter and less frequent, the air less humid, and the skies less cloudy. Looking in the semi-darkness at the branches of the trees waving in the light breeze, she thought how pleasant it would have been if Claire had not fallen ill and how they could have explored the countryside together.

Hearing footsteps on the stairs, Ruth hurried across, thinking Sushi was coming to ask her to return to Claire's room. She was surprised to see Jake Firman two steps below her when she reached the little landing at the top of the stairs. He stopped and for a moment or two neither spoke.

'Good evening, Ruth,' he said at last.

'Good evening, sir.'

'Come to pay my respects, Ruth.'

'Thank you, Master Firman. I must now return to my sister's room. I am sure you wish to return to your friends.'

'Hold hard, Ruth. I'm a man of taste. Not like Roland. Can't say I care for his dusky damsels. I prefer a paler shade of woman.'

'With your leave, sir. I wish to pass.'

'Don't be so hasty, my dear. You and I got unfinished business to discuss.'

'I think not, sir. The last time we met you insulted me. You doubted my honour.'

'I was overwhelmed by your beauty, Ruth. Didn't know what I was saying.'

'Your conduct was unbecoming a gentleman. If I had been a man, wearing a sword, I might have killed you.'

Jake laughed. 'I'm glad you aren't a man. Glad you're a woman. Come on. Let's kiss and make up and be friends again.'

'You are offensive, sir. I know you are a guest in Roland's house but you forget yourself. I must ask you to stand aside.'

---

'A girl of pluck and spirit. Just what I like.'

Jake took a step towards her and started to reach out his arms. Before he touched her Ruth stretched out her right arm to its fullest extent and pushed against his left shoulder. He stumbled and started falling down the stairs, shouting as he went. When he reached the bottom of the stairs he fell on his back. Ruth heard the thud as his head hit the ground. She hurried down the stairs, stepped over Jake's unconscious body, and met Roland coming through the archway, attracted by the noise.

'Attend to your friend,' she commanded. 'He has been involved in an accident.'

Although Claire became steadily weaker during the month of August, her mental faculties improved. It was almost as though her brain became accustomed to the large doses of morphine which Master Moxon prescribed for her. Because her lungs were becoming increasingly congested, she found it a strain to talk but she liked to have Ruth read to her, particularly from the four gospels of the New Testament. Each time Ruth took up her Bible to read to Claire, she glanced at her father's dedication, 'To my love, knowing you will be with me always'.

Master Boland was a frequent visitor to the bungalow and Claire became a regular communicant. He conducted a shortened form of the Holy Communion service for her and, to save her the effort of sitting up, would dip the host in the communion wine before placing it on Claire's tongue. Ruth sat through these bedside services, joining in the prayers but declining the offer of the consecrated bread and wine on the grounds that she had never been a member of the Church of England. She was escorting the chaplain through the courtyard one day towards the end of the month when he suddenly turned to her and asked, 'Do you plan to marry, Mistress Parker?'

'There is no prospect of that at present.' She shrugged her shoulders. 'If the right man comes along, who knows?'

'Your sister was married in my chapel. And don't forget, Mistress Parker, I'm the only person in Surat entitled to marry you according to English law.'

'I will remember that, Master Boland,' she smiled. 'Provided of course the prospective bridegroom is not a Catholic, Muslim or Hindu.'

The chaplain looked at her a little severely. 'It's not a thing to joke about. I know you to be a good Christian girl. Someday you will be the mother of a family. Would you want your children brought up outside the true church, not knowing the true word of Christ?'

'I mean no offence, Master chaplain.' She smiled sweetly at him. 'However, before you and I can talk about children, we must first find me a husband. If the bridegroom is an Anglican, I promise I will come to you to be married.'

He bowed slightly. 'I can ask no more at present. But I will remind you again soon.'

Ruth hurried back to Claire's room to find her foster-sister looking anxiously towards the door, awaiting her return. She sat on the side of the bed and took Claire's hand.

'You have no need to worry, sister. I'm never far away. Sushi will stay if I have to leave you.'

'I'll leave you soon,' Claire replied in a half-whisper. 'I'm going to die, aren't I?'

Ruth tried to keep her voice steady. 'We all have to die sometime, Claire.'

'Yes, but why does it have to be me? And why does it have to be now? Answer me that, Ruth?'

'I don't know, sister.' Ruth bent down and kissed Claire's forehead. 'We are all in the hands of God. Why not ask the chaplain for guidance.'

Claire waited a few seconds before replying. 'You were a long time with Master Boland. Were you talking about me?'

'No, Claire,' Ruth answered a little wearily. Her sister always became irritable just before her medicine was due. 'He asked me if I planned to marry.'

'What a thing to ask when I'm on my death bed.'

'Master Boland means well. He's very concerned about you.'

Sushi came in at that moment to remind them that the next dose of medicine was due. She placed the bottle down, measured out the dose and helped Ruth to lift her foster-sister into a sitting position. Claire was beginning to find it more and more difficult to swallow the liquid and gasped for breath as they laid her down again. Sushi stood near the end of the bed waiting to help but Ruth told her to leave for the time being. After the servant had gone, Claire said in a whisper which Ruth could hardly hear, 'You should have kept the bottle here.'

'Why?' Ruth asked, looking puzzled.

'You could have given me another dose. Then another and another and another, until it was all over and I was free from this awful pain.'

Ruth did not know how to reply. She knew it was wrong to take another life or help a person take his or her own life. Was it right, however, to let Claire suffer this pain when the inevitable end was such a short time away? If Claire had been a sick animal on her father's farm, Colonel Trent would have dispatched her without a second thought. The problem was solved for her by recalling the promise she had given to Master Moxon.

'I am sorry that you have such pain, Claire. But I gave my word to the physician that I would be responsible for seeing you took the correct dose.'

Her foster-sister started to cry. The crying turned into a whimper. 'You mean you won't help me. You've always been like a sister to me. Now you don't care any longer.'

'I gave my word to Master Moxon, Claire.'

The figure on the bed was racked with sobs. 'And your precious word of honour is more important than helping me. You don't really love me.'

Ruth could not reply. She had already made her mind up on what she must do. The dose of medicine was beginning to take effect and Claire became quieter. After each of her foster-sister's outbursts Ruth talked to her about the times when they were girls together on Colonel Trent's farm and before then at Aireton Hall. The recollection of their past life always seemed to make Claire more peaceful, almost as though her spirit was disembodied and travelling back in time to those carefree days just a handful of years ago. Ruth never mentioned Mark Fairbrother when she spoke to Claire about Aireton Hall but the hurt she felt at the time of his leaving still rankled, in spite of her foster-father saying that she would forget. After about half an hour of Ruth's talking, Claire fell asleep. Ruth sat in the room for another two hours and then saw Chand Narain walk past the half-opened door. She rose quickly and called after him as she left the room. When he turned round and came back to her, she asked him to fetch Sushi and told him she would have her evening meal now. He hurried away as she returned to the chair at the bedside. A minute or two later Sushi came in and Ruth asked her to wait until she returned at eight o'clock. Ruth ate the evening meal alone in her room. She was quite accustomed to solitary meals, partly because she seldom finished them before Claire was asking for her and also because Roland had become more irascible when he and Ruth ate together. Ruth preferred to eat alone in order to avoid the men friends and nautch girls who sometimes returned in the evening with Roland. After the meal was over, she sat dozing in the chair until Chand Narain came in carrying a lamp. She sighed inwardly. It would soon be dark. That meant another night of sitting in the darkness by Claire's bedside, waiting for the first, long, pale fingers of daylight to clutch at the black sky. Once the sun had set, Claire allowed them to remove the shutters from the windows, letting the dim light from the moon and stars illuminate the sickroom. Apart from that, the only light came from a small lamp which Chand Narain placed on the verandah outside the half-opened door. After a few minutes Ruth measured out a dose of medicine from the medicine bottle into the water in the beaker. She replaced the stopper, put the bottle into a pocket at the front of her skirt, picked up the beaker, and made for the door. Sushi got up as she entered Claire's room and asked, 'Shall I wait with you, memsahib? It is not yet time for medicine.'

'Yes, please,' Ruth replied. She looked at her foster-sister's still form. 'Hello, Claire. How are you feeling?'

Claire gave a wan smile which was difficult to see in the dim light. Ruth placed the beaker on the small table at the side of the bed. Claire lifted her head slightly and swivelled her eyes to look at the beaker. 'Is it time?' she asked.

'Not quite,' Ruth replied.

Claire lowered her head and stared at the ceiling. 'You sure?'

Ruth went to the door and looked at her watch by the light of the lamp. 'Yes,' she replied. 'Five minutes to go.' She sat in the chair and held her foster-sister's hand. 'Not long now.'

Claire closed her eyes. 'Why can't this pain go? Why won't it end?'

'Only God knows the answer,' Ruth replied quietly. She allowed a few seconds to pass. 'Do you remember how father used to read to us from the Book of the Revelation of St. John? The saint wrote about the new heaven and the new earth. How God will wipe the tears from our eyes because there will be an end to death. How there will be no more mourning, no more crying, and no more pain.'

'I remember,' Claire whispered. 'But I don't want to leave you.'

'I am going to give you the medicine a little early.' Ruth put her hand under Claire's shoulder. 'Sushi, come and help.'

The servant went to the other side of the bed and gently raised Claire into a sitting position while Ruth held the beaker to her foster-sister's lips. They slowly let Claire down again after she had finished taking the medicine. Ruth continued to hold the beaker as she told Sushi to leave now and return at midnight. She took the medicine bottle from the pocket in her skirt and placed it, together with the beaker, on that edge of the small table which was nearest to the bed. Ruth carefully removed the stopper and placed it down.

'I am very tired, Claire,' she said. 'I may doze off while I sit here.' She could dimly see her foster-sister's eyes looking at her. Ruth bent down and placed her cheek against Claire's, whispering, 'Sleep now, my sister. Step soft into that brief oblivion. The final sleep, which gently leads to a beginning. Born again into eternity. Reborn again, my sister, to wait for me.' She held Claire close in her arms and kissed her on both cheeks. 'Good night, Claire,' she whispered. 'God be with you.'

Ruth slowly straightened herself up. Claire continued to look at her but made no reply. Ruth leant back in the chair and closed her eyes. Within a minute or so, she was asleep.

\* \* \* \* \*

Ruth stretched her aching spine and pushed her shoulders back as she sat up quickly in the chair after regaining consciousness. The only noises she could hear were the rustle of the trees in the light breeze and the sound of laboured breathing from the bed. Ruth picked up the beaker. Although it was difficult to see in the quarter-light, it seemed to be empty. She picked up the stopper and replaced it in the neck of the thick, green, glass bottle, which she held up to see if any of the medicine had been poured out. It was impossible to tell inside the room. She tiptoed across to the door and stood so that the light from the oil lamp on the verandah shone through the glass. The medicine did not seem to have been touched. Ruth went back to the chair and returned the bottle to the table, aware of a feeling of anti-climax. She did not know whether to be glad or sorry that Claire had not been tempted to drink an overdose of morphine.

When she had left England at the beginning of the year, she had never visualised that eight months later she would be sitting alone in the warm darkness of an Indian night, watching her foster-sister's life draw painfully to a close. A slight feeling of resentment swelled up in her. Claire had begged to be given a massive overdose and yet could not make that choice of her own volition, after Ruth had carefully prepared her emotionally and put the means at her disposal. This was soon replaced by a feeling of guilt. Ruth wondered how she would react if she knew her own life was coming to an end after a painful illness. She tried to remember the New Testament descriptions of Jesus's last hours and wondered if she could have been as steadfast as him when he suffered. Ruth's train of thought was broken a few minutes later by the sight of Sushi in the doorway.

'You come quick, memsahib,' Sushi said in an anxious half-whisper. 'Medicine gone from your room.'

Ruth rose wearily. 'I have it here. I'm sorry, Sushi. It must have been left behind.'

Sushi came into the room. Even in the dim light, her expression was stern. 'I very worried. Surgeon sahib very cross when he find out.'

'I know, Sushi. It won't happen again. You pour out the medicine and make sure the bottle goes back to my room, ready for the four o'clock dose.'

Sushi picked up the medicine, a jug of water, and the beaker. She went to the doorway to take advantage of the light outside and started to pour out water and medicine. Ruth had very acute hearing and heard Sushi muttering to herself when holding the bottle against the beaker. It was obvious that Sushi was not pleased as she probably felt she had failed in her joint responsibility to take care of the medicine. By the time she returned to the bedside, Claire had been roused by Ruth. Claire kept her eyes lowered as the other two women lifted her up and Sushi gave her the medicine. After they had lowered Claire to the bed again Sushi picked up the bottle.

'I put bottle in your room, memsahib. Bring back in four hours' time.'

'I am very sorry I forgot to give it to you before,' Ruth replied. 'I must be more careful in future.'

She looked down at her foster-sister's face. Claire carefully avoided looking into Ruth's eyes, even when Ruth held her hands.

* * * * *

Claire was extremely quiet all the next day, engaging in only a desultory conversation with Ruth and exchanging a few words with the chaplain and the physician when they visited her. She became very subdued as dusk fell. When Ruth told her she would like to leave for her evening meal, Claire became wild-eyed, grasped Ruth's hands and said, 'Don't leave me. Please don't go. I've such pains in my stomach.'

'I will sit with you as long as you need me,' Ruth replied.

'It may be a long time. I feel as if I'm cut in half.'

'Try to lie still, sister. Your medicine is due in an hour's time.' During the next two or three minutes Claire lay motionless in the bed while Ruth sat quietly in the chair alongside. Suddenly, Claire sat up and began retching. Ruth ran aross to fetch the wash basin. She rushed back with it as a dark brown liquid began to stream from Claire's mouth. She held the basin steady, talking gently to Claire at the same time. The flow of dark brown liquid continued and she noticed tiny pieces of solid flesh among the vomit in the basin. She shouted loudly for Sushi and Chand Narain. Roland's bearer came in first, closely followed by Claire's maid. They both looked at her anxiously. 'Get Swamy,' she said to Chand Narain. 'And you, Sushi, get plenty of drinking water.'

The servants hurried out as Claire continued to retch into the basin. Sushi was the first to return carrying a serai of water in her hand.

'Put that down,' Ruth commanded. 'Come over here and support my sister's forehead.'

Moments later, Chand Narain returned. He was followed by the sweeper Swamy carrying a clean bowl. Swamy carefully removed the basin from Ruth's hands, replaced it with the clean bowl, and then went towards the door. He turned as he reached it and said to Ruth, 'I will give bowl careful clean. If memsahib permits, I will bring back for burra memsahib.'

'Of course, Swamy,' Ruth said a trifle impatiently. 'Come back as soon as the basin is clean. Don't wait to be called.'

Chand Narain stood looking at Claire in the fading light. Sushi was still holding her mistress's head but the vomiting had stopped for the time being and Ruth was wiping her foster-sister's mouth with a damp cloth. 'Sit my sister upright, Sushi. I am going to give her some water,' Ruth said. She poured water from the serai into a beaker, returned to the bedside and held the beaker up for Claire. Her foster-sister shook her head. 'You must drink,' Ruth told her sternly. 'Otherwise you'll get dehydrated. You've lost so much liquid.' Claire's eyes continued to stare straight ahead as Ruth held the beaker to her lips. At long last, she started to sip the water. With Ruth's encouragement she drank it all, taking three times as long as normal to finish. Ruth went across to fill the beaker again and brought it back.

'No, I can't, Ruth,' Claire said and started to retch again.

'Push her forward,' Ruth told Sushi, picking up the basin at the same time.

'How can I help. memsahib?' Chand Narain asked.

Dark brown liquid started to pour from Claire's mouth again and Ruth turned to Chand, telling him to send Ram Kopal for Master Moxon. The bearer hesitated.

'Tell Ram Kopal to go now,' Ruth shouted.

'Lockyer Sahib home soon. We wait for him, memsahib?'

'No,' Ruth replied firmly. 'If you will not send him, Sushi must ask him to come to me. I will tell him.'

'There is no need, memsahib. I get Ram Kopal to ride to English factory. I will tell Lockyer sahib when he returns.'

'Thank you, Chand. Please ask Master Moxon to come here when he is home.'

The next half-hour passed with Claire alternately drinking and vomiting. Roland had not been pleased to find his syce missing after he rode back from his day's work and was in a foul mood when he came into Claire's room. His expression softened a little when he saw Claire being assisted by Ruth and Sushi. He did not take up Sushi's offer to withdraw so that he could take her place, preferring instead to say he would wait outside until the physician arrived. Ruth could feel herself tiring with the strain of supporting Claire with one hand and holding the beaker in the other hand. Chand Narain had placed a lamp on the verandah by this time and, by its dim light, she could see Sushi smiling encouragingly at her from the other side of the bed. Sushi never seemed to tire and, as if in answer to Ruth's unspoken thought, she said, 'I stay here with Lockyer Memsahib tonight. We look after her together.'

'Thank you for the offer, Sushi. Let's wait to see what Master Moxon has to say.' Swamy peered cautiously round the door at this point. There was a slight lull in the flow of dark brown liquid from Claire's mouth and Ruth asked Sushi to help lower Claire gently on to the bed. She then told Swamy to come in, leave the clean bowl which he had brought with him, and to take the other one away. As Swamy left he was stopped by Master Moxon and Roland coming in. The physician went out on to the verandah with the sweeper, held up the lamp, and examined the contents of the bowl. Ruth and Sushi both rose as he returned, escorted by Roland.

'Can you bring me a lamp, please?' Master Moxon said to Sushi.

He asked her to wait outside when she returned with the lamp but suggested Ruth should stay as well as Roland, while he examined Claire. Master Moxon felt the patient's pulse, placed his hands on her forehead, and looked into Claire's eyes. He then placed his hands on Claire's distended stomach and she gasped with pain.

'Can you help me sit your sister up, please?' he asked Ruth and then tapped Claire's back below her shoulder blades.

'Say if that hurts, won't you,' he said continuing to tap with the end of his fingers.

'It does,' Claire whispered.

'Very well then. Lie back slowly. Your sister will support you. Now stay there.' Ruth strained to keep Claire up while

Master Moxon repeated the process at the front of Claire's chest. Before he had finished his examination, Claire started to be sick again. He held Claire forward with one hand, holding the bowl with the other. When Claire paused for a few seconds, he asked Roland to hand him a beaker of water. Claire protested that it would only make her sick but he insisted that she drank it and advised her to continue to drink after he left her. Master Moxon reached for his bag and told her he was going to give her belladonna and, after looking at his watch, also administer the evening dose of morphine. Sushi was asked to bring the medicine and stay while the physician gave Claire the required doses. After this was over, Master Moxon beckoned Roland and Ruth to follow him out. As they left, Claire told Sushi to take the lamp out of the room on to the verandah outside. Master Moxon's expression was grave as he stood in the courtyard. 'I am afraid your wife is deteriorating fast, Master Lockyer.'

'How d'you mean?' Roland asked.

'Her stomach's disintegrating and her lungs filling with liquid.'

'Is there nothing you can do?' Ruth questioned.

'You are more help to your sister now than I am, my dear. You were quite right to call me,' he replied, glancing at Roland. 'And you were very sensible in making Mistress Lockyer drink. Continual retching without any liquid in the stomach will strain the heart.'

'How long's she got?' Roland asked.

Master Moxon looked at him sharply. He shrugged his shoulders. 'Two weeks. Four weeks. Six weeks. I don't know. Do what you can for her. Let Master Boland know what I have said. I'd like to see that servant of yours before I go, Mistress Parker. How are the two of you coping? Would you like me to send somebody else to take care of your sister?'

'It seems such a short time to go,' Ruth answered slowly. She turned her head away. 'I think Claire would rather die with people she knows around her. I'll send Sushi to you now.'

She walked slowly into the room and told Sushi the physician wished to see her. As she sat in the chair Ruth looked into Claire's dull, hollow eyes. All the emotion seemed to have been drained out of them and she wondered if Claire guessed the substance of the physician's diagnosis. She took her foster-sister's hands in hers but neither of them spoke. Sushi came back into the room so quietly it was almost as though she glided. She sat on the chair on the other side of the bed, looked down at Claire's face for three or four seconds, and then raised her head. Ruth glanced across the bed as she sensed the slight movement. Her eyes met Sushi's and, to her surprise, she could see, even in the dim light, that the older woman's eyes were filled with tears.

\* \* \* \* \*

Ruth became increasingly tired during the next three weeks. She read to Claire during those daylight hours when she was awake and sat up with her all night. Her foster-sister was now so weak that she had to be carried in and out of bed and needed to be washed lying down. Claire's brain was still fairly lucid and Roland used to visit her from time to time. After one of his visits Claire said to Ruth that she had told him Ruth was to have all her jewellery after she died.

'Don't look so sad, Ruth,' Claire gave a twisted smile. 'If you don't take them, he'll only give them to those nautch girls. I won't have mother's jewels worn by a harlot.'

'If you want me to take care of them, I will. I promise you I will see they are treated with respect.'

'That's the spirit, little sister. I want you to know because I think my time is running out. First thing tomorrow, send Ram Kopal to Master Boland. I want to make confession and seek absolution.'

Ruth was too choked to reply. She held Claire's hand and nodded.

'I won't be able to talk much more.' Claire's voice croaked. 'I can feel the weight on my chest. Don't talk to me or I will think I have to answer. When you go back to England give my love to Mother and Frances and Anne.'

Ruth started to cry. 'I promised I would never leave you. How can I go back?'

'You must promise to take care of yourself. Make friends. Have a good life. Go and live near Anne and Benjamin. Watch their daughters growing up. I hope when your turn comes to marry you'll find a man who loves you. Who makes you happy. I'm sorry I've been so cross with you while I've been ill.'

'You have nothing to apologise for, dearest sister.' Ruth bent over and kissed her.

'Promise you'll go back ... go back, Ruth.' Claire was speaking very slowly and in a whisper. 'You must go back... Sell some of the jewels... to pay... for your journey... back home. I go on... a journey now... out of this vale of tears ...'

Ruth had been bending her head down to catch the last few words. Tears from her eyes dripped on to Claire's cheeks.

'Don't cry, sister ... I am waiting ... ' Claire whispered. 'For the angels ... to take me ... no more tears ... no more tears ... no more talk.' Claire shut her eyes and Ruth slowly raised her head up. When Sushi came in to give the medicine, Ruth told her to leave it. She was reluctant to wake Claire from her deep sleep.

\* \* \* \* \*

Master Boland was the first visitor to arrive the following morning. As Ruth left the room to seek out Roland, she felt overwhelmingly tired, not having slept for five days. Roland seemed irritated and short-tempered when she asked him to stay in the bungalow to be with his wife. Eventually, he reluctantly agreed to he guided by the advice Master Moxon would give after his visit to Claire that morning.

When Ruth met the chaplain coming out of Claire's room half an hour later, he looked extremely serious. He motioned her to a chair on the verandah and said, 'There is no need to go in straight away. Your servant is with your sister now.'

'How is Claire, Master Boland?'

'I have given her absolution. She is a virtuous woman. I am sure the Lord will deal with her kindly.'

'Did she understand you, Master Boland?'

'She only spoke once. But I am sure she understood.'

'What did she say? Or should I not ask?'

Master Boland gave a wry smile. 'Your sister had no dreadful sins to confess. She merely asked me to repeat the Nunc Dimittis.'

'What is that?'

'I am sorry, my dear. I forgot you're not an Anglican. We say it at Evening Prayer. It is that part of the service which is taken from the second chapter of St. Luke's Gospel. You may know it as the Song of Simeon. It begins, "Lord, now lettest thou thy servant depart in peace according to thy word. For mine eyes have seen thy salvation". Your sister asked me to repeat it. She was aware of what I was saying.'

Ruth lowered her head. She was too choked to reply.

'I feel your sister is not long for this world, Ruth,' the chaplain continued. 'But don't forget that by the resurrection of Jesus Christ we are promised life eternal. You will see your sister again. That we are sure of.'

Ruth's voice was subdued as she replied. 'I know, Master Boland. I never doubted that.'

He was about to offer more words of comfort when the physician came into the courtyard. Master Moxon took in the sight of the chaplain and Ruth together and hurried towards them. After the usual conventional greetings had been exchanged, Ruth and the physician went into Claire's room together. Claire was lying still and with her eyes closed. Master Moxon felt her pulse and her forehead. He sat by the side of the bed and spent some time listening to Claire's laboured breathing. When he looked across at Sushi standing near the door, he asked her, 'Can you fetch Master Lockyer, please?'

Ruth tried to talk to him but he put his finger to his lips and they remained in silence until Roland and Sushi came in.

'May I speak to you and Mistress Parker outside, Master Lockyer?' he asked. Master Moxon turned to Sushi. 'And will you wait with Mistress Lockyer, please?'

The three of them went into the courtyard and the physician told them that Claire was in a coma, which was the last stage of a terminal illness and lasted between twenty-four and forty-eight hours. He explained that he had brought them into the courtyard to talk because a person's hearing was the last sense to go. Even if Claire was lying with her eyes shut and not speaking she could still hear.

'There is no reason why you shouldn't talk to her when you sit by the bed. But don't expect a reply. Discontinue the medicine. At this stage, the body winds down and stops feeling pain. I will call again late this afternoon.'

Ruth sat with her foster-sister during the whole day, apart from two or three brief intervals when Roland came into the room and sat with his wife. She held Claire's hand and talked to her without obtaining any response. Once or twice Claire's grip on her hand seemed to tighten slightly when she stopped talking. Two or three times the ghost of a smile flickered across Claire's face when Ruth talked about the times soon after they moved to Aireton Hall and their elder sisters, Frances and Anne, were still unmarried.

When the physician came back about half past five in the afternoon she went outside in the courtyard to get some fresh air. Ruth was so desperately tired that she was almost disorientated. Master Moxon looked at her curiously when he left the sick room and advised her to try and get three or four hours sleep. 'How can I leave her now?' Ruth asked him.

'Your brother-in-law or your servant can stay with your sister. I have asked them to wake you if there is any change in Mistress Lockyer's condition. How long is it since you had a proper meal or a full night's sleep?'

When Ruth did not answer he made her promise to lie down for at least a couple of hours that evening.

'I will be here early tomorrow morning,' he told her. 'Remember you're my patient now as well as your sister.'

\* \* \* \* \*

Ruth went back to sit with Claire for the next three hours after the physician's visit. There was no response when she spoke softly to her foster-sister. She found it becoming increasingly hard to stay awake and was glad when Roland came in after his evening meal to say he would stay with his wife for an hour. Ruth found it difficult to eat the meal which Chand Narain brought to her. All her appetite seemed to have gone and it was an effort to get any food down. Even her movements were made as though she was swimming in liquid honey. She rose slowly and stretched, filling her lungs with air in an effort to make herself fully awake. Ruth walked up and down for a few minutes on the verandah, away from Claire's room at the opposite side of the courtyard. When, finally, the hour was up she went into Claire's room to relieve Roland. He was obviously ill at ease and, within a minute or so, left her and Sushi alone with Claire. Sushi looked at her anxiously and told her to go to sleep in the chair.

For a few minutes Ruth fought against sleep and then found herself falling into a black void. One uneasy dream followed another. In her most vivid dream she was floating on her back, about twelve feet above the ground, moving forward feet first, and looking at the starlit sky. As though from a far distance she could hear Sushi's voice calling, 'Wake up. Wake up.' The servant's cry became more persistent and she fought her way back to consciousness with Sushi shaking her and saying, 'Memsahib very sick. I send Chand Narain for Lockyer Sahib.' Ruth shook herself into wakefulness and could hear Claire choking as she fought for breath. She lifted Claire up and noticed yellow liquid pouring from her mouth. Ruth picked up a damp cloth from the bedside table and carefully wiped round her foster-sister's mouth. It seemed to sooth Claire, and for a moment or two her foster-sister opened her eyes but there did not seem to be any recognition in them.

'Bring that lamp in from outside, Sushi,' Ruth called.

When the lamp was carried in she saw that Claire's face was as white as a sheet and her forehead felt as cold as marble.

'Get some more water for me,' Ruth asked, cleaning Claire's lips and chin once more.

Roland entered, dressed in a gown as though he had just come out of bed, while Chand Narain stood in the doorway. He went across to the opposite side of the bed from Ruth and looked at her enquiringly.

'I think you should stay, Roland,' Ruth said. 'I don't think we'll have long to wait.'

He nodded briefly. Ruth continued to hold Claire in her arms but by now Claire's spasms were becoming more violent and more frequent. Claire opened her eyes again briefly, turned her head quickly towards Ruth, gave a prolonged choking sound, closed her eyes again, shuddered, and then stopped breathing. For several seconds nobody spoke. Ruth put her hand in front of Claire's nose and mouth but could feel no air being expelled. She took hold of Claire's wrist in the same way she had watched Master Moxon take the pulse and tried to feel if there was any movement but was unsuccessful. At last she lowered Claire's head gently to the pillow and said to Roland, 'Can you ask Ram Kopal to fetch Master Moxon?'

'Yes,' he replied. 'He'll be in bed, of course. It's after midnight.'

\* \* \* \* \*

After the physician paid a brief call an hour later, Sushi helped Ruth wash Claire's body. They dressed her in the white wedding dress, worn those few short weeks ago, and laid her back on the bed with fresh cotton sheets. Claire looked so young and peaceful again. All the strain of the last few months was gone and Sushi cleverly arranged Claire's hair so that it no longer looked dull and limp. The chaplain came in the morning to discuss funeral arrangements with Roland and Ruth was shocked to find that Claire would be buried the same evening. Sir George was among the stream of visitors who came throughout the day to pay their respects and offer their sympathy. He confirmed to Ruth that it was customary in India, even among the European traders, for funerals to take place within twenty-four hours of death. Fernando and Maria also came during the morning and Maria asked Ruth to come to Swally with her after the funeral service. Ruth thanked her for her kindness but excused herself from accepting the invitation for a few days. When Maria became more pressing Ruth said she was so tired that she would probably sleep for the next forty-eight hours and then help Roland clear up Claire's things. After that, she would be happy to stay with Fernando and Maria for a few days.

Towards the end of the afternoon, Chand Narain asked Ruth if the servants could see their mistress. After Ruth agreed they came quietly inside the bungalow. Claire's body had now been moved to an open coffin and they each placed a small garland of flowers around her neck, looking shyly at Ruth as they did so. About two hours before sunset Sir George Oxindon returned with eight East Indian factors who were going to act as pall bearers. A cart, pulled by two black bullocks and decorated with black crepe, was drawn up in front of the bungalow. Sir George came inside with Roland and the pall bearers and Sir George asked Ruth if she would like to go outside while they closed the coffin. Both men seemed a little surprised when she told them she would rather stay.

Ruth was too choked to talk during the short drive to the English chapel from the bungalow and Roland made no attempt to draw her into conversation. Master Boland met them at the entrance of the chapel and began reading the words, 'I am the resurrection and the life,' as the pall bearers carried the coffin down the aisle. Ruth could not help remembering that her sister had come down the same aisle as a bride only a few weeks before and the same group of friends were now sitting in the pews. She had only a hazy recollection of the rest of the service and the only part she could remember distinctly was the verse in the middle of Psalm 23. Ruth found the words 'Yea, though I walk through the valley of the shadow of death, I will fear no evil for thou art with me; thy rod and thy staff comfort me' going through her brain over and over again during the rest of the service.

At a sign from the chaplain the eight pall bearers lifted the coffin and started to carry it towards the door of the chapel. Roland took Ruth's arm and the two of them walked out of the chapel, following behind Claire's coffin. It was only a short distance to the European cemetery. Ruth had never been there before and was surprised to see the long lines of gravestones, with the large number of burial plots far outnumbering the small European population in Surat and Swally. As the party halted beside the open grave which had been already prepared, she thought how appropriate were the words 'In the midst of life we are in death' which she heard the chaplain saying.

Roland released her arm and stood by the grave as the coffin was lowered in. He threw a handful of earth on Claire's coffin as Master Boland read the words, 'We commit her body to the ground; earth to earth, ashes to ashes, dust to dust; in sure and certain hope of the resurrection.' Ruth stood quite still while the chaplain continued and as other mourners threw pebbles or earth into the grave.

She noticed that Roland was wiping his eyes with a handkerchief and Lady Oxindon and Maria were weeping but she felt no emotion on her own account. Sad though she was at being parted from Claire, Ruth could not feel sorry that Claire's pain and suffering were at an end.

After the mourners had joined together in the familiar words of the Lord's Prayer, the chaplain read two more short prayers and then the blessing. Ruth was aware of Jacoba Streynsham putting a bunch of flowers in the grave and then found herself surrounded by a small group of ladies who embraced and kissed her. She was surprised to see Lady Oxindon red-eyed and weeping. Even Jacoba was in tears. While she was prepared for Maria's grief, the tears of Mistress Robertson and Mistress Farmerdale surprised her. Ruth thanked them for their sympathy but felt unable to shed any tears for Claire's death. She stood on the same spot when the ladies' husbands came to offer their condolences and then to escort their wives away. During a brief time when Ruth was alone Jake Firman came to offer his sympathy. He was both respectful and subdued and Ruth felt it would be churlish not to offer her hand. Jake took it and gave the briefest of handshakes before bowing and withdrawing again.

By now the majority of the party had started to drift away and Roland was standing a little way off talking to a few of the remaining mourners. Ruth saw that Sushi and the other servants were standing about twenty yards from the grave, holding garlands in their hands. She motioned them towards her and Chand Narain asked if it was permitted for them to place their garlands into the open grave. Ruth nodded and the servants stood around the grave in the gathering dusk. As they dropped the flowers on to the coffin there was a slight murmur as they recited a short Hindu prayer. They paused for a brief time and then slowly walked off, apart from Chand Narain who stood about five yards from Ruth. When Roland joined her Chand Narain started to lead them along the long, winding path out of the cemetery. As Ruth looked back into the dim light she could see two men with spades by Claire's grave, ready to cover the coffin before the last traces of daylight disappeared.

Roland's carriage was waiting for them outside the cemetery gate, with Ram Kopal standing alongside. Much to Ruth's surprise Roland helped her into the carriage and then excused himself, saying that he was visiting some friends that evening. She was too tired to make any comment and went to bed as soon as she returned to the bungalow.

It was nearly noon on the following day before she woke up. She still felt slightly sleepy and very hungry. When she asked Chand Narain where Roland was, he replied that his master had not yet returned.

\* \* \* \* \*

Another three days went by before Roland came back to his bungalow. He looked thoroughly dissipated and worn out as he sat drinking coffee. His balding head was not covered by the wig he usually wore, there were heavy dark lines around his eyes, and he did not appear to have changed his clothes for some time. Ruth was surprised at the alteration in his appearance and asked if he was unwell when she went to join him.

'I've been grieving,' he replied. 'You ought to know how I feel.'

'I am glad you're back,' Ruth answered mildly. 'Perhaps I can help you sort out Claire's belongings some time tomorrow.'

'You're a cold fish, aren't you? Never shed a tear at the funeral. Now you want to go through my wife's things.'

'I have no intention of upsetting you, Roland. Claire indicated some of her wishes to me before she died. But it might be easier to discuss this tomorrow.'

'Wishes? What wishes are these? Talking about my property behind my back.'

'Please Roland,' Ruth could feel herself becoming angry. 'Let's leave it until tomorrow.' She rose from her chair and started to move away.

'You stay here,' he shouted. 'Don't make vague hints, then go. You got anything to say, you say it now.'

Ruth sat down once more. 'Very well, Roland. I only wish to help. Someone will need to write to Claire's relatives,' she said wearily. 'Her dresses and shoes will have to be sorted out. There may be toiletries and small personal items which are of sentimental value. These could be sent back to her family in England. Claire said she had told you that she wished me to have her jewellery.'

'So that's your game,' he sneered. 'All my wife's things belong to me. Even if Claire said anything to you, she was half-demented towards the end. Enough to drive anyone out of their mind. You and that native servant clucking round her all the time. Like a couple of vultures outside the Parsee towers of silence.'

Ruth's face was red with anger. She stood up and, in as calm a voice as she could manage, said, 'I am not sure whether it is opium or alcohol disturbing your brain. I can see there is no point in continuing to talk to you now. So I bid you good day.'

\* \* \* \* \*

Another week passed before Ruth saw Roland again. She had always finished her evening meal long before he arrived back at the bungalow at night. He did not seem to rise until late in the morning and, as a result, Ruth breakfasted alone while Roland was still in bed. Much to her surprise, he still occupied the room next to her own, the room which had been Claire's when the two girls first arrived in India. In the absence of Roland's permission she felt unable to go into the room which he and Claire had shared together. She hoped a favourable opportunity would arise in future to speak to him again on the subject of the clothes and jewels. Ruth could understand why Roland was disinclined to move back into the room where he had started married life but felt that the longer he left making the move, the greater the effort he would need to make to return. On this particular evening she was reading on the front verandah when Roland rode up on his horse. Contrary to his usual practice, he did not shout for the syce until Ram Kopal came from the direction of the stables. After the horse had been led away he came up the steps and greeted Ruth pleasantly.

'Do you mind if I join you this evening when you eat?' he asked.

'No. I will be pleased to share the meal with you, Roland.'

'Very well, then. I'll get Bhadre to get some water for me to bathe, ask Chand to help me change, and I'll be with you in about forty minutes.'

Ruth looked at him impassively as he took his leave. It was always possible that he had turned over a new leaf. Roland had such a volatile nature, however, that Ruth found it hard to be convinced that any change could be permanent. She found it impossible to continue reading after her conversation with Roland. Instead she studied the trees surrounding the bungalow, waving gently in the warm evening breeze. The monsoon was now over and Ruth thought she had never seen the foliage looking so green. She could just hear the noise of bullock carts moving slowly along the main road some distance from the bungalow, behind a screen of palm trees. From far away she heard a muezzin calling the faithful to prayer. The sound must have come from the minaret of the mosque which stood at the edge of the public park nearby. Ruth was suddenly overwhelmed by the strangeness of it all and a wave of homesickness swept over her.

She shook herself mentally. This was not the time for weakness. There would be a time to feel sorry for herself, a time to grieve, a time to make a fresh start, when she was on her way back to England, away from the bitter memories of the past few months. Ruth's one regret was that Claire's illness, combined with Roland's insensitivity over the use of his carriage during the rainy season, had prevented her from seeing more of this strange but beautiful country. She wished she had been able to see some of the sights which Sir George, Fernando, and Master Moxon had mentioned to her. Ruth shrugged her shoulders. It was unlikely to happen now. She rose from her chair and went to her room to wash and change.

\* \* \* \* \*

Roland seemed very cordial as he joined her for the evening meal. Although he appeared to be drinking rather more wine than she had anticipated he was still able to maintain a steady flow of small talk, telling her the latest news of their mutual friends. Towards the end of the meal his tone became more serious.

'Are you lonely, Ruth?' he asked.

She hesitated before replying. 'I miss Claire. But I need to make a new life for myself. That's what she wanted.'

'And that's what I want too,' Roland answered earnestly. He paused as if expecting a reply and then continued. 'I'm lonely too, Ruth. I know I've not been good company lately. But I've always been fond of you. Why don't we console each other. Then you can have those jewels you want.'

Ruth was too stunned to reply. It was only a fortnight since Claire's funeral and she was still recovering mentally from the months of nursing her foster- sister. In addition, she was only just regaining her physical strength after the weeks of sleepless nights and insufficient meals. Roland looked across the table enquiringly, 'What d'you say, Ruth?'

'Your wife has only been dead a fortnight,' was the only reply she could think of on the spur of the moment.

Chand Narain came in at that moment carrying a tray with a decanter of brandy and a glass.

'Not now, you fool. Later,' Roland snarled.

The interruption and his change of tone gave Ruth a chance to gather her thoughts together. She studied this man who was not only nearly twenty years older than herself but looked like a fat, dissolute, middle-aged man. The skin on his face was crossed by deep lines above a straggly beard which was streaked with grey. When she looked at his soft, plump hands she shuddered inwardly as she compared them with the strong, firm hands of her foster-father.

'If you're worried about what people say we could even marry,' Roland said ingratiatingly. 'But we don't need to marry straight away. Ought to leave it for a few months. Be friends in the meantime.'

'I have no wish to hurt your feelings, Roland,' she answered coldly. 'But I cannot take your wife's place.'

'Can't? You're not in the church's table of kindred and affinity. You ain't my wife's sister. What d'you mean, you can't?'

'I mean I cannot love you, Roland. You must understand that. Even if I felt it was possible to love you, Claire would always come between us.'

Roland's face was becoming red and flustered by this time.

'I don't understand,' he shouted. 'You could love me in the future. And I'm willing to marry you. Later on.'

'No, Roland,' she replied firmly. 'I promised Claire I would never marry a man I did not love.'

'It's true what Jake says. You ain't a real woman. You're made of ice' he sneered.

Ruth rose from her chair, her face white with anger by this time. 'Your pardon, Roland. I will take my leave. I am not interested in the opinion of your drunken friends.'

She walked towards her room as she heard him say, 'You'll get no jewels from me.' The lamp had already been placed on the table beside her bed and she knelt to pray. Sushi came in a few minutes later and paused in the doorway as she saw Ruth on her knees.

'Come in, Sushi. I had already finished,' Ruth told her, rising to her feet.

'I help you wash and change now,' Sushi replied.

'Thank you, Sushi. I need some help. I'm tired and want to sleep.'

\* \* \* \* \*

Ruth found sleep difficult even though she was tired. Roland's proposal still staggered her and, she had to admit to herself, frightened her a little. He had such a volatile nature that he was somewhat unpredictable as he vacillated between two extremes of behaviour. She spent a long time going through her prayers again, asking God for guidance. However often she closed her eyes, sleep eluded her, driven away by the thoughts of how quickly Roland's pleading had turned to anger. One leaden hour was followed by another before Ruth drifted off into an uneasy, dream-filled sleep. She fought her way back to consciousness, aware that someone was pressing down the edge of her bed. Ruth sat bolt upright, suddenly awake. As she moved, Roland's head came crashing down on her pillow. There was only the dim light from the moon shining through her window but it was sufficient to see that the rest of Roland's body was partially on her bed. One of his feet was still on the floor and he was endeavouring to lift the remainder of his body by pushing down with his foot. He reeked of brandy.

Ruth quickly lifted the sheet and one thin blanket and leapt out of bed. 'What in the name of God are you doing, Roland? For the love of Christ, go at once.'

'Don't you be crosh, Roosh. Come to shay I'm sorry.'

'Get out, you drunken sot,' Ruth hissed.

'Don't be like that,' he whined, rolling over the edge of the bed. 'Lesh be frens. Friends.'

Ruth's reply was cold and contemptuous. Her voice was harsh and monosyllabic as she said, 'If you do not get out now, I will scream. Do you hear me?'

Roland fell off the edge of the bed, uttering curses as Ruth moved away towards the window. He rose from the floor slowly, swaying all the while. 'Why don't you shtay in one plaish?' he muttered. 'How can I speak to you when you move? Move all over.'

'I warn you, Roland. Take one step towards me and you'll regret it.'

'Regresh? Wash that?' He staggered towards her, holding out his arms as he came. His action took Ruth by surprise and she could feel his hot, sweaty hands round her waist and his alcohol-laden breath on her shoulder as she turned her head away.

'Just a little kish, Roosh. For old times sake,' he muttered.

Ruth forced her arms upwards in front of his chest and grasped one of Roland's ears in each of her hands. She pulled down hard and then jerked his head back. He uttered a strangled curse as he released the hold on her waist. Ruth still held his ears, pulling his head downwards as she raised her right leg, bringing Roland's nose down hard against her knee. Even in the dim light, she could see that her nightgown was spotted with blood and Roland staggered back against the wall, swearing as he did so. Ruth ran to the door shouting, 'Sushi,' as she went down to the courtyard. She raced through the archway and ran towards the servants' quarters. She was still calling Sushi by name and expecting Roland to follow in hot pursuit.

Sushi came to the doorway of her little hut and in a voice filled with concern asked, 'What is wrong, memsahib?'

Ruth burst into tears, 'Let me stay with you. Till morning, please.'

Sushi looked at Ruth's bare feet, her dishevelled, blood-spotted gown and held her in her arms. 'I will watch over you like a daughter, Mistress Ruth,' she said very slowly and carefully. 'You come inside now.'

She led Ruth into the tiny hut, passing through the cooking and washing room into the small bedroom. Ruth clung tightly to her, crying copiously for the first time since Claire's funeral. 'You stay here. You safe here,' Sushi said quietly. Ruth continued crying until she was emotionally drained. She expected Roland to burst in at any minute but could only hear the soft whispering of the trees in the wind and the far-off sound of a jackal howling. As her sobs abated she was pushed towards the only bed in the room.

'You lie here. I sit on bench. Watch over you,' Sushi said softly.

Ruth sank down on the small bed and stared out through the open doorway as if expecting to see Roland's ample figure blocking out the dim light. Sushi squatted on her heels beside her and gently smoothed her forehead, crooning a lullaby as she did so, almost as if she were calming a small child. The night hours dragged by interminably and Ruth never knew how long it was before she fell into an uneasy sleep. Bright sunlight was streaming through the window when she woke and, through the open doorway, she saw the ground outside bathed in strong light. The air felt hot and still as she sat upon the small bed. Sushi sat on a wooden bench by the wall, looking grave.

'Thank you for looking after me, Sushi. I must go back into the house now, Ruth said.

'That is not possible, Mistress Ruth.'

'Not possible?' She was suddenly wide awake and looked hard at Sushi. 'Why do you say it is not possible?'

'Chand Narain come to see me this morning. He tell me Lockyer Sahib very angry. His master tell him to burn all your books. All your clothes. All your shoes. He and Swamy have to do it together.'

'Oh, no!' Ruth exclaimed.

'Chand Narain not bad man. He only does what his master wants. He save me pair of shoes for you.' She held out Ruth's Bible. 'And also holy book. He says Lockyer Sahib tell him you not allowed in house.'

Ruth's head was spinning. She felt unable to understand Roland's action. What was there about her that seemed to bring out the worst in men? Henry Fairbrother, Jake Firman and now Roland had all reacted in the same way towards her. She swung her legs off the bed and stared at the mud floor of the hut between her feet. After a few seconds she raised her head again to find Sushi looking compassionately at her. 'What will you do now, Mistress Ruth?'

'I don't know,' Ruth answered dully.

'When Des Raj come to bring me wages from Ferrara Sahib, I give him news, I tell him to ask Ferrara Sahib to speak to Lockyer Sahib.'

'No, Sushi. You mustn't do that,' Ruth said in sudden alarm. 'In Master Lockyer's present frame of mind there is no telling what he might do. He could become violent towards Senhor Ferrara. I would never forgive myself for that.'

Sushi thought hard for a few seconds. 'I lend you clothes, I come with you. We see President Sahib. He know what to do.'

Ruth crossed to the bench where Sushi was sitting and hugged her. 'I will be proud to wear your clothes. But I must not go to Sir George Oxindon.' Her voice became firm and strong as she continued. 'I cannot let Master Lockyer beat me. He has tried to rape me after failing to seduce me. He has thrown me out of my sister's home. He has cheated me of the jewels which my sister gave me. How can I allow myself to be defeated by a man like him?'

Sushi smiled. 'You like my daughter, Mistress Ruth. You speak like true Maratha. We never rest until we avenge insult. We never allow ourselves to be dishonoured.'

'Please let me stay with you, Sushi,' Ruth pleaded.

'I get Chand Narain to bring bed for you. You eat with me. Go to market with me for food. We join gowns together. Then other servants know you my daughter. They not interfere with you then. You stay here until Lockyer Sahib say he sorry. Until he give you sister's jewels.'

# 12

## OCTOBER 1663

The six weeks following this incident passed very quickly. After the first few days, the other servants accepted Ruth and she was able to move relatively freely round their quarters when Roland was out. She never went inside the bungalow now and she suspected that the servants maintained a conspiracy of silence. They never mentioned their master to her and she assumed that they did not speak of her to Roland. When Ruth went to the native markets with Sushi she attracted a number of curious glances from traders and bystanders, but escaped attention from any Europeans by pulling her sari over her head like a cowl and following closely behind Sushi in a deferential manner. It sometimes amused her to think how Roland could explain her absence from the company of her fellow Europeans.

Ruth became used to eating only two meals a day, once in the middle of the morning and again after sunset. Sushi never ate meat and their diet consisted of millet, rice, flour, herbs, vegetables, ghee, and a little salt. Ruth spent a great deal of time reading her Bible and found that she was more relaxed than at any time since she left England. It was almost as though she was recuperating after the tensions of the past year. She found herself thinking less and less about the future and even the recollection of Roland's behaviour was beginning to fade. Ruth was brought abruptly back to earth at the end of the six weeks' period.

She was sitting on a bench outside Sushi's hut late one morning, reading her Bible. Ram Kopal hurried past her as they both heard the sound of a horse stopping in front of the bungalow. Ram Kopal reappeared a few seconds later leading a horse towards the stables at the back of the servants' quarters. Fernando Ferrara walked behind him, looking very angry. He came towards Ruth, taking in her native dress, the wooden bench and the servant's hut in one glance. She rose to greet him as he said, 'Good day, Ruth.'

He seemed far from friendly when she replied 'Good day, Fernando. Have you come to see Roland?'

'No,' he replied, almost curtly. He briefly kissed her hand. 'Where's Sushi?'

'She's with Bhadre, our dhobi, Fernando.'

'Fetch her, please,' he replied.

'May I know why, Fernando.'

'I very angry with her. And with you also, Ruth. You live like this for six weeks. Not tell me or Maria. Sushi not tell us either. I get truth from Des Raj. He not lie to me.'

'Don't blame Sushi. It was my choice to live with her, Fernando. She has been kindness itself. Been like a mother to me.'

Ram Kopal must have told Sushi that Senhor Ferrara had arrived because she hurried round the corner and then stopped suddenly. He barked abruptly at her, speaking in Portuguese as he did so. Sushi muttered three or four words in Portuguese by way of reply and then hung her head. Ruth hurried across to Sushi and took her hand.

'If you wish to speak to Sushi in my presence, Fernando, please use English or Marathi,' Ruth said, a little astringently.

'I am sorry, Ruth. I should not be angry with Sushi. But you made promise to Maria. You say you let her know if you in trouble. She very upset.'

'Sushi has taken good care of me. As for Roland, that's a matter which I must settle with him in my own way.'

Fernando's tone became exasperated. 'All your friends worry about you. When we ask Roland he say you leave his house. Nobody see you since funeral of Claire. Why not come with me? Stay with Maria. I speak to Roland if you like.'

'I mean no disrespect, Fernando, but do not speak to Roland. He is a violent, dangerous man. I do not wish anyone to interfere on my behalf.'

'Then come back with me, Ruth. Bring Sushi as well.'

'I have unfinished business here. When that is over I will be glad to accept your hospitality. Until then my place is here. With Sushi.'

'You stubborn girl, Ruth.' He looked at Sushi. 'You tell her to come with me.'

'She very proud woman, Senhor Ferrara. Like Maratha. Never leave here until Lockyer Sahib leaves. Unless Lockyer Sahib say sorry.'

Fernando was puzzled by this reply. 'I do not know you and Senhor Lockyer quarrel. At least, let me bring some clothes and some food.'

'You are very kind, Fernando.' Ruth turned to give a warm smile in Sushi's direction. 'I have all I need here.'

'What do I say when I get back? Maria ask how you are? Maria ask why you not come?'

'Say I am well, Fernando,' she replied calmly. 'Tell her I will come soon.'

He looked thoughtful for a few seconds before he nodded to Sushi. 'I tell Pushpa you stay here.' He picked up Ruth's hand and pressed it to his lips. 'I also tell Maria you stay with Sushi.' Fernando smiled slightly as he released Ruth's hand. 'I not speak to Roland. But I see you again soon.'

\* \* \* \* \*

Two mornings later Ruth and Sushi were chatting together by the door of their hut when they heard the sound of a carriage pulling up outside the bungalow, accompanied by two outriders. Ram Kopal hurried past them and this time did not reappear. Ruth dismissed the thoughts of the carriage from her mind, thinking it must be Roland returning from Surat or the port. She was surprised, therefore, to see the agitated figure of Chand Narain walking towards them. 'You come quickly, memsahib,' he said, stopping in front of her. 'English President here. English President want to see you.'

'You may bring him here, Chand,' Ruth replied.

The bearer looked shocked. 'No. You come with me. He be very angry if you not come.'

'Chand Narain speaks truly,' Sushi added. 'President is burra sahib. You go to him now.'

Ruth was reluctant to agree but she realised how important it was for Sir George to maintain his position and she rose from the bench on which she had been sitting. 'I'll come,' she said, flatly. Chand Narain was visibly relieved as the two of them walked round the corner. Ram Kopal stood by the coach, talking to the two horsemen and the coachman. Sir George was sitting on a chair just inside the verandah at the front of the house. He rose to greet Ruth but she stopped at the foot of the steps.

'Good day, Ruth,' he called. 'Come up here.'

'Good day, Sir George. I prefer to stay where I am.'

He looked long and hard in Ruth's direction and then joined her at the bottom of the short flight of steps.

'What's got into you?' he asked. 'Why won't you come on to the verandah?'

'I have made a vow never to go into that bungalow again.'

Sir George glanced at his two outriders and the coachman in conversation with Ram Kopal, who were looking from time to time in Ruth's direction. He saw the cheap, cotton sari which she was wearing and sighed, 'We have all been concerned about you. Why did you tell nobody where you were?'

'I have been in good hands, Sir George.'

'This is purely an informal visit, Ruth,' he said, looking again at the small group standing by the horses. His tone became almost acid. 'But don't you see that even my travelling without the usual escort causes comment. If you can't go into the bungalow, sit in my carriage.'

He started to walk towards the carriage, galvanising the coachman and outriders into activity. He gave a brief word of command and then stood back to allow Ruth to get inside. Sir George took up a position facing Ruth after he took his place in the carriage.

'Your perverse behaviour has made me angry, Ruth,' he began.

'I am sorry, Sir George. But Fernando had no right to tell you where I was.'

'On the contrary. His actions were impeccable. You are under age. An orphan. An unmarried English girl in a strange country. Who else should Senhor Ferrara go to for advice but the leader of the English community here?'

'He gave me a promise not to tell.'

'His promise was not to speak to Master Lockyer. Senhor Ferrara is a man of integrity and kept his word. But he did not promise not to tell me.' Ruth realised the truth of Sir George's comments. She had been lulled into a false sense of security when Fernando talked to her.

'Why are you living like this?' he asked. 'Dressed like a native.'

'Master Lockyer knows.'

'Don't be difficult, Ruth. I'm trying to help you. If you've quarrelled so badly with Master Lockyer that you don't want to stay in the same house, collect your things together and I'll take you back to the English factory.' Ruth hung her head. 'Say something, for pity's sake, Ruth. If you don't want to go back in there, your servant can bring your clothes outside.'

'It's not that easy.'

'Why not?'

'Roland burnt all my clothes, my books and my shoes. Apart from one pair of shoes and my bible which Roland's bearer put on one side for me.'

'Did he, by Heaven?' When Ruth did not reply, he continued. 'All the more reason to get you away from here.'

'No, Sir George. I will not leave unless Roland apologizes or unless he leaves this bungalow.'

'You're a stubborn girl, Ruth. The sooner you marry and have someone else who can be responsible for you, the better I shall be pleased. What am I to do with you?'

'Leave me here with my servant Sushi. She has been like a mother to me, Sir George.'

'You must see that this dispute between you and Master Lockyer has to be resolved.'

'Indeed. Roland knows what needs to be done.'

Sir George Oxindon thought carefully for a few moments. 'I will see Master Lockyer this evening. The company wishes to establish a new factory in Hubli. I will tell him to leave in seven days' time with the party which is sailing for Goa, in preparation for travelling to Hubli.'

'But I may not see him again!'

'Quite so. In which case, there is no point in staying here.'

'I'm sorry, Sir George. There is more than just an apology needed from Roland. Claire asked him to give me my mother's jewels. And he refuses to give them to me.' She lowered her head. 'Unless I dishonour myself.'

Sir George's face was impassive. He had obviously guessed this was no ordinary quarrel.

'Without a written will, the jewels are his. Tell your servant to follow us to the factory.'

'You're a hard man, Sir George.'

'When it is necessary,' he replied calmly. 'I know Master Lockyer's reputation. So does Senhor Ferrara. If you had stayed with the Ferraras after the funeral, this would not have happened. I'm not prepared to have you staying here any longer.'

Ruth felt trapped. After a few seconds' deliberation, she said, 'I will come with you on one condition. And only one condition.' She paused but Sir George did not interrupt. 'I want Roland to stay in Surat. If he leaves I will never obtain my mother's jewels. I promised my sister I would ensure they were not flaunted by some harlot.'

'If you wish him to stay, he will stay. Provided you leave here at once. I need an interpreter. We have an envoy coming from Shivaji in a few weeks' time to discuss a commercial treaty. Maratha called Narainji Pandit. I want you to interpret

*Rough Winds*

for me. You'll be paid five rupees a day while working for the company.' He looked distastefully at Ruth's cheap, cotton sari. 'I'll give you an advance to buy some clothes.'

Ruth tried hard to suppress a tear. She turned her head away so that she could look through the door of the carriage at the bungalow which had been her home since she had landed in India. She drew a deep breath, turned back to Sir George, and said, 'I will tell Sushi to follow me. Just give me a minute or so and I will be ready to leave.'

'Take your time, Ruth,' he replied gently. 'I will stay here.'

She descended from the carriage to the ground and walked slowly away. Ruth turned the corner of the bungalow and Sushi hurried towards her. There was a look of concern on Sushi's face as Ruth stopped a few yards from the servants' quarters.

'I am going to the English factory to work for Sir George Oxindon. You are coming as well. Sir George is taking me in his carriage. Can you follow us later with your possessions?'

'I get Ram Kopal to bring things to English factory. I be there very soon. Lockyer Sahib stay here?' Sushi asked.

'Yes, Sushi. I am going now.' Ruth turned and started to walk towards the carriage. After she had taken three or four paces she looked back to see Sushi gazing after her forlornly. Ruth ran back, kissed Sushi on both cheeks, and held her tightly. 'You will always be dear to me. I love you so much, Sushi. Nothing will ever change that.'

Sushi stood quite still and made no reply.

# 13

## JANUARY/FEBRUARY 1664

Nobody in the English factory had slept on Tuesday and Wednesday night. Sir George had called his factors and their families together on Tuesday morning to give them the news that four thousand troopers of Shivaji's cavalry were just ten miles from Surat. The only absentees were Lady Oxindon who was on a visit to Swally and Roland Lockyer and another factor who were transacting business in Bombay. Fourteen of the Indians who usually provided the President's escort and performed guard duties at the factory decided to leave, together with most of the Indian servants. Six of the President's escort remained behind with a handful of servants. All the factors volunteered to stay and, in spite of much pleading from their husbands, the wives of Luke Farmerdale, Thomas Robertson and Peter Streynsham said they wished to remain at their husbands' sides.

'You don't need to stay, Ruth,' Sir George told her. 'You have no husband to worry about.'

Ruth flushed slightly. 'That is true, Sir George. But these people are my people. I could not leave them now. Perhaps I can load a musket for someone. Cook meals now that most of the servants have gone.' Her expression clouded. 'Even do nursing.'

'It won't be easy. You sure you won't change your mind?

Ruth laughed. 'You always said I was obstinate. I'm proud too. How could I face Jacoba if I came back here after all the danger has passed?'

Sir George coughed slightly to hide his emotions. 'Stay close to me then. I may want you as an interpreter.'

Throughout Tuesday thousands of refugees streamed past the factory, carrying their belongings with them. Sir George gave strict orders that no refugees were to be admitted, remembering how Shivaji had recaptured Poona from Shayista

Khan by disguising his men as a funeral procession, traders, and travelling musicians. Those of the refugees who had money bought passages on fishing boats and canoes to escape to the sea along the River Tapti. The remainder scattered into the countryside, hoping to find safety in wadis or among woods. By Tuesday afternoon the Marathas had reached the walls of the city and, throughout the rest of the day, scattered musket fire could be heard from the city walls and the citadel as the Mogul troops fired on the besiegers. Shivaji presented an ultimatum to the imperial governor, asking for three of the wealthiest Mohammedan merchants to act as hostages and to ransom themselves and the other citizens of Surat. When this demand was rejected Sir George ordered everybody to stand to throughout the night, expecting Shivaji to give immediate permission for the city to be sacked. In the event, the Marathas did not attempt the assault on the city gates until noon on Wednesday. The light resistance put up by the Moguls at the gates was quickly brushed aside and the remainder of the imperial troops withdrew to the citadel. The city was almost deserted by early afternoon and the only noise to be heard was the occasional boom of a gun from the citadel walls. In the middle of the afternoon, a Maratha officer demanded to enter the English factory but was refused permission.

Soon afterwards several hundred Maratha lancers galloped through the open space between the French and English factories. They circled to the rear of the English factory, effectively cutting it off from access to the road to Swally. A short time later the fleur-de-lis was hauled down from the walls of the French factory and replaced by the ochre flag of the Marathas, to the disdain of the watching Englishmen. A few minutes afterwards Peter Streynsham gave the alarm when about fifty Maratha troopers, carrying spears and swords, came out of the French factory and began walking in a column towards the gate of the English factory. Sir George sent Peter Streynsham to the parapets and told him that the men there must not open fire until those under Sir George's command withdrew through the gateway. Sir George led the six guarding the archway outside, lining them up in single file in front of the gate. The Marathas continued to advance over the ground between the two factories. When the front of their column was about fifty yards away Sir George shouted to them in Urdu telling them he would fire if they did not halt. There was a momentary pause in the Maratha ranks and then they advanced once more as an officer gave another command.

'Fire!' shouted Sir George. 'Reload!' he ordered, as the smoke cleared. The advancing column came to a halt, paused for two or three seconds and then moved forward again as the English factors heard a second shouted command. Sir George pulled a brace of pistols from his belt and fired them in quick succession into the advancing column. This was quickly followed by another shouted command and the Marathas withdrew, carrying their dead and wounded with them.

'Stand easy, men!' Sir George shouted. 'Hold your fire!'

After the Marathas had retreated into the French factory, Sir George took his men back inside the gateway and sent a message for food to be brought to them and taken to those on the roof.

'Nobody is to leave his post,' he ordered. 'If I know Shivaji's troops, they'll be back.'

\* \* \* \* \*

An hour later one of the handful of Indian women servants who had stayed behind came into the storeroom which was being used as a temporary kitchen. She looked round the room until she saw Ruth and Sushi sitting together and said, 'President Sahib wants you to go to gate quickly, memsahib.' Ruth got up quickly and hurried into the courtyard with Sushi following behind. When they came into the gateway Ruth saw a group of about ten Maratha soldiers who had halted about fifty yards away. Two of them were carrying a flag of truce and another, who seemed to be in command, stood a yard or so in front of the group. Sir George and Luke Farmerdale were in the gateway with the rest of the small archway guard standing behind them.

'Tell me what the fellow's saying, Ruth. We don't seem to understand each other.'

'Ram, Ram, Sirdarji,' Ruth shouted as she moved alongside Sir George.

'Jai Ram,' the officer answered.

'The President Sahib has requested me to ask what it is that you wish to say, Sirdarji.'

The Maratha officer looked hard at Ruth and asked, 'Are you English? You speak good Marathi.'

'Yes. I am English,' Ruth answered. She pulled Sushi to her and put her arms around the older woman's shoulders. 'But I have a Maratha mother.'

The officer seemed puzzled by this reply and waited for a few seconds before asking, 'May I come nearer? I will come alone.'

Ruth turned to Sir George and repeated the request in English. Sir George nodded. 'Please ask your men to stay where they are when you approach,' she replied. The Maratha moved cautiously forward until he stopped about five yards in front of the gateway. He stared curiously at Ruth and Sushi standing together between Sir George and Luke Farmerdale.

'Is your Maratha mother here?' He asked Ruth, looking at Sushi.

'Yes.'

'Then you will not want to see blood shed between Englishmen and Marathas.'

'No, Sirdarji. But tell me what else you wish to say to the President Sahib.'

'I come with a message from Shivaji. He commands me to say that the English President must not obstruct our troops.'

Ruth carefully translated this for Sir George who asked her to reply that, while he had no wish to obstruct the Marathas, he could not allow them into the English factory. It was a matter of honour for the English to defend their flag and the goods belonging to the company with their lives.

'We have an army of four thousand in this city,' the officer answered. 'You would be throwing away your lives to resist us.'

When Ruth translated this for Sir George, he looked at the composed, expectant look on her young face. 'How should we answer that, Ruth?' he asked.

'We can only do what is right, Sir George. According to our own consciences.'

'Yes, Ruth. Tell the officer we will oppose any move into our factory. We will not budge from here and we stand ready for all that may happen.'

After Ruth had finished translating this for the Maratha, he bowed, turned round, rejoined his men, and then turned round once more to face the little group standing in the gateway. He saluted, gave a command to his troops, and began walking back towards the French factory.

\* \* \* \* \*

Ruth snatched no more than a few minutes' sleep on Thursday afternoon before Sushi woke her to say that a single man had left the French factory, carrying a flag of truce. The two of them hurried to the gateway again to find Peter Streynsham pointing a pistol at a man standing about twenty yards away. Two of the archway guards had also levelled their muskets at the man. He looked about twenty-two years of age, was clean shaven and shaven-headed and appeared unconcerned at this display of firearms. He was dressed in an ankle-length robe made from a single piece of yellow silk.

'A Brahmin,' Sushi whispered.

'Where's Sir George?' Ruth asked Peter.

'He's coming now. Let's hope this is not another of Shivaji's tricks.'

'The Maratha looks pretty harmless to me,' Ruth replied.

She glanced across at the French factory. Shivaji's yellow ochre flag was still flying from the ramparts and she could see Marathas moving on the walls. Sir George hurried towards them and, as soon as the man saw the English President, the Maratha started walking forward.

'Halt or I fire!' Peter shouted.

'I come in peace. I am Narainji Pandit and serve my master Shivaji.'

'Peace be with you, Panditji,' Ruth replied. 'But please stand still.' Narainji Pandit stopped. He smiled. 'You speak our language well. If only all foreigners were like you.'

'I have a good teacher.'

'What's he saying, Ruth?' Sir George asked impatiently.

'We were exchanging pleasantries,' she replied. 'May I ask him to come nearer?'

'Yes,' Sir George said. 'One man alone can hardly be a threat.' Ruth asked Narainji Pandit to come to the gateway and the muskets and pistol were slowly lowered as he stopped a yard in front of Sir George.

'My master Shivaji has been told of your bravery, President Sahib,' the envoy began. 'He only wishes this courage had been used against our enemies and not against our troops.'

When this command was translated for Sir George, he asked Ruth to say that the same determination would be shown against any who tried to interfere with the English flag, lives or property.

'Shivaji has asked me to escort you and any two companions of your choice to his headquarters. He wishes to discuss a truce with you, President Sahib,' Narainji Pandit said.

'If I refuse?' Sir George asked when Ruth had relayed the request.

The envoy shrugged his shoulders and smiled. 'So long as you are in our camp, no attempt will be made to take over your factory. I have taken an oath on that.' He nodded towards Sushi. 'That woman is Hindu. She will tell you a Brahmin never takes an oath which may be broken.'

'What if we are held hostage? Prevented from returning?' Sir George asked Ruth.

'I am your safe conduct, President Sahib,' Narainji Pandit answered. 'I will not eat, drink or sleep until you are back in your English factory.'

'Wait here,' Sir George replied. 'I will be back in a few minutes.' After this information had been given to the envoy, Sir George asked Luke Farmerdale to stay on guard and requested Peter Streynsham and Ruth to follow him back into the courtyard. When they were inside, Sir George turned to his deputy and said, 'I must go. It will delay any further attack on us. And the Moguls must come soon. Shivaji's lightly armed, half-starved cavalry can't hold the city against the imperial army. But who do I take with me? You must stay here of course, Peter.'

'Heaven knows we need every man,' Peter replied. 'Shall I ask for volunteers?'

'Yes. They'll be unarmed, of course,' Sir George said.

'Why don't you take me and Sushi with you?' Ruth asked. Sir George and Peter looked at her in open-mouthed astonishment. Before they could raise any objections, Ruth continued. 'Sushi used to take me to the markets dressed in a sari. Nobody noticed me when I pulled it over my head.'

'Good God, Ruth,' Sir George replied. 'They're a bunch of half-naked hillsmen.'

'All the more reason for taking us instead of two men. Sushi told me that the Marathas respect women, which is more than you can say for the Moguls. Maratha women have never tolerated purdah and suttee is virtually unknown among them, unlike the Rajputs.'

'You'd make a good diplomat,' Sir George said.

'I know. And you'll need an interpreter as well.'

'I don't like it,' Peter Streynsham interrupted. 'Shivaji is still holding those four factors from Rajapur as hostages.'

'Don't worry, Peter. It's better if we go,' Ruth told him. 'Rather than taking two men from the factory walls. Give me ten minutes to change into a long- sleeved blouse, sandals and a sari. Let me mix some charcoal with water to put on my hands, face and feet and you won't recognise me as Ruth Parker. I'll be Sushi's daughter once more.'

'You're a brave girl, Ruth,' Sir George said. 'If you and Sushi are willing, I'll be proud to escort you.'

'Ten minutes time then, Sir George. Are you coming, Sushi?'

'You know I can refuse you nothing, daughter of my heart,' Sushi replied, speaking to Ruth in Marathi so quickly that neither of the men could understand.

* * * * *

Sir George and Narainji Pandit pushed through the throng so that Ruth and Sushi could follow them into Shivaji's tent. Although large, it was already quite crowded. There were half a dozen guardsmen, as well as two unarmed officials dressed in long, yellow robes, who Ruth thought must be Brahmins. Sir George greeted Shivaji by bowing slightly while the two women greeted him by putting the palms of their open right hands to their foreheads and bowing three times. There was silence for a few seconds. This gave Ruth a chance to lift her head slightly and look at the man who inspired fierce loyalty on one hand and terror on the other. He was shorter than she had anticipated and looked younger than she had imagined. His body was broad and powerfully built, with long arms hanging down his side. Ruth noticed that his face was covered by a thick, black beard and moustache. On his head he wore a plain, orange-coloured turban. Shivaji must have been aware that Ruth was looking at him. He suddenly turned in her direction and she found herself gazing at a pair of fine, brown eyes, either side of his curved, aquiline nose. The expression in them was surprisingly soft, while at the same time quick and searching. She lowered her head and moved close to Sir George.

Shivaji's eyes ran over the little group standing close together in front of him. 'This is your deputation of three?' he enquired, talking quickly in Marathi.

Ruth whispered the English translation in Sir George's ear. 'Yes, Raja,' he replied. He turned to Ruth, speaking in English at a slow enough speed to allow her to translate. 'As you see,

Highness, I carry no sword. Nor, unlike Afzal Khan, do I bring a swordsman such as Bandu with me. I bring two women with me because I know that you and your troops honour and respect women and would cause them no harm. We seek only peace between us. We honour you as a great leader, Raja, and we only wish to have your assurance that our lives and our goods are safe in your hands.'

'Your men fired on my troops,' Shivaji answered.

'I regret that as much as you do, Highness. A column of them approached our factory. They demanded entrance saying you had given them authority to sack the city. When we replied that this was the factory of the East India Company and they should not enter, the officer in command said that the French had allowed them to occupy their factory. I replied that while the French factory might be full of monsieurs, it had very little cash or goods, Raja. The officer insisted that he and his troops must come in. I answered that it was more like Englishmen to make ourselves ready to defend our lives and goods. I told him, Raja, that we had to consider the honour of our nation, that we were ready and resolved not to allow him or any of his men to enter. A group of his troops approached and we were forced to open fire, Highness.'

'Why, then, did your men fire on the Marathas who were sent to the house of the rich merchant Said Beg? He is a Mohammedan. His house is not in your factory.'

Sir George spoke very deliberately, allowing Ruth plenty of time to translate. 'Said Beg put himself under the company's protection. Is it not right, Raja, that you were going to hold him and two others as hostages? And keep them until a ransom was paid. Did you not also, Raja, take four of our factors hostage at Rajapur and keep them hostage to this very day? How could our honour permit us to allow you to take as a hostage one who has sought our protection?'

'Your musketeers killed eight of my men,' Shivaji replied.

'For that I am sorry, Raja. I mourn the loss of every single life in conflict, be they English, Maratha or Mogul. But I do not think of you as an enemy and hope you will regard us as your friends, Highness. Once this wretched business of the four hostages taken at Rajapur is settled, there need be no further dispute between the company and any who live in the territory under your control, including its most illustrious ruler.'

'Will you waive the claim for compensation for the destruction of the warehouses at Rajapur?'

Sir George hesitated. He realised that he needed all his diplomatic skill. 'There is still the matter of your claim against the company, Raja. Those factors are servants of the company but disobedient ones. They disobeyed our orders for them to remain neutral in the war between you and the Sultan of Bejapour. When you hand them back to us they will be punished. If you waive your claim against the company for a breach of neutrality, a claim which the company does not accept, release the four factors, and order your men to withdraw from the vicinity of the English factory during the present occupation of Surat, the company will waive its claim for compensation for the loss of our warehouses.'

One of the Brahmins went to Shivaji's side and a whispered consultation took place. 'I accept,' Shivaji said. 'The factors will be sent back to you and my troops will be withdrawn from near your factory. Keep your men alert, President Sahib. Some irregulars ride with us who are not as disciplined as the main army. There are also looters around as well as bandits coming in from the countryside.'

'Thank you, Raja. May the blessings of peace and friendship strengthen the ties between our two peoples, illustrious ruler.'

Shivaji's face broke into a warm smile as Ruth finished translating the last sentence. Even his eyes were smiling and she looked down as she said 'illustrious ruler'.

He turned to address Sushi directly. 'What is your name? Are you this woman's mother?'

'I am Sushi from the village of Lalhulla. She is not my flesh, Raja. But we tied our robes together. She is the daughter of my heart.'

'She does not carry the sign that she is married,' he said reflectively. 'Why is she with you and the President Sahib?'

Before Sushi could answer two messengers came into the tent in a state of high excitement. They bowed and raised their open hand to their forehead in a gesture of salute. When one of the Brahmins asked the reason for their intrusion into an already crowded tent, they replied that an officer from the imperial army had arrived to discuss the surrender of the fort and the rest of the town by the remnants of the Mogul Emperor's garrison.

Ruth thought how young the imperial officer looked. He could not be more than a boy. She sensed the tension in the young man as he greeted Shivaji with the Mohammedan salaam. His voice was agitated as he began to speak.

'My master has ordered me here to discuss terms. We wish to negotiate the surrender of the fort, which will be yours, if we are allowed to leave honourably.'

'You serve a coward,' Shivaji replied.

'The governor is not a coward, Shivaji. He has proved himself as a soldier in the service of Emperor Shah Jahan and Emperor Aurangzeb.'

'He was too afraid to come on his own. English President came on his own to talk to me.'

'My master is not afraid,' the young officer answered. 'He wishes to save the lives of those under his command and the lives of your men. Many will die if you attack our citadel.'

'Your master sits quietly in his castle like a weak, timid girl.' Shivaji nodded in Ruth's direction. 'English President brings women with him to talk to me. Governor sends girl to discuss terms.

'We are not all women,' the officer replied angrily.

'Sultan of Bejapour, Sultan of Golcanda, Emperor Aurangzeb, Shayista Khan, Governor of Bengal. All women.' Shivaji answered contemptuously. 'Served by girls.'

The young officer drew a dagger from a scabbard on his belt and ran at Shivaji, intending to kill him. A Maratha guardsman standing to the left of Shivaji sprang forward and cut off the officer's hand with his sword. Such was the speed at which this had taken place that the officer closed with Shivaji and the two of them fell together to the floor. The two rolled over until the young officer was pinned in Shivaji's arms. Another guardsman stepped forward and with one sweep of his heavy sword cut straight through the helmet underneath the officer's turban, splitting his skull in two. Shivaji's turban and the rest of his clothes were covered in blood and Ruth could hear people outside shouting that he had been assassinated. Narainji Pandit came across to her and whispered quietly. 'Tell the English President to keep with me. You will be safe if we stay together.'

She nodded in answer as Shivaji got to his feet. He dashed out of the tent with his bodyguard, his officials, and Sir George's party following. For the first time since the attack on Surat began, Ruth was really frightened. Neither Sushi nor Sir George showed any emotion and she determined to copy them. All round her she could hear savage cries of vengeance. The shouts came not just from the wild hillsmen who had joined Shivaji after the attack on Surat but also from the better dressed and better disciplined troops of the regular Maratha army. Shivaji ran through his camp, shouting to make himself heard. Swords, lances and spears were being waved wildly in the air, with their owners demanding blood. He commanded them to return to their posts, repeating his command time after time. Although his picked, uniformed, personal guard gradually became calmer, the shouts for vengeance, made by the wilder elements, were becoming more hysterical. Narainji Pandit and another Brahmin stood each side of Sir George, with Ruth and Sushi directly behind them, forming a little phalanx of order in an ocean of seething hatred.

Shivaji shouted that he would order amputation of the right hands of twenty-four imperial prisoners and the execution of four Moguls. Although his decision on the scale of retribution was only heard by those immediately around him, the message was passed quickly through the remainder of the camp. It had a calming affect and the forest of lances and spears was gradually lowered and the swords sheathed.

'Please tell your President to stay close to me,' Narainji Pandit whispered to Ruth. 'It would only need one false move to cause another tragedy.'

'I will do as you say,' she replied. 'You are very thoughtful.'

'You came here under a flag of truce,' he answered. 'I gave the English President my word. I must protect him with my life.'

It seemed an interminable time before the crowd of several hundred was relatively quiet. For the first time for several minutes it was quiet enough to hear the occasional rattle of musket fire and the intermittent booming of the guns from the imperial fort. A space was gradually cleared in front of Shivaji's tent, and the troops and irregulars waited expectantly for the imperial prisoners to arrive. There was a hush as the group of twenty-eight prisoners appeared in single file, with guards on either side of them to prevent their escape. As the first prisoner was ordered to extend his right arm, a guard quickly severed the hand at the wrist. The prisoner was led away for the wound to be dressed and the flow of blood staunched. After this had happened six times, Ruth felt she had to look away. The sight of so much blood sickened her and she was angry at the impassive way in which the file of prisoners moved forward to accept the punishment of dismemberment.

'That part's finished,' she heard Sir George say.

There were only four prisoners now left in the line. The first of them was ordered to remove his turban and then kneel. Almost before his knees had touched the ground, his head was severed from his body by a single stroke of a sword. She continued to stare in fascinated horror as the second and third prisoners were despatched in the same way. The fourth prisoner seemed taller than the others. He carefully removed his turban and then looked slowly round the crowd.

'Oh, no!' Ruth heard herself saying. 'You can't. You mustn't.' She moved forward until she was only a yard from the prisoner.

'Who speaks for this woman?' Shivaji demanded.

Sir George and Sushi moved alongside Ruth.

'The English President speaks for her, illustrious Highness,' Sushi replied.

'And you speak for her also, woman. Is she not your daughter? Is your life to be forfeit too?' he asked angrily.

'I speak for my daughter, Shivaji Raja. If my life is to be forfeit, I am content to obey your wish, Highness.'

Ruth held her breath, wondering what would happen next. Shivaji looked fixedly at the prisoner, back to Ruth and then stared at the prisoner once more. 'Are you a Frankish soldier?' he asked, talking to the prisoner in Urdu.

'No. I am an Englishman,' the prisoner replied.

Ruth could sense Sir George shuffle slightly.

'You know you are to be executed?' enquired Shivaji.

'Yes. I have seen what happened to my fellows.'

'You cannot execute him now, Highness,' Ruth called out, speaking in Marathi.

'Cannot, woman?' Shivaji asked, in a voice filled with surprise.

Ruth could hear the buzz of excited discussion in the crowd.

'When you gave your commands, Shivaji Raja, you said four Moguls would be executed. This man is English. He is not a Mogul.'

'And you want his life?'

'If your Highness will only exercise the prerogative of mercy for which you are famous throughout this land, I will be the first among women to sing your praises.'

'You shall have him,' Shivaji paused, 'if you marry him today.'

Even as she replied, 'I will take him for my husband, merciful ruler,' she could hear the laughter in the crowd.

The tension was suddenly eased and she could feel the waves of hatred which had swept the crowd dying down. Shivaji turned to the prisoner and asked, 'Where will you lie tonight, Englishman? The grave or the marriage bed?'

Ruth stepped forward and took his hand. She could feel him trembling but at her touch he became still.

'Don't be afraid, Mark,' she whispered. 'It's me, Ruth Parker.' Mark looked down. All he could see was the cowl of a native woman standing beside him. It must be an hallucination. Perhaps he was already dead. The pressure on his hand became more insistent. He heard a second whisper. 'Say something, Mark. I really am Ruth.'

'Shall the executioner do his duty, Englishman?' Shivaji asked.

'No, Shivaji,' Mark replied. 'I take this girl for my wife.'

A ripple of cheering and laughter swept through the crowd. Although only the nearest had heard all the interchanges, the message was quickly passed along. It appealed to their sense of fun that an English prisoner's life had been spared on condition that he married a native girl he had never seen before. 'A wise choice,' Shivaji said laconically. 'You must marry today. And leave the Mogul army. Have I your word on both these?'

'Yes, Shivaji,' Mark answered. 'You have my word of honour.'

'Take this man, President Sahib,' Shivaji said, addressing Sir George Oxindon. 'He is in your charge. See he is married today. If not, his life and the lives of these two women will be forfeit. Leave us now. Your safe conduct, given under our flag of truce, extends to this man also.'

Sushi whispered a translation in the President's ear.

'I will carry out your wishes, Raja,' Sir George answered, speaking in Urdu. He bowed slightly as Ruth and Sushi put the open palms of their right hands to their foreheads and bowed three times in the usual Maratha greeting.

'Ram, Ram, Highness,' they both said, moving backwards

as they did, keeping their heads well down and covered by their cowls. Mark turned on his heels and took his place beside Ruth. Narainji Pandit had previously been into the tent to bring out the white flag of truce which had been left behind. He handed it to Sir George and smiled.

'Go in peace, President Sahib,' he said. 'You and your party will be safe now.'

'Thank you for your help,' Sir George replied. Narainji Pandit's only answer was another smile.

Sir George moved off slowly with Sushi by his side. Ruth and Mark followed in their immediate wake. As well as a good deal of shouting and laughter, soldiers in the crowd yelled out ribald comments as they passed. Sushi shouted back in a good-humoured way from time to time as cries of, 'Fall in, wedding party,' were heard. The crowd roared with laughter at one of their comrades when he lost a verbal interchange with Sushi. Although Ruth could not understand all the rough dialect spoken by the hillman in this exchange of banter, she blushed under her cowl. It seemed that Sushi had told them that a strong, healthy woman like her daughter would suck a puny monkey like him dry in three days. That was why she had chosen the English prisoner.

The crowd thinned out as they approached the edge of the camp. Sir George stopped when they were about two hundred yards clear of the perimeter. The occasional musket shot could still be heard as well as the infrequent boom of the citadel's cannon.

'We still have to go very carefully from here,' he said to the other three. 'It will be dark soon and I want to get back to the factory as quickly as possible. None of us is armed but we should be safe if we stick close together. Although it's occupied by the Marathas at the moment, our most direct route is through the French factory. If we are separated, go to the French factory. Stay there until I can get a message to you. Do you all understand?'

They all murmured their agreement.

'Have you a priest in the English factory, Master President?' Mark asked.

'A priest? What the devil do you want a priest for at a time like this? And the way people address me is Sir George, lad. Not Master President.'

'To get married, Sir George.'

The President looked astounded. 'Married? Married? In Heaven's name, you're not serious, are you? To a girl you've never met before. When my factory may be burning even now and I need every able-bodied man who can fire a musket or hold a sword.'

'I gave my word,' Mark replied quietly.

'To a brigand like Shivaji. You must be mad, lad. In a few days' time, if we all live that long, the imperial army will relieve Surat. Shivaji and his wild hordes will retreat and no one will really care whether you're married or not.'

'But I will, Sir George. I repeat, have you a priest in your factory?'

'You don't have to go through with it, lad. Not just for Shivaji. As it happens, it's out of your hands. Our chaplain's confined to bed with a fever. Come on, let's get started or we won't be back before dark.'

Sir George started walking at a brisk pace, leaving the others to hurry after him. Mark, with his long strides, quickly caught him up. Narainji Pandit passed Ruth and Sushi, walking in the same direction as they were going, and nodded to them in recognition. From fifteen or so yards away, Ruth could just hear Mark telling Sir George that he would have to go back to the Maratha camp because he had given his word of honour.

'Don't let him go back, Sir George,' she cried out to them.

Sir George stopped dead in his tracks, allowing Ruth to catch him up. 'Good God, Ruth,' he said. 'Have you gone mad as well?'

'No, Sir George. But I gave my word also. If he goes back, I go back. And Sushi's life will be forfeit too.'

'I can't let you do it. For a man you've never seen before.'

Ruth threw back her cowl and stood up to her full height. Her long, fair, curly hair fell round her shoulders as she did so. She moved in front of Mark so that she looked him squarely in the eyes. She smiled at him as she started to say, 'I am no sacrificial victim, Sir George. I think I have loved this man from the first time he kissed me, five and a half years ago. I think I have always known I would be his woman one day.' She half turned to Sir George. 'During the Commonwealth it was possible for two people to marry by making a declaration before a Justice. Can Mark and I do this before you, Sir George?'

'That is no longer possible. A declaration of that sort is not recognised as legal under the Crown.'

'Very well,' Ruth replied. 'I would prefer your blessing but even without it, I must know Mark tonight. My honour is worthless if his life is forfeit.' The blood rushed to Mark's face as he looked at Ruth. The pretty girl he had once kissed was taller and had grown into a beautiful woman, even in spite of the dark colouring on her skin. The small breasts he remembered had become larger, rounder and firmer. She really was lovely. Mark could feel his heart pounding and his breathing becoming heavy.

'I don't like it,' he heard Sir George say, as if from a far distance, 'but if you're determined to go through with it, Ruth, I'll do it, so help me God. You must see the chaplain as soon as he's better.'

Ruth went towards Sir George and kissed him.

'Thank you, Sir George,' she said.

'Now that's settled, let's get started, everybody,' he replied, beginning to walk in the direction of the French factory. Before they had gone more than a few yards, Mark was at his side again.

'I'm sorry, Sir George,' he said. 'I can't let Ruth do it.'

Sir George exploded with rage. 'In the name of Christ, man, what's wrong with you? You have your life spared for you today. You have a pretty woman who is prepared to bed down with you tonight. What more d'you want? Don't answer that! Just leave me! Sushi, you come and walk with me. Ruth, you walk with Mark. See if you can talk some sense into this idiot.'

He started to walk forward quickly, still holding his white flag. In a moment of exasperation, he flung it to the ground.

'No one will be able to see it soon in this light,' he exclaimed.

Sushi quickly picked it up and hurried after him. Ruth caught up with Mark and slid her arm across his back, giving his right shoulder a squeeze as she did so.

'Put your left arm around my waist, Mark,' she said. 'We can follow the others like this.'

She felt the tentative pressure of his arm on her body becoming more confident as they walked in the wake of Sushi and Sir George. She took her arm from his shoulder and put it across his left arm and around his waist.

'You're doing this just out of pity, aren't you, Ruth?' he asked.

'Pity!' she exclaimed. 'Pity is the last emotion I feel with your arm around my waist.'

'You're sure now?'

She pulled him closer to her. Ruth could feel their thighs touch through her thin cotton sari. 'How many more times do you need to be reassured?' she answered a trifle astringently. 'I have an interest in this as well. We both gave our word that it would be either the grave or the bed for you tonight. Am I so repulsive that you can even contemplate the alternative to marrying me, according to the custom of the Commonwealth?'

He stopped and looked straight at her.

'No. No, Ruth. You're beautiful. But I have nothing to give you. Nothing at all.'

'You have yourself,' she answered quietly. 'That's all I ask. All I need. Nothing else matters. Money, position, family are unimportant. All I want is here beside me. Now and always.'

Mark's head moved towards hers and their lips were locked in a lingering kiss. After what seemed an eternity to Ruth, they heard Sir George shouting and their lips separated. He and Sushi were standing almost fifty yards ahead. Ruth took Mark's hand and together they ran towards the others, laughing as they did so. They were breathless when they reached them and as bubbly as two young children coming out of school.

'I see your eloquence persuaded him,' Sir George remarked drily.

Ruth smiled by way of answer. Sushi looked both disapproving and pleased as Ruth told her, 'Mark is coming with us.'

'Right,' said Sir George briskly. 'We're two hundred and fifty yards from the French factory. Just outside the range of musket fire. We'll go through there, hoping they'll honour our flag of truce. It's three hundred yards to the other side to get to our own factory. Our men can cover us with their fire once we're clear of the French walls.'

He turned to Ruth and Sushi. 'Mark and I will lead the way. You two ladies follow. That way if anyone is hit, it will be the two of us in front.'

'No, Sir George,' Ruth contradicted firmly. 'You've done enough. Mark and I will go in front. If I'm going to lose him again after all this time, I would rather go with him.'

Sir George gave her a long, searching look. 'If that is your wish. You must know that I can't ask Sushi to go in front.'

'Come on, Mark,' Ruth said, taking hold of his left arm. He turned to look at her and could feel the blood rushing through his veins and the muscles in his body tightening up as he saw the expression in her eyes. He kissed her briefly on the forehead.

'I'm ready,' he said in a husky voice, as they went forward into the dusk, arm in arm. After they had gone about twenty-five yards they heard the others following behind. They walked ahead slowly and deliberately, observing the buildings burning for two or three hundred yards each side of the French factory.

A few seconds after they started a gun on the citadel wall opened fire, followed by a volley of musket shots from the garrison. Ruth felt Mark's arm become tense but he did not alter pace or direction.

'No need to be concerned on my account,' she said. 'I'm not afraid. Not while we're together.'

Mark's only reply was to whisper, 'Ruth, dearest,' and to continue to look and walk straight ahead. After a few more seconds had elapsed he said, 'Providence.'

'I know, darling,' Ruth replied. 'I was thinking the same thing. There must be something more in store for your life. I can't think God wants us to die in a foreign land. So far from home.'

'Do you remember how we used to walk together before?' he asked. 'Through the gardens of Aireton Hall, I mean.'

'Yes, Mark,' she laughed. 'Look at us. Me, the Puritan maiden. You, the dashing Cavalier. But that doesn't matter now. What is important is that the two of us are together again.'

They were silent, lost in their own thoughts for half a minute or so, as they approached the gateway of the French factory.

'Keep walking straight on,' Mark muttered.

Ruth noticed three Maratha soldiers had appeared and were levelling spears at them. She thought the pair of them must present a strange sight to the sentries. Mark was in the uniform of a Mogul officer, apart from a missing turban, while she was dressed in the traditional sari worn by a Maratha woman. When they were about thirty yards from where the sentries were standing one of them called out a Marathi command to halt. Another, who had obviously been taking lessons from one of the French factors, shouted 'Qui va la?'

Mark's quick response of, 'Nous sommes Anglais. Pas des Moguls,' met with complete silence. It was obvious that the sentry did not understand the answer but as Ruth was about to reply in Marathi, Sushi could be heard shouting from behind, asking the soldiers if they were blind or drunk. They must be if they could not see the flag of truce the English President Sahib was carrying after his meeting with their commander Shivaji.

The mention of the name Shivaji caused a certain degree of consternation. There were calls for the guard commander and shortly afterwards a black-bearded Maratha captain appeared. He motioned them forward, looked at the quartette carefully and ordered the sentries to lower their spears. After a brief glance again at the two men, he gave careful scrutiny to Ruth and Sushi. The news of the release of the imperial prisoner must have reached the garrison occupying the French factory. Perhaps the message had been relayed by Narainji Pandit who had passed them while they were on the way.

The captain turned to Sushi and asked, 'This woman your daughter?'

'My adopted daughter,' Sushi replied.

The officer looked at Ruth's fair hair and appeared dissatisfied by the reply. He turned to Sir George and, speaking to him in Urdu, asked, 'This man the English prisoner?'

'He is no longer a prisoner,' he replied. 'Your commander released him into my custody.'

The Maratha still looked in a puzzled way from Sushi to Ruth and back again. He spoke once more to Sir George, 'Which woman is to marry this man?'

Sir George moved to Ruth's side 'This lady is to be married.'

'I was told a Maratha woman was to marry him,' he replied, looking at Sushi.

'I assure you, captain, Shivaji asked this lady to marry this man.'

'Tonight?' the officer asked mischievously.

'So it was agreed,' Sir George answered, impatiently. 'May we go now. It will be dark soon and my men will not see who is approaching.'

'In a moment, English President.' The Maratha captain stared hard again at Ruth's long, fair, curly hair and blue eyes. He looked at the mark on Sushi's forehead. 'Are you Hindu?'

he asked Ruth tentatively, switching to Marathi.

'No, captain,' she replied.

'English?'

'Yes, captain.'

His face broke into a broad smile. He started speaking in Urdu once more. 'You may go now, English President. I will send some of my men with lamps to escort you to the gate of the factory. The other three stay with me. I will personally escort them to your factory later.'

'That I cannot allow, captain,' Sir George answered. 'These ladies are under my protection and this man has been delivered into my charge. Why do you wish to keep them?'

The captain dismissed the sentries who were listening to this conversation with growing interest. 'Please follow me,' he ordered Sir George and his party. They moved from the area near the gate into a large warehouse. It had obviously been recently cleared of goods. Once inside, the captain's face became wreathed in smiles again.

'We have a Frankish padre here, English President. I get him to marry this man and this woman. Bride's mother stays as well. I send three of my men back with you now. They stay in English factory with you. I bring these three later and take my three men back with me. Tell your men not to shoot us.'

At the mention of the words 'Frankish padre', Ruth's hand had reached out to Mark's. It must mean there was a Catholic priest nearby. If only he could be persuaded to marry them. She nodded and smiled at Sir George as he looked across at her.

'I don't like it,' he said.

'You must go back, Sir George. Otherwise Master Streynsham will think the Marathas have broken the truce. I will be alright with Sushi.'

'It seems you can go now or later, English President. What is your choice?' the captain asked.

'Very well, then,' Sir George said. 'If these three are not back inside my factory in two hours time, my men and I will come looking for them.'

'Please,' the Maratha officer replied, 'enough blood has been shed already.' The noise of gunfire could still be heard from the direction of the citadel. 'And is still being shed. I assure you there is no need to break the truce between us.' He made a signal to Sushi and led Sir George away. 'Are we to stay here, Sushi?' Ruth asked.

Sushi embraced her. 'You are to be married, daughter of my heart,' she answered smiling. 'But you have not eaten or drunk for five hours. I must ask the captain if his soldiers will give us food.'

'We are not Catholics, Ruth,' Mark said seriously, after a brief pause.

'I know that. Does it matter?'

'We have our children to think of, Ruth,' Mark blushed slightly as he spoke. 'You'll have to marry me again afterwards. Would you mind?' She hugged him, her eyes bright with happiness. 'Mind, my dearest idiot? Of course, I will marry you again. A dozen times over if you want me to.'

He kissed and held her and continued to hold her, only releasing her when the Maratha captain returned.

'My name is Abiji Sing. I will help you,' the officer told them. 'But you two stay now. You, mother, you come with me.'

Sushi followed him outside the door and Ruth could hear the murmur of their conversation from a little way off. They were speaking too rapidly and too softly for her to catch any of the words. Both of them returned after a short time. Sushi's face was wreathed in smiles and the captain looked very pleased with himself.

'You follow me now,' he said. 'I take you to my quarters. You have food and drink. Afterwards, Frankish padre come to see you.' He led them to a storeroom at the side of the warehouse. Inside was a little table, four small chairs, and a wooden-framed string bed with a blanket folded at one end. It was almost dark by this time and, as if in answer to their unspoken wish, an orderly appeared carrying an oil lamp.

'Food will be coming soon,' Abiji Sing said. He grinned. 'Soldiers' rations only.'

'Sushi and I are used to Maratha food, captain,' Ruth replied. 'Thank you for your hospitality.'

'Maratha food very simple.' He looked wickedly in Mark's direction. 'Not like pilaus and other rich Mogul food.'

Mark lowered his eyes. It was as though he was trying to forget that he had ever served in the Mogul army.

'I bring some sweetmeats,' Abiji Sing continued. His tone became confidential. 'One of my soldiers found them in an empty baker's shop today. He took them to stop them being looted.' He laughed, 'You know how it is when a city is sacked. All sorts of bad characters around.'

The necessity for a reply was avoided by two orderlies coming in with a tray of rice and a dish of herbs. As they left, they bowed and saluted by touching their foreheads with their open right hands. A third orderly followed with a large tray bearing French plates, mugs, and a serai full of water. He bowed and saluted in the same way as he left.

'You are my guests,' Abiji Sing said. 'Please start. I have already eaten. I go now to see the President and the padre.'

'Why does he need to see the President?' Ruth asked after he had gone. Sushi merely smiled enigmatically.

'Maybe the President will act as a witness,' Mark mused.

The three of them lapsed into silence. They were hungry and thirsty, with nerves strained to breaking point by the events of the afternoon and evening. The sounds of musket shots and cannon fire had subsided now but, even in this small storeroom, they could see the dull red glow from the countless fires burning in the city. It would only take another incident, like the attempted assassination of Shivaji that afternoon, for these wild hillsmen to put to the sword those few inhabitants who remained in the city.

Just before they finished their meal, Abiji Sing returned. He was followed by an orderly carrying a dish of sweetmeats. Behind the orderly came a white- haired man dressed in the habit of a French Capuchin missionary. The orderly placed the tray on the table, saluted, and withdrew.

'This is the Frankish padre,' the captain said. 'I leave you now. I return later.'

The priest spoke to them in French and Mark replied in the same language. He then turned to Ruth and addressed her in Marathi. 'I am Father Dellon. You are English, are you not? I am sorry I spoke in French, my child. The captain told me a European man and woman wish to marry. Europe is so far away to these people. But who are we to think they are ignorant because they do not know the difference between the King of France and the King of Spain. Or between the King of England and the King of Portugal. How many people in Europe know who the Mogul Emperor is, or can tell the difference between the Sultan of Bejapour and the Sultan of Golcanda? Please forgive me for interrupting your meal.'

'Please join us, Father,' Ruth replied. She paused for a few seconds and then said cheerfully, 'I understand Latin.'

The missionary's face brightened considerably. He answered her in the Latin tongue.

'That will be better when we talk about preparation for the sacrament of marriage.' He turned to Mark. 'Do you speak Latin, my son?'

'Not a great deal, Father. I studied it until I was twelve. After that I had to leave my home. I went to France with my brother when I was fourteen. Ruth studied it until she was past that age.'

'Very well, my son. I will talk to you in French when we come to your preparation. It will be easier for us all than speaking in Marathi.' They continued eating the sweetmeats for a minute or so in silence. Sushi seemed a little lost and ill at ease hearing the French conversation, followed by Ruth speaking in Latin. Eventually the missionary turned to Sushi and spoke to her in Marathi.'

'Captain Abiji Sing told me you are the mother of the bride.'

'Mother of Ruth is dead,' Sushi answered.

'How well do you know the bride?' the missionary asked cautiously.

'I was her servant?' There was a long pause. 'Then she lived with me. We tied our robes together. Became like mother and daughter.'

Father Dellon gave an almost imperceptible sigh. He took Sushi's hand in his and said gently, 'When you have finished your meal, will you wait outside, please?'

'I have finished now,' Sushi replied. She went quietly out.

'So have both of us, Father,' Ruth added.

The missionary waited for a few moments as if uncertain how to proceed. 'I will speak in Latin, if I may, my children. Please stop me if there is anything you do not understand. I must confess my head is spinning.' Father Dellon paused.

'I have heard a story from the captain which is quite incredible. That you, my son, were to be executed. Pardon was granted on condition that you married a Maratha girl who now turns out to be English. Captain Abiji Sing also told me that the girl's mother was here and it now seems that she is the bride's Hindu servant.'

'Every word is true, Father,' Ruth answered. 'And the wedding must be tonight.'

'Must be, my daughter?' he asked, gently.

'We gave our word.'

'To whom, child?'

'Shivaji, Father.'

'Shivaji,' the missionary snorted. 'That hill chieftain! That robber!'

'Yes, Father.'

'But is it necessary, my child, to keep your word to a man like that?'

'We gave our word in the eyes of Almighty God,' Ruth answered.

'And do you feel equally strongly, my son,' he asked, addressing Mark in French.

'Yes, Father,' Mark replied, in Latin.

'You are English, are you not?' Father Dellon hesitated. 'Are you both Catholics?'

'No, Father,' Mark answered.

'Neither of us is a Catholic,' Ruth added.

'You know, my children, that any marriage I might perform between you will not be binding in the eyes of your church or your king?'

'We know that,' Ruth replied.

'And you still wish me to proceed? Do you not wish to wait until the English chaplain marries you?'

'The chaplain is ill,' Ruth answered.

'It is true he has a fever,' Father Dellon said. 'But Master Boland should be well enough to marry you in a week or two.'

'You do not understand, Father Dellon,' Ruth replied. She was beginning to feel exasperated. 'Mark and I must be husband and wife tonight.'

The missionary smiled. 'But I do understand, my daughter. Sometimes we have to fight against the weaknesses of the flesh. It is not that I will not, my child. It is that I cannot marry people who are not Catholics, without good reason.' Ruth stood up. 'Goodbye, Father Dellon. Thank you for your time.'

'What will you do now, my daughter? But please sit down before you answer.'

'I must keep my word. If we are not joined together tonight, Mark will go back. He will regard it as a point of honour. His life will be forfeit.'

'You realise, my child, that you will sin?' Neither Ruth nor Mark answered.

'Listen to me, my children. Fornication is a mortal sin. You will be in peril of losing your immortal soul.'

'I think not,' Ruth replied curtly. 'You may not understand. But God will. God will forgive us. To save the life of a man I love, I am not asked to kill. I do not need to lie. I am not being compelled to cheat or to steal. Neither will I be asked to deceive or bear false witness. I am not being forced to cause pain and suffering to others. I will only be asked to follow the command of my Lord Jesus Christ. Which is to love one another as he loved us.'

Father Dellon was visibly moved. He waited several seconds before replying. 'You claim wisdom beyond your years, my daughter. You think you know the mind of God. I have tried for sixty years and I still do not know or understand the workings of God's mind.' He stopped to recover himself and then looked Ruth straight in the eyes again. 'To save this man, you would risk your immortal soul?'

'Yes, Father,' Ruth answered quietly. 'He is my man. For as long as he lives.'

The missionary spoke to Mark in French. 'Have you understood what I said?' he asked.

'Yes, Father.'

'And do you realise that not only your immortal soul but the soul of this girl could be in danger?'

'I am her servant,' Mark answered. 'I owe my life to her. It is hers to command. Now and always. If it is her will to know me tonight, I must obey.'

'Bless you, my children,' Father Dellon replied. 'I will take you to our chapel in the factory. You must know that unless you promise me that your children are brought up as Catholics, any marriage ceremony I perform cannot be valid in the eyes of the Church.'

He paused as if hoping for a response but none came.

'Your own church and king do not recognise my power to marry you and you must ask Master Boland to marry you as soon as possible after you leave here. But I can go through the wedding ceremony here. Although you will not be married in the eyes of Church or state, your union will be blessed in the eyes of God.'

'That is all that matters to Mark and me. Thank you, Father,' Ruth replied.

'Follow me then, my children.'

The three of them went outside into the warehouse. In the dim light they saw that a rather plump, European gentleman, with a pointed, dark-haired beard, was talking to Abiji Sing, with Sushi standing a little way apart. Three pairs of eyes turned in their direction as Father Dellon led the way towards the little group. The European gentleman hurried towards them. He seized Ruth's hand and bowed to her. 'Good evening, Mademoiselle,' he said, speaking in English. 'I am Monsieur Villeneuve, President of the French factory. I am at your service. Until you go to English factory.' He kissed her hand before releasing it.

'Thank you, Monsieur,' Ruth replied.

'And you, Monsieur,' the President said to Mark. 'You are lucky man.' He lowered his voice slightly. 'You escape from Shivaji into the arms of a beautiful demoiselle. What fortune. I look after you. You come with me when the good father has finished with you.'

'Thank you, Monsieur Villeneuve,' Mark answered, a trifle stiffly. 'Ruth and I are obliged to you.'

'Obliged, Monsieur? It will be my pleasure! Come, we must not keep the good father waiting.'

He murmured a few words in French to Father Dellon and the whole party moved off. After leaving the warehouse, they went through a series of rooms. They saw a number of armed Marathas who saluted their captain as the group approached, giving curious glances to the remainder of the party at the same time. Ruth was surprised at the absence of Frenchmen. When they were coming to the end of a long corridor, Father Dellon said, 'My chapel is directly ahead,' and stopped. The Maratha captain spoke briefly to Sushi and she embraced Ruth saying, 'All my blessings on you, daughter.'

'You will have to let Mademoiselle go, Monsieur,' the President said. 'It will only be for a short while.'

Mark released Ruth's arm reluctantly and then followed Father Dellon into the chapel. A momentary panic seized Ruth. It all seemed so unreal. Was she dreaming? Was it just an act being put on for her benefit? Monsieur Villeneuve seemed to understand her mood. He took her arm and said gently, 'I will take you to his side, my dear. I will be with you in the chapel.'

'Yes, Monsieur. But he's so alone in there.'

'Alone, Mademoiselle?' Monsieur Villeneuve chuckled. 'Oh, no. Every man in my factory is in the chapel tonight. They all heard the story about you and Monsieur. When they see you, they think what a lucky dog he is. They all wish they could take his place.'

Ruth smiled. She could feel the tension draining from her. They began walking slowly towards the chapel door. A sudden thought struck her. 'Do you need to exchange rings in a Catholic marriage, Monsieur?'

'It is customary. But sometimes only the bride has a wedding ring.'

'But Mark has no ring.'

'Do not worry, Mademoiselle,' the President replied. 'My deputy is with him now. I am sure one of our congregation will provide one for a lovely lady such as yourself.'

They paused at the door of the chapel. In the dim light, she could see Father Dellon standing in front of the altar screen. Mark had his back to her. She and Monsieur Villeneuve walked slowly up the aisle. Ruth was aware of faces in the congregation being turned towards her and could hear audible sighs of appreciation. All the time she was walking up the aisle, Mark stared fixedly ahead, as if afraid to turn around. The President stopped alongside Mark. He released Ruth's arm and then moved round, so that she was at Mark's side. Ruth took his hand. She was surprised to find that he was trembling. The gentle pressure of her hand soothed him. Mark looked at her and they smiled at each other. She squeezed his hand tightly and suddenly realised that Mark had a signet ring on the little finger of his left hand.

'The ring,' she whispered. 'We'll need a ring. Take off your signet ring.' He allowed two or three seconds to elapse before replying. It was as though so much had happened that he could not comprehend what she was saying.

'My signet ring?'

Ruth grasped the ring between the thumb and first finger of her right hand. It felt quite loose. She moved it up and down. 'Take it off. I'll give it back to you later.'

He nodded. It was difficult to get it past the knuckle of his little finger but at last it was free.

During the time that this whispered conversation had been taking place, Father Dellon had been reading introductory prayers from his missal. Ruth felt detached from reality as the rest of the service proceeded. The Latin liturgy was unknown to her and she relied on prompting from Monsieur Villeneuve to give the correct response. At last the ring was on her finger, Mark had kissed her, and they were going back down the aisle to a buzz of conversation from the worshippers. Ruth was surprised to see Sushi and Abiji Sing in earnest conversation about twenty yards away as she and Mark left the chapel. They were part of her existence about which she had completely forgotten.

An excited crowd was now coming out of the chapel. A few pressed forward to shake Mark's hand while some bowed low in front of Ruth before kissing her hand. They stepped back at their President's command and formed two ranks with a space between. Ruth and Mark followed Monsieur Villeneuve through the path between the well-wishers to the sound of cheers and words of encouragement. The President nodded to Sushi and Abiji Sing, who came to stand behind the bride and groom.

'Follow me,' Monsieur Villeneuve commanded.

He led them up a flight of stairs and then along a corridor, pausing outside a door at the end. He made a low bow and smiled broadly.

'My private apartments. They are at your disposal, Madame and Monsieur.' He nodded in the direction of the Maratha officer, 'Captain Abiji Sing tells me you leave in an hour. Until then, this is your home, Madame. No one will disturb you. If I do not see you before you go back to your own factory, I wish you many years of happiness. Au revoir, Madame. Au revoir, Monsieur. My compliments to Sir George Oxindon.'

---

He bowed, smiled at the bridal pair for three or four seconds, turned round, and walked away.

'I come back in an hour's time,' the Maratha officer said.

'Thank you,' Mark answered.

'Ram, Ram, Captain Abiji Sing,' Ruth added, holding her hands together in the Maratha greeting.

The captain's eyes sparkled in the dim light. 'A thousand blessings on you and your husband. I go now.'

Sushi opened the door and followed them into the apartment. A lamp was burning on a table in the sitting room. An opened bottle of wine stood beside the lamp, together with two glasses.

'While you talk to padre, President Sahib bring me here,' Sushi said. She pointed to the wine. 'Come now. He say everything here for you to use. Follow me. I show you.'

Sushi opened another door and led them into a bedroom. It was well furnished with chairs, a commode, and a dressing table. A large portable mirror had been placed on the dressing table, together with a basin and a jug of water. A lamp was burning alongside. There was a large, freshly made bed in the corner of the room. Sushi moved across to stand by it.

'President Sahib most clear. He told me all things here for you.' She walked back to Ruth and embraced her. Turning to Mark, she said, 'Be kind to her, my son.'

Mark took her by the shouders and kissed her on both cheeks. 'Thank you for everything, Sushi,' he said.

Ruth instinctively followed Sushi back into the sitting room and Mark came after her. 'Where will you be, Sushi?' Ruth asked.

Sushi pointed to the door of the President's apartment.

'I stay outside, daughter. I see no one comes in,' she answered in a fierce voice.

Ruth smiled. It would take considerable force and determination to get past that formidable lady. Sushi turned just before she reached the door to look at Ruth once more.

There was such love in her eyes that Ruth felt compelled to run across to her. Sushi held her arm out and pushed the younger woman away. 'You go to your husband,' she said, trying to sound cross. 'You married woman now.'

She opened the door and was gone. Ruth and Mark were alone at last. For a few seconds neither spoke. Each was suddenly shy in the presence of the other. Mark broke the spell by reaching across to the bottle and pouring out two glasses of wine. He handed one of the glasses to Ruth and raised his own. Ruth could see the soft, warm and so gentle expression in his eyes as he proposed the toast, 'To us ... and our future.'

'To us,' Ruth responded and they both took a sip of wine. 'As far as the future goes, that can take care of itself.'

They stood, smiling at each other, glasses in their hands, uncertain what to do next.

'I'm so happy for us, Mark,' Ruth said. 'I wouldn't care if we died together now.'

Mark raised his eyes and swallowed a mouthful of wine. 'Not before ...' His voice trailed off and he lowered his eyes.

Ruth laughed. She took a sip of wine from her own glass, and placed it down on the table, took Mark's glass and placed it deliberately alongside her own. She chuckled and took his hand in hers, leading him into the bedroom and glancing at the bed as they came through the door.

'You're right, Mark,' she pushed her nose into the side of his neck. 'Not before.' Slowly and deliberately, she started to take her sari and blouse off. Mark moved in front of the dressing table and removed his tunic, followed by his shirt. He sat on a stool in front of the dressing table and bent down to take off the sandals he was wearing. He slowly unfastened his breeches and started to stand up. As he did so, he looked in the large portable mirror on the dressing table. Ruth was standing at the side of the bed, looking at him. She was perfectly upright, quite calm, and absolutely naked. Mark could feel himself shudder and started to tremble. It was with a certain amount of difficulty that he finished removing his breeches. He turned round very slowly and saw that Ruth was now sitting up in bed, with her firm, round breasts showing above the blankets, their whiteness contrasting with the darkness of her face and neck. Mark hesitated, as if undecided about the next step. Ruth stretched out her arms to him, smiled, and called, 'Mark'. He slipped into the bed and lay on his back alongside her.

Ruth could feel he was trembling. She held his hand and they lay still for a few seconds. The trembling gradually subsided and she could feel the tension leave him as he lay beside her. His breathing was becoming more normal and the pounding of his heart was slowing down.

'Thank you for everything, Ruth,' she heard him whisper. 'For my life, for you, for your love.'

She turned on her side towards him, kissed him gently on the cheek and then nuzzled her nose on to his cheekbone. Mark turned on his side to face her and slid his arm around her neck. He gently kissed her forehead.

'You're so beautiful, Ruth,' he said in a husky voice.

She put her arm around him and pressed her breasts against his chest. Her face was pressed against Mark's and she could feel him hesitate.

'I'm glad you're still clean shaven,' she said softly. 'I would have hated it if you had grown a moustache or a beard. But I wish you'd been able to shave this evening.'

Mark laughed and it broke the tension in him. 'So do I,' he replied. Ruth moved on to her back, half pulling, half encouraging Mark to follow across to her side of the bed. She felt his body gradually sink down on hers. Now they would really be husband and wife, in spite of all the French priest had said. Ruth felt Mark's body become tense again and then he gradually lifted himself off her.

'What's wrong, darling?' she asked anxiously. 'Please tell me what's wrong.'

'I don't want to hurt you,' was Mark's half-strangled reply.

Ruth raised her head, searching for his lips with her own. When her mouth found his, she lowered her head, bringing his head down with her, their lips still locked together. She folded her arms around his shoulders, coaxing his chest down towards her. Gradually her hands slid down past his waist to the small of his back. Gently her hands moved lower and, as they reached Mark's pelvis, she pulled him into her.

# 14

They lay side by side in each other's arms, without needing to say anything. Ruth had gradually become aware of the slight smell of smoke from the burning buildings and the noise of the exchange of gunfire between the besieged in the citadel and their besiegers. During that explosion of love she had been oblivious of all else apart from joining together with Mark. Now they really knew each other. Now they were one person and would remain so always. Mark's hateful brother Henry came into her thoughts even though she tried to push him out. He had thought he could buy her body with jewels, money and fine clothes. Then there was the despicable Roland Lockyer and his contemptible friend Jake Firman. Both of them had accused her of being frigid and less than a woman. They had all been wrong, she thought. She had been proud to take Mark when he had nothing to give her but his love.

Ruth leant over Mark and pushed back the dark curls from his damp forehead. She looked at his face and thought how the years seemed to have rolled away. The hardness, the tension and the strain had gone, leaving him as she still remembered him from the first time they walked arm-in-arm. She bent to kiss his forehead and he smiled up at her.

'Thank you for making a woman out of me, Mark,' she whispered. 'The girl that you knew is no more.'

'Darling Ruth. Dearest sweetheart,' he murmured in reply, gently pushing her on her back.

Ruth laughed. 'Not now, darling. Captain Abiji Sing will be here soon.' Mark moved away from her and she could feel the disappointment in him. 'Don't be so heartbroken, Mark. We don't have to tell Sir George that the French President lent us a room. All we need to say is that we are married. Sir George is hardly likely to want us to spend our wedding night apart.'

'You're quite right, wife,' he replied with a chuckle.

They lay together without speaking for a quarter of a minute.

'When did you get this signet ring?' Ruth asked suddenly.

'Mother gave it to me the day before I returned to Sweden. It belonged to my brother Edmund. Just before he died he asked that it be kept for me to wear when I was old enough. It has the Fairbrother family crest on it.'

'Oh, Mark darling, I'm sorry. I didn't know. I hadn't seen you wear it before.' She started to slide it off the third finger of her left hand. 'Here. Take it, Mark. I can't possibly keep it. It's not meant for me. It's for you ... and your son, if we have one,' she said shyly.

'Wear it for tonight at any rate, sweetheart. Otherwise Sir George won't think we've been married.' He grinned wickedly. 'And he won't offer us a room. And you know what that will mean, don't you?'

He playfully tipped Ruth on to her back and started to make threatening motions towards her.

'Alright, darling,' she laughed. 'I didn't know you could be so masterful.' A gentle knock came on the door. It became more persistent until Ruth went into the sitting room to answer Sushi who told her, through the closed door, that they must get ready to leave. As she went back into the bedroom she saw that Mark had already moved across to the dressing table and picked up his shirt. At the sight of her standing in the doorway he dropped the shirt and went across to hold her in his arms. The feel of his strong, young body pressed against hers made Ruth weak with longing.

'Sushi says we must go now,' she told him in a voice between a whisper and a croak. He kissed her gently and then pushed her away.

'I'm sorry, dearest,' Mark said. 'You looked so lovely standing there.' For a brief moment Ruth felt afraid. It was a terrible responsibility to have to shoulder. Securing another human being's happiness. Caring for him for the rest of his life. She went past him to pick up her clothes from the side of the bed and, in as matter-of-fact voice as she could muster, she said, 'I won't be long, Mark.'

Ruth picked up the jug from the dressing table, poured water into the bowl, and washed off the dark stain from her hands, neck and face. Mark was dressing quickly in the meantime. As Ruth finished washing she picked up a cloth and dried herself. Mark looked in her direction and said softly. 'Now you look just as I remember you, darling.'

Ruth chuckled. 'Not quite, darling. That would have caused a scandal.'

He moved across quickly and placed his hands on the small of her bare back. 'You're just as I've always imagined you, sweetheart,' he said in a husky voice. 'As I've always longed for.'

Ruth pushed him away gently. 'Our hour is nearly up, Mark. I must get ready to go.'

He released her reluctantly. 'Of course, dearest.'

After they were both dressed they opened the door to find Narainji Pandit, Sushi and Captain Abiji Sing standing outside. The Maratha officer carried a lamp and a spear to which a white flag was attached. Sushi hurried past them into the bedroom and came out half a minute later carrying a white sheet under her arm. She embraced Ruth and said, 'May your children bring you much joy, my daughter.'

Narainji Pandit looked enquiringly in Sushi's direction. She handed the sheet to Abiji Sing and drew herself up so that she was standing erectly. 'You take this to Shivaji tomorrow,' she said. 'You tell him Sushi of Lalhulla village is proud to have a daughter who keeps her word to Shivaji. Now none of our lives will be forfeit.'

Captain Abiji Sing stared at Ruth for a few seconds, noting the change in her appearance. Then he nodded and turned to Mark, 'May you have many sons, Englishman.'

'Thank you, Captain,' Mark answered.

Ruth blushed and lowered her eyes. She had not realised that her union with Mark was going to be a subject for such public scrutiny. The sooner she and Mark were inside the English factory the better.

'We are ready to move off now. Follow me,' the Maratha officer commanded. The small party followed in silence, taking a different route from the one taken when they left the chapel. They came out on the opposite side of the French factory and saw the English factory about three hundred yards in front of them. Captain Abiji Sing positioned them in a line of four, with Mark and himself in the centre and Sushi and Ruth at opposite ends of the line. Narainji Pandit bowed and went back inside.

'We will walk forward together,' he ordered in a brisk, military style. 'Keep in line. Only stop if I tell you to or you hear the English sentries.'

It seemed to take an age to cross the flat piece of ground between the two factories. They could hear movement inside the English factory when they were about fifty yards away and five seconds later they stopped as they heard the cry of, 'Halt, who goes there?'

'Friend,' Mark shouted out.

'Advance friends. One by one. To be recognised,' came the reply.

As Mark stepped forward there was a second cry of, 'Halt,' followed by a call of, 'Women first.'

Mark stopped dead in his tracks and allowed Ruth to pass him. When she was about ten yards from the gate she shouted out, 'It's Ruth Parker. I mean Ruth Fairbrother.'

The figure of Sir George Oxindon appeared in the gateway.

'Make your mind up, Ruth. Come on now. We were going to send a search party for you.' He took a step or two outside the gateway and waved the others on. 'Very glad to see you all here,' Sir George said a trifle gruffly. 'We thought you'd never come.'

The three Maratha soldiers appeared from behind Sir George, looking very relieved. They saluted their officer and moved about ten yards away in the direction of the French factory. Captain Abiji Sing started to talk to Sir George in rapid Marathi but was obviously not making himself understood. 'Ruth,' Sir George called. 'What's the fellow say?'

She listened carefully and translated for Sir George's benefit. Captain Abiji Sing said that as the first part of the truce agreement had been honourably complied with, his troops would be withdrawn from the vicinity of the English factory with strict orders given not to open fire on the English. To avoid any further clash he would also withdraw from the French factory. He was going to report to Shivaji and arrangements would be made for the four captured factors held hostage to be returned to the English factory as soon as possible. 'Tell him that sounds satisfactory,' Sir George said.

The four Marathas took their leave when Ruth had relayed Sir George's agreement to them. Ruth watched them walk slowly back across the open space, moving inside the pool of light cast by the single lamp which one of the soldiers had taken from Captain Abiji Sing.

'Let's get inside, everybody,' Sir George called.

Ruth saw Peter Streynsham standing a little way back from the gate. Sir George stopped as they passed him and said, 'Make sure our men stay on guard, Master Streynsham. No relaxing now. I won't be happy until Shivaji leaves Surat.'

'Yes, Sir George,' Peter replied. 'We'll keep the same watch.'

Ruth thought how tired Sir George looked as they entered the building. The events of the last few days, the negotiation of the truce, and the shocking punishment inflicted on the prisoners had taken their toll.

Sir George turned to Sushi. 'Got to write to London about you.' He coughed. 'Tell them how brave you've been. The company's in your debt.' Sushi's eyes were bright with pride. 'Ruth was the brave one, President Sahib.'

'Well, I'll write to them about her,' he said, a little gruffly to hide his feelings. 'You run along now, Sushi.'

'What are we going to do about you, young fellow?' Sir George asked Mark. 'You can't rejoin the Imperial Army. Even if you wanted to, the Citadel is surrounded by Maratha troops.

I might lend you a fast horse and you could make a break for Bombay.'

'I'm a married man now, Sir George. I couldn't leave Ruth.'

Sir George looked searchingly at Mark. 'What's your other name, lad?' he said.

'Fairbrother, Sir George.'

'Yes. That's the name Ruth used when she was challenged.'

Sir George turned to Ruth. 'What did that Maratha captain mean? About first part of truce agreement being honourably complied with. What's the fellow getting at, Ruth?'

'I presume it means Mark and I being married by a French priest.'

'I suppose so,' Sir George replied. He looked at her roguishly. 'So you really went through with it? You had a proper Catholic wedding, Mistress Fairbrother?'

'Yes, Sir George.'

'You know a Catholic wedding doesn't count in English Law.'

'In the eyes of God, Mark and I are man and wife.'

'You're a stubborn girl, Ruth,' he said. 'And dogged with it. You always get your way. I'll lead the way to my private apartments. I'll let my bearer know you can use my private rooms tonight. That is if you wish.' He grinned across to Mark. 'You may prefer to wait until our chaplain is better.'

'I speak for both of us, Sir George,' Ruth answered. 'We accept your offer.'

'Well, your husband will have to work for it, Mistress Fairbrother. Stand to at four in the morning. Report to Master Streynsham for orders. It will be different from the Mogul army, Master Fairbrother. We have half a dozen native chaukadars with spears but the rest of the men manning the walls are Englishmen. Not like those French over there. Allowing the Marathas to occupy their factory. Whatever your political views, suppress them. I know Ruth's a Cromwellian but I'm not going to ask you what you are. We have royalists and Fifth Monarchy men mounting guard together. Former soldiers of the King's army standing shoulder to shoulder with veterans of the New Model Army. Monarchists taking orders from Republicans and Roundheads from Cavaliers. There are no differences between them here. They're all Englishmen facing a common danger.'

'I am an Englishman too,' Mark answered quietly. He smiled at Ruth. 'And my wife is an Englishwoman.'

'Thank you for joining us, Mark,' Sir George said. 'I'll go on my rounds now. Ruth knows the layout of my private apartments. I'm sure you'll both be anxious to get some sleep after the day we've all had. Good night.'

\* \* \* \* \*

Ruth opened the door and turned to Mark with a gleeful look on her face. 'I said it would be alright, darling.'

'It was touch and go.'

'No, Mark. You don't know him as well as I do.'

'Where's his wife?'

'She was visiting a friend in Swally when the Marathas attacked and cut off Surat. She must be worried about her husband. If I knew my husband was in danger,' Ruth said. 'I'd want to be with him.'

'Dearest,' Mark said softly. He kissed her and fumbled with the top of Ruth's sari without achieving anything. Ruth pushed him away.

'Don't be so impatient, Mark,' she laughed. 'There's a special way. It's easy when you know how.' She gave a slight tug and the sari began to slide slowly towards the floor. Mark stood transfixed. 'Hurry up and get those clothes off, darling. It will be four in the morning soon.'

Within a few seconds their clothes were in crumpled heaps on the floor. They stood looking at each other, giggling like two truant schoolchildren. Ruth took Mark's hand and led him towards a long couch on which some blankets had been placed for their use. This time there was no hesitation in their coming together.

\* \* \* \* \*

Ruth was woken up from a sound sleep by the noise of a loud explosion. Mark moved restlessly as he lay in her arms but did not wake. There was silence for a few seconds and Ruth lay absolutely still. She opened her eyes to see that the red glow in the night sky seemed much brighter. There must be fresh fires burning now. The silence was broken by the sound of musket fire, followed by the boom of one of the citadel guns. Mark began moaning as he lay in her arms and she held him close to comfort him. The noise he made was almost like a beaten puppy whining until suddenly he began shouting in a language which Ruth had never heard before. Ruth kissed him on the cheek and shook him gently.

'Mark. Mark,' she said softly. 'What's the matter?'

She shook him slightly more vigorously to rouse him. He looked at Ruth as he opened his eyes. She thought he looked frightened and said, 'It's alright, Mark. There's nothing to worry about. You're with me.'

Mark stared uncomprehendingly at her. He still seemed half asleep. 'Your wife, Ruth. Ruth,' she emphasised.

His eyes opened wide, he gave a little sob and buried his face in her shoulder. 'I'm with you now, Mark, darling. We're together now. I'll never leave you.' She caressed his head and held him as gently as if he was her child. 'That's better. Isn't it? No more need to worry,' she crooned as she continued to caress his head, which still lay buried in her shoulder. 'Tell me what's wrong, Mark. Then I can help you.' Mark made no reply. 'Look at me, darling. I want to help you. I'm your wife now.'

He raised his hand slowly and looked at her as though he was a whipped dog.

'Please, Mark,' Ruth said, 'what's wrong?'

'I had a dream,' he answered in a hesitant voice. 'I thought I was back in Denmark again. It all seemed so real.'

'I'm no dream. You're here beside me now, Mark.'

He tried to lower his head again but Ruth took his chin in her hand and kept it steady.

'Look at me, darling. You're my husband now. Hold on to that.'

'I know,' he replied. 'I'm not worthy of you.'

'Not worthy? What do you mean?'

'I'm sorry I woke you because of my dream. I'm sorry you saw me looking afraid.'

'After all you've been through today,' Ruth replied. She held him close to her. 'You've no need to apologise. I love you. That's all that matters.'

'Yes. But a man shouldn't be a weakling.'

'A weakling!' she exclaimed. 'You're not a weakling. You're a real man. It needed a real man for me to become a woman tonight. My man.'

Mark still looked crest-fallen and depressed.

'A weakling?' Ruth said, squeezing the muscles at the tops of his arms. 'I'd say there's a real man here.' In the dim light she saw Mark smile wanly as her hands caressed his forearms. 'I love those hairs on your arms,' she said. Her right hand moved across to his chest and started to move her fingers lightly through the hairs on his breastbone. 'I've never seen a man with hairs on his chest before. Dark and curly. Like the hair on your head,' she whispered gently, giving one of the hairs a slight tug.

'Don't do that. It hurts.'

'And who is going to stop me?' she teased, pulling gently at another hair on his chest.

Mark laughed. 'I will.'

Her hand still rested on his breastbone. 'I dare you to,' she said mockingly.

'If you don't stop, I'll have to take my will of you,' he replied half-jokingly.

Ruth tweaked another hair and said, 'I know, darling,' as her lips reached for his.

When they lay in each other's arms a few minutes later, Ruth's mood was more serious. They had so many years of their young lives still to spend together that they needed mutual support.

'Be proud, Mark,' she whispered in his ear. ''Be proud of the strength which you as a man gave to me as your woman. Just as I'm proud of you and will add my strength to yours.'

'I will always love you, dearest,' he said softly. 'I promise you that.' Ruth held him close and together they drifted off to sleep again.

\* \* \* \* \*

Ruth was woken up by the sound of prolonged knocking on the door of Sir George's private apartment. It was still night but she could see quite well from the dull red flow in the sky. As she looked across the city she could see there were many fires burning still. She hurriedly slipped on her clothes and opened the door to find Sushi standing outside.

'Very sorry, daughter of my heart,' she said. 'President Sahib wants your husband.'

'Yes, Sushi. I will wake him.'

'I wait here. You go with your husband. When you go, I will tidy rooms of President Sahib.'

Even in the dim light, Ruth could see Sushi's face smiling with happiness. When she had been a young girl, dreaming of her wedding day, she had never imagined that her wedding night would be spent in surroundings like this. How different it had been for Frances and Anne. Even Claire, sad though the outcome had been, was able to go to her wedding in peace and tranquility. She had no regrets, however. Whether she and Mark died that day or lived another fifty years, she knew how right were the words which her father had written in her mother's Bible, 'To my love, knowing you will be with me always'.

Ruth saw Mark was still sleeping on the long couch, when she went back into the apartment. She moved the lamp across to look at him more closely. All the strain and tension had gone. He looked so tranquil. Whatever the difficulties of their life together, she would always remember how he looked now. Ruth felt reluctant to wake him. She put the lamp down again and kissed him gently on the forehead. He stirred slightly but did not open his eyes.

'Mark, darling,' she said. 'Time to get up.' He opened his eyes and she saw recognition dawn.

'Ruth, dearest.' He sat up and put his arms round her shoulders.

She hugged him briefly and said, 'Quickly, Mark. Sir George is asking for you.'

A look of regret crossed his face.

'There will be plenty of time for us to be together when this is over,' she said. 'Be patient, my love. Sir George has had no sleep for four nights now. And some of his men have fared no better.'

'Of course. You're quite right, Ruth. I'll get up now. I know where my duty lies.'

Mark washed and dressed quickly and three minutes later he and Ruth were down in the courtyard talking to Sir George Oxindon and Peter Streynsham.

'Hope you had a restful night, Mistress Fairbrother,' Sir George said. 'Had to blow up some nearby houses during the night to act as a fire break. Hope the noise we made didn't wake you.'

Peter Streynsham grinned and Mark felt too embarrassed to reply but Ruth said cheerfully, 'I had an excellent night, Sir George. Best one for ages.'

He looked at her sharply. 'Good. Well, stay in the warehouse with the other ladies. Don't want any more heroics like yesterday. If the Marathas attack again, I don't want you rushing up to hold Mark's hand. They won't harm the women if you're all together but if you're with your husband you might get killed in the confusion.'

'I wouldn't care, Sir George. It wouldn't matter if ...'

'Don't argue, Ruth,' he snapped, interrupting her in mid-sentence. 'Do as I tell you for once. God knows what sort of life you'll lead Mark if we ever get out of this.' He paused but the only answer he received was a seraphic smile from Ruth. 'As for you, Mark. Peter Streynsham suggests you take charge of the six native chaukadars we have left. Most of them went away just before Shivaji's troops started sacking the city. Can't say I blame them. We're asking them to defend foreigners against men of their own race. Master Streynsham's been looking after them until now. He's also my deputy and it's too much for one man. You're experienced in commanding native troops while most of my factors here can hardly string a sentence together in the native dialect. You'll get no pay, of course. I have to account for every rupee I spend. But it will be a privilege for us to have you in our garrison.'

'It will be an honour to serve under your command, Sir George.'

'Right. I'll leave you in Master Streynsham's hands. He'll find you a hat to shelter your head from the sun. The clothes will have to wait. You come with me Ruth and change back into European clothes.'

Ruth put her arms round Mark and kissed him. 'Always remember I love you, darling,' she said.

'Come on, Ruth,' Sir George said gruffly.

* * * * *

Peter Streynsham led Mark away to the corner of the courtyard where half a dozen Indians were holding spears.

'As Sir George said, Master Fairbrother, this is all that's left of them. Do what you can.'

'Yes, of course,' Mark replied.

The Indians looked suspiciously at Mark as he approached. He was still wearing the uniform of a Mogul officer, apart from the missing turban. Peter Streynsham introduced each of the Indians to Mark in turn. There were two Marathas named Nabha Sing and Hira, two Gujeratis called Kashi Mathura and

Jaswant, a tall Pathan whose name was Sher Dil, and a fierce-looking Afghan named Ahmed Khan. Mark knew little Marathi or Gujerati and was glad that they all appeared to understand when he spoke to them in Urdu, the common language of the Mogul Empire.

'Very well, Master Fairbrother,' Peter Streynsham said after the introductions were completed. 'You and your men will be responsible for seeing nobody comes through the gate into the courtyard. The men who have been keeping watch at the moment have been on duty for forty eight hours without sleep. You can let any Europeans through but, if any Indians approach, call for me or Sir George.'

'What about weapons, Master Streynsham?' Mark asked.

'They have their spears. All of them are trained for close quarter work.' He grinned. 'Mind you, crowd control's a bit different from facing Shivaji's army. Anyway, I'll bring you a sword and a brace of pistols from the armoury. And let you have one of my hats as well. Can't let you have a musket, I'm afraid. They've all been sent up to our men on the roof. But I'm sure you'll give a good account of yourselves if the worst happens.'

Mark made no reply. He had looked too often into the eyes of that harlot, Danger, to be afraid now on his own account. He was thinking of Ruth and all the things he would have said if only he had time to spare.

'I'll be making my rounds again now. Be back in a few minutes time,' Peter Streynsham continued. 'I leave it to you to organise your watch. But make sure you and your men get some food soon. Good luck.'

Mark called the Indians to him after Peter Streynsham left. He divided them into two watches with Sher Dil, Nabha Sing and Jaswant in one watch and Ahmed Khan, Hira and Kashi Mathura in the second watch. He then took the first three towards the gate and introduced himself to the three Englishmen standing guard, each armed with a brace of pistols and a sword. They obviously remembered him from the previous night because the one who appeared to be in charge held out his hand and said. 'I'm Luke Farmerdale. Glad you're with us, Master Fairbrother.'

'Thank you,' he said as they shook hands. 'My name's Mark.' He looked at the other man's face. The chin was black with the stubble of about three days' growth of beard and there were heavy, dark lines of weariness underneath Luke Farmerdale's eyes. 'You look as though you need some help.' Luke smiled feebly. 'Master Streynsham has arranged for me and the squad of Indians to relieve you. I'm sure you'd welcome some sleep.'

Luke and his two companions nodded and moved off wearily, leaving Mark and his group to take over. It was becoming brighter by the minute and Mark looked across to where the Maratha flag still flew from the roof of the French factory. Somehow, it seemed a shorter distance from the English factory than when he had been crossing the open space in the dark. The walls of the French factory now looked menacingly close. Mark felt naked, going on guard duty without any side arms of his own. A few minutes later, Peter Streynsham returned with the sword, hat and pistols he had promised. He looked briefly at the three Indians guarding the gateway and seemed satisfied by what he saw.

The morning dragged slowly by. Mark's men went off in turn to eat and Ahmed Khan brought back some food for him from the kitchen. At about eleven in the morning, Maratha soldiers began pouring out of the French factory three hundred yards away. Mark quickly called the remainder of his group to him, lining them up across the gateway. He sent Kashi Mathura to fetch Sir George and Peter Streynsham. He gave a few words of encouragement to his men, feeling that he needed encouragement as well. Peter Streynsham hurried over to be told the news and asked Mark to let Sir George know he was going on to the roof in order to organise the defences.

Half a minute later Mark left the gateway to meet Sir George hurrying across the courtyard, with Ruth and Luke

Farmerdale following behind. Sir George and Luke both had a brace of pistols in their belts and were carrying swords. Mark outlined briefly what he had seen and where Peter Streynsham had gone. 'Perhaps the Marathas want to parley,' said Sir George. 'But it looks unlikely.' After a short pause, he went on to ask, 'Can't you do anything with that wife of yours, Mark. Flatly refuses to stay behind with the rest of the women.' Mark looked at Ruth and smiled. She was in European dress and had washed, combed, and brushed her hair. She looked even lovelier than on the previous day.

His reverie was disturbed by Sher Dil calling out, 'Captain Sahib.' Mark hurried forward to the gateway with Sir George forcibly restraining Ruth.

'What's going on, Mark?' Sir George called out.

'It's Captain Abiji Sing standing in front of his troops. I estimate there are four hundred of them lined up in ranks in front of the walls of the French factory. Abiji Sing is walking over here alone. Now he's stopped. Given a salute and walked back again.'

The Maratha troops let out a roar of 'Hurr. Hurr. Mahdev.' It was the Maratha war cry which had so often struck terror into the hearts of their enemies. Ruth broke free from Sir George's grasp and ran towards her husband.

'Don't come any closer, Ruth,' Mark shouted as he pulled the two pistols from his belt. 'Stay where you are, Ruth.'

To Sir George's great surprise, she stopped. Mark slowly replaced the pistols in the belt round his waist.

'What's going on now, Mark?' Sir George shouted.

'The Maratha captain's talking to them. They all look very cheerful. Now he's given a command. They've turned to their left and are moving off. I do believe they're going away. The yellow Maratha flag's come down from the French factory, Now someone is putting up the fleur-de-lis instead. They must be keeping to their agreement to leave us alone.'

'Christ be praised,' Sir George answered. He looked at Ruth, still standing motionless five yards behind Mark. 'You can go to your husband now, Ruth. I'd never have believed it possible.'

Ruth ran towards Mark and put her head on his shoulders. 'Oh, Mark,' she said. 'I thought they were going to attack us. I thought you'd be killed.'

'So did I, dearest,' he whispered softly. His wife's voice reminded him so much of the hills and green dales of the country he had left so many years before.

Ruth started to cry. 'I wanted to die with you.'

Mark held her in his arms as she continued to sob. 'Remember what you said last night?' he whispered. 'About us giving strength to each other.'

She nodded. 'Let me go now, Mark. I'll be alright.'

Sir George had been waiting a few yards away. He came up slowly when they separated.

'Sorry I'll have to leave you on duty, Mark. Rest of my men are dog tired. This may be another of Shivaji's stratagems. Until his troops leave Surat, we'll still have to mount guard.'

'I understand, Sir George,' he answered quietly.

'Ruth,' Sir George called.

'I'm coming,' she replied. She smiled wistfully at her husband and then started to walk slowly away, side by side with Sir George.

Mark stood looking at her as she walked across the courtyard. Now that she was dressed in European clothes, she reminded him so much of the shy, young girl he had known during those few, precious, sunlit days so long ago. The metamorphosis from the strong-willed, self-confident, self-sufficient young woman, dressed in native costume, who had dared to outface the dreaded Shivaji, was complete. Mark felt very humble that he could have such an effect on another human being. She had given him his life, his will and his strength, at the price of her own. It was up to him to see that she was protected from all harm in future. She had told the French priest that she was prepared to sacrifice her honour, even her immortal soul, on his behalf. How could he ever repay such devotion?

He was recalled to the present by the sight of the guards at the gateway gradually drifting away. Mark issued a sharp word of command and lined them up in front of him, telling them that the President Sahib had not yet ordered them to stand down.

\* \* \* \* \*

The next forty-eight hours were eerie in the extreme. Ruth saw only brief glimpses of Mark from time to time. He was on duty constantly, only snatching an hour or so of sleep each night. By Friday afternoon, a large part of the town had been destroyed by fire and Sir George went out on several occasions to make fire breaks by blowing up nearby houses in order to protect the English factory. He also went out a number of times to rescue people whose houses were being attacked by looters.

The smoke was so thick that it hung like a cloud over Surat and the night was almost as bright as the day. The imperial soldiers besieged in the fort were still shooting down at the Maratha troops. At infrequent intervals the imperial artillery also opened fire from the walls of the fort without inflicting any real damage on the Marathas and only adding to the general confusion. The noise rose to a crescendo on Saturday evening and stopped suddenly just before midnight. As the day dawned, Mark sent a message asking Sir George to come to the gate quickly. Ruth accompanied the President and when they arrived they found Mark and his men trying to hold back hundreds of refugees who had come back from the countryside and were trying to force their way into the courtyard. The distraught crowd was yelling that an imperial army was on its way to the relief of the city and a battle would soon be fought. Ruth told Sir George that the people were begging for English protection.

'Tell them the women and children can come in first, Ruth,' Sir George said. 'The men will have to be searched by your husband and his guards.'

Sushi had also arrived by this time and when Ruth relayed this news to the crowd Sushi shouted out that real men would stand back. They would not want their wives and children trampled on. The sight of a Maratha woman standing alongside the English President had a calming effect on the crowd and they allowed the women and children to file quietly past the guards. The men followed one by one after they had been searched for weapons.

'Ruth,' Sir George asked. 'Can you get Jacoba to organise some food for these people? Take Sushi with you. Jacoba can't speak good English. Let alone understand what the natives say.'

The next two hours Ruth spent in reassuring the women that they would be safe in the factory, while she and Sushi helped to feed the families and to care for the children. In the middle of the morning, the vanguard of the imperial army reached the French factory and a Mogul officer came to pay his respects to Sir George Oxindon. The officer looked a little curiously at Mark, dressed in the uniform of the imperial army, wearing a European sword, carrying a brace of pistols in his belt and wearing a European hat. Before Sir George came to reciprocate the courtesy, the imperial officer was surrounded by a group of refugees cursing the governor, praising the English and only held back with difficulty by the men under Mark's command. After a brief word or two with Sir George, he beat a hasty retreat.

A few minutes later they heard a volley of shots from the direction of the fort. Mark called his group together again and the factors ran to their defences once more, to the accompaniment of shrieks from the refugees saying that the battle had already began. No more shots were heard, however, and the streets were soon filled with angry people. As far as Ruth could make out, the governor had left his fort when the imperial army arrived, only to be greeted with hisses and shouts of abuse. These cries turned to curses as the governor ordered the garrison under his command to open fire on the crowd. Two demonstrators were killed and several injured. That evening the general commanding the relieving force called on the President. He told Sir George that a deputation of worthy citizens of Surat had called on him to complain about the cowardice of the governor and his men and to contrast the conduct of the imperial officials with that of those in the English factory. The deputation had asked if the English President could be given some reward as a mark of respect for his bravery. When the general offered Sir George a jewelled sword, a gold vest and a horse, Sir George declined the gifts. When pressed to accept them, he said, 'These gifts are becoming to a soldier like yourself, general, but we are merchants in this factory.' The only request he made to the general was that Mark should be formally discharged from the imperial army.

* * * * *

Two days after the relief of Surat, Lady Oxindon returned to the factory from her involuntary stay in Swally. She told her husband that Maratha patrols had been seen on the outskirts of Swally during her stay and that a detachment of Shivaji's cavalry had camped by the road to Surat at one time. Apart from that, they had escaped the attentions of Shivaji's tribesmen. The handful of traders was still standing guard in the English factory, together with the men under Mark's control. This was necessary because of outbreaks of looting in the city, in spite of the presence of imperial troops. The fires had now been extinguished and life was gradually returning to normal as the refugees returned.

When Lady Oxindon enquired how everybody had fared during the siege, she was intrigued by the news of Ruth's marriage. She gave an approving nod when Mark was introduced to her and wished him and Ruth happiness. According to Lady Oxindon, Maria Ferrara had heard of Ruth's past difficulties and had asked that Ruth and Sushi should stay with the Ferraras. When Sir George learnt of this invitation, he told Ruth to go to the Ferraras for a week, taking Mark with her, and then return in a week's time. Luke Farmerdale lent Mark some clothes and Sir George arranged for one of the company's bullock carts to take them from Surat to Swally. Peter Streynsham gave Mark a brace of pistols from the armoury, in case they met stragglers or looters, and said he looked forward to seeing them at the end of seven days.

As the bullock cart trundled slowly along towards the Ferrara's bungalow, Ruth thought how different it had been the last time she went there with Claire on the eve of her wedding day. She squeezed Mark's arm and when he looked at her, he saw tears in her eyes.

'What's the matter, darling?' he said. 'What's wrong?'

'I was thinking about Claire,' she replied. 'I promised I'd never leave her.'

Mark was silent for a few seconds. 'I know Claire would want you to think of the future, not of the past. I'm sure your Portuguese friends would say the same thing.'

Ruth made no reply and as the bullock cart turned on to the track leading to the Ferrara's bungalow, Sushi said 'Pushpa will be pleased you marry husband. She will be sorry she was not there.'

Ruth smiled slightly. 'Tell your daughter not to worry. I will get married again just so you can both see me.'

The bullock cart drew up in front of the bungalow and the syce called out. One of the bearers left the bungalow to greet Ruth and Sushi while Des Raj came from the direction of the stables. He greeted his mother-in-law as the bearer went inside to fetch Maria. Des Raj called out to his wife after he had greeted Ruth and then looked enquiringly in Mark's direction.

'This is my husband Mark, Des Raj.'

'Your husband!' His face broke into a broad grin. 'Pushpa not believe it.'

'It's true. Sushi was there.'

'I very happy for you both.' He turned to Mark. 'A thousand blessings on you, sahib.'

'Thank you,' Mark replied.

Maria came out of the bungalow at that moment and Pushpa walked towards them at the same time. The next minute passed in a furious exchange of words between Maria and Ruth on one hand and Pushpa and Sushi on the other hand. It seemed to Mark that all four were talking at the same time. There were tears in Maria's eyes as she clung to Ruth while Pushpa smiled broadly at seeing her mother and Ruth again. Maria asked Des Raj to look after the luggage, gave Sir George's syce a small tip, and escorted Ruth and Mark into the bungalow.

'Lady Alice not say you married, Ruth,' she said, looking in a half-accusing way at Mark.

'I know, Maria. It happened during the siege.'

Maria looked down at Ruth's left hand and noticed the absence of a wedding ring. Ruth laughed. 'Mark and I really are married, Maria. You ask Sushi.' Maria looked embarrassed. 'I no think you naughty girl, Ruth,' she replied defensively. 'Just when Claire married, many people there. You marry Mark and I not there.'

'I'm sorry, Maria. It was all such a rush. Father Dellon, the Capuchin missionary, married us.'

'I know him. He comes to our Church sometimes,' she said, continuing to look at Mark in a slightly hostile fashion.

'I know you're Ruth's oldest friend in India, Senhora Ferrara,' Mark said. 'Neither Ruth nor I are Catholics but Father Dellon married us because the English chaplain was ill at the time.'

'But why you marry so quickly?' Maria asked, not really convinced by his explanation.

'That's a long story. May we tell you and your husband when he returns from the port? I assure you Ruth and I will marry again. In our own church this time. And you and your husband will be the guests of honour.'

'Fernando will be so pleased for Ruth. We were sad when we hear about Claire and how Ruth was treated. My husband will be so glad for Ruth now. And for you too, Mark,' she added hastily.

\* \* \* \* \*

Fernando returned from the port area in the early afternoon. It was obvious that Maria had told him the news before they came in together to the courtyard where Ruth and Mark were sitting. He shook hands warmly with Mark, kissed Ruth's cheeks, and offered both of them his warmest congratulations.

'I am so happy for you, Ruth. For both of you,' he continued. 'I tell you, you like Mumtaz Mahal, Ruth. Wife of Emperor Shah Jahan. Nearly twenty when you marry.'

'You were quite right, Fernando. And when the English chaplain marries us, we want you both to be our guests of honour,' Ruth replied.

'It will be our great pleasure,' Maria said. 'You wish to come to my house on day before wedding? Like Claire?' she asked mischievously.

Ruth blushed slightly and took hold of Mark's hand. 'Thank you, Maria. It will not be necessary. But thank you for the thought.'

'You are fortunate man, Mark. Not only do you choose most lovely girl in Surat but Ruth is also one of the most clever.'

'I know I'm lucky, Fernando,' Mark laughed. 'Ruth chose me for a husband. I had no choice.'

Fernando raised his eyebrows and looked enquiringly at Ruth.

'I had no choice either, I assure you,' Ruth said. 'But let Mark tell you and Maria how it happened.'

They listened intently as Mark told the story of how he and Ruth first met, their long separation, the different ways in which they had come to India, his capture by the Marathas, and how Ruth had saved him from execution. He then described their marriage in the French factory and the events of the past five days. When Mark finished, Maria rose from her chair, embraced Ruth, and kissed her on both cheeks.

'You both have special angels guarding you,' Fernando said seriously. 'God must mean you to have very happy life together. He take so much trouble to make you husband and wife. My home is yours. For as long as you wish.'

'Thank you for your kindness, Fernando,' Mark replied. 'But we've promised Sir George Oxindon that we'll return to Surat in a week's time.'

'I think of Ruth like my daughter,' Maria said, looking at Mark. 'Now I think of you like my son. You will always be welcome in our house.'

'And what is news of husband of Claire?' Fernando asked tentatively.

'He is still in Bombay,' Ruth answered. 'He went there two days before we knew Shivaji would attack Surat. He has not yet returned.'

'I see,' Fernando paused. 'Please tell me if you need help again.' Ruth took Mark's hand and smiled at him. There was no need to reply.

'This young man and young woman only have few days with us,' Maria intervened. 'We make them happy times,' She smiled at Ruth. 'I put you and husband in room you and Claire shared.'

Ruth grimaced momentarily, thinking of the two small beds in which she and Claire had slept. She recovered herself quickly and said, 'Thank you.'

Maria laughed. 'You look disappointed, Ruth.' She looked across at Fernando. 'I remember when I was young. I see you get matrimonial bed.'

Ruth blushed slightly and lowered her eyes. 'I tell servants to make room ready for you,' Maria continued. 'Make it fit for new bride and husband.'

\* \* \* \* \*

The next six days were the happiest that Ruth and Mark had known until that time. Maria and Fernando had evening meals with them but, apart from that, left them entirely to their own devices. Sushi kept a discreet distance, contenting herself with arranging for Fernando's dhobi to have their clothes washed, the sweeper to keep the floor of their room clean, supervising Ruth's daily bath, and beaming approvingly at Mark each time she saw him.

For the first three days they were content either to sit on the verandah, telling each other of their lives since they last met, or to walk hand in hand through the Ferrara's garden. As if by unspoken agreement, they never discussed the future. On the evening of the third day, Fernando told them that the area was now clear of looters and stragglers and he offered to lend them his carriage so that they could travel round. Ruth declined the offer, saying she would rather walk with her husband as they had done when they first met.

The weather next morning was perfect as they set out together. It was no warmer than a day in early May in England. They walked hand in hand under the trees beside the bank of the River Tapti. The brilliant sunshine reflected on the water, making constantly changing patterns of dancing lights. Ruth felt herself smiling as she recalled how gauche Mark had been when they first met and how naive she had been about her own feelings. Mark sensed what was going through her mind and placed his right hand over hers as it rested on his left forearm. He turned his head towards her and smiled as they continued walking.

'This is so right,' he said.

'Yes, Mark,' Ruth replied. After three or four seconds, she said thoughtfully. 'If I had been a couple of years older, I would have fought to have kept you in England. It would have saved you all those years of danger and exile.'

'If I'd been wiser,' he answered. 'I would have stayed. None of us knows what the future holds but we've our future together now. For always. Don't let's always regret lost opportunities, dearest.'

'I promise, darling.'

They walked on towards the quayside. It was the first time Ruth had seen it since she had arrived with Claire eight months before. There were fewer ships riding at anchor, presumably because their masters had sailed after hearing of Shivaji's attack on Surat. Over fifty vessels were still left in the harbour, however, and the godowns of the foreign traders seemed almost as busy as ever.

Each foreign trading company flew its own national emblem over the godowns it owned and all the European ships flew their own national flags. There were three English ships at the quayside, flying the flag of Saint George. Ruth could hear the excited shouts of the English sailors as she and Mark walked close to one of these ships. She laughed. 'Does it make you feel homesick?'

'Homesick? No. My home is where my heart is. And my heart's right here beside me.'

'Darling,' she whispered, as she squeezed his arm. 'Would you mind if I wrote to Elizabeth?'

'Elizabeth? I hadn't thought about it. Last letter I had was a year ago. Told me that Henry was a member of Parliament now. That world seems so far away.'

'I'd like to write, Mark. And I think you ought to write to your mother.' They reached the end of the quay and started to retrace their steps.

'Mother knew how I felt, sweetheart. How d'you suppose she'll feel now?' he asked bitterly.

'You're her son, Mark. Her flesh and blood. I'm sure she believed she was acting for the best then. But if you don't tell Lady Catherine, she'll resent us both.'

'I'm sure you're right, my dearest. I'll send a letter to her as soon as we've been married by the English chaplain. You write to my sister at the same time, Ruth.'

'You remember the long gallery at your home, don't you, darling?'

'How could I forget?' Mark asked. 'You and the posy of lily of the valley flowers!' They both laughed.

'Two years after you went back to Sweden, Mark, your mother and I were walking arm in arm in the long gallery.'

He stopped the two of them in their tracks and turned to look at Ruth with an expression of surprise on his face. 'You haven't told me that before.'

'I know, darling.' She ran her hands down the side of Mark's chest and rested them round his waist.

'Your mother had a sixth sense of what would happen even then.' Ruth looked Mark straight in the eyes, smiling at him broadly. 'You ought to write to her now, you know. She told me that I had good, childbearing hips. Let's not walk back, Mark. Let's get a tonga to Maria's house. Let's see if your mother was right.'

'Yes, sweetheart,' he answered huskily.

\* \* \* \* \*

When they were sitting in the courtyard with their hosts after the evening meal on the sixth day of their visit, Fernando told them that he had sent a message to the English President that day. He wrote to Sir George to let him know that there was no need for a bullock cart to be sent for Ruth and Mark as he, Fernando, would bring them back in his carriage.

'Thank you for your kindness, Fernando,' Mark said. 'But you needn't have troubled.'

'It is my pleasure to help Ruth and her handsome husband. I also tell Sir George I wait until he sees you. Otherwise I take our friend Ruth back.'

Mark looked puzzled. 'Surely there's no need to bring Ruth back here?'

'I mean no disrespect Mark. You ask me to be like father of bride when English chaplain marries you. Very well. I speak like father of bride. How you look after Ruth? I promise Senhor Lockyer last year I pay Sushi her wages for twelve months. That time soon up. How you pay wages for servant of your wife?' Mark looked crestfallen. 'Maria and I very fond of Ruth,' Fernando went on. 'She very much in love with you and I know you make good husband for her. But you ask Sir George what he do for you and for Ruth.'

'Yes, I know, Fernando. I'll speak to Sir George. I realise you're only thinking of Ruth's future.'

'Cheer up, darling,' Ruth said brightly. 'We're both young and fit. I'm sure Sir George will find something for us to do.'

'Sushi is worried,' Maria said after a brief pause.

'Worried?' Ruth asked. 'What on earth is she worried about?'

'She thinks you and Mark get bungalow of your own. You will have other servants. Other servants not understand how Sushi and you like mother and daughter, not like servant and mistress.'

'I'll tell her she mustn't worry,' Ruth replied. 'Even if Mark and I have a bungalow it will be sometime in the future. And Sushi will always be very dear to me. I must go to her now.' She rose from her chair.

'No, Ruth,' Maria said firmly. 'Sushi is quite right. Stay where you are. I know you both very fond of each other. But other servants not understand. I will tell Pushpa tonight. She tell Sushi to go back with you tomorrow. You talk to her on way. But Sushi thinking of you always. You no longer little Ruth who stay here with sister. You Senhora Mark Fairbrother to my servants from now on and in future.'

'I want to go to her now. She must be very unhappy.'

'Maria is right,' Mark interrupted gently. 'Please sit down, Ruth.' He waited until she resumed her seat. 'Sushi knows it's different now you're my wife. If we have other servants, we can't treat her any different from the rest. The others wouldn't think it fitting. I have lived among these people for three years. They have a great sense of position and feeling for place.'

Ruth's eyes filled with tears. She was remembering the harsh words used by Lady Fairbrother, reminding her to remember the station in life to which God had called her. She recalled that she was an orphan, brought up as a foster-child by the Trents, sent out to India with Claire because there was no room for her with her foster-sister, Frances, and then abandoned and humiliated by Claire's husband. What was her position? What was her place?

'Excuse me, Maria,' she said. 'Excuse me, Fernando. I'd like to go to bed now.'

Mark and their hosts looked anxious. Mark sprang to his feet saying, 'Of course, darling.' He turned to Maria and Fernando with a look of concern in his eyes. 'Please excuse us.'

'Goodnight, Ruth.' Fernando stood up as Ruth rose from her chair. 'Goodnight, Mark.'

'Holy Mary and all the angels will watch over you,' Maria said.

'I take you back in the morning,' Fernando added.

Mark slid his arm round Ruth's waist and they walked slowly towards their room. As he opened the door, she burst into tears.

'Darling, what's wrong?' he asked.

'Who am I?' she sobbed.

'I don't understand,' he said, holding her in his arms. 'You're my wife.'

'I know that, Mark. But before that I was a nobody. I was poor. I had nothing. Sushi cared for me when I was an outcast. Why can't I be friends with her now?'

'You can always be friends with Sushi, dearest. But she can't be your servant if you have other servants in the house. Maria is right. And so is Sushi.'

'What am I to do, Mark? Please tell me.'

'Hold me tight, dearest. That's what you're to do. Remember you're Mistress Fairbrother now. I know the Ruth Parker who saved my life will always be by my side and I will always remember you that way. But other people will forget Ruth Parker and think only of Ruth Fairbrother. Be patient, darling. We both have to see it through other people's eyes. Fernando does not know the boy who ran, laughing, hand in hand with a girl, up the steps of Aireton Hall. He sees only a man, with a hostage to fortune in the shape of a wife. Other people do not know the brave girl who dared to defy Shivaji to save the life of a foolish youth she had once known. They see only the wife of a rather ordinary man.'

'You're not foolish, Mark. You're not ordinary.'

'That's because you see me with special eyes. As I see you with the same special eyes. Our memories are our private secrets because they've made us what we are.

'But what's to become of me, Mark?'

'Darling,' he whispered softly. 'That's in God's hands. But I'll give him a little help. Trust me. Remember our first night together. You said that the girl that I knew was no more. You can't look back now.'

Ruth pressed herself tightly against him.

'I know Mark. I do trust you. I meant it when I said thank you for making a woman of me. Let me thank you again, darling. Kiss me, please.'

# 15

Sir George rose from his chair as Mark and Ruth were shown into his private drawing room. Although he still appeared to be a little tired, the strained look on his face, which Ruth had seen when they left seven days earlier, had gone.

'Where's Senhor Ferrara?' Sir George asked after the exchange of conventional greetings.

'He's sitting outside in his carriage,' Mark replied.

'He wrote to me. Seems to be taking a great deal of interest in the welfare of you two young people.'

'He and his wife have been very kind to Ruth and I,' Mark replied.

'Well, we don't want him taking Ruth back with him, do we? I've thought a great deal about the two of you in the last week.'

Sir George hesitated for a few seconds.

'You'll be glad to hear the four factors who were held hostage are being released. They've been kept in the far South of Shivaji's territory. Also a courier has brought a note from Shivaji waiving any claim for compensation. I wrote to London about it. Difficult to explain to them why we should be arguing with Shivaji for three years and now it's all settled in a matter of hours. They're probably thinking I'm writing a work of fiction. Especially when the directors won't be able to read it for another three months.'

The President then went on to say that Thomas Robertson's tour of duty in Surat was now over. He would be returning to England with his wife to take up a post at the East India Company's office in London. They had arranged to leave on the 'Eagle' which would sail in six days. Their bungalow was owned by the company but the furniture inside was their own. The Robertsons were quite happy to sell their furniture to Ruth and let her stay with them until they left, although there was insufficient room for Mark as well. All their existing servants were prepared to stay, apart from the syce, who had been with them for five years but now wanted to go back to his family and his farm.

'How will I pay for this?' Ruth asked. 'And the servant's wages?'

Sir George told her there was money due to her for acting as his interpreter. The rest of the money required could be an advance against her husband's wages.

'But I don't work for the East India Company, Sir George,' Mark said.

'That's what I want to talk to you about. What's your military experience?'

Mark outlined his service in the Swedish army, giving details of the two campaigns in Jutland during the Baltic wars. He then told Sir George about his service with the Mogul army, beginning with the suppression of the Pathan rebellion, garrison duty in Delhi and Agra and, finally, forming part of the imperial garrison in Surat.

'How did a man with all your experience manage to get himself taken prisoner?' Sir George asked.

Mark's cheeks flushed and Ruth could feel the tension rising in him. 'I had eight men on picquet two miles from Surat. My job was to keep a watch out for the Marathas and send a message to the fort when I saw them. About five hundred of their cavalry came galloping towards us and I sent a man on a horse to ride towards the town. They cut him down before he had gone three hundred yards. These hill ponies they have move very fast. They can travel sixty miles a day during a campaign. Anyway, the Maratha squadron leader called on us to surrender and I ordered my men to lay down their arms.

'I see,' Sir George replied.

'I've known too much blood shed in hopeless situations,' Mark said defensively. 'My seven men wouldn't have delayed Shivaji's cavalry for more than a few seconds.'

'I know, Mark. You can be as brave as anyone when it's needed. I saw you standing in our gateway when we all thought the Marathas were going to attack. Master Streynsham was also very impressed by the way you took command of what was left of our Indians here.'

Sir George then went on to say that he was planning to recruit twenty Indians to protect the factory from future attack. They would be used for ceremonial duties as mace bearers and pikemen but, in addition, would be taught to handle muskets.

'I want you to command them, Mark. And to train them. I'll write to London telling the directors I'm engaging you with the temporary rank of Captain. Your pay will be one hundred and forty rupees a month. Less than your pay in the imperial army but then our men will only be used for ceremonial or defensive purposes, or as escorts. And the East India Company will pay you when it's due. You won't have it months in arrears. What do you say, Mark?'

'I accept, Sir George.'

'Good, Captain Fairbrother. I'll give you an advance of pay so that you can buy clothes for Ruth and yourself and settle up with the Robertsons. Stay in the factory while Ruth and Sushi are with the Robertsons. Master Streynsham will arrange quarters for you.' He grinned. 'You're a soldier, of course. You're used to living rough.'

Ruth spoke up before Mark could reply. 'Wherever my husband is, I want to be with him,' she said firmly.

'We're not used to catering for ladies here,' Sir George replied. 'All the wives live outside the factory. It's going to be pretty uncomfortable for Mark.'

'My heart will be desolate if I am not at his side,' Ruth answered.

Sir George looked at her with a mixture of amusement and respect.

'You two will be glad to hear that Chaplain Boland is nearly recovered from his fever. I suggest you see him during the next two or three days. If you really want to rough it in here with Mark, see Peter Streynsham. He'll probably find a storeroom you can share.'

\* \* \* \* \*

Fernando congratulated Mark on his taking service with the company. He was extremely pleased to hear that they would take over the Robertsons' bungalow in six days' time and asked if he and Maria might call on them when they were settled in.

'Of course you may come. Maria is my oldest friend,' Ruth replied. 'I'll stay with Mark in the English factory for the next week. Could you take Sushi back with you and return with her in six days time?'

'If this is your wish, Ruth.'

'You cannot send me back!' Sushi interrupted angrily. 'You have your izzat to think of. You Captain Memsahib now. Burra memsahib. You cannot stay in factory without servant to look after you. All people think you too poor to have servant.'

'But, Sushi. You will have nowhere to stay,' Ruth said. 'My husband and I will have one small room. Where will you go?'

'I stay in factory like I stay when Shivaji here. I stay outside your door like time you get married.'

'Let her stay, Ruth,' Mark said. 'We go to the bungalow in six days' time. The Robertsons' servants will look after us then. The only one who is leaving is the syce.'

Ruth looked from Sushi to Mark and back again. Although Sushi's expression was angry, her eyes were pleading. As Ruth continued to look at her, Sushi's expression softened. Ruth remembered only too well the dark days which followed when she fled Roland Lockyer's house into Sushi's arms and how Sushi had held and comforted her. She recollected how Sushi had asked Chand Narain to save her Bible and a pair of her shoes from the possessions which Roland had ordered the servants to burn. How could she forget such kindness? How could she refuse anything to someone who had been as dear as a mother to her? She put out her arms and Sushi came forward to embrace her. Neither woman spoke for a few seconds. It was sufficient just to be held in Sushi's arms. 'Go to your husband now, daughter of my heart,' Sushi said to her at last.

Late in the following afternoon Mark was sitting in the factory's small armoury with Ahmed Khan, the Afghan, one of the chaukadars who had served under him in the siege of the factory. They had just finished checking the quantity of arms and powder for which Peter Streynsham had previously taken responsibility. It had been a tiring morning going round the factory with Peter, examining their defences, not just against a possible renewal of attack by the forces of Shivaji but the more immediate threat of thieves breaking in. He was glad to see that the armoury was reasonably well provided with muskets, pistols and blunderbusses, as well as with a variety of swords, halberds, pikes and spears. Tomorrow he would start teaching his men how to handle muskets. In the meantime, there was the chance to relax and drink the tea which Nabha Sing, one of the Marathas, had brought for him. His peaceful mood was suddenly shattered by the sound of shouts and screams from the floor below. Mark went to the door, followed by Ahmed Khan, as the cries from the courtyard became more hysterical. Kashi Mathura, one of his Gujeratis, came running towards him. As soon as he saw Mark, he called, 'Come quickly, Captain Sahib. A mad dog has bitten two children.'

'Ahmed. Kashi. Take a spear each,' Mark ordered.

He loaded a pistol, locked the door of the armoury and ordered the two chaukadars to follow him. When Mark reached the ground floor he was surrounded by about a dozen weeping Indian women, who were accompanied by about twenty frightened children and half a dozen men. Two of the children had been badly bitten on the legs and arms. Ruth and Sushi had come from the storeroom which was Mark's temporary home and were trying to comfort the women.

'Ruth,' Mark called out. 'Get these children to the physician. The dog may be rabid.'

'You men! Come with me!' he shouted to the men who had accompanied the women and children. 'Bring lathis with you. We must find the dog!'

Ruth looked concerned when Mark was issuing these orders but made no attempt to interfere.

'Sushi!' Mark called across. 'What are these women saying?' She hurried across and told him that the dog was roaming the servants' quarters at the side of the factory. It had run, snarling and foaming at the mouth, from the direction of the fort but did not belong to anyone who worked in the English factory. Mark divided the men into two groups, with one group led by Ahmed Khan and the second group by Kashi Mathura.

'Follow me,' he commanded, making towards the archway. 'You come as well, Sushi,' he said. 'I may need an interpreter.'

Some of the men appeared reluctant to accompany him and stopped just outside the factory.

'Be proud,' he said, addressing them in Urdu. 'You are men. Do you want to cower away from one dog while your children are in fear? How will you earn your children's respect?'

'If there are any of you mice who want to stay behind with the children, give me your lathi,' Sushi said, talking to them in Marathi. 'I, grandmother Sushi, will be at the side of Captain Fairbrother. Any of you who lags behind me is not man enough to share his wife's bed tonight.'

There was a certain amount of muttering as Mark led the men off but none stayed behind. When they came to the row of huts he spread the men out in line abreast, with Ahmed Khan and Kashi Mathura at opposite ends of the line and himself in the middle. They moved forward slowly and carefully. Each hut they came to was approached cautiously and the line stopped until the 'all clear' was given. Just as Mark began to think they would have to search elsewhere, two of the men dropped their lathis and started to run, pursued by a large, white dog. Kashi Mathura shouted and the dog turned towards him. He stood in the open doorway of one of the huts and, as the dog leapt at him, Kashi Mathura stepped smartly to the left of the door. The dog landed on the floor of the hut and turned round, by which time Kashi Mathura had closed the door behind it. Mark called the rest of the men to him. Ahmed Khan spoke contemptuously to the two men who had run away and they picked up their lathis, looking somewhat shamefaced as they returned. Mark said that these two men would go to the rear of the hut with Kashi Mathura. The other four men were to stand in a protective square round Sushi. Mark said he would be immediately in front of the door, with Ahmed Khan directly behind him. He told the men who were going to the rear that they should bang on the walls and window frame. When the dog leapt at the window Kashi Mathura, and only Kashi Mathura, was to shout out. Mark would then open the door and, as the dog came towards him, he would try to shoot it with his pistol. If he missed and the dog landed on him, Ahmed Khan was to kill it with his spear. In the event of the dog escaping from the hut, the other four men were to beat it with their lathis, in order to protect Sushi. She translated Mark's orders into Marathi for the benefit of those who had not understood his instructions in Urdu, adding her own comment, 'Let me see you acting like men this time, not behaving like chickens.'

Mark spoke to Kashi Mathura and he led the other two men to the rear of the hut. The remaining four closed round Sushi, while Mark and Ahmed Khan moved towards the door. The sound of lathis being banged on walls and window frames could be heard and then a loud snarl, with a simultaneous shout from Kashi Mathura. Mark opened the door and went down on his right knee. The dog turned and leapt at Mark with its mouth foaming and eyes blazing. Mark braced himself, aimed his pistol at the dog's chest, and fired at point-blank range. As he did so, Ahmed Khan moved his spear forward over Mark's shoulder to protect him. The dog fell about eighteen inches in front of Mark's left foot, gave a strangled bark and then lay still. Nobody moved during the several seconds which elapsed until Kashi Mathura came running from the back of the hut. He stood at Mark's left side, pointing his spear at the dog. Mark rose to his feet slowly and gingerly. He moved back two or three paces, took a lathi from one of the men, and pushed the dog on its back.

'It's dead,' he said, handing the lathi back. He turned to Ahmed Khan. 'Get two sweepers to bring a blanket and tell them to take the body of the dog to Moxon Sahib. You wait here, Kashi, until Ahmed Khan returns. No one is to touch the dog until Moxon Sahib has a chance to examine it. The rest of you can go back to your wives now. Thank you for your help.' There was a torrent of laughter and conversation as the tension broke. The relief showed itself in the cheerful smiles on the men's faces and their effervescent talk. They shouted loudly as the party went through the archway and saw the fear disappearing from the wives' faces as their men returned. Several of the women looked shyly in Mark's direction as he heard their husbands saying that the Captain Sahib had killed the wild dog. Ruth was holding two of the children when she saw Mark but gave them back to their mothers as Mark led his small party back.

'I was worried about you, darling. Thank goodness you're safe,' she said.

'You don't need to worry, dearest. I had a pistol. Sushi didn't have any weapons,' Mark replied. 'Apart from her tongue, that is.'

\* \* \* \* \*

'You are to be commended,' Sir George said when Mark was called to see him the following morning. 'Master Moxon says that the dog had rabies. It's unfortunate, but the children who were bitten will almost certainly die. The dog bit several people in the town as well, before it ran into the servants' quarters.'

'I'm sorry to hear that, Sir George,' Mark replied.

'One good thing is that your prompt action, taken on your own initiative, stopped a panic and probably saved other lives.

I want everyone to know about it, including the directors in London.'

'I couldn't have done it without help. I'd like Kashi Mathura and Ahmed Khan to share any credit. Not forgetting the six men who acted as beaters. And Sushi who encouraged them, of course.'

Sir George smiled, 'Yes, I'm sure Sushi was a great help. But you were the one who led the others.' He waited for two or three seconds and then continued. 'Now that Master Boland is well again, will you and Ruth be seeing him?'

'We are meeting him in two hours time,' Mark replied. 'We'll ask him to call banns on Sunday.'

'Good.' Sir George hesitated. 'I suppose Roland Lockyer could claim to be her nearest relative. Will he be asked to give the bride away?'

'No.' Mark said abruptly. 'He'll not be at the wedding.'

Sir George did not appear surprised at this reply. 'May I know who Ruth has in mind?

'Of course. Maria Ferrara is the friend she's known longest here. Maria will be her matron of honour. Ruth thinks it appropriate for her husband to stand in place of the father of the bride.'

'A good choice,' Sir George replied. 'Fernando Ferrara is a sound man. What about your own choice, Mark?'

'My own choice?' He sounded puzzled. 'I agree with Ruth.'

'No. I mean, who will be your supporter?'

'I don't know, Sir George. The only people I know well are in the imperial army. I can hardly ask them.'

'Peter Streynsham speaks well of you. He's only four years older than you. Why not ask him?'

'Thank you for the suggestion, Sir George.' Mark answered. 'I hadn't thought of him.'

* * * * *

Four days after Mark killed the rabid dog, he and Ruth walked in the bright, early morning sunshine for the two hundred yards which separated the factory from the English chapel. Ruth was blissfully happy. They were taking over the Robertsons' bungalow on the following morning and Sunday night would be the last night which she and Mark would spend in the small storeroom before moving into their own home. The morning's Eucharist was the first service Ruth had attended at the English chapel since Claire's death. Their banns were to be called for the first time before the service began and Master Boland had told them that he would marry them fifteen days after the banns were read out for the first time. Several of the younger male members of the congregation were standing outside the chapel door. They gave admiring glances in Ruth's direction and raised their hats as she approached. Mark greeted them politely and then escorted Ruth into the chapel. After he had taken Ruth to her pew, he excused himself and went up the aisle to speak to Peter Streynsham. When Mark had finished speaking, Jacoba and her husband both turned to smile and nod at Ruth. After the blessing had been given at the end of the service, Ruth knelt in prayer. She was unaware of the rest of the congregation filing out. The words of her namesake kept coming back to her over and over again. Ruth was only aware of her husband at her side as the words of the Old Testament book repeated themselves in her mind.

'Entreat me not to leave thee or to return from following after thee; for whither thou goest, I will go; and where thou lodgest, I will lodge; thy people shall be my people, and thy God my God; Where thou diest, will I die, and there will I be buried; the Lord do so to me, and more also, if ought but death part thee and me.'

When Ruth rose from her knees and took her seat again she was surprised to find that she and Mark were alone in the chapel. Mark stood up, moved into the aisle, bowed his head to the altar, and then stood back to allow Ruth to leave the pew. Ruth took his arm and they walked together towards the chapel door. 'I feel like a bride. Walking down the aisle like this with you,' Ruth said quietly.

'You'll always be a bride to me, dearest,' he answered softly.

The congregation had already dispersed from outside the chapel, apart from Jacoba and Peter Streynsham who stood talking to the chaplain. Master Boland shook both Ruth and Mark by the hand and asked them if a rehearsal of the wedding on the morning of Saturday, 6 February would be convenient for everybody.'

'Convenient for my wife and I,' Mark replied.

'Yes,' the chaplain said. 'Father Dellon told me that he had already married you both in a Catholic ceremony. Because it's not valid in English law, I had to call your wife by her maiden name when I read the banns.'

'I understand, Master Boland. We both look forward to your blessing. As far as the rehearsal is concerned, I wished to ask Master Streynsham if he would be my supporter.' Mark turned to Peter. 'Will you do us this honour of attending the wedding as my supporter, Peter?'

'I will be privileged, Mark?'

'How you know I not ask you to marry me on same day?' Jacoba teased her husband. 'Make double sure of you. Like Ruth here.'

'We can solve that problem if I have you as one of my matrons of honour, Jacoba,' Ruth said. 'Then you can imagine you and Peter are getting married once more. I'll marry Mark again every week, if he wants me to.'

Jacoba looked at her husband. 'I vonder if he marry me again if I ask. Vot you think, Ruth?'

'I'm sure your husband marries you again every day in his heart,' she replied. 'I tink I not ask him,' Jacoba said with a laugh. 'Maybe he say no to me.'

'It seems February 6 is a convenient day for Master Streynsham and his wife as well,' Master Boland said drily. 'Who will be father of the bride?'

'Senhor Ferrara,' Mark answered. 'And Senhora Ferrara will be another matron of honour.'

'Good. I'll assume that they will be able to attend the

rehearsal. Unless I hear from them I will expect them to attend. May I bid you all good day.' The chaplain took his leave of them and Mark and Ruth started to walk away accompanied by Peter and Jacoba. The Streynshams asked if they would like to come back to their bungalow for a while but Mark and Ruth declined, explaining that they had arranged to call on the Robertsons. Mark went on to say that he and Ruth were to meet Sushi in the factory and then the three of them would go to the Robertsons' bungalow. They were to take inventory there and arrange to settle by means of a note which Sir George could draw on the company's bank in London.

'I be glad when you and your husband in your own home, Ruth. You set good example to other people. Too many of zees men spend all time drinking, smoking tobacco, and going with nautch girls.'

Ruth laughed. 'Mark is the one who will be setting the good example.'

'You all vaze be good vife to him,' Jacoba said seriously. 'You help him keep on narrow path.'

'Like you have with me?' Peter asked.

'Zat is right. You vicked man,' she said, giving a playful tap on her husband's shoulder.

\* \* \* \* \*

An hour and a half later Mark and Ruth said goodbye to the Robertson family. Mark and Thomas Robertson had agreed a price for the furniture and other items which were to be taken over. They confirmed that Mark would ask Sir George to draw a promissory note on the East India Company's bankers in London and give it to Thomas Robertson in settlement. A corresponding sum would be regarded as an advance of Mark's pay. Ruth and Sushi met all the servants in the Robertson household to find out their names and the wages they were to be paid. Even the syce and his wife said they would defer their plans to return to their farm until the Fairbrothers could arrange a replacement. It had been a very successful morning and Ruth still felt in the happy mood with which she had started the day. She asked if they could make a slight detour and go through one of the public parks on the return to the English factory, instead of taking the direct route.

The grass was at its best at that time of the year. With the temperatures rising between February and May, the grass would become withered and scorched while the earth became cracked and hard. The ground was likely to become a quagmire when the monsoon rains of June and July fell. Even as late as September and October, the lawns in the parks might be soggy and difficult to walk on. Now the park was a delight to spend time in. Mark and Ruth walked slowly through the avenues of jacaranda trees and silver-grey pipal trees, past fountains and the pools which the Indians called tanks. Neither was in any hurry to get back to the tiny storeroom which would be their home for another twenty-four hours. Sushi walked discreetly a few yards away from them. Their peaceful mood was suddenly shattered by a cry of, 'Good day, Mistress Parker.'

Ruth looked across to see three men sitting on the ground several yards away. One was Jake Firman, another Roland Lockyer, while the third was a stranger to her. They had glasses and bottles of brandy on the ground beside them. Jake rose to his feet and called out, 'Good day, Mistress Parker,' again.

Mark touched his hat. 'Your pardon, sir. This lady is my wife, Mistress Fairbrother.'

Roland went on all fours and started to bark. He paused and then said, 'Good day, Captain Doghunter.'

Mark did not reply. Sushi had come to his side by this time. Roland rose unsteadily to his feet.

'Why don't you come over here, Ruth? Stay with real men,' Roland said. 'Doing work. Not dog catching.'

Ruth could sense that Mark was becoming angrier as he turned to Jake Firman. 'Your friend appears to be drunk, sir. I suggest you take him home to sober him up. In the meantime, my wife and I will take leave of you.'

---

'Wife? Wife? What wife? Master Boland called banns for Ruth Parker. There she is.' Roland laughed. 'Lived alone with me in my bungalow. Frigid bitch though. You ask Jake as well. Now the vixen's a real whore. The whole world knows she sleeps with you.' His voice rose to a shout. 'The whole world knows Ruth Parker's a whore.'

Mark broke free from Ruth's restraining arm, stepped forward and struck Roland across the mouth with his open hand. 'Shut your mouth, Master Lockyer,' Mark said in a voice full of fury.

Roland staggered back one or two paces. 'Look at the whore,' he shouted. 'Not good enough for real men. Had to have a dog catcher when the bitch came on heat.'

Mark stepped forward again, struck him on the jaw with a closed fist and Roland fell to the ground. He turned his back and began walking away as Roland staggered to his feet and drew his sword. The third man in the party rushed toward him. 'No, Roland,' the other man said, as he held his sword arm, 'he's not armed.'

Mark had rejoined Ruth and Sushi by this time and was standing between them.

'You're a coward,' Roland told him. 'Hitting a man when you're not wearing a sword.'

'Gentlemen do not carry swords when visiting a public park,' Mark replied icily.

'Give him your sword, Henry,' Roland said to the man who was still holding his arm. 'Let's see the colour of Captain Dogkiller's blood.'

Mark carefully removed his coat and hat and took the sword which the other man handed to him. Ruth kissed him on the cheek and said, 'God will give you victory, Mark.' Her voice became a whisper as she added, 'But please be careful, my love. Please be careful. He used to be in Prince Rupert's cavalry.'

From the other side Mark heard Sushi say, 'My blessings on you, my son. Shiva and Krishna will protect you.'

Ruth and Sushi moved back while Mark remained motionless, waiting for Roland to make the first move. After a moment or two of hesitation, Roland rushed forward and thrust at Mark, who quickly parried. Roland's attack was so fast and furious that Mark was forced to give ground slowly. Mark could tell that his opponent had been taught to fence and contented himself with a purely defensive posture. He reasoned that Roland was likely to tire more easily and gradually become more prone to make mistakes as the fight wore on. The clash of steel had attracted a small crowd of spectators, including some Europeans.

After just over a minute had elapsed, Mark could see beads of sweat appearing on his opponent's forehead. It seemed that Roland realised that time was running out for him because he intensified his attack, with his breathing becoming heavier as his sword strokes became more rapid. Mark had the measure of Roland's prowess by this time and stood his ground. This seemed to infuriate Roland even more and his attacks became frenzied in the extreme. Mark stepped aside to avoid a furious lunge and, as he did so, Roland slipped, dropping his sword to the ground. Mark quickly brought his heel down on his opponent's sword, breaking the blade in two. 'You are disarmed, Master Lockyer,' Mark said. 'I assume you will now apologise.'

Roland's wig had fallen on the ground when he slipped, showing his bald head. The small amount of hair which remained was grey. His shirt was damp with patches of perspiration and there were beads of sweat on his face. Roland looked a pathetic figure as he used his hands to slowly lever himself to his feet, breathing heavily as he did so.

'Give me a brandy, Henry,' he called.

Mark lowered his sword and stepped back. Roland swallowed the large brandy in one gulp. He waited a couple of seconds and snarled, 'Give me your sword, Jake.'

There was a murmur of disapproval from the crowd as Jake handed over his sword. Above the noise made by other spectators, Mark heard two Mogul officials say, 'Ab khutam hogia.' They, at any rate, thought that honour was satisfied and the fight was finished.

Mark stood quietly. He raised his sword as his opponent advanced towards him. There was pure venom in Roland's eyes as their blades clashed once more. Roland's attack seemed even more frenzied than before but this time Mark did not give way. He sensed Roland was becoming desperate and that it was only a question of time before Roland staked everything on trying to achieve a quick kill. The sweat was now glistening on his opponent's right hand and wrist, as well as on the forehead. His breathing was becoming increasingly erratic as each second passed and he started to tire. Mark was quick to follow up but Roland parried and the two men stood toe to toe, with their swords pressed together.

They remained like this for about three seconds until Roland took a pace back, lunged at Mark but missed. Mark lifted his sword over his opponent's guard, thrust the blade into Roland's right shoulder just above the collar bone, quickly withdrew the sword and stepped back. Roland gave a cry of pain as the air hit the wound. He dropped his sword, sank slowly to his knees, and rested the palms of his hands on the ground. The blood from his shoulder was beginning to stain his shirt.

Mark brought his heel down sharply on Jake's sword, breaking it in two. The first six inches of the blade of the sword which he had borrowed from Henry were covered with blood. He thrust it down into the ground until only half the blade was exposed. Jake was glaring malevolently at him but Mark gave no acknowledgement that he was aware of this. Henry had come to support Roland by this time and Mark said to him, 'Your sword is here, sir. I suggest you get Master Lockyer to a surgeon.'

Ruth came to Mark's side while Sushi followed carrying his coat and hat. She looked contemptuously at Roland, who was now sitting on the ground with his legs stretched out, and at Jake, who was standing behind his friend. Ruth put her arms round Mark's waist and kissed him full on the lips, aware of the baleful looks given her by Roland and Jake. She continued to hold her husband even after their lips separated. Ruth pulled him towards her and whispered in his ear, 'Let's go back quickly, Mark. I love you so much, darling. Please let's go back quickly.'

\* \* \* \* \*

Next morning Ruth and Mark were summoned to Sir George's office.

'This is an official visit, Captain Fairbrother,' Sir George began. 'I've been to see Master Lockyer this morning. I also saw Monsieur Villeneuve, the French President, who was in the park at the same time as this regrettable incident. It's unfortunate because there are few enough English here, God knows, without quarrels among ourselves. One of the Mogul officials who was there also sent me a report. I'd like to hear your side of this affair.'

Mark related the events of the previous morning, helped by two or three comments interspersed by Ruth. Sir George looked pensive for a few seconds. 'I discourage my factors from wearing swords while they're in Surat. These views have been expressed to Master Lockyer. One of the good things about the Commonwealth was that duelling was made illegal. I regret that it's creeping back following the Restoration and it's now fashionable to wear swords again. I commend you for not wearing a sword when off duty. I hope the day will never dawn when we have to put on a sword to go to church or walk in a public park. You were placed in a difficult position, Mark. However, a sword fight in a public place, or indeed anywhere else, is still regrettable.'

'You can't blame Mark, Sir George,' Ruth interrupted. 'He couldn't stand by when my honour was impugned.'

'So I've heard, Ruth,' he replied smoothly. 'I suppose you'd have killed Master Lockyer if he'd been at the point of your sword.'

'Roland hates me!' Ruth answered vehemently. 'Not just because I refused to submit to him while his wife was still alive and after she died, but because I know how he treated my sister. That's why he picked a quarrel with Mark. He wanted to hurt me by killing my husband.'

'I know there's been bad blood between you and Master Lockyer.' Sir George looked searchingly at Ruth. 'And I suspect Master Firman has behaved badly towards you.' She lowered her eyes to avoid looking at him.

'You handled yourself well, Mark,' Sir George continued. 'You exercised self-control when Master Lockyer was at your mercy, after he had dropped his sword. Yet the whole of Surat now knows that your wife's honour is safe in your hands. And I will be spared the duty of writing to my directors to say that one of my factors has been killed in a brawl with the captain I appointed to protect us. There's no reason why they need be informed about this duel.'

'Thank you, Sir George.'

'We now have the future to think about. When did Master Boland say he was going to marry you?' he asked.

'In fourteen days time,' Mark replied.

'Good. And the Robertsons hand over their bungalow today?'

'Yes. Master Robertson will be calling to collect the promissory note for the furniture later on.'

'The sooner you two get down to some serious married life after the excitements of the past three weeks' the better,' Sir George said drily. 'I saw Master Moxon this morning,' he continued. 'Master Lockyer should be fit again in ten days time, although he may have to keep his arm in a sling for a day or two after that. Now that we seem to be on reasonable terms with Shivaji,' Sir George looked straight at Ruth, 'and our hostages are going to be freed, thanks to your help, we can start rebuilding our warehouse at Rajapur. I'll ask Master Lockyer to supervise the work. Get him to leave in ten days' time.' Sir George grinned wickedly. 'You weren't going to invite him to the wedding, were you?'

Ruth shook her head vigorously. 'I despise him. I didn't plan to invite him even before he insulted me and called my husband a coward.'

'I'll see him today,' Sir George continued calmly. 'Try and get him to apologise to both of you. As for Master Firman, I shall tell him to make Goa his base in future. If the Sultan wants to trade with the company in future, he'll have to do it through Firman's deputy. I'll tell Master Firman now that I think his behaviour was unworthy of a gentleman. I won't go into anything that happened between you before yesterday. But I'll tell him it was ungentlemanly to call you by your maiden name when we all know Father Dellon married you during the siege. His conduct in giving Master Lockyer a sword was inexcusable. Mark had clearly won a victory in a fair fight, honour was satisfied, and it was only thanks to Mark's self-restraint that nobody lost their life as a result of Firman's irresponsibility. He won't be coming to your wedding either, I suppose.'

'Indeed not!' Ruth answered savagely. 'I'd rather Mark and I stayed as we are if I thought that contemptible man would be in the congregation.'

Sir George looked at her with a smile. 'You and your husband move into that new home of yours today, don't you, Ruth?'

'Yes, Sir George.'

'Take my advice,' he said. 'Let yourself give full vent to your emotional feelings within those walls. Perhaps then you'll feel more at peace with the world outside.'

Ruth blushed and lowered her eyes. 'You misjudge me, Sir George. I am at peace with the world now. I love our Lord and Saviour Jesus Christ but I love my husband also, as God commands me. Mark is the only man whose wife I have wished to be. He is the one man in my life I have wanted. I thank the Good Lord in my prayers every day that we have found each other again. I remember John Milton's rendering of Psalm 136, which Master Phillips, my tutor taught me to say,

> *'Let us with gladsome mind*
> *Praise the Lord, for he is kind.*
> *For his mercies, aye endure*
> *Ever faithful, ever sure.'*

Why should I not be at peace with the world, Sir George?'

He looked curiously at Ruth. 'You're a funny mixture you know, my girl. Half an intensely passionate, impulsive woman. Half a rigid Puritan.' He turned to Mark. 'So long as you keep on loving your wife, my lad, you'll have a wonderful life. Christ help you, because no one else can, if you ever stop loving her.'

\* \* \* \* \*

Two days after they moved into the Robertsons' bungalow Sir George sent for Mark and Ruth again. This time he asked if Sushi would come with them. Sushi was asked to wait in an ante-room when they arrived, while Ruth and Mark were shown into Sir George's private drawing room. He rose to greet them and, after the normal greetings were exchanged, handed Ruth the box of jewelry which had belonged to Claire. 'Master Lockyer sent this,' he said laconically. 'By way of apology.'

Ruth was too choked to speak. She stared at them for a few seconds, only raising her eyes when Sir George said, 'You may wish me to look after them for a few days.'

'Why is that, Sir George?' Mark enquired.

'I have a mission for you. It will take you away from Surat for about five days. Knowing how you two feel about each other, thought you might insist on going as well, Ruth.'

'What does the mission consist of?' Mark asked.

'I'd better start at the beginning,' Sir George replied. He went on to say that the four factors who had been held hostage had ridden into Surat an hour before. Their two escorts would begin the journey back to their own territory the following day. Peter Streynsham had suggested a small escort should be provided for them. It meant a five day round trip into the hills and neither Peter Streynsham nor Sir George could spare the time. Mark had nearly four years experience of living with native troops, could speak good Urd,u and was felt to be the obvious choice to command a small escort for the Marathas.

'Is it safe for Mark?' Ruth asked.

'Would I ask your husband to go if it was unsafe?' Sir George asked. 'A party of five armed men will be safe from any stray robber, while the Moguls won't interfere with a group travelling under the emblem of St. George, commanded by a European. They might detain the envoys if they travelled alone, however, and all our good relations with Shivaji would be spoiled.'

'May I go too?' Ruth asked.

Sir George smiled, 'I thought we'd get round to that. I'm sure you'll be useful. You speak good Marathi. But take Sushi with you. Don't want to have you on your own in those hills. Sushi's a farmer's widow. Knows that country well. Do you ride, Ruth?'

'Yes, Sir George. I learnt to ride at an early age and used to ride round my foster-father's farm.'

'Good. It's a little different in the Western Ghats. You go up from the coastal plains to four thousand feet high in just a few miles. It's quite cold in the hills at this time of the year. Almost wish I was going myself. What do the two of you think about it?'

Ruth and Mark looked at each other for a moment or two. There was no need to say anything or even nod.

'Yes, Sir George. We'd like to go,' Mark replied.

'Right. You leave early tomorrow. See Peter Streynsham about the arrangements for the trip and come to see me this evening to talk over the plans. You both have a busy day ahead of you.'

'Yes, Sir George,' Mark replied.

'How old are you, Mark?'

'Twenty-five.'

'And I know Ruth is nearly twenty.' Sir George paused for reflection. 'It's a responsible mission but you both have old heads on young shoulders.' He rose from his chair. 'Come with me. The Marathas have something for Sushi. I may need you to interpret, Ruth.'

The two of them followed him out into the ante-room where Peter Streynsham, an Indian official of the East India Company and Sushi were all waiting. 'Everything's ready, Sir George.'

'Right. Follow me then,' he replied, leading the way into the large reception room used for important visitors.

Ruth saw Luke Farmerdale at the other end of the reception room, talking with another Indian official of the East India Company, together with two Indians who had their backs to Ruth. They turned round as Sir George and his party entered the room and bowed slightly. Ruth instantly recognised Narainji Pandit by his distinctive, yellow, ankle-length, silk robe and his clean shaven face and shaven head. He gave a brief smile in recognition. The other man had a thick, black beard and was dressed like a Maratha farmer. He had a flat, orange turban on his head, was wearing a knee-length divided skirt, together with an olive-coloured jacket and heavy brown cloak thrown over one shoulder. Narainji Pandit's companion gave no sign of recognition but it suddenly dawned on Ruth that he was the Maratha officer who had arranged for her to be married by the Capuchin missionary.

Sir George stopped and, speaking first in English, then in Urdu, asked for everyone to be seated. When Sushi showed a reluctance to take a chair, Ruth whispered, 'Sit down. This is for you.'

The little ceremony began with Luke Farmerdale getting up to ask if he could present an envoy from Shivaji Raja. Permission was granted and Narainji Pandit stood up to speak in faultless Urdu, repeating himself in Marathi. He said that his companion had been glad to escort the four factors back to Surat as a token of the present good relations between his ruler and the English. He was sure that friendship would grow between their two peoples and asked if the English would allow their coins to circulate in the Maratha territories. His ruler was unable to mint sufficient coins of his own and the people were forced to use those of the Mohammedan oppressors.

Sir George reciprocated politely by speaking in somewhat laboured Urdu, then in English, which he asked Ruth to translate into Marathi. He explained that he would give a considered answer to the requests before the envoys returned in the morning. He mentioned that, in recognition of certain actions of the English during the recent siege of Surat, the Mogul authorities had decided to reduce to $2^1/2\%$ the tariffs on English goods imported into imperial territories. It would be a gesture of goodwill if a similar reduction was made in the tariffs on imports into the Maratha territories. Narainji Pandit thanked the President cordially. He said he would submit his proposal to the Maratha Council of Nine the moment he returned to his capital. In the meantime, he had a pleasant duty to perform. During the recent attempt to assassinate him, Shivaji Raja had been impressed by the fortitude shown by the older Maratha woman accompanying the English President. In recognition, his ruler had sent Captain Abiji Sing with a silver bracelet as a reward. He read out the Marathi inscription. 'To Sushi, the tigress of Lalhulla, whose cub carried off a man. From Shivaji.'

For the first time since Ruth had known her, Sushi seemed embarrassed. She lowered her face and pulled the top of her sari over her head like a cowl. Ruth rose from her chair as soon as she had finished translating the inscription into English and went across to Sushi, kissing her on both cheeks. Mark started to clap his hands and was followed by a ragged applause from the others present.

'I think that concludes the more formal part of the meeting,' Sir George said ironically. 'Captain Fairbrother will be in charge of the escort for the two Maratha gentlemen. Please present him to the two envoys, Master Streynsham.' Sir George rose from his chair and went across to congratulate Sushi. After he had finished he said to Ruth, 'I think this is about the most informal presentation ceremony I have ever attended.'

Peter Streynsham brought Narainji Pandit and Abiji Sing across to meet Mark.

'We meet again, Englishman,' Abiji Sing said after the formal introductions had been made.

'Yes,' Mark replied. 'It will be a privilege to escort you. I will be able to repay some of the debt I owe to you.'

After Narainji Pandit excused himself by saying that he wished to talk to one of the company's Indian officials, Peter asked Mark to call on him in an hour's time to discuss the arrangements for the escort. He motioned across to another of the company's Indian officials and introduced him to Abiji Sing saying, 'Babu Kishan Chand will look after you in my absence, Captain Sing. Please excuse me for the moment.'

The babu bowed to Abiji Sing, said, 'I will wait here Captain Sahib until you finish talking to Captain Fairbrother,' and then moved back to about ten feet away.

'Ram, Ram, Captain Abiji Sing,' Ruth said as she came up, arm in arm with Sushi.

'Ram, Ram, daughter. Ram, Ram, mother. Last time we met your daughter wore a sari.'

He smiled broadly. Sushi appeared too overwhelmed to speak. She kept looking at the bracelet on her wrist.

'The last time we met,' Ruth said with a laugh, 'we were both dressed differently.'

'This time I am in mufti,' Abiji Sing replied. 'As the Moguls say.'

'Sushi and I will travel with you when you return. Should I wear a sari then?' Ruth asked.

Abiji Sing's eyes opened wide with astonishment. 'We Marathas respect women. Not like Mohammedans. But no women are allowed to travel with Maratha soldiers. East India Company like Moguls,' he said. 'They allow wives and children to travel with army. So do Sultans of Bejapour and Golcanda. And camp followers too. I hear all European armies like that as well.'

'Yes,' Mark answered.

'No. There were no women allowed with the New Model Army,' Ruth said impulsively. 'Not like the King's troops.' She could have bitten off her tongue at the end of the sentence. Mark turned and gave her a piercing look but made no comment.

Abiji Sing looked puzzled. He thought for a few seconds before asking, 'The New Model Army. I do not understand. What is that?'

Mark waited for Ruth to reply but she did not answer. After a short pause he said, 'An army which fought against the King of England in the Great Rebellion.'

'Like us and Emperor Aurangzeb?' Abiji Sing asked. When neither Mark nor Ruth replied he said, 'Was the New Model Army victorious?'

'Yes. The King was defeated,' Mark replied.

'As we Marathas will be victorious over the Mogul Empire,' Abiji Sing replied.

'Perhaps,' Mark answered. 'But victories won with the sword seldom last. You may destroy the Mogul Empire yet find someone else will enjoy the fruits of your labours.'

'Better that, Englishman, than spend our lives in fear under the yoke of an intolerant tyrant like Aurangzeb. But we will have plenty of time to talk as we ride together.'

# 16

Early next morning Mark went to the English factory, accompanied by Ruth and Sushi. Preparations were already far advanced for the start of their journey. Ahmed Khan, the Afghan, saluted Mark and said the escort was ready to leave. Mark checked the matchlock muskets, horse pistols, powder, shot, swords and other equipment carried by the escort and then made sure that each of the horses was fit for the journey. While this inspection was taking place, Ruth noticed Peter Streynsham approaching, accompanied by the two Marathas. Narainji Pandit bowed gravely to her while Abiji Sing placed the palms of his hands together as he greeted Ruth and Sushi. Abiji Sing smiled when he saw Ruth glance at the heavy sword he was wearing. He touched the hilt and said, 'Your husband and I must see you ladies are both protected. Narainji Pandit and I will be your guarantees of safe conduct when we are in the territory under Maratha control.' As Mark approached, Abiji Sing gave a Maratha salute and asked him, 'May I ride with you at the front of the column? I can help in finding the way.'

'Yes, of course,' Mark replied.

'You will be in command all the time but some of my own men will meet me when we reach Maratha territory.'

'I am obliged to you, Captain,' Mark answered. 'My men are ready to leave now.'

'Can you delay for five minutes, Mark?' Peter Streynsham asked. 'Sir George wants to see you off. I'll fetch him now.'

After Peter left, Mark ordered the handful of his men who were staying behind to line up in a single file by the factory gate. He then proceeded to organise the column of those who were travelling with him. Everyone mounted their own particular horse, with Mark and Abiji Sing riding at the front. They were followed by two of Mark's men, Sher Dil and Ahmed Khan, with Ruth, Narainji Pandit, and Sushi riding in the middle of the column. Three pack ponies came after them, carrying their supplies of food, blankets, and warm clothing. These ponies were led by Mohammed Ali, the syce selected for them by Peter. The tail of the little procession was brought up by two more of Mark's men, Nabha Sing, one of the Marathas, and Kashi Mathura, the Gujerati who had been with Mark when he shot the rabid dog.

Sir George was in a small procession which came out of the factory to bid farewell to the travellers. A standard bearer carrying the flag with the cross of St. George, a mace bearer and two trumpeters preceded him. Peter Streynsham and a number of the company's Indian officials followed him. As Sir George came through the archway on to the open space in front of the factory where Mark's column was drawn up, Mark called the men standing in file by the gate to attention. Mark was aware of Abiji Sing looking at this display with a professional eye and also studying the accoutrements of the mounted escort. Sir George looked at the escort and said to Mark, 'Congratulations. You've picked the best men to provide your escort. Good luck.' He then shook Mark and Ruth by the hand, wishing them both a safe journey. Sir George also wished a safe journey to the two Marathas but, following the Maratha custom of avoiding physical contact with all but intimate friends, he did not extend his hand to them. They bowed gravely in return and said they would convey Sir George's expressions of friendship to Shivaji. Sir George stepped back, Mark gave the word of command for the column to advance, the two trumpeters played a resounding call on their instruments and Mark and Abiji Sing both saluted as the column moved forward.

\* \* \* \* \*

Ruth was fascinated by the days that followed, even though the hard riding was tiring. She noticed that Abiji Sing kept the party off the main roads, where they might encounter patrols of imperial troops. When they stopped it was at small, isolated villages which Abiji Sing had reconnoitred previously. While one or two of the menfolk had seen an occasional European man, none of the villagers had ever seen a European woman. Ruth found herself the centre of attention whenever she stopped. The village women plied her with questions about her clothes and her bungalow in Surat. After they had shyly asked if she had any children, they seemed surprised when she told them she was nearly twenty years old before she married. The women took great pride in showing Ruth their clean, tidy homes, with freshly plastered and painted walls, and their kitchens, with rows of gleaming brass pots standing on the well scrubbed floors. Sushi and Nabha Sing were always careful not to upset any religious susceptibilities. With one exception, all the party ate the same simple, country fare which the villagers prepared. Nabha Sing and Sushi brought the food to Mark and Ruth so that they could eat apart. Ahmed Khan, Sher Dil and Mohammed Ali formed a little group, who also ate separately the food prepared for them by the villagers. The extrovert Abiji Sing seemed completely at ease when eating either with the villagers or with Kashi Mathura and Nabha Sing, or chatting to the Mussulmans.

Narainji Pandit, however, remained isolated. He had some cold chapattis and maize cakes which he ate frugally whenever the party stopped and he carried his own drinking vessel with him. When Sushi was asked by Ruth why Abiji Sing seemed quite happy to eat with the rest, although he was an officer, she replied that he was a Prabhu, not a Brahmin like Narainji Pandit. Sushi gave a slightly cynical smile as she went on to say that having envoys of two different castes reduced the possibility of treachery.

During the afternoon of the second day they had moved out of the coastal plain with its mango groves, palm trees, jacaranda trees and fields of sugar cane, maize and rice. It became noticeably cooler as they left the fertile, yellow-coloured fields below. Ruth was glad to be wearing a cloak over the sari into which she had changed that morning. When they stopped that evening, Abiji Sing asked Ruth if he could join her and Mark for their meal. She noticed that a rapport had been established between her husband and the Maratha officer during the two days they had been riding together and readily agreed, asking Nabha Sing to bring extra food for Abiji Sing. While they were eating their simple meal of rice and vegetables together, he told them they would be leaving Mogul territory early next morning. He said it was unlikely any Mogul patrols would be encountered as he had chosen a route to avoid imperial frontier posts and their guards. After they entered Maratha territory, he would take them on a detour, lasting most of the day, before sending them into Mogul territory by a different route. He grinned. 'We do not want these followers of the prophet to know the way I go back into and come from their country, do we?'

The party made a very early start the following morning. Even Narainji Pandit seemed more relaxed now that they were entering his own territory. He had not initiated any subjects for discussion during the journey and Ruth found conversation with him hard going. They were now moving slowly through the cold, morning mists. The higher they climbed the more barren the earth became. Here and there, patches of wild begonias could be seen, living precariously on the dry earth. As they approached a narrow pass through a high escarpment Abiji Sing slowed down and suggested they should proceed in single file. A hundred yards further along the winding trail, they entered a belt of trees. The jungle was so thick that no light of the thin morning sun penetrated the foliage. Mark ordered the column to close up as he did not want to lose anyone in this forest. His words were hardly out of his mouth before a horseman came from the trees a few paces ahead of them, rode up to Abiji Sing and saluted. Abiji Sing gave a shouted word of command and a dozen other horsemen appeared from either side of the path alongside which they had travelled.

'No need to be alarmed,' Narainji Pandit said reassuringly to Ruth and Sushi. 'These men are troops under Abiji Sing's command.'

He smiled as Ruth said, 'Now I can see why the imperial army finds it so difficult to defeat the Marathas.'

She noticed that the horses the Maratha troopers rode seemed thin and large-boned compared with the Arab mounts belonging to the party from the East India Company. Their only weapons were swords and their only uniforms were the quilted jackets which they each wore. The party rested for a few minutes while the Maratha troopers ate a meal of black peas and cold boiled rice, giving Abiji Sing time to change from his peasant dress into the uniform of an officer in Shivaji's regiment of guards. He caressed the spare horse which his men had brought along, talking softly to it all the time he stroked it. The horse whinnied two or three times while this was taking place, almost as though it was a pet dog being reunited with its master. After a minute or so of patting the animal, Abiji Sing saddled and mounted his horse. In answer to Mark's unspoken question, he replied, 'The horse lent me by the East India Company is good but my horse can stop on a mountain track when there is any danger without needing any command. It is like having another eye.' The horse formerly ridden by Abiji Sing was now taken over by Mohammed Ali and his own inferior mount placed among the group of packhorses.

By this stage of the journey, Mark and Abiji Sing were on first name terms. 'I will now lead you to a road, Captain Mark, which will take you to a more direct route back to Surat.' Abiji Sing said. 'It is a few miles away and may take us several hours to reach there.'

During the day, they moved more slowly than at the start of their journey. The thick jungle on the lower slopes alternated with bare, rocky plateaus higher up. Several times they descended from uplands, on which the only sign of vegetation was a group of stunted, leafless shrubs in patches of yellow spear-grass, to forests carpeted with decaying leaves. Sometimes the horses were able to travel three or four abreast but often Abiji Sing took them through ravines so narrow they were forced to move in single file.

Towards the end of their long day the landscape changed and they rode gently downhill over heaths on which bracken was growing in abundance. On the horizons above them, the hills were coloured purple with growing heather. Abiji Sing held up his hand to stop the column and gave orders for his troopers to pull over to the side, to allow the party going back to Surat to close up.

'Go due west from here, Captain Mark. Soon you will reach a road which will take you to Daman by midday tomorrow. Follow the coast road north from there and you will be in Surat by evening the day after tomorrow.'

'Thank you, Abiji. I shall miss your company on the way back,' Mark said.

'This is where we say goodbye, Captain Mark'. He leaned forward in his saddle and extended his arm. As Mark took his hand, Abiji Sing shook it warmly. 'When you go back to that land of mists and cold, beyond the far seas, remember me to your sons.' He saluted as Mark released his hand, turned to Ruth, saluted her and said, 'My blessings on you, Captain Memsahib.'

'Thank you for everything,' Ruth shouted after him as he rode to join his troops.

Narainji Pandit bowed his head gravely to Mark and said, 'Thank you for escorting us. My compliments to Sir George Oxindon.' He then turned and bowed to Ruth, saying, 'Thank you for your company.'

'A safe journey to you,' Mark replied, giving the command for his column to move off. As Ruth looked back she could see the Maratha horsemen galloping away up the slopes behind her.

\* \* \* \* \*

Mark was pleased with the progress they made towards the road Abiji Sing had indicated. The ground sloped gently downhill towards the fields of the coastal plain and it took only half an hour to cover the five miles between the point where the Marathas had left them and the road. The surface of the road had been baked hard by the heat of the previous September and October, and Mohammed Ali was able to make even the pack horses break into an easy gallop. Mark had been told there was a government rest house about ten miles further on from where his column had joined the road. With reasonable luck, they ought to reach it before dusk fell.

Two miles down the road, their luck changed. As they came alongside a small, imperial frontier post at the side of the road, the guards manning it ordered them to stop and dismount. Mark thought it would be no more than the perfunctory inspection usually given to travellers by the frontier guards. The officer in charge seemed unusually agitated, even when Mark explained that they were all servants of the English East India Company, apart from the two ladies they were escorting.

The reason for the tension was apparent when a cloud of dust was seen on the road and a squadron of Mogul cavalry came into view. Mark and his party were soon surrounded and, after a hurried discussion with the frontier guards, the officer commanding the cavalry asked him where his column was heading.

'I am on my way to the English factory in Surat,' Mark replied.

'Why was the English factory saved when the rest of the city was looted by the Kaffirs?' the Mogul officer asked.

'Because our men fired on the Marathas. These men all wear the cross of St. George on their jackets. They stayed true to the company during the siege.'

'Are these men Nazarenes? Or are they Hindu spies? Will they report to that mountain rat Shivaji that even now an assault is planned on Sinhgad?'

'I am Nazarene. As is my wife. Some of these men are followers of the prophet and know the words spoken by Mohammed. Do they look like Hindu spies?' Mark asked.

The Mogul officer gazed sourly at the little party. While Ahmed Khan and Sher Dil looked like Mohammedans, there was little to distinguish Kashi Mathura, Nabha Sing and

Mohammed Ali. The Mogul's gaze shifted to Sushi. He looked with distaste at the painted mark on her forehead and the silver bracelets round her wrist.

'This woman here. She does not wear the Nazarene cross. How do I know she will not tell her infidel masters that even now regiments of Prince Muazzam' s army are crossing the frontier to finish Shivaji once and for all?'

'She is no spy,' Ruth said angrily. 'I am the daughter of her heart.'

'Is this Nazarene woman really your daughter?' the Mogul officer asked Sushi, with a sneer on his face. 'And also the wife of your commander?'

'Yes,' she replied firmly.

The Mogul thought carefully. 'If she is your true daughter let me see you kiss each other. Not just on the cheeks but full on the lips.'

Mark held his breath. He knew that for a Hindu to kiss a non-Hindu in this way was just as much an infringement of caste rules as eating food or drink prepared by a non-Hindu. Atonement could only be obtained by long and costly penances. Even if they had been of the same religious belief and the same caste, it was a public humiliation to be asked to kiss in the presence of so many men. Mark felt anger boiling up inside him. He saw the two Hindus in his party turn their backs to avoid embarrassing Sushi.

There was no need for either woman to speak as they looked into each other's eyes. Ruth stood quite still as Sushi came towards her. They both realised how closely the Mogul officer was watching every facial expression but neither showed a moment's reluctance as they put their hands on each other's shoulders. Just for a second, Sushi hesitated. Ruth lowered her head, slid her arms around Sushi's shoulders and gently placed her lips against the lips of the older woman. Sushi put her arms round Ruth's waist and pulled Ruth towards her, pressing their lips together fiercely and defiantly. She clung to Ruth so hard, it almost seemed as though she was trying to squeeze the breath out of both of their bodies. Several seconds later she released Ruth from her grasp, looked round proudly and contemptuously at dozens of pairs of male eyes gazing at the two women, and asked the Mogul officer, 'Are you satisfied, son of a dog?'

He turned to Mark. 'You may go, Nazarene. And take this unbeliever with you.' Nobody in Mark's party spoke until they reached the government rest house, eight miles further on.

\* \* \* \* \*

On the afternoon of the day after they returned to Surat, Sushi came to Ruth with a broad smile on her face and her eyes bright with excitement. She was speaking so quickly that Ruth was forced to ask her to slow down. When Sushi resumed speaking at a more normal pace, it was to tell Ruth that Roland Lockyer was leaving for Rajapur the following day, but only Chand Narain was going with him.

'Master Lockyer's movements do not interest me,' Ruth said abruptly.

'I spoke to Chand Narain in market of Surat,' Sushi continued, ignoring Ruth's interruption. 'He said he only go to Rajapur with Lockyer Sahib because he has eaten the sahib's salt and he ashamed of burning your books and clothes.'

'Chand Narain is a good man.' Ruth's voice became astringent. 'However, whether he goes or stays is not our concern.'

'None of other servants go with him. They all want to stay in Surat. When I heard this I went to Lockyer Sahib's house. Spoke to Ram Kopal. He will be very happy to work for Ferrara Sahib as syce.'

'But Des Raj is Senhor Ferrara's syce.'

'I know.' Sushi looked at Ruth with a patient expression on her face. 'I will speak to him today. Tell him he come to work for Captain Fairbrother and Pushpa work for Captain's memsahib.'

Ruth smiled. 'You've got it all worked out.'

'Ferrara Memsahib old woman now,' Sushi said. 'I make her good servant. You are young woman. You want young girl for servant. Someone who treats burra memsahib with proper respect.' Sushi tapped Ruth playfully on the arm, as if to hide her true feelings. 'Pushpa not like me. She good girl. She will do what you say.'

'You realise, of course, my husband may not want Des Raj as his syce.'

Sushi chuckled. Her eyes were bright with laughter. 'You tell Captain Sahib tonight. He young husband. You tell him tonight. He does everything you ask.'

Ruth could feel herself blushing slightly and turned her head away. After a sufficient time had elapsed to enable her to recover, she turned to look at Sushi again. 'Senhor Ferrara will have to be asked. He will need to see Ram Kopal. And, of course, Senhora Ferrara will need to see you, Sushi.'

'I come with you to English chapel on Saturday. When you practise for wedding on Monday. I tell Ferrara Sahib and his wife.'

'No, Sushi,' Ruth said firmly. 'You must not tell Senhor Ferrara what you have organised. I will ask him if he agrees to the plans you have made.'

'You ask Ferrara Memsahib. She like me. You like daughter to her,' Sushi smiled. 'Soon we both be grandmothers to English grandson.'

'What am I to do with you?' Ruth asked. 'I ought to be cross with you.'

'After wedding I go to house of Ferrara Sahib. You no longer cross with me then because Pushpa be with you. She do everything you say. No arguments between you and her. Make no plans for you. You be proper burra memsahib then.'

Ruth looked wistfully at Sushi. 'I shall miss you, Sushi. We've been through so much together.'

'I miss you too, my daughter.'

Ruth was surprised to see tears in the older woman's eyes. There had been a subtle change in the relationship between them since their journey into Maratha territory. The old warmth was still there but they seemed reluctant to show any emotion towards each other, especially when others were present. Ruth remembered how Mark had tried to thank Sushi when they reached the government rest house, after their encounter with the imperial cavalry. He thanked her for obtaining their release from the Moguls, speaking to her in English so that nobody, apart from Ruth, would understand.

Sushi had shrugged her shoulders almost dismissively. 'I not think of you, Captain Sahib. Ruth and I kiss to get away quickly from those cow-killers. My daughter Ruth ready to give herself to you to save your life. Kiss between mother and daughter nothing.' She continued perfunctorily. 'No need to tell President Sahib.'

'But I'm very grateful …' Mark had said.

Sushi's interruption was almost brutal. 'Mussulmans not care. Kashi Mathura and Nabha Sing tell me they see nothing. Why President Sahib know your wife kiss her mother?'

Mark had taken her by the shoulders, kissed her gently on the forehead and said, 'You're quite right, mother.'

Ruth reached out to take Sushi's hands in hers. She squeezed them as she told Sushi, 'I will speak to Senhor Ferrara and his wife on Saturday.'

\* \* \* \* \*

Saturday morning saw Ruth and her group of friends assembled outside the door of the chapel. Ruth could not help feeling regret as she remembered the rehearsal for Claire's wedding just those few months ago. There had never been the same warmth between Roland and Claire as there was between her and Mark. From the second time they met, when she was just a girl and Mark a gangling youth, they had shared a common sympathy which was conspicuously lacking in the relationship between Roland and Claire. Ruth looked at Fernando and Maria and then at Peter and Jacoba. There was a subtle closeness between both couples, which she had not been aware of with her foster-sister and Roland. Each had the ability to converse by means of non-verbal signals and to know instinctively what their partners were thinking, a closeness and ability which she and Mark shared. After the conventional greetings had been exchanged, the conversation continued on the subject of the wedding arrangements. When Peter asked Mark if the wedding ring was available, he replied that Ruth wanted to wear Claire's ring.

'It's a link with my sister,' Ruth said simply. 'Claire was also Elizabeth's best friend. She's Mark's sister and I feel this ring is a link between our two families as well as a symbol for Mark and myself.'

Mark looked down at the signet ring with the Fairbrother crest, which he wore on the little finger of his left hand.

'I'd like the chaplain to bless this ring as well, Peter. Father Dellon blessed it and I put it on Ruth's finger the night we were married in the French factory. After I told her it belonged to my eldest brother, Ruth insisted on my taking it back the next morning. I want her to give it back to me during the marriage service.'

'You, you are …' Jacoba began. 'Vot is zat word I look for, Peter?'

'Sentimental,' her husband replied.

'Zat is right. You sentimental man, Mark. I suppose you vont Ruth to vear vite gown for bride.'

'No!' Ruth said firmly. 'I shall wear my gold bridesmaid's gown. This time I have put a few light blue trimmings on it. I am no hypocrite. I shall not pretend to be something I am not. I want everyone to know I was proud to take Mark as my husband, even if we were not married in the English church.'

'Sorry, Ruth,' Jacoba said. 'I only ask because Senhora Ferrara and I vont to know vot ve vear on Monday.'

'Of course, Jacoba,' Ruth replied. She turned to Maria. 'Why not wear the matron of honour's gown you wore at Claire's wedding? You can put some silver trimmings on it. In your case,' she said, looking at Jacoba, 'Wear something which will go with that colour scheme.'

Ruth was saved any further embarrassment when discussion stopped as Master Boland came out of the door of the chapel. Unlike the rehearsals for Claire's wedding there was no need to make any introductions because all those present were known to the chaplain.

'I understand you will be Captain Fairbrother's supporter, Master Streynsham,' the chaplain said.

'Yes. That's correct,' Peter replied.

Master Boland turned to Ruth and Mark who were standing together. 'I have just received copies of the new prayer book. You two will be the first couple I will have married using the new service. But I'm sure we'll all manage. And you, Senhor, must be acting as father of the bride,' he said to Fernando.

'I have that honour, father,' Fernando answered.

'If you, Master Streynsham, and Captain Fairbrother will go into the chapel and stand in front of the altar screen, I will be with you in a moment.'

Mark and Peter went through the chapel door and Master Boland asked Fernando to stand, with Ruth holding his left arm, facing the chapel door. The chaplain asked if Maria and Jacoba were matrons of honour and requested them to stand a yard behind Ruth and Fernando. He threw a quick glance at Sushi who was about three yards away.

'I not come in today,' Sushi said.

'Perhaps I come in on Monday. When my daughter marry before I only stay little while. Not understand what any one says.'

Master Boland smiled. 'That service was in Latin. The service on Monday will be in English.'

Ruth turned round. 'I would like you to come in on Monday, Sushi. Please tell me that you'll come.'

'Then I come on Monday,' Sushi answered. 'I wait now. See Ferrara Memsahib later.'

'We mustn't keep the gentlemen waiting,' the chaplain interrupted. 'I'll go into the chapel now. Give me a few seconds, then start walking up the aisle. Bride and father first. Matrons of honour following.'

'Yes, father,' Fernando replied. 'I will lead these ladies into your church.' After a few seconds, Ruth and the others went through the door. Fernando walked with her up the aisle in the same unhurried way which she remembered from Claire's wedding. They stopped alongside Mark and he gave her a warm smile as Fernando moved to her left side.

'Will you two matrons of honour please sit in the front pew now?' the chaplain asked. He turned to Mark. 'Some people choose to have hymns when they marry. Have you any special favourites?'

Mark thought carefully for a few seconds. 'It didn't cross my mind, Master Boland. There are two hymns I quite like. One begins, "Christ is our cornerstone, On him alone we build". The other starts off, "Praise to the Lord, the Almighty, the King of Creation".'

'Both quite suitable,' the chaplain replied.

'May we have the hymn written by John Milton? The one based on Psalm 136?' Ruth asked. 'The first verse of it goes like this,

> *"Let us with gladsome mind*
> *Praise the Lord, for he is kind*
> *For his mercies aye endure*
> *Ever faithful, ever sure".'*

The chaplain looked startled. 'But he was a Puritan. Cromwell's Latin Secretary. He was lucky not to be hanged.'

'I know, Master Boland,' Ruth answered. 'I am not trying to turn my husband into a dissenter.' She blushed slightly and lowered her eyes. 'When we have children they will be baptised into the Church of England. I remember the words of Ruth the Moabite, 'For whither thou goest, I will go; and where thou lodgest, I will lodge; thy people shall be my people, and thy God my God'. But I was brought up as a Puritan and that hymn was a favourite of my foster-father.' Ruth took a handkerchief from her sleeve and dabbed her eyes. 'None of my family will be at my wedding. I want to feel my foster-father is present in spirit.'

'I would like the congregation to join in singing Colonel Trent's favourite hymn as well, Master Boland,' Mark said.

'Very well, Captain Fairbrother. If that is your wish. I will see it is included in the order of service.'

The rest of the rehearsal went without a hitch. Master Boland was quite happy to agree on the blessing for both Claire's wedding ring and Mark's signet ring. It was decided that Peter and Maria would sign the register as witnesses, and then the little procession formed in the aisle, with Mark and Ruth in front, followed by Fernando and Maria, who were followed in turn by Peter and Jacoba. They moved slowly down the aisle, went through the door and were welcomed outside by Master Boland. The chaplain was smiling and relaxed, the other participants in the rehearsal were carefree, and Ruth thought how different it was from Claire's rehearsal and her subsequent marriage. The question of making room for Sir George's carriage was raised by the chaplain and Peter answered by saying, 'Leave it to me, Master Boland. I will make sure all is in order. I don't think Sir George will be in any great hurry. Ruth is a great favourite of his.'

'Excellent,' the chaplain replied. He turned to Fernando and Maria. 'I look forward to seeing you at nine o'clock on Monday morning.'

'Yes, father,' they both replied.

Master Boland beamed at the other two couples. 'And the rest of you good people at half past nine tomorrow morning. I will bid you all good day now.'

He shook hands with the six of them and went back into his chapel.

'Come over to have tiffin with us after service at the chapel tomorrow. You and Jacoba,' Mark said to Peter.

'We'd love to do that. If there are any last minute arrangements we can sort them out then,' Peter replied.

'Well you won't have to fill me with Dutch courage,' Mark said, grinning at Jacoba. 'Ruth and I are an old married couple.'

'You naughty man,' Jacoba said. 'Ruth is too good for you.'

'Will you and Maria stay with us overnight on Sunday?' Ruth asked Fernando.

'It will be a pleasure,' he answered. 'After all, you no need to come to my house this time. You already married by Catholic priest. No need to marry any more.'

'Fernando!' Maria exclaimed. 'If Ruth want to marry Mark again, do not try to stop her. May we bring Pushpa and Des Raj with us. Pushpa help Sushi take special care of you. Des Raj prepare carriage for the bride.'

'Of course,' Ruth replied. 'There is room enough in the servants' quarters for them.'

At the mention of the names of her daughter and son-in-law, Sushi moved forward. 'I speak to you about Pushpa and husband, memsahib,' she said, addressing Maria. 'When marriage finished they stay with Captain Fairbrother and young memsahib.' Both Maria and her husband looked startled.

'Do they know this?' Fernando asked.

'I tell them two days ago. They not glad to leave your home but they happy to be with the young sahib. I come to look after Ferrara memsahib. Be good servant if you take me back with you.'

'But Des Raj is a good syce!' Fernando exclaimed. 'I want him to stay.'

'I get you good syce, sahib.' Sushi persisted. 'Ram Kopal, syce of Lockyer Sahib, not want to go to Rajapur with his master. He very happy to work for you, sahib. I spoke to him three days ago. He very good man. You ask Fairbrother Memsahib.'

Fernando laughed. 'You have been busy with your plans. What do you think about this, Mark?'

'It would solve a problem for us. The Robertson's syce and his wife want to go back to their farm. They're only staying until we get a replacement.'

'What about Sushi, Ruth?' Fernando asked.

The two women looked at each other for three or four seconds before Ruth replied. 'I don't want her to go. I said I would speak to you about her plans but I want her to stay.'

'I get cross with you,' Sushi said. 'Captain's memsahib should have young girl for servant. Not old woman like me. I not want to stay with you any more. You burra memsahib now.'

Both Fernando and Maria appeared shocked at this outburst. Peter and Jacoba, who had seemed disinterested in the conversation up to that point, looked surprised. 'Sushi and Ruth are both in a difficult position,' Mark said gently. 'The other servants we took over from the Robertsons can't understand why Ruth allows Sushi to talk to her like that. They can't see why she is dealt with in a different way to the other servants. Sushi and Ruth are very close but I'm sure Sushi would be more settled if she came to you. And Ruth could still see her from time to time.'

'You be good servant to me, Sushi?' Maria asked. 'Not cross at all?'

'I be special servant to you, memsahib. You be Ferrara Memsahib to me. Not like daughter to me,' she said softly.

'I get husband to bring Pushpa and Des Raj with him tomorrow. You make sure your English daughter is beautiful bride and we take you back to Ferrara house.'

\* \* \* \* \*

By just after eight on Monday morning, everybody was ready. Peter and Jacoba Streynsham had come to the bungalow to join them for breakfast. Jacoba was wearing a pale yellow silk gown, with a pale blue girdle tied round her waist. Peter wore highly polished boots, blue silk breeches, a brown jacket with a large white lace collar round his neck and large white lace cuffs round his wrists. He had pinned silver coloured lace ribbons to the sleeves of his jacket and to the sides of his breeches. There was a certain amount of jocular banter at the ability of the bride and groom to eat a normal meal. After breakfast was finished, Mark, Ruth and Maria went off to change while Peter, Jacoba and Fernando sat on the verandah watching Des Raj and Ram Kopal decorating the carriages with the help of the other servants. In addition to the large carriages belonging to the Ferraras and the Streynshams, there was the small two-seater vehicle which Mark had bought from the Robertsons with the help of the advance of his pay. A few minutes after breakfast was over, Mark joined his guests.

'We'll travel to the chapel in your carriage, Mark,' Peter said. 'Jacoba and Maria will go in mine. You take Ruth in yours, if that's alright, Fernando.'

'Of course, Senhor Streynsham. It will be my pleasure. And Sushi and Pushpa will sit on top with Des Raj.'

'When the service is over, you and Ruth will return here in the President's palanquin,' Peter continued.

'What!' Mark exclaimed.

Peter smiled. 'Sir George is very fond of Ruth. Even though you were married in the French factory during the siege, he wants to make sure today will be a day to remember. For both of you.' He chuckled. 'And Lady Alice approves of you. Now that Ruth has met her handsome prince, she wants Ruth to be treated as a princess, if only for a day. Mind you, you'll have to treat her as a princess for the rest of your life.'

Mark waited a short time, as if uncertain how to reply. 'I will always be in my wife's debt.'

Fernando sensed that the conversation was becoming too serious and asked, 'How many guests you bring back here after the wedding?'

'Eighteen.'

'And how many go as well to the English chapel.'

'I don't know,' Mark replied.

'I think over a hundred.'

'What!' Mark exclaimed. 'Why so many?'

Fernando laughed. 'You famous man. Everyone in Surat know of Captain Fairbrother, saved by beautiful English senhora from hands of wicked Shivaji. They also know of fight with Senhor Lockyer. To defend not your own but honour of your wife. All people. Dutch, Portuguese, French, as well as English come to see lucky man who marry lovely English girl.'

'I didn't know,' Mark answered lamely.

'You don't need to look sorry,' Peter said. 'Everyone wishes both of you well. Especially the ladies. They now understand why Ruth did not marry before.'

Mark looked slightly embarrassed. Jacoba chortled. 'Ven all those ladies look at handsome Captain Fairbrother, zey know vy. Zey all be jealous of your Ruth.' She smiled across to Peter. 'Apart from Maria and me, of course.'

Fernando rested a hand on Mark's shoulder. 'Let's go into the courtyard,' he said. 'And leave Des Raj and Ram Kopal to their work.'

After a few minutes, Peter and Jacoba followed them into the courtyard, to be followed soon afterwards by Maria and Pushpa. Maria was wearing the gold bridesmaid's gown she had worn at Claire's wedding, together with a silver-coloured, silk girdle round her waist. Pushpa wore a new, bright, gold, silk sari, with silver threads in it. A minute or so later, Ruth and Sushi appeared. Sushi was wearing a new, silk sari of the same colour as that worn by her daughter. Ruth wore her gold, silk gown, with a few light blue trimmings. When he saw her, Mark went across and kissed her, whispering, 'You look so beautiful, dearest,' in her ears.

Jacoba moved over to kiss Ruth on the cheek so that all five women were standing together.

'Look at them!' Fernando exclaimed, waving his arms in their direction. 'Like a group of golden suns. Brightening the days of us poor men. Warming our cold hearts.'

'Vy not you say like that, Peter?' Jacoba asked.

'Fernando is a poet. I'm only a simple merchant,' he replied.

Fortunately, further controversy was stopped by Mai Nayah, Mark's new bearer, appearing with posies of flowers. He bowed gravely to the gentlemen and then asked Mark, 'I give flowers, sahib?'

'Yes, of course, Mai.'

The bearer handed posies to Ruth, Maria, Jacoba, Sushi and Pushpa in turn. After he had finished, Ruth turned to Mark and said excitedly, 'I'd like Sushi and Pushpa to follow me into the chapel. Behind Maria and Jacoba. Would you mind, Mark?'

'It's a little unusual,' he replied. 'What do you think, Peter?' Peter looked across at Jacoba who nodded slightly.

'Provided Sushi and her daughter don't feel out of place, I'd have no objection.'

'How would you like to walk with your daughter behind Senhora Ferrara and Mistress Streynsham?' Mark asked. 'And sit with them on the front seat in the chapel.'

'We both be very happy, Sahib,' Sushi replied. 'I like to give present.' She placed the flowers she was carrying on a chair behind her and produced a necklace of black onyx beads. 'You Christian, but you still my daughter. I want you to have this. Hindu ladies wear these when they marry, Ruth. You keep still,' she said to Ruth. 'How I put this on if you move?'

'Thank you,' Ruth said, kissing Sushi lightly on the mouth as Sushi's hands were behind Ruth's neck, putting the necklace in place. 'You wait here a minute.'

She hurried away and returned shortly afterwards with the pearl necklace which Roland had given Claire. 'This is for you, mother.'

Sushi lowered her head. 'You keep still this time.' Ruth continued, 'How can I put it on?'

When Ruth's hands were behind Sushi's neck, putting the pearl necklace in place, Sushi raised her head and kissed Ruth firmly on the lips. Ruth's arms moved around Sushi's shoulders and held her close. Even after their kiss finished, Sushi still clung to Ruth, with their cheeks pressed together. 'You still my daughter,' she whispered in Ruth's ear. There were tears in the servant's eyes and on her cheeks. It was the first time Mark had ever seen Sushi cry.

'I think you and I ought to go to the chapel, Mark,' Peter said quietly. 'Fernando can cope with everything that needs to be done here.'

Ruth was surprised by the large crowd of Europeans and Indians waiting outside the English chapel when she drove up. She could not understand why the Europeans made no move to go inside the chapel when Fernando took her arm and Maria and the other women fell into line behind her. The crowd pressed forward as Fernando moved forward and there was barely enough room for Ruth and her attendants between the crowds on either side of the chapel door. As the little party entered the chapel, Ruth could see that not only was every seat taken, apart from the pews in the very front row, but a number of people were standing along the side walls. Fernando paused a few feet inside the door to allow the two matrons of honour and two servants to move closer. When he was satisfied they were all in position, he started walking slowly down the aisle.

Ruth thought the words of the marriage service were the most beautiful words she had heard in her life When the chaplain asked, 'Mark, Wilt thou have this woman to thy wedded wife, to live together after God's ordinance in the holy estate of matrimony? Wilt thou love her, comfort her, honour and keep her, in sickness and in health; and forsaking all others, keep thee only unto her, so long as ye both shall live?' Mark's answer was a loud, clear 'I will' which could be heard by everyone in the chapel.

The answer to the question, 'Ruth, Wilt thou have this man to thy wedded husband, to live together after God's ordinance in the holy estate of matrimony? Wilt thou obey him, and serve him, love, honour, and keep him, in sickness and in health; and, forsaking all others, keep thee only unto him, so long as ye both shall live?' was an equally decisive 'I will.'

Ruth smiled encouragingly as Mark took her right hand in his. There was no hesitation or pause as he began, 'I Mark, take thee Ruth, to my wedded wife, to have and to hold from this day forward, for better for worse, for richer for poorer, in sickness and in health, to love and to cherish, till death do us part, according to God's holy ordinance and thereto I plight thee my troth.'

It was Mark's turn to smile encouragement as Ruth said in a firm voice, 'I Ruth, take thee Mark, to my wedded husband, to have and to hold from this day forward, for better for worse, for richer for poorer, in sickness and in health, to love, cherish, and to obey, till death us do part, according to God's holy ordinance; and thereto I give thee my troth.'

Master Boland had already blessed Mark's signet ring and the wedding ring. She lifted Mark's ring from the chaplain's prayer book and slipped it quickly on to Mark's little finger. Mark held Ruth's left hand in his and lifted the wedding ring from the prayer book with his right hand. He started to slip the wedding ring on to the third finger of Ruth's left hand. Mark began confidently enough to repeat after the chaplain the words, 'With this ring I thee wed.' His voice wavered as he repeated the phrase, 'With my body I thee worship' and Ruth squeezed the thumb of his right hand between the thumb and little finger of her left hand. Mark's voice became clearer and louder as he finished off, 'And with all my wordly goods I thee endow: In the name of the Father, and of the Son, and of the Holy Ghost. Amen.'

As they went on their knees together in front of the altar screen to join the rest of the congregation in prayer, Ruth reached out for Mark's right hand and continued to hold it until the prayers were over. At last the service was finished and Peter and Maria followed them into the vestry to sign the register. The chaplain finished writing out the marriage certificate and handed it to Ruth with a smile, saying, 'This is for you, Mistress Fairbrother.'

Ruth thanked him as she shook his hand and then they went back into the chapel to join the rest of the congregation. She took her husband's left arm and waited for Fernando and Maria, Peter and Jacoba, and Sushi and Pushpa to line up behind, before walking slowly down the aisle, towards the chapel door. Although there were a few familiar faces and some more people whom Ruth remembered from Claire's wedding, most of the congregation were strangers. Everybody seemed to be smiling as the small party made its way out of the chapel. She stood in the doorway and saw that the men who had escorted them into Maratha country, as well as those Mark had commanded during the last days of the siege, were drawn up in two small ranks to form a guard of honour, each holding a spear.

Sir George's palanquin was about twenty yards away, surrounded by a large crowd. After Mark and Ruth had passed the guard of honour, the spearmen pushed in front of them to form a small phalanx and started to edge forward slowly towards the palanquin. Ruth could hear cries of 'Vive la belle Madame' from the excited, young French factors in the crowd and single flowers kept being thrown in their path. When the spearmen reached the palanquin they moved back so that Mark and Ruth could take their places inside. The two of them remained standing outside so that they could greet well-wishers. Des Raj and Ram Kopal were already near the palanquin holding garlands of flowers in their hands. Each of them shyly placed a garland around Mark's neck and then handed garlands to Sushi and Pushpa who had pushed their way to the front of the crowd. Pushpa raised her garland up, held her arms out straight, and placed the garland of flowers around Ruth's neck. Sushi repeated the process and when she had finished, she placed a little dab of paint on Ruth's forehead, looked at her and smilingly said, 'Everybody know you married woman now, daughter.'

A moment or two later Sir George and Lady Oxindon came up to congratulate them. Sir George shook Mark's hand and kissed Ruth lightly on the cheek. He looked at them carefully and said, 'You really are a striking couple.' After a slight pause, he continued, 'And you set a good example to my young factors. Far too many of them have, well, unofficial arrangements with native women.'

'I am sure if we had more girls like Ruth in Surat, Master Boland would find himself extremely busy marrying them off,'

Lady Alice said. 'Once you have settled in your bungalow, we must see more of you two. I haven't seen much of you since your sister's illness and that unhappy business with Master Lockyer.'

'Thank you, Lady Alice,' Ruth replied. 'How will you and Sir George get to our bungalow if we have Sir George's palanquin?'

'We will ride with Master Streynsham. In his carriage,' Sir George answered. 'Today I want everyone to know you both have my wholehearted approval.' Ruth could see the French President standing just behind Sir George. As she caught his eye, he bowed slightly to her and Sir George turned to greet Monsieur Villeneuve. After the conventional greetings had been exchanged between the two Presidents and their respective wives, Monsieur Villeneuve kissed Ruth's hand and then presented her and Mark to Madame Villeneuve. Ruth was a little puzzled when the French President's wife spoke to Mark in French and he replied in the same language. After Mark had finished speaking, Madame Villeneuve laughed and apologised to Ruth.

'Pardon, madame. You have husband who is so beau, I think he must be Frenchman.'

Ruth smiled. 'No, madame. He is as English as I am.'

'When my husband tell story of young English demoiselle who argue with the wicked Shivaji to save life of young man, I think how brave. How romantic.' Madame Villeneuve continued, 'I tell my husband, I must see this man.' She looked at Mark and smiled. 'I not disappointed. Un beau soldat. Pardon, madame. I speak in French. He is so handsome, I think he must be French. I know you both very happy.'

'Thank you, madame,' Ruth replied. 'And to you Monsieur Villeneuve, for your kindness to Mark and me.'

'Enchanted, madame,' the French President answered with a low bow.

The crowd of well-wishers was pressing round and Sir George seemed to become slightly anxious. 'I think, Monsieur,' he said, addressing the French President, 'we should allow this young couple to take their leave of us.'

'Of course, Sir George,' Monsieur Villeneuve answered.

'You must come to see me, Madame Fairbrother,' his wife quickly intervened. 'Tell me full story. You know these men. Only say half of things.'

'I will be delighted, Madame Villeneuve,' Ruth replied.

Mark took his wife's hand, helped her into the palanquin, and then took his place beside her. He noticed that a rider on a large, white Arab horse was in front of the palanquin, closely followed by a standard bearer carrying the flag of St. George. Eight porters lifted the palanquin from the ground and the six spearmen formed up on either side. Sir George gave a brief word of command to the rider and the procession started to move off slowly. Instead of going straight out of the square in front of the chapel, the procession made a complete circuit, going through the lines of the crowd, so that everybody could see the bridal pair. Those of the wedding guests who had no carriage started to walk behind the palanquin as the little procession left the square. They were followed by the carriages of the more important guests, as well as a few individual horsemen. A small crowd of spectators, made up of people of a variety of nationalities, followed in the wake of the procession as it moved along the road. By the time the last of the congregation had left the square, the procession had increased to a considerable size. Trading ceased as they passed through the market, with traders and customers craning their necks to see who was being escorted by so many people. Even the Mogul officials and soldiers, going about their business, stopped briefly to see if the English had a new President. Bullock carts, carrying the produce of local farmers, and carriages belonging to European traders, all stopped at crossroads as a mark of respect, allowing the palanquin to make an uninterrupted progress to the bungalow occupied by Ruth and Mark.

Just before they arrived, Ruth turned from looking at the crowd on both sides of the road and smiled at Mark. 'I feel like a queen.'

'You will always be my queen,' he replied earnestly. 'Queen Ruth. I will always be yours to command.'

'Never talk of commands between us, my love,' Ruth answered softly. 'You are my husband. Not my servant. I am your wife and will work alongside you.' Mark leaned across and tried to kiss her.

'Not now, Mark. We're nearly there. Think of your guests.' He sat upright again.

'Don't be disappointed, darling.' Ruth smiled and squeezed his hand. 'We'll still be together. Once the guests have gone.'

'And for the rest of our lives,' he answered softly.

\* \* \* \* \*

The reception was much quieter than the one which had followed the wedding of Claire and Roland. Mark and Ruth stood in the doorway to greet their guests as they arrived. Tanadai, the Robertson's syce, had agreed to remain for a few more days and he, Des Raj, and Ram Kopal looked after the carriage horses as well as the mounts of individual riders. Mai Nayah, Mark's new bearer, arranged for food to be available outside the servants' quarters for the porters, spearmen, and other attendants.

Sir George and Lady Oxindon led the guests into the courtyard after shaking Mark's hand and kissing Ruth's cheek. Apart from Jacoba Streynsham, Maria and Fernando Ferrara, the remainder of the guests were English people, working for the East India Company, and their wives. During the wedding breakfast Mark replied to the toast of 'The bride and groom', Fernando replied to the toast as the father of the bride and Peter Streynsham replied to the toast 'The matrons of honour'. Just before the meal ended, Sir George rose to his feet and asked the guests to drink the health of the king. They all stood up raised their glasses and said, 'His Majesty, King Charles the Second'. When Ruth sipped the wine from her glass, she became aware of Sir George, looking in her direction. She caught his eye and he gave an almost imperceptible bow before resuming his seat.

Once the meal was over, the guests began to circulate and it was several minutes before she found herself talking to Sir George. After he had asked her to compliment the cook on the meal, Sir George said quietly, 'I observe you now drink the king's health. During your sister's reception, you left your glass on the table during the loyal toast.'

'That is so, Sir George. I am not inconsistent. Both my father and my foster-father were enemies of the old king. As a dutiful daughter, I shared their opinion. My husband is a loyal subject of Charles the Second. Is that not sufficient reason for me to drink the king's health?'

'Yes, but what do you think, Ruth?' Sir George asked.

'I think it is possible for me to be a loyal subject without believing that the king has the divine right to rule as an absolute monarch. The people of England are not serfs or vassals!'

'Gently, Ruth,' Sir George said, 'I am sure most of us would agree.'

'Indeed, that is so, Sir George. The king and the people of England are one nation under God and the king cannot rule without the consent of his people. When I drink the health of his majesty, it is to wish peace and prosperity for our country, praying that God will keep us from civil war.'

'If you were a man, you'd make a good diplomat. I must remember that,' Sir George smiled. 'I do not wish you to neglect your other guests, but if I ever again need to send someone on a mission, I might call on your services.' A few minutes past midday, Sir George asked the guests to drink a final toast to the happy couple before leaving them to their own devices. After the guests had finished drinking the health of Mark and Ruth, they crowded round the two of them to repeat their good wishes. Mark made his way to the verandah, bringing Ruth with him, and they stood together as their friends' carriages and horses were brought round to the front of the bungalow.

At long last even the high-spirited young factors were gone. The only carriage left was the one belonging to the Ferraras, with Ram Kopal on the coachman's seat and Sushi standing beside it. Maria and Fernando waited just behind Mark and Ruth until the other guests had gone. Fernando shook Mark's hand and then Maria kissed him on the cheek. She laughed. 'I hope you remember to take good care of Ruth. You lucky man. She good woman. Too good for you, perhaps.'

Mark looked at Ruth before replying, 'She is more precious to me than my own life.'

As if to hide her emotions, Maria embraced Ruth, whispering in her ear, 'I very happy for you now. You not alone any more.'

There were tears in her eyes when she released Ruth. Fernando took his wife's arm and led her gently towards his carriage, with Mark and Ruth following discreetly behind. Fernando helped Maria into the carriage and then kissed Ruth lightly on the cheek. He stood aside to allow Sushi to get into the coach but she shook her head.

'I sit with Ram Kopal, sahib. I memsahib's servant now. It is not fitting for me to sit with you. You lose izzat.'

Ruth looked across to Sushi. Although her face was lined and her hair grey, she still stood as erect as a young woman. Ruth moved towards her and took Sushi's hand in hers. 'Thank you for everything,' she said. 'You will never be a servant in my eyes.'

'You remember you married woman now,' Sushi answered, almost gruffly. 'I hear from daughter Pushpa if you not care for Fairbrother Sahib.'

Ruth released her hands and the older woman stepped back only to be stopped again by Ruth's left hand reaching out to hold her shoulder. She lifted the bottoms of the long garlands of flowers and placed them over Sushi's neck, so that the two women were enclosed by a single circle of flowers.

Mark saw Sushi's face looking over his wife's shoulder and then she lowered her head as if to hide her emotion.

'Remember how we tied our robes together, Sushi?' Ruth asked. Sushi nodded. 'I will take this garland this afternoon and place it on Claire's grave,' Ruth continued. 'Then we'll all be united.'

For a few seconds nobody spoke, until Sushi lifted the garland of flowers off her shoulders and, with tears in her eyes, said, 'Your sister is happy now, my daughter. She is with bride of Shiva. The Daughter of Snows. I go now. You say prayer for Lockyer Memsahib for me.'

Ruth still held Sushi in her arms and kissed her on the cheeks, before whispering, 'I will never forget you.'

Sushi walked quickly away, and climbed to sit beside Ram Kopal, looking straight ahead as she took her place. Fernando took his seat in the carriage as it moved slowly forward. Mark could see the Ferraras looking back as their coach pulled away but Sushi did not even give a backward glance.

# 17

## AUGUST 1664

Ruth felt the child growing bigger inside her each day. Although the heat worried her a great deal, she was pleased when Master Moxon said that he thought her child, Mark's child, would be born in December. This was the best month for a European child to be born in India, as it gave the baby a chance to become strong in advance of the disease and heat of the few weeks preceding the monsoon. It seemed strange that both she and Pushpa should become pregnant while in the new bungalow. Perhaps there was something in the old saying 'New house, new baby.'

Mark had been consideration itself ever since they had received confirmation of Ruth's condition from Master Moxon. Although he had his work, training and exercising the new squad of men the East India Company had recruited for defensive purposes, Mark spent every minute of his spare time with Ruth. Her heart leapt as she saw him ride up in front of the bungalow. Des Raj hurried forward and took the horse to the stables to be rubbed down and fed. Ruth got up as Mark ran up the steps and they kissed.

'You're a little earlier than usual, darling,' she said.

'I know. Sir George sent for me. He wants to see you in his reception room at nine tomorrow morning. Do you feel up to going, sweetheart?'

'Of course I'll go. Apart from this heat, I feel as fit as a flea.'

'Curious thing is, he wouldn't tell me why. Wants Fernando to bring Sushi as well.'

'Sushi?' Ruth asked quietly.

'Yes. Strange, isn't it?' Mark replied.

Her thoughts wandered over the past six months since her marriage in the English chapel. Sushi came on fortnightly visits to their bungalow but the purpose was always to see Pushpa and Des Raj. She congratulated Ruth warmly when told the news of her pregnancy. Although Ruth told Sushi then to visit her whenever she wished, they had not been alone together at any time. Ruth exchanged a few words with her each time she and Mark visited the Ferraras' bungalow but someone else was always present. It seemed as though they were destined to drift apart.

'Stop day-dreaming, dearest. We ought to think about something to eat.'

She laughed. 'You're quite right, darling. Must keep up all our strengths.'

\* \* \* \* \*

Peter Streynsham met Mark and Ruth at the factory just before nine the following morning. Sushi and Fernando arrived just as they were being led into the reception room. Fernando kissed Ruth on both cheeks and shook Mark warmly by the hand. He asked about Ruth's health and general well-being, leaving just enough time for Ruth and Sushi to hold hands, before Peter re-entered the room, bringing Sir George with him. After he had asked them all to be seated, Sir George said that although this was a private presentation it was, nevertheless, a very important occasion.

'I propose to pass this information on, not just to my own factors but to the Presidents of the other trading companies in Surat. The directors of the East India Company have decided to honour three people for services to the company during the recent seige. One of these persons is Mistress Ruth Fairbrother.' Ruth gave a slight gasp and Mark squeezed her hand. 'The second person is the Maratha lady, Sushi.' Ruth looked across to Sushi and smiled.

'I have been commanded by the directors to honour both these ladies by giving each of them a silver medal, struck in her honour by the Council. These medals bear the Latin inscription, 'Pro meritis contra Sevageum'. If you two ladies will step forward it will give me great pleasure to present you with these decorations.'

Ruth and Sushi went in front of Sir George and he opened the two presentation boxes to show them the silver medals inside, each with a long silver chain. 'My congratulations to you both,' he said, handing the boxes to them. Mark rose from his chair as Ruth returned.

Before she could sit down, he took the medal out of its case, hung it round her neck, kissed her and, still holding her in his arms, said softly, 'I'm so proud of you, dearest. My brave darling.' He was quickly followed by Peter and Fernando coming to add congratulations by kissing her cheeks and then Sir George came across to enlarge on his formal good wishes. Sushi looked a little forlorn as the small group congregated round Ruth. Mark went across to her, pulled her from her seat and kissed her gently on the cheek.

'I am puzzled, Sir George,' Fernando said. 'You say East India Company honour three people. Only two persons here. Why is third person not here, Sir George?'

Sir George looked embarrassed and hesitated before replying, 'I must correct you, Senhor Ferrara. The third person is here. The directors of the company have sent a gold medal for me.'

Mark hurried across to join in the general congratulations for the President. He heard Sir George saying, as he looked at Ruth wearing her medal, 'Women can carry off the wearing of a medallion and chain to perfection. But the wearing of jewelry is not becoming to a man.'

Ruth glanced across at Sushi. She looked so lonely on her own. Ruth went over to Sushi, held her by the shoulders, and kissed her on the cheek.

'Let me put your medal on for you. Then we will both be alike,' she said to Sushi. She took the medallion out of its presentation case and slipped the chain over Sushi's head. Ruth continued to hold her arms around Sushi's shoulders and asked 'Do you remember how you said, "I speak for my daughter," when Shivaji asked if your life was forfeit too?'

Sushi nodded and pressed her cheek against Ruth's.

'How you cared for me when I had nowhere to go?' Ruth asked, in a whisper. 'Remember how you stayed outside the door of my room when we were in the French factory.'

She giggled and pressed her forehead against Sushi's. 'And that sheet you gave to Abiji Sing?'

Sushi smiled and kissed Ruth's cheek. They held each other without speaking, each conscious of the memories they shared. Sushi moved her head so that she could look directly at Ruth.

'I have missed you, my daughter.'

'I have missed you too, mother,' Ruth answered. They stood close together, looking at each other, almost as if wondering what to do next. 'Why have you not come to see me on my own since you have been with Senhora Ferrara?' Ruth asked.

Sushi lowered her head and then lifted it again to look at Ruth. 'How could I come to you? My daughter Pushpa is your servant now.'

Ruth smiled and kissed Sushi on the forehead. They continued to hold each other close in spite of the pressure on Ruth's enlarged abdomen. Suddenly, Ruth could feel her child kicking inside her. Sushi must have felt it too, because she loosened her hold.

'Even if you are Senhora's servant now, you will always be Mother Sushi to me and Grandmother to my child.' Ruth said, pulling the older woman towards her and kissing her again on the forehead. 'You come to see me soon.'

Ruth became aware of Mark coughing discreetly at her side and turned her head to see her husband and Fernando standing together.

'Come on, you two,' Mark said smiling, 'Thought you'd never finish.' Ruth released Sushi from her embrace but still continued to hold her hand.

'Sushi and I were just congratulating each other on getting our medals. I asked her to come to see me soon. We hope we haven't kept you waiting.'

'Not at all,' Fernando replied, gallantly.

'We didn't know if you were going to be hugging all day,' Mark said, a little ungraciously.

The harsh words of Lady Fairbrother's that the Fairbrothers were not a kissing family went through Ruth's mind. She released Sushi's hand, put her arms round Mark's waist, pulled him to her, and kissed him fiercely. She paused after several seconds, looked Mark squarely in the eyes and laughingly asked, 'Would you mind if we hugged all day, darling?'

'Well,' was the only word he could speak before Ruth kissed him again. This time it was Peter Streynsham's turn to cough discreetly in the background.

'Sir George wishes to take his leave,' he whispered as Ruth released Mark from her arms.

They took two or three seconds to recover and then the five of them moved to the other side of the room where Sir George was standing.

'Sorry to hurry along the exchange of felicitations,' he said drily. 'I expect you young people will find a way to celebrate in your own time, but we all have business to attend to.' He turned to Sushi. 'May I say again, Sushi, how grateful the company is to you. We will always be in your debt. And to you, Mistress Fairbrother.' He looked at Mark. 'For more than one reason. I am obliged to both you ladies. Thank you for bringing Sushi along today, Senhor Ferrara.'

'It was my great pleasure, Sir George,' Fernando replied. 'Nevertheless, I am obliged to you. And will not forget.I will say good day to you all now.' He bowed to Sushi. 'Good day, Sushi. And thank you once more.'

'Good day, Sir George,' she replied very quietly.

'Good day, Ruth. Thank you,' he said, shaking her hand.

'Good day, Sir George.'

After the other leave takings had finished, Fernando took Sushi to his carriage as Mark helped Ruth into theirs. Before Mark could begin the journey back to the bungalow, Fernando hurried across to them.

'I have business to attend to in Surat, Mark,' he began. 'It is likely to take about two hours. Would you mind if Sushi stayed at your bungalow during that time?'

'Of course she can stay, Fernando. But I will be returning here as soon as I have taken Ruth back.'

'That is no matter. I can easily collect Sushi when my business is finished. I bring her across to your carriage now. I think she and Ruth have plenty to say to each other.'

At the end of this conversation, Ruth got out of the carriage again to tell Des Raj this was to be a special visit for her alone, not for him and Pushpa. 'Yes, memsahib,' he said as Sushi walked across the space between the two carriages, with her face beaming.

'Careful, Sushi,' Ruth said when Sushi started to embrace her. 'Ram Kopal.'

Sushi looked round quickly to see Fernando's syce looking down with a surprised look on his face.

# 18

## JUNE 1665

There was no need for lamps or candles to be lit after Lady Fairbrother and Elizabeth finished their evening meal. The long sunset of a midsummer day in the North of England meant that darkness did not fall until well into the evening. Because the day had been hot, the two women decided to sit outside on the terrace at the back of Aireton Hall, while they waited for Sir Henry to arrive. It was pleasant just to be there, looking out over the small formal garden and the rose garden beyond. The steward's lodge, in which they had lived until five years before, was screened by the trees of the Elm Walk, which were now in full foliage. In the near distance, sheep could be seen grazing in the meadows belonging to the estate farm.

Digby Foster coughed discreetly from behind and told them that Sir Henry's carriage had just arrived at the front of the house. Lady Fairbrother helped Elizabeth from her chair while the steward stood holding open the door which led into the dining room. As they went into the house, Sir Henry came into the dining room from the hall.

'Hello, Mother. Hullo, Sister,' he said, kissing each of them in turn.

'It's good to see you, Henry. But you must let one of the footmen help you out of those travel clothes and then Digby will bring you something to eat.'

'That can wait a minute or two,' he replied. 'Fact is, got two letters here. One in brother Mark's handwriting, addressed to you, Mother. Both got the Fairbrother crest impressed on the wax. Both from the Indies. Other one in another handwriting, addressed to you, little sister. So it's probably from the Parker girl. The Member of Parliament I'm friendly with, who's a director of East India Company, knew I was coming here for a short time to let off some of the land for rent. Devilish expensive being at court and a Member of Parliament too. Anyway, he thought it'd be quicker than sending them by ship to Hull and then overland here. They've been delayed. Ship carrying them was in a storm off West Africa. Had to put into Azores for repairs. Stayed there a month.' Sir Henry handed the letter to his sister. She broke the seal and her eyes opened wide. When Sir Henry handed the other letter to his mother, she looked at it wistfully for two or three moments.

'It's been a long time since we heard from Mark,' Lady Fairbrother sighed. 'I wonder how he is now.'

'My letter's from Ruth,' Elizabeth interrupted. 'She says she and Mark have a son John,' she continued excitedly. 'Wants me to know how happy they both are.'

Sir Henry's face went red. Lady Fairbrother sat down quickly with Mark's unopened letter still in her hands.

'The little vixen,' Sir Henry shouted. 'Well Mark won't get a penny out of me for the brat.'

'Why don't you see what Mark has written?' Elizabeth asked, with unaccustomed spirit. 'I thought you'd be glad. Should he have married one of those dusky maidens? He and Ruth were always fond of each other.' She sighed, 'I wish I was in Ruth's place. Nobody is ever likely to marry me for love.'

'What sort of future can Mark and his son have now?' her mother asked. 'Married to an orphan from a poor family.'

'Mark was always an impulsive romantic.' Sir Henry gave a slight sneer. 'Perhaps you'd better see what he's got to say for himself, Mother.'

There was silence for half a minute or so as Lady Fairbrother read the letter from her son and Elizabeth finished reading Ruth's letter.

'My first grandchild,' Lady Fairbrother whispered abstractedly. 'When I first saw them together I knew Ruth would have a child by Mark. I could see the way they looked at each other from the moment they met.'

'Don't expect me to make the Parker wench welcome,' Henry stormed. 'Or her brat.'

'I think you're very cruel,' Elizabeth said angrily. 'Mother knew how they felt about each other before you came back with King Charles. That's why she encouraged Mark to go back to Sweden. I thought you'd be glad he's happy now. I'm sure she's a good wife and mother.' She started to cry. 'Nobody is going to give me the chance to show I love them and to give them children of our own now I'm twenty-four.'

'Don't be sentimental, Elizabeth,' her mother told her. 'If you can't control yourself, go to your room!' She turned to her son. 'You know what this means, don't you, Henry?'

He looked puzzled. 'How does it affect me?'

'Uncle George was rather pinning his hopes on you or Mark. Since your brother put himself out of the running by marrying Ruth Parker, the coast has always been clear for you. Marriage to Sophie could make you a very wealthy man in time.'

'I need money now. That's why I came home for a few days. To arrange about those lets. And collect the midsummer rents. Can't waste time on plain, little Sophie. Too much unfinished business in London.'

'But Henry, why go back to London now that the plague has reached the city?'

'Just a few cases,' her son replied. 'Maybe I'll stay here for a bit longer until it blows over. Be finished in a month or so.'

'Won't you even consider calling on your Uncle George and Sophie while you're here? If you leave it too long before you marry, Henry, one of these days Mark will be master in your place.'

Sir Henry shrugged his shoulders.

'Or Ruth Parker's son could be the master of Aireton Hall one day,' Lady Fairbrother said.

Her son looked startled. 'In God's name, I never thought of that. Perhaps I'll marry after all. When I've done my business in London.'

Just before breakfast on the following morning, Lady Fairbrother gave the news to Digby Foster. When he offered his felicitations, she told him that Sir Henry did not consider congratulations to be in order. 'Do you wish me to keep the news to myself, your ladyship?' he enquired.

'No, Master Foster. You may tell the other servants. Mistress Ruth's foster-sister still lives in the area. No doubt it will soon be all over the district that the ward of their former Cromwellian governor has a child by my youngest son. I would rather the servants heard the news from you instead of picking up gossip from strangers.' She paused briefly. 'John is the first of the new generation.'

'As you say, Lady Fairbrother.' He hesitated. 'Will Master Mark be coming home? And Mistress Ruth?'

'No. I'm sure Sir Henry will say she is not welcome here.'

'I see. And Master Mark, your ladyship? And Master John?'

Lady Fairbrother's face softened. 'My youngest son has always been soft-hearted. He won't return here without his wife at his side.' She sighed. 'My grandson is unlikely to come here without his mother.'

# 19

## JULY 1666

The monsoon was late that year, making the air humid and oppressive. This was Ruth's third summer in India and she was becoming acclimatized, although her son John sometimes found the heat trying. He was twenty months old now, two months younger than Lakshmi, Pushpa's daughter. They had been constant companions ever since they had been able to crawl together. Sushi liked nothing better than to be with the two children, singing and talking to them in Marathi. She had infinite patience with them and John was never fractious with Grandmother Sushi. Des Raj often went to the Ferrara's bungalow to collect his mother-in-law, so that Sushi was a frequent visitor to the Fairbrother bungalow and had been since the day of the medal giving ceremony nearly two years ago. She was very careful never to show familiarity in the presence of other servants, apart from Pushpa, but the same old easy warmth existed between her and Ruth when they were alone together. Ruth looked across the room now and a wave of affection swept over her. Sushi was crooning to the two children playing happily on the floor beside her, laughing and cuddling together. The grey hair Ruth had first seen when Sushi arrived at Roland Lockyer's bungalow three and a quarter years ago had now turned to silver. Sushi's face was deeply lined, her breasts were now flat and arms wrinkled, but her body was still slim with the back as straight as ever.

Although Sushi never admitted to it, Ruth often suspected that Sushi favoured John over Lakshmi, her own granddaughter. Two months after John's birth, Des Raj was driving Ruth back from a visit to Lady Oxindon when the carriage horse went lame. Des Raj got down, took hold of the horse's head and started to lead it. Progress was painfully slow and, knowing how restive John became if he was not fed in time, she walked the rest of the way. Ruth hurried across the courtyard to her own room, knowing that John would be waiting for her there at this time of the day. Because they had not heard the sound of a carriage pulling up, the servants were taken by surprise. John was being fed by Pushpa and had a contented look on his face. Lakshmi was crying with hunger and thirst and refused to be pacified by Sushi. Pushpa lowered her eyes and half turned in an effort conceal her exposed breast.

'Why are you feeding my son instead of your own child, Pushpa?' Ruth asked angrily.

Before she had a chance to answer, Sushi interrupted, saying, 'I tell her to care for son of Captain Fairbrother before her own unworthy daughter.'

'All children are the same in the sight of God. Give me Lakshmi!' Ruth commanded.

Sushi knew it was better not to argue at this time. She helped slip the gown from Ruth's shoulder and watched as Lakshmi's mouth closed eagerly round Ruth's nipple. Pushpa stared in wide-eyed wonder as she saw her daughter being suckled at her mistress's breast.

When John grew older, Sushi had fiercely opposed his wearing swaddling clothes, as was customary with other European children. John usually wore loose fitting native dress, with sometimes no more than a loin cloth in warm weather. The exposed parts of his body had become brown under a tropic sun. John was tall for his age and had dark hair, so it was easy to take him and Lakshmi for siblings.

Ruth smiled on hearing the first clap of thunder because John instinctively followed Lakshmi's example and clung to Sushi. They heard a coppersmith bird give a menacing hoot to warn of the onset of the rain and after half a minute, the dark clouds opened. Ruth picked up John to cuddle him, only to be greeted by the sound of Lakshmi wailing for similar treatment. Sushi gave a serene smile as John snuggled happily in her arms after being handed over, while Ruth comforted Lakshmi. A minute later they heard the sound of a horseman riding up to the bungalow. A short time after, Mark burst into the living room where Ruth and Sushi sat with the two children. He looked anxious and agitated. The rain dripped from his wet clothes. 'What's wrong?' Ruth asked, a look of concern on her face. She handed Lakshmi to Sushi and got up to stand in front of Mark.

'Bad news, I'm afraid,' he replied.

'Do you want to tell me in another room?' Ruth asked, looking across at Sushi.

'No. Everyone should know as soon as possible. I must go back to England at once.'

'Now?' she asked incredulously.

'Yes. I have a letter here. Henry has died.'

She put her arms round Mark and held him tenderly in her arms. 'I'm so sorry, Mark. And you so far away. When did it happen?'

'The end of last summer.'

'The end of last summer?' Ruth was unable to believe her ears.

'Yes. The letter Mother wrote and the letter from the directors of the company about me were put in a ship which foundered. It was not reported overdue until it failed to dock in Surat. Mother had to write a duplicate which came out by a second ship in April.'

'I'm sorry, Mark.' She held him tight. 'So very sorry. Both for you and for your mother. And Elizabeth too. When we wrote at Christmas we didn't know anything about it.'

'I'm alright now, dearest.' He freed himself from her arms. 'Read Mother's letter yourself, Ruth.'

She opened the letter and read through it carefully. It told Mark that Henry had died of plague the previous summer. His mother said it was desperately important that he returned to England as soon as possible. Henry had allowed the estate to run down and Lady Fairbrother was unable to cope with the running of the property on her own. Henry had some influence with the East India Company when he was a Member of Parliament and she had asked them to release Mark from his contract.

Ruth took a handkerchief from her sleeve to wipe her eyes. This time it was the turn of Mark to do the comforting. 'Just like my mother and Frances's two boys,' Ruth said.

Mark held her tight. 'Yes. They died of plague too. It must have been terrible.'

Ruth broke free of Mark's arms to wipe the tears from her eyes once more. After a short pause, she said, 'Your mother only mentions you. She hasn't mentioned John or me.'

'Do you think I'd go back without you?' he asked, loudly and fiercely. 'Do you believe I want to leave my wife and son behind?'

'No, Mark,' Ruth replied quietly.

'I'm sorry, dearest. I didn't mean to shout. There is so much to do before we leave for home.'

Home. What was home to her, Ruth thought. The farm on which she had lived as a small girl so many years ago or the house to which her foster-parents had taken her and from which she had been brutally evicted six years ago? It did not mean the house in London where she lived on sufferance or, even worse, the bungalow belonging to Roland Lockyer from which he had so violently expelled her. The only real home she had known was here in Surat, with her husband and son, with Sushi and with the gentle Pushpa, who had almost taken her mother's place in Ruth's affections.

She let Mark take her in his arms again and looked up again into his anxious face. 'I will always be with you, darling. You know that,' she said. 'Wherever we go.'

He bent his head slightly and kissed her. As she felt the gentle, reassuring pressure of his arms she knew, with absolute certainty, that home could only be where Mark was.

'When do we leave?' she asked.

'As soon as possible. Would you mind?'

'Of course not, darling.'

'Will you come to see Fernando with me this afternoon. Luke thinks he has a friend who has just arrived from Portugal and is looking for a bungalow.' Ruth looked across to Sushi in the corner of the room with the children playing happily beside her. She had obviously heard the conversation because her face was sombre.

'Yes, Mark. Can I tell all the servants?'

'They ought to know. I'll change now. Let's have a meal and then we'll leave for Fernando's in an hour. We can take Sushi back with us.'

After Mark had left the room, Ruth went across to Sushi, held her hands and told her the news.

'You going home,' Sushi replied flatly.

'No, Sushi. I shall always think of this as my home. But I must go with my husband.' The older woman's lips started to tremble and her eyes filled with tears. She looked suddenly old and frail. Ruth's heart was filled with love for this woman of a different race who had cared for her when she needed help most, who had given Ruth affection when the world seemed a hostile, dangerous place, and had given Ruth's son a love as great as or even greater than the love she gave to Lakshmi, her own granddaughter.

When Pushpa came in she was surprised to see her mother and Ruth weeping copiously on each other's shoulders, with the children looking puzzled and near to tears themselves. She hovered round them, a look of concern on her face, unsure of whether to try to comfort them.

'What is wrong, memsahib?' Pushpa asked anxiously.

'I am going back to England. With my husband,' Ruth answered with a half-sob.

Several seconds passed before Pushpa found the words to reply. 'I hope you are very happy there. As happy as me here,' she said shyly. 'I hope you have been very happy here too.'

Ruth took her arms away from Sushi to look at Pushpa and saw tears in the younger woman's eyes also. 'I shall miss you, Pushpa,' she said.

'I miss you too, memsahib.'

'I miss you daughter. And my grandson.' Sushi interrupted. There was a fresh outburst of tears and she cried out, 'I lose my three sons. Now I never see grandson again.'

Ruth took her hands as the tears streamed down Sushi's face. 'Don't cry. My son and I will never forget you.' She held Sushi close to her, kissing the wetness of her cheeks and saying, 'Don't cry. My son and I will always love you.'

'I say goodbye now,' Sushi told her. 'Last time I say goodbye. Then no more.' Ruth looked at Pushpa for support but she stood transfixed by her mother's emotional outburst.

'You swear, Ruth. You promise me.' Sushi repeated more urgently. 'No more goodbyes.' Ruth bent down gently and kissed the wrinkled forehead, just below the line of the other woman's silver hair. 'I promise, mother.'

\* \* \* \* \*

The journey to Fernando's bungalow took place in almost complete silence. Mark, Ruth and Sushi kept their thoughts to themselves. Even if they had wished to converse, the hard rods of rain, beating on the roof and sides of the carriage would have made any conversation difficult. Sushi hurried off when they arrived.

Fernando and Maria were surprised to receive a visit at that time in the afternoon. They both extended their condolences to Mark on the loss of his brother, saying they were sorry not only to hear of his death but because it would take Mark and Ruth back to England.

'It will be better for John in England,' Maria said suddenly.

Ruth had a mental picture of row upon row of young children's graves in the European cemetery with Claire's grave in their midst.

'Yes,' Fernando agreed quietly.

'Luke Farmerdale mentioned to me you had a friend looking for a bungalow in Surat,' Mark began tentatively.

'Yes,' Fernando replied. 'He and his wife stay with me. Senhor Cabedo work for Portuguese trading company in Surat. I be very happy to bring him and Senhora Cabedo to your bungalow. Can Maria come with them?'

'I'd be greatly obliged, Fernando. Will tomorrow morning be convenient?' Fernando looked at Ruth and she nodded. 'I bring them then,' he replied.

'One other favour,' Mark began. 'Luke Farmerdale asked to see Sushi. I don't know why. Could you combine the visit with taking her to the English factory?'

'Of course. Senhor Cabedo hire carriage since he landed. He be pleased to take Maria back to Swally. I take Sushi later.'

When Mark mentioned that there would not be a ship belonging to the East India Company sailing for at least a fortnight, Fernando said that a Portuguese vessel would be leaving Surat for Lisbon in three days time. It was a fast ship and the one in which Senhor and Senhora Cabedo had travelled out from Portugal. Fernando was sure there would be no more than a delay of a day or two before they found a ship for England after they arrived in Lisbon.

'It is very quick, I know. I arrange passage with master of ship.' Fernando told them. 'Is that too soon for you?'

Mark and Ruth exchanged looks. There was no need for words.

'We'd be grateful if you could help us,' Mark said. 'We have many friends here but we'd like to go quickly. Even if we wait for an English ship to take us home, it will stop at Madeira, or Lisbon, or Oporto on the way back. Changing ships at Lisbon won't cause any delay.'

Fernando laughed. 'I have busy day tomorrow. Go to ship 'Bom Jesus', then English factory, then to Fairbrother bungalow.'

'Should you not bring Maria, Senhor Cabedo and his wife here first?' Ruth asked. 'We will have to see Sir George in the morning to discuss our leaving in three days' time. You and Sushi can see Luke Farmerdale while we're talking with Sir George and I will be able to see Sushi when we're all in the factory.'

'Yes, I will do that. It makes no difference.' Fernando replied. 'Except Senhor and Senhora Cabedo no need to wait for me in Surat.' He smiled. 'Or Maria.'

'You are very fond of Sushi, Ruth,' Maria said. 'When you go back to England you become very fond of Mark's mother. You be great comfort to her.'

'Sushi is very dear to me,' she replied. 'And you two are my oldest friends in Surat. Please come to visit us tomorrow.'

'We will be glad to come,' Maria answered. 'We must see as much of each other as we can before you leave.' She hesitated, looking first at Mark and then at Ruth. 'May I come to put flowers on Claire's grave?'

Ruth got up. She put her arms round Maria's shoulders and kissed her cheek. 'Claire was very dear to me,' she replied. Ruth took a handkerchief from her sleeve and wiped her eyes. 'And I promised I would never leave her.'

\* \* \* \* \*

'Good day, Lady Fairbrother. Good day, Sir Mark,' Sir George said as they walked into his small private office.

Ruth's hand shot up to cover her mouth as she said 'Ooh!'

'Good day, Sir George,' Mark replied quickly.

'What's wrong, Ruth?' Sir George smiled as he asked the question.

'I hadn't thought of that. You didn't warn me, Mark.'

'You'll have to get used to it, my girl. Always on the cards while your brother-in-law was a bachelor. Had some influence as Member of Parliament. I think the company hopes Mark will take his place. That's why they want him back.'

'Senhor Ferrara is arranging a passage for the three of us on a Portuguese ship leaving in two days' time. Would that be convenient, Sir George?' Mark asked diffidently.

'It's a little quick but we can manage. I'm sure your Ensign Butterworth is itching to show us how they organised things when he was with the king's troops in Bombay. I'll give you a promissory note on Child and Co. in London for the balance of your pay. How about your bungalow? And the furniture?'

'Senhor Ferrara brought a friend and his wife round to see it this morning before we came. They are very happy to take it.'

'Belongs to the company, of course. But if they are friends of Fernando Ferrara I'm sure Luke Farmerdale can arrange a year's lease, against a guarantee from Senhor Ferrara. Luke's very good at that kind of thing. Furniture's yours of course.'

'Yes,' Mark replied.

'Well, when you've agreed a price and the friend of Senhor Ferrara pays the money over to Luke Farmerdale, he'll give you another promissory note on London. Save you carrying cash with you. If the friend hasn't got his funds through yet, Luke can still arrange a promissory note, against an indemnity from Senhor Ferrara. He's a very sound man.'

'Thank you, Sir George,' Mark answered.

'Luke Farmerdale's seeing Sushi at the moment, as I think you know. He wants to see you when you leave me, Ruth.'

'Why is that, Sir George?'

'East India Company's decided to distribute some of its large profits. Going to pay small pensions to a few people who were here during the seige. Includes those given medals. Not much. Twenty pounds a year or equivalent in rupees. Means Sushi will never starve. What are her plans now? Do you know, Ruth?'

'She's with the Ferraras but she's getting quite old. I think she would like to go back to her village.

'Has a small farm, hasn't she?' Sir George asked.

'Yes. Her two eldest daughters, their husbands and her five granddaughters live on it. She had three sons but they all died. Her youngest child Pushpa is my servant.'

'Any chance of her living with the youngest daughter?'

'No.' Ruth replied. 'Her son-in-law Des Raj is our syce. He's an orphan and has no land.'

'Hmm,' Sir George said. 'That's probably why she became an ayah. Too many mouths to feed. Not enough land. It's poor soil in those hills. Back-breaking work just getting enough to eat. At least with the company pension she'll never go hungry, as I said. By the way, can you come to dinner tomorrow evening? I'm sure Alice wants to see you both before you go.

I'll ask Peter and Jacoba. And Luke and his wife. Get Senhor Ferrara and his wife as well. They've always taken a great interest in you.' He smiled roguishly. 'And Monsieur Villeneuve and his wife. You have a lot to thank the French President for.'

'Thank you, Sir George,' Mark replied.

'If you're off on the day after, won't keep you up too late. Let me know which dock your ship sails from and I'll come to see you off.' Sir George rose from his chair and extended his hand. 'We'll miss you in Surat. Both of you.'

\* \* \* \* \*

'You should have warned me, Mark,' Ruth said, as they walked arm in arm along the corridor leading to Luke Farmerdale's office.

'About what, sweetheart?'

'Well. You know. About Sir George calling you Sir Mark.'

'I'm sorry, Ruth. I didn't give it a thought. I suppose I should have warned you. Somehow, it didn't seem important.'

She squeezed his arm and they walked on a few paces.

'Don't take it seriously, dearest, Mark told her. 'Ruth Parker, Mistress Ruth Fairbrother, Lady Fairbrother, they're all the same woman. If we were at home now, I'd prove it to you.'

She giggled, pushing her nose into the side of his neck, slightly dislodging his hat. 'They weren't quite all the same.

'Shush,' he replied. 'Here's Fernando. And Sushi.'

As Fernando approached he swept off his hat, grinned, made a low bow and said, 'Good day, Sir Mark. Good day, Lady Fairbrother.'

'Hullo, Fernando,' Mark answered with a broad smile. 'Hullo, Sushi.'

'Good day, Fernando,' Ruth said. 'Hullo, Sushi.'

Sushi was looking very glum and was reluctant to take Ruth's hand. 'Can we speak now about details of your passage?' Fernando asked. 'I had no chance when Senhor Cabedo at your home.'

'Only if you promise not to call me Sir Mark.'

The two of them started chatting together and moved a yard or so away from the two women. Ruth suggested to Sushi that they should walk up and down along the corridor until Mark was ready to take her into Luke Farmerdale's office. Sushi was reluctant to take Ruth's arm saying, 'I promised I not touch you again. Otherwise I cry.'

Ruth laughed. 'I am not going to kiss you, Sushi. There are too many people about. Anyway, you made me promise as well. But you can hold my arm.

Sushi lowered her head and stared at the ground. 'Farmerdale Sahib say you great lady now. Captain Fairbrother now great lord with big mansion and much land.'

Ruth laughed again. 'Is it that which worried you, Sushi? Listen! I am still little Ruth, daughter of your heart, whom you sheltered when Lockyer Sahib attacked me, whom you cared for when Lockyer Sahib burnt my clothes, whom you claimed as your daughter when Shivaji said our lives were forfeit. Did I not claim you as my mother when the Mogul cavalry surrounded us on the Damon road? Have you not been grandmother to John, son of Captain Fairbrother, son of your daughter Ruth?'

'It is true what you say. But Farmerdale Sahib still say you great lady.'

'Let us at least walk together, mother. I will tell you of my husband's land.' Ruth told her that the land round Aireton Hall was mainly farming land, which Mark's brother had allowed to run down. She and Mark would have to work very hard at it so that John would inherit the estate as a worthwhile farm when he grew up.

Sushi smiled for the first time that day. 'I know my grandson would be a farmer.'

'How did you know that?' Ruth asked.

Sushi looked slightly embarrassed. 'If you are my daughter, I must tell you truth. Soon after John born, Pushpa and I bring Hindu priest to him for good luck. We lay him on carpet. We put quill for clerk, scroll for scholar, Captain Fairbrother Sahib has sword. We have net for fisherman, spade for farmer, money for trader. We put sword and all other things together on carpet. Priest watch where grandson point with fingers. He tells us fingers point to spade and child will be farmer, not soldier like father. I always believe he will be farmer.'

'And that's what my husband will be. And I will be a farmer's wife, mother.'

'You still great lady.'

'You will make me angry, Sushi. What must I do to show you nothing has changed. Between us, between your grandchildren and between me and your other daughter Pushpa. Do you want me to leave with sad memories of our last days, our last hours together? I want us all; you, Pushpa and I to part with happy memories. What do you want me to remember about you? About your country? When I am old I want to remember our last days together with happiness and pride.'

'Sorry, dearest,' Mark said, coming up to them. 'Fernando's got to go off. He'll drop you off at our bungalow, Sushi. You can see Pushpa. And Des Raj will take you back to Senhor Ferrara's bungalow when we return.'

'Yes, Sir Mark.'

'Goodbye, Sushi.' Ruth said.

'Goodbye, Lady Fairbrother.'

Ruth seized hold of Sushi's hands angrily. 'Look what you've made me do now. Made me break my promise. Remember what I said. I want us to have happy memories.'

'Yes, Ruth.' The expression on Sushi's face softened. 'You still my daughter.'

'That's better, Mother. If I hadn't given my word, I'd kiss and hug you now, cross as you have been.'

'Now isn't that much better?' Ruth said, releasing Sushi's hand.

Fernando, who had been waiting patiently in the background, seized the chance to say, 'I see you later this morning, Ruth. And you Mark. When I collect Sushi. You need not send Des Raj back to Swally until later.'

'Yes, thank you, Fernando. Thank you for everything,' Mark replied.

He held his arm out for Ruth to take. They paused momentarily to smile at Sushi and Fernando, turned and walked slowly together down the corridor to Luke's office.

* * * * *

'Good day, Sir Mark,' Luke Farmerdale said, with a broad smile crossing his face. 'Good day, Lady Fairbrother.'

'Not you, please, Luke,' Mark replied. 'The first time we met I hadn't shaved for nearly two days and you lent me a hat.'

'And that goes for me too,' Ruth said. 'I don't know what will happen when I get back to England but here I'm Ruth to my friends. Sir George is asking you and Peter and your wives to dinner with us tomorrow. If we don't see Peter or Jacoba before then, could you say we want everything to be kept as informal as it always has been.'

'Of course, Ruth. Just a little joke. Senhor Ferrara tells me he has arranged for you to leave in two days' time.'

'Yes, on a Portuguese ship.' Mark replied. 'We have to be on the quay at one. It sails at two in the afternoon.'

'It's going to be a rush but I understand you've seen a friend of Senhor Ferrara about the bungalow and the furniture. He will also buy your carriage and horses, I'm told. If you agree a price let me know. I can smooth out any details with Senhor Ferrara and let you have the promissory notes tomorrow evening when we dine with Sir George.'

'Yes. Thank you for all your trouble, Luke,' Mark said.

'Sir George mentioned your small pension, didn't he, Ruth?'

'Yes,' she replied.

'I will write and tell the directors in London you're going back. You can arrange to have it paid to you regularly when you're home.' He looked at Mark and then grinned at Ruth. 'It'll be useful pin money for you.'

'I suppose so,' Ruth answered. 'I hadn't really thought that far ahead. How are you arranging payment for Sushi?'

'There's no difficulty there. She can draw from us on a regular basis. If she goes back to live in her village, we can pay it yearly or half-yearly. She can collect it from us or get someone else, like your servant, to collect for her. We can either pay it in rupees or in English gold guineas. They've become very popular in the hills since we started importing them two years ago.'

'I'm glad she's being looked after,' Ruth replied quietly.

'No pension for you I'm afraid, Mark,' Luke said. 'You weren't with us during the whole of the siege and you're leaving before your present contract's up.' Luke sighed. 'In some ways I envy you two going back, even if it is to an English winter. Your place is somewhere in the chilly North, isn't it, Mark?'

'Yes.'

Luke paused reflectively. 'Every time the monsoon comes I think I can't stand another summer in this benighted country. And then the winter comes and I think this is the loveliest country in the world.' He shrugged his shoulders. 'Enough of my thoughts. If any urgent problems crop up, let me know. You'll be around here tomorrow? Handing over to Master Butterworth, aren't you, Mark?'

'Yes, Luke.' Mark smiled. 'Ensign Butterworth is always very correct but I'm sure he's itching to take command.'

Luke got up and held out his hand. 'We'll all miss you both. Goodbye for now.'

\* \* \* \* \*

'Would you mind very much, darling?' Ruth asked.

'I think you're very generous,' Mark replied, non-committally.

It was difficult to see Mark's face inside the carriage. The dusk was gathering fast and it would be dark before they arrived at Fernando's bungalow. 'But you do see, don't you? We've both known what it's like to be poor. I want Sushi to have a secure old age. She was the only person who took me in when I needed shelter. She has been like a mother to me. Sushi had no money for a dowry when Des Raj married Pushpa. That's why Des Raj was chosen. He was as poor as they were. An orphan. I've known what it is to be an orphan. Sushi's farm is too small for Pushpa to go back there. So what future have they? Being servants all their lives, until they are too old to work. And then thrown out. What chance has Lakshmi without a dowry? Unless the parents get themselves into debt.'

'Those jewels are worth a lot of money, Ruth.'

'Not to me. I only wanted them because Claire gave them to me in trust. She didn't want Roland to give them to some nautch girl in payment.' She paused. 'As he was going to give them to me. For favours received.' She shuddered slightly.

Mark put his arm round Ruth's waist and whispered, 'Darling, that's all over now.'

'Every time I look at them I think of you risking your life.'

'Not for the jewels, sweetheart.' He kissed her lightly on the forehead. 'For your honour. And would do so again.'

'I know that darling. But when I left home … our home, Aireton Hall, I left with nothing. Let me go back with nothing.' Ruth's voice softened. 'Apart from you. And your son. How could I live in comfort knowing Sushi and Pushpa and Lakshmi might be in need.'

Mark turned his head towards her. 'I can never refuse you anything,' he said, after he had finished kissing his wife.

'I'll make it up to you. I promise you.' Ruth answered eagerly. 'You can have my East Indian pension. I'll work on the farm. I worked hard on Colonel Trent's farm.'

Mark laughed. 'I know Henry was a spendthrift, Ruth, but I don't think we've reached quite such a desperate pass.' His voice became serious. 'You'll be my right hand in running the estate and the managing of the house will be left to you. But I know everyone would be surprised to see Lady Fairbrother ploughing a field.'

'I could do it, Mark,' Ruth said, spiritedly.

'I'm sure you could. We'll have to tell Maria, of course. It's only right she should know.'

'Yes. I hope it's not too much of a shock. Ask her not to tell Sushi yet.' They heard Des Raj shout as the carriage slowed down outside the Ferrara's bungalow. Fernando's bearer appeared on the front verandah with a lamp and by the time Des Raj reached the door of the carriage, Ram Kopal and Sushi had come from the servants' quarters to greet them. The bearer led them into the courtyard, leaving Des Raj in conversation with his mother-in-law and Ram Kopal.

Maria and Fernando greeted them both warmly and led them to a table under the covered verandah where dinner was to be taken. Conversation over dinner was mainly on the topic of Mark's plans for the future, how he would revitalise the Aireton Hall estate, the way Ruth would look after the Hall and the gardens, and the way they would bring up and educate John and any other children.

'I tell you when I first see you,' Fernando said. 'A special Providence watches over you and Ruth. God, in his wisdom, take your brother from you. That way you take young son back to England. Very few European children live through more than three monsoons. You have special guardian angels looking after you and your son.'

Maria took out a handkerchief and started to wipe her eyes. Ruth got up from her chair and went across to comfort her. She heard Mark talking in an undertone to Fernando and then Fernando saying more loudly, 'Yes. I think it best.' Ruth looked round to see both men looking at her and she resumed her seat.

'I am all right now, Ruth,' Maria said. 'I did not mean to spoil your meal with us.'

'I think I am the one to do that,' Mark said, hesitantly.

Fernando sat impassively. It was obvious he knew what Mark would say next. There was silence as the other three waited for Mark to continue. 'Could you let Sushi come to us early tomorrow, please?' Mark asked.

When her husband made no reply, Maria asked, 'Why is that, Mark? I was going to bring her across in the afternoon. Before I go with Ruth to the European cemetery.'

'Ruth wants to give her some of her jewels,' Mark replied. Maria still looked puzzled. 'The jewels which belonged to Claire are quite valuable.' Mark continued. 'Ruth wants to give half to Sushi and half to Pushpa. There are enough to buy a farm for Pushpa and her husband while Sushi's share will be sufficient to buy more fields to add to her farm. She could go back to her village. I'm sorry if it means your losing Sushi. We thought you ought to know as soon as possible.'

'Does Sushi know?' Maria asked him.

'No. Ruth wants them to be together when she tells them.'

'Are you sure you make right decision, Ruth?' Fernando asked.

'Yes,' she replied firmly. 'I know neither I nor my children will go hungry in my husband's house. Why should I not follow the teachings of Our Lord and give what I have to the poor? Will not that gold and those stones give more happiness to one who has been like a mother to me, and to her daughter, than to me, wearing them round my wrists and neck?'

'When Ruth has made up her mind,' Mark said quietly, 'you won't change it.'

'I see they get a good price,' Fernando told them. 'I look after those two for you.'

'Thank you. Now you see why I want to tell them together,' Ruth said.

'You are lovely girl, Ruth. You also naughty girl. Now I lose good servant because of you.

'I'm sorry, Maria.'

'Perhaps it was for the best,' Maria answered. 'Senhora Cabedo has own new maidservant. A girl from Goa who has been working for Portuguese family in Surat. I know Senhora Cabedo worried what to do about Pushpa. Now you very kind to her. Pushpa get farm of her own. She went across to Ruth, hugged her and started to cry. 'When you go to Heaven, you get special place among angels. Near Our Lady,' she said through her tears.

'Don't cry, Maria,' Ruth said. 'Please don't cry.'

'I think you so good. You never do anything bad,' Maria continued.

'Come on now. You should see me when I'm in a temper.'

Maria gave a half smile. 'That's better,' Ruth continued as Maria wiped her eyes.

'What time shall we expect Sushi?' Mark asked, trying to bring the discussion down to a more practical level.

'I get Senhora Cabedo to share servant with me. She will not mind. Sushi can go back with you this evening. Stay with you until you go day after tomorrow. Then she come back with us,' Maria answered. She looked thoughtful. 'Senhor Cabedo need new syce. When he get new man, Pushpa and husband stay here until they go back to village with Sushi.'

'You are very kind, Maria,' Ruth answered. 'And you too, Fernando.'

\* \* \* \* \*

The air felt very hot and sticky the morning after the visit to the Ferraras and Ruth decided to wear a cotton sari after she bathed. Mark left the bungalow immediately after breakfast, saying he wanted to get to the factory before the rain started. In the event, heavy rain started coming down almost as soon as he left and Ruth told Sushi to bring the two children into John's room, rather than let them play in the courtyard. She also asked her to collect Pushpa. Ruth had been the object of Sushi's constant attention since waking that morning and Sushi had obviously told her daughter to stay in the background until called. A clap of thunder was heard as the servants came through the door together. Ruth had already placed her box of jewels in the middle of the table and now asked Pushpa to bring in two more chairs so that they could all sit down. When Pushpa returned and the three of them sat round the table, Ruth opened the box. Neither servant seemed surprised. They had seen the box of jewels often enough.

There was a puzzled look on Sushi's face as Ruth began dividing the jewels into two piles of roughly equal value. She had been mystified by being brought from the Ferrara's bungalow without explanation and was equally baffled to know why Ruth should want anyone to watch her examine her jewels.

When the division was finished, Ruth sat back and looked at the other two women still waiting patiently for her to speak. She repeated the conversations she had had with her husband and the Ferraras, telling them that Senhor Ferrara had offered to help them get a good price for the jewels. As Ruth explained her plans, their eyes became wide-eyed in amazement. She was listened to in incredulous silence by both the servants and the only sounds heard, after Ruth finished, were made by the two children playing together. The period of shocked silence lasted for about fifteen seconds. Ruth began to wonder whether she ought to have prepared the ground more carefully before making the announcement. She asked herself if she should say more now.

Pushpa was the first to recover her wits. She rose from the chair, moved towards Ruth and made a low bow. As the other girl's head almost reached Ruth's knees, she became aware of the subtle perfume she always associated with Pushpa. The servant's eyes were still wide open with wonder when she raised her head and said, 'I am very happy, Lady Fairbrother. Des Raj will be very happy too. He always wanted farm of his own. And we give good dowry for Lakshmi.'

Ruth rose from her chair to face Pushpa and replied, 'May you have many children, Pushpa. Especially sons.'

'Yes, Lady Fairbrother. And you, too.' She lowered her eyes. 'We both have strong, young husbands.'

Ruth turned to Sushi, expecting her to speak. Her eyes were moist but she seemed too shocked for words. Ruth took her hand but Sushi snatched it away, kicking her chair over as she got up.

Sushi pointed to John and Lakshmi, laughing and cuddling on the floor. 'Look at your children,' she shouted in Marathi. 'They are showing you how to say thank you. Look at Lakshmi, daughter.'

Pushpa looked surprised while an expression of bewilderment crossed Ruth's face. 'Please, Sushi,' Ruth asked. 'What's wrong?'

Sushi glared at her. 'Are you so proud now you want my Maratha daughter Pushpa to bow to you like a sweeper woman?'

'Of course not, Sushi.'

Pushpa had an amazed look on her face as her mother shouted, 'And you, Pushpa. How do you say thank you to my daughter Ruth? Your sister who gives you jewels to buy a farm. By bowing to her? Do you think she is Lady Oxindon?' There was another clap of thunder and the children clung to Sushi's sari. She continued speaking in Marathi. 'How will my daughters have happy memories of each other, if one sister does not know how to thank the other.'

Pushpa was quite motionless. She stared at her mother as the tirade continued. 'You have lived here together for more than two years. Your children play together. They bathe together.' She paused as if waiting for a response but none came. 'There is no one here to see you thank your sister, Pushpa,' she pleaded in a much gentler voice. 'Nothing to be afraid of. Do you think your sister is a nautch girl?'

When neither girl made a move, Sushi gave Ruth a hard push in her daughter's direction. Ruth had to hold on to Pushpa's arms to prevent herself falling. She felt the younger woman tremble slightly. Ruth looked at Sushi and saw her eyes were filled with tears. She recalled that Sushi had sworn not to touch her. Ruth realised that Sushi wanted Pushpa to be her surrogate to express the feelings which Sushi had vowed not to express. She knew she had been right to change into one of her cotton saris that morning. Perhaps it would be easier for Pushpa if she could think of Ruth as a woman of her own race.

John started to cry and Sushi picked up both children, holding Lakshmi in her right arm and John in her left arm. She spoke to the two of them in Marathi. John understood this as well as he understood English and stopped crying. 'Your mothers show you they are really sisters now,' she said to the children. 'You will always be part of my family John. You and Lakshmi are like brother and sister.'

The two young women stood motionless for several seconds. Ruth smiled encouragingly but Pushpa lowered her eyes. It was obvious that, as a strict Hindu, she was concerned about losing caste. The eighteen years of her life had not prepared her for being expected to show affection for a European in the way her mother wanted. Sushi became impatient at the delay. She moved her arms across her chest so that the foreheads of the children touched. They giggled, and as Sushi lifted them up gently, Lakshmi kissed John.

'You see, daughters. Your children show you how.'

Pushpa jerked her head and shoulders backward as a flash of lightning was followed soon afterwards by a very loud clap of thunder. The rain became much heavier and Pushpa lowered her eyes and took her daughter from her mother's arms. When Ruth looked at Sushi there were tears streaming down the older woman's face. She took John from Sushi's arms.

'What is the matter?' Ruth asked.

'I am very sorry,' she sobbed. 'I did not want to cry when I said I would cry no more. I am sorry my grandson go back. But I know you, my daughter, must go back with your husband. I make you sad when you should be happy.'

Ruth kissed her very tenderly on the cheek.

'I love you, Mother. You are very dear to me. That is why I want to do this for you. This afternoon Senhora Ferrara and I will go to the grave of my sister Claire, Lockyer Memsahib, whom you cared for and nursed until she died.' Ruth was near to tears herself. 'My sister would want you and your daughter to have those jewels which belonged to her. She would want us all to have happy memories of each other.'

Ruth began to cry. 'I will go now. Look after John for me, Pushpa.'

'Yes, Lady Fairbrother,' Pushpa replied, still with her eyes lowered as Ruth hurried from the room.

After a few minutes Ruth recovered and went back to collect her son. She saw that Pushpa's eyes were red rimmed as though she had been weeping heavily but Ruth made no comment, being fully wrapped up in her own thoughts. Sushi was nowhere to be seen.

# 20

Ruth and Maria spent a desolate afternoon. Although the monsoon rain stopped around midday, it began again soon after they reached the cemetery. They left Maria's carriage at the entrance after telling Ram Kopal they would return around an hour later. Ruth carried a large bouquet for her sister's grave. Maria carried five small posies, one for each of her four children and a fifth one for Claire.

The cemetery was a melancholy sight. Rain dropped from the trees on to the wet gravestones, and Ruth and Maria were the only living people there. They walked in silence along the wet paths, past the rows of tiny graves. Among the scores of names in the English section she noticed two with the names of the Streynsham children and others with the familiar names of Oxindon, Robertson and Farmerdale. So many young lives shrivelled up so far from an England they would never see or know. When they came to Claire's grave, Ruth bent down to place her flowers in front of the headstone. A few seconds afterwards, Maria placed her small posy beside it. 'I leave you now, Ruth. You want to be alone with your sister. I go to graves of my children to say prayers for them.' Ruth was too choked to speak. She held out her hand. Maria gave it a quick squeeze and said, 'I go now. I come back in a few minutes time.'

Ruth did not know how long she stood in silent prayer. After she opened her eyes she saw Maria quite still about twenty yards away. She was on the edge of the Catholic section of the cemetery in front of a row of small graves. Maria made no attempt to come towards her and Ruth looked down at Claire's grave again. The tears began to flow as she remembered the bond of affection there had been between her and her foster-sister and the love which had been shown to her by Sarah Trent, her foster-mother. They would never know that Mark was now her husband and John her son. Ruth felt her heart being torn in two. She had promised her foster-mother she would never leave Claire and had repeated the same promise to Claire. Now she must break that promise in order to follow her husband back to England. Ruth realised the emotional trauma Sushi must be suffering now. Sushi had been like a mother to her, while Ruth was the only adult European who had shown her real affection. She worshipped John with an almost fanatical devotion. It was as though John had taken the place of her own three dead sons. Now both the woman she regarded as a daughter and the boy she regarded as her only grandson were to be torn from her, never to be seen again. Ruth did not wonder that Sushi found her share of Claire's jewels poor recompense.

Mark and John were now her family but Ruth knew that Mark also had a loyalty to his mother and sister. Ruth began to pray for guidance again. She prayed that in time she would come to feel the same love for Lady Fairbrother as she had felt for her foster-mother and now felt for Sushi. She prayed that she would feel the same affection for Mark's sister Elizabeth as she had felt for Claire. Ruth asked God to give her the same qualities of gentleness and patience shown by Pushpa for her and prayed that she might show the same tenderness towards Elizabeth as Pushpa had shown for John.

A loud peal of thunder heralded the start of another heavy downpour of rain. The initial drops were warm but the rain gradually turned tepid as it became heavier. After a quarter of a minute Maria moved across to stand beside her. They remained silent for a short time until Ruth, still looking at the wet, cold earth of the grave, said, 'She's so alone there.'

'No,' Maria said firmly. 'My children are lying quietly beside her.'

'But I promised I'd care for her. I said I'd never leave her. What can I say to Frances and Anne?'

'Listen to me,' Maria said. 'When you go home – and you must go home – you and your son, you tell your family you left your sister in good hands.'

Tears mingled with the rain as Ruth turned to look at Maria. 'I don't understand.'

'I will look after your sister's grave.'

'But what happens when you go back to Portugal? Who will be with Claire then?'

'I went home three years ago. No more. I stay here with my children. When I die I be buried near them. Close to your sister. I lie down quietly with my friend Claire.'

Ruth put her arms around Maria. As she bent her head to rest it on Maria's shoulder, Ruth could feel hot tears running down her cheeks. Maria held her very gently and after half a minute or so placed her hand under Ruth's chin. 'We go now,' Maria said. 'The rain is so heavy.'

She spoke as softly and gently as though she was talking to a child. 'We must go now. Think of Mark and John. When we get back to your bungalow we change wet clothes. Mai Nayah will bring us some hot tea. Then I go home and you see me again this evening.'

Ruth nodded and allowed Maria to put her arm round Ruth's waist, guiding them over the soggy ground towards the path leading to the gate of the cemetery.

\* \* \* \* \*

Pushpa knocked on the door and then came in with an oil lamp in one hand and a small bottle of perfume in the other hand. She placed them on the side table and smiled as Ruth looked round from where she was sitting in front of the dressing table.

'Thank you for bringing that, Pushpa. I could hardly see.'

The rain which had been falling all afternoon had now stopped but the sky was still filled with heavy, black clouds. Although it would soon be dark, inside Ruth's room it was warm and humid and she still wore the sari she had put on when she returned from the cemetery.

'John is asleep now. I come to help you change, Lady Fairbrother,' Pushpa said, hesitating a little over the title.

Ruth smiled encouragingly and answered Pushpa in her own tongue, to free the other girl from embarrassment. 'I am going to Sir George Oxindon's soon. There is not much time, Pushpa, because my husband will be here in a quarter of an hour.'

Pushpa came across the room and stood beside Ruth, looking at the reflection in the portable mirror on the dressing table. She produced a silver bracelet from a concealed pocket in her sari, holding it over Ruth's shoulder for her to see. 'Mother asked me to give you this. She said she could not give it to you herself. She has sworn not to touch you again because she did not want you to see her cry. She is very proud.'

'But that bracelet is the one Shivaji gave her, Pushpa. She must keep it.'

'Mother is an old woman now. She wants you to wear it in memory of her.'

Ruth stood up and looked down at the other girl's hand. 'If that is what she wants, I will always wear it.' She raised her eyes and looked at Pushpa. 'It will remind me of our mother.'

'Let me put it on for you.'

Ruth held her right wrist out. Pushpa took it in her left hand and slowly eased the bracelet on to the wrist with her right hand. She continued holding Ruth's wrist for a moment, as if lost in thought. 'You have the same perfume you wore this morning, Lady Fairbrother,' she said shyly.

Ruth laughed softly. 'Yes. Lavender water. I bought some from a merchant who imports from England. I will give you a bottle, Pushpa.' She picked up a bottle from among those on the dressing table and handed it to the other girl.

'I have a present for you also.' Pushpa went across to the side table by the door and carried across the small bottle of perfume which had stood there previously.

'Is this the same perfume you were wearing this morning?' Ruth asked.

'Yes. White Jasmine and Sandalwood. Please accept this gift as very small thanks for your gift of jewels to me and Des Raj.'

'Of course I will accept it, Pushpa. As it is a gift from you, I will wear some of your perfume when I visit the English President.'

Pushpa gave a gentle laugh. 'He will think you are a Maratha lady instead of Lady Fairbrother.'

Ruth became aware of Pushpa looking intently at her as she stood in front of her. When she saw the gentle eyes of the Indian girl, Ruth realised she had never seen this appealing expression on Pushpa's face before. Neither of them spoke for several seconds. Ruth reached out her hands to take Pushpa's hands in her own. She wondered what Sushi had told her daughter that morning to make her cry.

Pushpa slowly lowered her head and said quietly, 'We must not forget our husbands. Sir Mark will come soon to take you to Sir George Oxindon. Des Raj will drive you there.'

'Yes.' Ruth smiled as she reverted to English. 'It's a pity I won't be wearing a choli and sari. It would not take so long to dress.' She tried to release her hands but Pushpa lifted her head slowly and squeezed Ruth's hands at the same time.

'Mother told me today we are both her daughters,' Pushpa said slowly and deliberately, gazing intently into Ruth's eyes as she did so. 'And your son John and my daughter Lakshmi are both her grandchildren.'

'She is right, Pushpa,' Ruth replied in Marathi. 'But mother should not be cross with you.' She remembered how Sushi had tried to make the two young women embrace in the same easy way in which their children had kissed as they played together. It suddenly dawned on her how desperately Sushi wished Ruth's memories of an Indian woman in the years to come, when memories began to fade, to be that of Pushpa and not that of an aged woman. Sushi wanted her to remember the long, black, shiny hair, reaching to the waist; the firm, round breasts in the elegant, symmetrical figure; the smooth, firm arms; the sweet, gentle face with its delicate, finely chiselled features; and the graceful walk of her youngest daughter.

'You lived with mother like her Marathi daughter, though you are Nazarene and we are Hindu,' she heard Pushpa saying softly, with the same warm, tender expression on her face which Ruth knew so well. 'But I have always been your servant as mother wanted and you have lived with Captain Sahib. Now you are great lady.' Pushpa was three inches shorter than Ruth but the same height as Sushi. She wore a similar black, onyx necklace to that worn by Ruth and had silver bracelets on both wrists. As Ruth continued to look at her, she realised that Pushpa was standing in the same proud, straight, erect way in which her mother had stood when Ruth first met her. Pushpa was quite calm and absolutely still. The words Ruth had said to Sushi the day before, that she did not want them to part with sad memories, came back to her. Ruth knew she could not force Pushpa to break caste.

Keeping her voice as steady as possible, she said, 'It is almost time for me to change.'

Sushi could not expect Pushpa to think of Ruth as a sister. Only Claire had ever called Ruth sister before. While Frances and Anne had been affectionate enough, they had always used her Christian name. Now Claire was lying alone in the cold, wet grave which Ruth had seen that afternoon. This brown-skinned girl who stood in front of her, looking with soft, brown, unwavering eyes, might be daughter of Sushi, mother of her heart. But Ruth was no longer the young orphan, wearing the black necklace given to her by her mother on her wedding day. To Pushpa she was Lady Fairbrother, soon to return home as the mistress of Aireton Hall, who would be dining with Sir George Oxindon in half an hour's time.

Ruth put her hands gently on the other girl's shoulders. She looked into Pushpa's gentle, dark eyes and kissed her lightly on the forehead.

'I will always remember you as you are now,' Ruth told her.

Pushpa's eyes were filled with love as she said, 'Thank you for everything. I will always remember your kindness.'

'I am the one who should thank you, Pushpa,' Ruth answered. 'I will never forget you or your daughter Lakshmi. I will remember you as you are today and when you were fifteen. Do you recall how it was when we first met? You tried to speak to me in Portuguese. You knew so little English and I knew so little Marathi.' The two young women giggled and pressed their foreheads together. Pushpa reached with her right hand for the long, fair hair hanging behind Ruth's back. Ruth's right hand imitated the action so that Pushpa's long, sleek, waist length, black hair finished up hanging down Ruth's back.

'Tell Mother we are both proud to be sisters now,' Ruth said, looking intently into Pushpa's eyes so near her own. They remained absolutely still for a few seconds until Ruth lifted her hair from the other woman's shoulder and gave a soft laugh. 'Look at my hair. You will have to comb it for me, Pushpa, if I am to be ready in time.' Pushpa smiled, hesitating for a brief time before replying.

'Your husband will be here soon, sister.'

'Yes.' Ruth laughed and reverted to English. 'Why can't I go in my sari, Pushpa?' she asked, pulling the two of them together.

'Sir George Oxindon would not think it fitting, Ruth,' Pushpa replied, gently trying to break free.

'You're quite right.'

Ruth released the younger woman, went to the wardrobe and took out an underskirt, together with her shoes and gown. This time she avoided looking round at Pushpa.

\* \* \* \* \*

Their request must have been passed on to those invited to dine with Sir George. Apart from the French President, the other guests all greeted Mark and Ruth by their Christian names. Ruth had visited Madame Villeneuve frequently since her marriage and they were soon on Christian name terms. Monsieur Villeneuve addressed Mark as Captain Fairbrother and hesitated uncertainly before addressing Ruth as Madame Fairbrother. The only indirect reference to Ruth's new status was made by Lady Oxindon.

When Ruth said, 'Good evening, Sir George,' and, 'Good evening, Lady Alice', Lady Oxindon told her, 'You must now call me Alice, my dear.'

Ruth noticed how the long, highly polished, teak dining table shone in the soft light of the candles burning in a score of silver candlesticks. As Sir George escorted her into the dining room she had seen that several gleaming, imported Venetian wine glasses were placed at each guest's place. Like other functions which Ruth had attended at Sir George Oxindon's, she found the conversation lively and easy but the meal very heavy going. She did not eat a great deal of meat normally and found the succession of meat courses tiresome. A fresh wine was always served with each course and Ruth did no more than sip the different wines poured into her glasses. After the last course was cleared away, Sir George called out 'Master Streynsham, The King' to his deputy, sitting at the opposite end of the table. Peter rose to his feet and called 'Ladies and Gentlemen, His Majesty King Charles the Second,' at which everyone rose to drink the loyal toast. Sir George remained on his feet as the other diners resumed their seats.

'Please join me, ladies and gentlemen,' he asked, 'in a toast to our departing friends, Sir Mark Fairbrother and his wife, Lady Ruth Fairbrother.'

Mark and Ruth remained in their places as the toast was drunk and when the other guests sat down, Mark murmured, 'Thank you, everyone,' by way of acknowledgement.

There were muttered cries of, 'Speech,' which gradually became louder as Mark showed no sign of compliance. Eventually, Sir George looked across and said, 'You ought to say something, Mark.'

He rose to his feet. 'I know you won't want me to bore you by talking about the time Ruth and I have spent in India. You know it well enough already. Instead of that I'll tell you about my family and the way my path and the path of my wife have crossed.'

Mark related how his family's fortunes began on the return of a crusader ancestor from the Holy Land. Additional grants of land were given to members of the family following their services in various foreign wars. During the reign of Henry VIII, his great-great-grandfather had acquired substantial property belonging to local monasteries, because he had abandoned his religion to take an oath of loyalty under the Act of Supremacy, unlike most of the landed gentry in his area. His grandfather was given a baronetcy after he made substantial loans to King James I, grandfather of the present king, when he had been short of money. The family's luck changed during the Civil War, when they chose the losing side. As a result, Ruth's foster-father had taken over Aireton Hall and he and his family were compelled to leave their home. Roles were reversed on the restoration of the king, with his brother Henry expelling Ruth and her family from Aireton Hall. Mark looked at Ruth and smiled. 'We both regard it as our home. That is where we first met and the only way Providence could resolve the dilemma is by having us both live there as husband and wife. I was the youngest of three brothers. I never expected to become master of Aireton Hall.' Mark paused briefly. There was dead silence among his listeners. Ruth could feel the emotion in his voice as he continued. 'Ruth was the foster-child of an enemy of my family. When she was driven out of her home, she did not expect to return as mistress of Aireton Hall.' Mark's voice became almost choked as he continued. 'Our son will always be aware that he will be master one day. I know Ruth will teach him to be honest and true in all his dealings so that future generations can look back on an inheritance they can be proud of.'

There was silence for several seconds as Mark sat down. Monsieur Villeneuve was the first to speak. 'Bravo, Sir Mark. It was indeed the hand of fate bringing you, charming Lady Ruth and Father Dellon to my factory.'

'I always say to you, Ruth,' Madame Villeneuve said, as her husband finished, 'Your story so romantic. A husband who is so beau. And now you are among the nobility of England. It is like some fairy tale.'

'Not nobility, Madame Villeneuve,' Mark corrected gently. "My son may inherit a title but he will be a country gentleman like me. As my own father was,'

'Ladies, I think we should leave the gentlemen to their tobacco and brandy,' Lady Oxindon said, anxious to avoid embarrassment by curtailing further discussion.

'Of course, my dear. We will not be more than a few minutes,' Sir George said, as he rose from his seat. The rest of the gentlemen followed his example by standing, as Lady Oxindon led the other women into the ante-room and then across into her drawing room.

There was only one lamp burning in the room when Ruth entered with Maria at her side. Lady Oxindon clapped her hands irritably, demanding "more light" when a bearer appeared. Because all available punkah wallahs had been used to pull the cords of the hand-operated fans in the dining room, none had been available to keep the air circulating in Lady Oxindon's drawing room. The air inside seemed hot and sticky while the dim light given out by one small lamp made the drawing room appear gloomy. Ruth moved across to the window in search of fresh air. The heavy, dark monsoon clouds were building up above, preparing for the rain of the following day, obscuring both the moon and the stars. Ruth looked up into the vast, black, velvet sky overhead. The night air on her cheeks was the same temperature as warm milk. When she looked into the darkness of the Indian night, she thought of the large cities, hundreds of miles away, which Sir George, Fernando and Master Moxon had visited. She remembered the stories told to her, taught to Sushi by the Hindu priests, of a huge range of snow-covered peaks at the edge of the Mogul Empire, a thousand miles away. Further still, there was a limitless snow-covered plateau at the very roof of the world. The immensity of the Mogul Empire overwhelmed her and she felt suddenly afraid of the vastness of this alien land.

Ruth turned to see two bearers, each carrying two oil lamps in their hands. She shivered slightly and Maria, who was standing nearby, placed her hand on her arm. 'What is wrong, Ruth?' she asked.

'I don't know, Maria.'

'Come and sit down. The heat at this time of year always plays funny tricks.' They went to sit a little way from where Lady Oxindon was chatting to the three other ladies.

'I wish Mark hadn't talked about John like that over dinner,' Ruth said.

'Why not? Your husband is very proud of your son.'

'Perhaps I have been in India too long,' Ruth replied. 'I begin to believe in their gods of the hills, the forests and the streams. The Hindus believe if you praise your children too much or too well, the gods become jealous. They take the children away.'

'Oh, Ruth,' Maria said reproachfully, 'you are true Christian, believing in our Lord Jesus, Holy Mary, and all the blessed saints watching over you and your son.'

'I am a young woman, Maria,' Ruth answered. 'Perhaps I do not understand. Perhaps I still remember Claire's grave and all those graves this afternoon. Look at those women over there. They are all older than I am. They have all had children. Where are they now? Is it because India has no place for us Europeans? Are we only allowed to stay here for a while if we render the gods of Hindustan a tribute of tiny children?'

Maria put her arms around Ruth's shoulders. 'I will pray to Our Lady tonight. I pray she keep you and your son safe from harm. You pray too, Ruth.' Ruth nodded, 'Thank you, Maria. I will pray also. But I am afraid. Not for me, but for John. How many European children do you know in Surat? When is the next tribute due? Have I to leave part of my body here in payment for my time in this foreign land?'

Maria hugged her. 'You must have faith, Ruth. Your son is strong.' She smiled. 'I am sure Saint John takes special care of your son. Saint Mark takes special care of your husband. Saint Joseph sits among the angels, with Our Lady. He has special care for you. You have same name as Ruth the Moabitess, mother of Obed, from whom he descends.'

Ruth felt tears coming to her eyes and was aware of the curious glances being given to her by the group around Lady Oxindon.

'Ruth has been affected by the heat,' Maria told them by way of explanation. Lady Oxindon hastily summoned a bearer, directing him to bring a basin of cold water and a cloth for Lady Fairbrother. When the others in the group moved towards her, Lady Oxindon asked them not to crowd round. She cooled Ruth's face with a fan until the bearer returned, carrying the basin of water and a cloth. Lady Oxindon dipped the cloth into the basin, wrung it out, and then rested it across Ruth's forehead. It felt almost ice-cold.

Ruth realised the water must have come from one of the large earthenware jars, filled with water every day, where the slow evaporation of the liquid kept the water cold. She smiled and said, 'Thank you, Alice. I'm feeling much better now.'

'Too much excitement for you in the last two days,' Lady Oxindon said briskly. 'That's your trouble, young woman. When other people go back to England, they know weeks, even months in advance.' She took the cloth off Ruth's forehead, dipped it in the bowl, wrung it out once more, and placed it back above Ruth's eyes. 'As soon as your husband appears, I'll get him to take you home. We can all see you again tomorrow morning. If it's convenient to you,' she added hastily.

'We have to be on the quayside at one o'clock,' Ruth replied.

'I know,' Lady Oxindon said. 'Peter Streynsham has arranged a little leave taking ceremony at the factory at half past eleven.' She looked round at the half circle of other women standing around the two of them. There was a murmur of assent.

'I must admit it has been a bit of a rush,' Ruth said.

'Sit here quietly, Ruth,' Lady Oxindon replied. 'I'll get a message to your husband.' She rose, went to the door and spoke to a bearer outside.

'You have nothing to worry about,' she continued after she returned. 'Peter Streynsham will send a company bullock cart to your bungalow at ten o'clock in the morning to collect your luggage and take it to the ship. My husband will take you in his own carriage to the quayside. Leave everything to us.'

'Fernando will have an agent on the quay. Agent will look after your luggage,' Maria said. 'My husband will go himself to meet you before you go on to the ship.'

'Thank you,' Ruth answered. 'Thank you. Both of you.'

Mark hurried through the door at that point, a look of concern on his face. A few seconds later, the other guests and Sir George entered at a more leisurely pace.

'What's wrong, dearest?' Mark asked as he reached Ruth's side.

'I'm alright, darling. Just a touch of the heat, I expect.'

'You leave everything to us,' Lady Oxindon said. 'Just take good care of your wife. You're a fortunate young man.'

'I know and I will, Lady Alice,' he replied. 'Would you mind if we left now? Do you feel up to going, Ruth?'

'I would like to leave quickly, Mark,' Ruth answered.

'Of course you must both go now,' Lady Oxindon told them, a little sharply.

They bid hasty farewells amid shouts of, 'See you both tomorrow morning.' A message must have been passed to Des Raj because their carriage was waiting for them when Sir George and Lady Oxindon bade them 'Good night' on the steps of their bungalow. As the horse trotted along the dark road taking them back to their own bungalow Ruth said, 'I wish Des Raj would go faster.'

'What's the matter, sweetheart?' Mark asked.

'I'm remembering Claire's grave. Do you think I'm fanciful?'

'Fanciful?' Mark sounded puzzled. 'In what way?'

'In thinking of the Mogul Empire as a swallower of children. English children. Is it John's turn next?' Mark held her by both shoulders. 'Darling, we go home tomorrow. Plenty of sea air for the three of us. Back in England in time for the long autumn evenings. With the winds sweeping way down from the far North across those moors.'

Ruth pushed her face into his chest. Her voice sounded muffled as she said, 'I'm so glad we are going home. I want John to grow up in the house we both know so well.'

'And so he will, dearest wife,' Mark said gently. 'We're nearly back at the bungalow now.'

They sat in silence for the rest of the short journey. When the carriage stopped, Ruth did not wait for Mark to get out of the carriage first so that he could help her down. She ran through the archway, making for John's room, adjacent to their own. Sushi got up from her chair as Ruth ran towards the half opened doorway of her son's room. There was a lamp burning on the verandah and Sushi looked at Ruth curiously in the half-light. She placed her finger over her mouth and then said very quietly, 'He is asleep.'

Ruth stopped. 'Is he alright?'

'Yes. I knew you were worried. When you go to President Sahib I come to sit by my grandson.'

Ruth went through the door and looked at John. He was lying on the bed with just a sheet covering him and only wearing a cotton loin cloth. His breathing was regular and he looked perfectly tranquil. She picked him up and covered his face with kisses. John grumbled a little as he struggled to semi-wakefulness. His body felt quite cool to his mother's hands.

Mark came through the door, closely followed by Sushi. 'Whatever's wrong?' he asked.

'Thank God he's alright, Mark,' Ruth said and burst into tears.

Sushi took John from his mother's arms and began to croon softly to him. Mark put his arms round Ruth and said, 'Dearest. Of course, he's alright. Sushi would have told us if there was anything wrong.'

Ruth could hear Sushi in the background talking quietly to John and then putting him back to bed. The flow of tears gradually stopped and Ruth wiped her eyes and blew her nose.

'I am sorry, Mark. I think Lady Alice is right. The last three days have been too much.'

'I'm a brute,' he replied. 'Thinking only of myself. I should have waited. We can still wait for an English ship.'

'Oh, no. I want to go quickly. Not for us, darling, but for our son.'

'I stay with John tonight,' Sushi said quietly from the side of the bed. Ruth ran across and held her by the arms. 'Will you, Sushi? Please.'

'You made promise not to touch me any more,' Sushi said, but made no attempt to remove Ruth's hands from her arms.

'I know. I'm sorry.'

'I stay with my grandson like I stay with your sister. I make sure he comes to no harm. Tomorrow, after you leave, I sleep.'

Ruth put her head on Sushi's shoulder and began to cry again. 'Thank you, Mother,' she said.

Sushi looked appealingly at Mark and then back to Ruth. 'You make me cry. You go to husband now, Ruth. I see you in the morning.'

Mark took Ruth gently from Sushi's arms and led her into their own room.

\* \* \* \* \*

Ruth slipped out of bed very quietly before Mark was awake. She moved slowly across the room to pick up her dressing robe and sandals and then opened the door. Sushi stood up from her chair outside John's room and waited until Ruth put the sandals on her feet, placed the arms in the sleeves of her gown and then tied the belt. Neither spoke as Ruth went through the door into John's room. Her son was still sleeping peacefully as Ruth bent over him, with Sushi standing in the doorway looking at them both. This time Ruth did not disturb him and went back on to the verandah again. When Sushi sensed that Ruth wanted to talk, she moved about five yards away so that their conversation would not disturb either Mark or John.

'Thank you for staying with my son. I am so grateful,' Ruth told her. Sushi shrugged her shoulders.

'I was worried. I would not have slept, Sushi, if you had not been there.'

'I knew you were afraid,' Sushi told her gently.

The first thin streaks of daylight were beginning to cut through the dark curtains of the night. Sushi began speaking in Marathi in the way she always did when she spoke to Ruth as a woman rather than as a European mistress. 'We learn to listen to Mother Earth, my daughter. Our priests tell us to listen to the songs which the gods of the streams and the trees sing. If we take our sorrow and our fear to Mother Earth, my daughter, she will answer us. I listened to the gods talking in the trees last night. They told me not to be full of sorrow for my daughter who goes back across the sea. They sang to me that I must not be afraid for my grandson. He will grow to be a great lord with many sons.' Ruth stretched out her arms and took Sushi's hand in her own. This time the older woman did not try to snatch them away. Above the sounds of the birds singing their dawn chorus, the sounds of the first stirrings of movement in the servants' quarters could be heard.

'I was sorry when you said you were leaving me but the gods tell me you must return with your husband,' Sushi continued. 'Now I am filled with joy for your kindness to me and to Pushpa. She and Des Raj will have a farm of their own and live near me when I go back to our village.'

'Mother, Mother, I have so much to be grateful to you for. I wish I could do more for you and Pushpa.'

Sushi looked at Ruth searchingly. 'We both have much we must thank you for, daughter. Pushpa should have thanked you properly yesterday morning.' Ruth could only smile back. It was difficult to know what to say. She tried to pull Sushi towards her. Sushi released her hands and half turned saying, in a mixture of English and Urdu, 'Mai Nayah come soon. He bring chota hazri for you and Captain Sahib.'

'I will tell my children and grandchildren of you, mother,' Ruth replied.

'And Pushpa will do the same,' Sushi said, reverting to Marathi. 'When she is old like me, Pushpa will tell her grandchildren of a girl from a land far across the sea. With hair of spun gold, eyes like the sky in spring and breasts like the clouds of autumn. Who lived first with her mother, then with her and how they became sisters. Pushpa will tell her grandchildren how the gods did not want the girl from the far country to marry until she was quite old. She will say to her grandchildren that her beautiful sister refused other suitors until one day her sister and her mother went to see Shivaji Raja, Great King of all the Hindu lands. And her sister asked the great Shivaji to spare the life of a handsome prisoner who was going to be executed. The great king was merciful. He spared the prisoner's life but only if her sister married the prisoner that day. And the gods favoured the handsome husband of Pushpa's beautiful sister. He had a fine son and became a great lord in his own country far across the sea. And her sister became great lady, much loved by all people. To show her love for Pushpa and her mother, her beautiful sister gave them many jewels so that her mother bought other fields for her farm. And Pushpa and Des Raj bought a farm of their own, near Pushpa's mother, Sushi.'

Ruth laughed. 'They will think she is telling a story.'

Sushi's tone became serious. 'All the best stories are true. That is why you must not be afraid for your son, my daughter. You and John have found favour with the gods. Your grandsons and your grandsons' grandsons will keep your husband's land for many generations.' Sushi paused briefly. 'Pushpa spoke to me after you went to see President Sahib.' She continued to look Ruth squarely in the eyes as Ruth put out her right arm to show the silver bracelet on her wrist.

'I will always wear this,' Ruth said. 'When I look at it I will think of my wise mother, Sushi, and her gentle daughter Pushpa.' She bent forward to try to kiss Sushi on the cheek but the older woman was not caught unawares.

Sushi pushed Ruth gently away and told her, 'You promised not to touch me. That is why I wanted Pushpa to thank you for both of us. For me as well as her. When you go home you must remember Maratha woman as young woman. Like your sister Pushpa. Not like old woman mother Sushi.'

Ruth looked across to see Mark's bearer coming through the archway. He was carrying a tray containing tea, fruit, and sweetmeats. It was decorated with flowers.

Mai Nayah nodded to the two women standing a few yards along the covered verandah. He went quietly into the bedroom to wake Mark.

'You go back to your husband,' Sushi told Ruth. 'I get John ready for his bath now. Pushpa will come to see you soon.'

\* \* \* \* \*

Ensign Butterworth called the small company of troops to attention and gave the order 'Present Arms' as Sir George's carriage began its journey from the factory to the port. It was completely covered by the flowers which Mark's servants had used to decorate the carriage on its arrival at the bungalow.

Sher Dil, Ahmed Khan, Nabha Sing and Kashi Mathura, the four men who had escorted Mark and Ruth into Maratha territory, insisted on their right to accompany their former commander and were now riding on either side of the carriage on its way to Swally. John sat on Ruth's lap, facing Sir George, and looked uncomfortable and faintly ridiculous in the unfamiliar European clothes he was wearing. While Mark and Sir George engaged in a sporadic conversation on the opposite seat, John played with the silver medallion on the long chain which Ruth wore round her neck.

She had been cajoled into wearing it at half past ten that morning when Sushi and Pushpa appeared, dressed in their best costumes. Over a scarlet silk blouse, Pushpa wore the bright gold silk sari with silver threads, which she wore at Ruth's wedding ceremony. Sushi wore a green silk blouse under the gold silk sari which she had also worn at Ruth's wedding. Over the sari, she was wearing the pearl necklace Ruth had given her on the day of the wedding. Sushi told her she would never part with the necklace and that it would pass to Pushpa on Sushi's death. She also wore the silver medallion awarded her by the East India Company. Sushi did not insist on Ruth wearing her own medallion but emphasised that she wanted to remind Ruth of happy memories. Much to Ruth's embarrassment, Mark produced her medallion from his pocket and suggested she wore it. Although John played with the silver medallion itself, the chain was completely covered by the two garlands remaining from those placed round her neck by the servants when she and Mark left their bungalow.

The steady 'clip clop' of the escorts' horses, combined with the rumble of the wheels of the carriage on the road had an almost soporific affect on Ruth. She did not anticipate any difficulty in sleeping once on board the ship. Up till now the day had gone very well. Pushpa had been initially shy when she first met Ruth that morning but Ruth quickly put her at ease. Other people were always present when the two of them were together so that, apart from smiling at each other from time to time, their behaviour was perfectly normal.

Maria had arrived at their bungalow at about a quarter to eleven so that she could say goodbye to Ruth and take Sushi back with her. Sushi refused point-blank to go, saying she would wait for the carriage to come for her later in the day, unless Pushpa and Lakshmi came with her. This was because John kicked up such a fuss when asked to say goodbye to Sushi. Maria relented, saying she would take Sushi with her to the factory and hastily agreed to Pushpa and Lakshmi coming as well when John's attention had been diverted by the arrival of the President's carriage and the sight of the horses being unhitched. After Mark gave out small presents to them all, apart from Des Raj and Pushpa, the servants attached ropes to the carriage and covered it with flowers. Maria told Ruth she would follow with Sushi and Pushpa, leaving Ruth, Mark, and

John to get into the President's carriage and be pulled by the servants for the first quarter of a mile of the journey, to the sound of cheers and other encouragement from servants in other bungalows. The horses were hitched up for the next half mile and then the process was reversed. Mark's small company of troops was drawn up on the side of the road, a quarter of a mile from the factory. They fastened ropes to the carriage as the horses were untied and pulled the carriage as far as the factory gate, to the accompaniment of applause from the waiting Europeans.

Ruth remembered how emotional her friends had been when she said goodbye. Almost all of them held handkerchiefs to their eyes as Ruth kissed them on the cheeks before leaving. Ruth gave each of her friends one of the garlands of flowers given by the servants until just two were left. Only Sushi and Pushpa seemed cheerful as they waited, a little apart from the others, each holding one of John's hands. Five minutes before the carriage was due to leave, Ruth went across to them to say goodbye. John let out such a howl of rage at the thought of being parted from his grandmother that Maria had raced across and hastily agreed to take Sushi to the quayside, so that the goodbyes could be said there. Sushi, just as before, flatly refused, saying she would wait at the factory unless Pushpa and Lakshmi came to the dockyard with her. Maria reluctantly agreed, saying she would send Pushpa and Lakshmi back to the Cabedo bungalow later.

John seemed quite relaxed at present and Ruth wondered whether it would not have been better to have been firmer with him in the factory or bungalow. There were three months ahead during which she would be in sole charge of John. Fond though she was of Sushi, she had the feeling that John might become spoiled if left too long under Sushi's influence.

She stared out of the carriage, realising that she was seeing the Indian countryside for the last time. Ruth thought of the faces of those she had left behind. She would almost certainly never see them again and most of them would leave their bones in India. She gave John a hard squeeze and he let out a little squeak of protest.

'That's a fine lad you have there,' Sir George said.

'Yes, Sir George,' she answered. Ruth made no attempt to elaborate on this and he did not pursue the subject. Apart from a little desultory conversation between Mark and Sir George, the rest of the journey continued in silence. As they approached the dockyard gate, Ruth saw Fernando and Peter mounted on horseback, waiting to meet them. They turned their horses round and led the carriage and its escort past the Mogul customs house where Ruth and Claire received their first impressions of India. Though it seemed only yesterday to her, three and a quarter years of her life had passed since then. The godowns of the foreign trading companies were much busier than when she and Mark had walked this way during their stay at Fernando's, just after the siege. The quaysides were crowded with Arab and European traders mingling with Indian merchants, together with swarms of labourers shifting cargoes of goods and Indian clerks checking the loads. Every dock was occupied by shipping of all nationalities, flying every sort of flag and emblem. They passed a packed crowd of several hundred Indians, waiting with their luggage beside some Arab dhows.

As he saw the puzzled look on Ruth's face, Sir George said, 'Pilgrims on the way to Mecca. They assemble a pilgrim fleet here once a year. Take a good look, Ruth. There's real religious faith for you. They save up for years just so they can risk their lives sailing two thousand miles across the ocean in an open boat, three or four feet out of the water.'

The press of people on the quayside was so great that their carriage was slowed to a walking pace. Even so, their escort was forced to use all manner of threats and imprecations to keep the way open for the President's carriage and Fernando's carriage following close behind. Their pace quickened as they came nearer to that part of the port where the large, merchant ships were moored. Fernando held up his hands when they arrived at a relatively uncongested part of the quayside. He and Peter both took their horses to a hitching post and the coachman opened the door for the President and his passengers to descend. Sir George gave the order for his escort to dismount and to lead their horses out of the sweltering sun. Fernando seemed surprised at the presence of Maria with the two servants and Ruth noticed him in hurried consultation with his wife. Peter Streynsham joined Sir George, Mark, and Ruth as Fernando and Maria were talking in rapid Portuguese. 'I am sorry Jacoba was so upset, Ruth,' Peter said.

'She wasn't the only lady who was, Peter,' Sir George added.

'I know, Sir George. Ruth is a very popular girl. She'll be sorely missed,' Peter replied. 'And you too, Mark,' he added hastily.

Mark laughed. 'Don't worry, Peter. I know I can never be more than a moon to Ruth's sun.'

'There's something about the East which gets hold of you after a time,' Sir George said reflectively. 'Are you upset at the thought of leaving, Ruth?'

'No, Sir George,' she answered quietly. 'I am not upset. I'm glad to be leaving with Mark. If I was alone, I might be able to make my home among these people. But Mark could never do that. His heart has always been among the hills and dales of the West Riding. That's where he wants his son to grow. Among English fields and under an English sky.' There was a loud clap of thunder followed by heavy spots of rain. 'No. Sir George. I promise you. I won't be upset to live no longer under this alien sky.'

Fernando hurried across at this point, leaving the other three women standing a few yards away. 'I very sorry, Sir George. I not prepared for Maria to come as well.'

'Don't mention it, Senhor Ferrara. Very good of you to take this trouble.' Fernando pointed to a four-masted galleon at the quayside. 'The "Bom Jesus", Mark and Ruth. It will be your home for the next few weeks.'

Ruth could feel the warm, heavy rain begin to penetrate her thin gown. 'At least it will be dry, Fernando,' she said.

'My agent saw your luggage taken on board. I go to your cabin to see bags you want for voyage taken there.'

'Thank you, Fernando,' Mark said. 'We can't thank you enough.'

'It is my pleasure to be of service to you and to Ruth, Mark. Captain of "Bom Jesus" say all passengers must be on board by one o'clock. Visitors allowed on board until then.' He looked meaningly at the rain coming down and the heavy rain clouds above.

'Shall we go aboard, Sir George?' Peter asked.

'If you and Ruth will permit, Mark,' he answered. 'It will get us out of the rain.'

'Of course, Sir George,' Mark replied. 'You are very welcome.' Fernando called across to Maria in Portuguese and she and the two servants joined the rest of the party. He made his way up the wooden gangway and spoke briefly to a ship's officer at the top. The rest of the group were then directed to come up. Mark insisted on carrying John up the gangway himself. When he reached the deck he was greeted by Sushi, saying in an aggrieved voice, 'I thought you did not want me to say goodbye to my grandson.'

Mark laughed and handed John to her as Fernando led the way down a flight of steps to the deck below. They walked along a narrow passageway with Fernando still in the lead. A member of the crew approached them but withdrew quickly when Fernando spoke to him in Portuguese.

'He is Manuel, your steward,' he told Mark. 'You be glad to hear he speak some English.'

'Thank goodness for that,' Mark replied.

A little further on, Fernando opened the door into the cabin which was to be their home for the next ten or eleven weeks. Mark opened the porthole, fanned his face with his hat and said, 'It will be cooler when we're at sea.'

'I'll be glad to get out of these damp clothes,' Ruth said.

A fresh clap of thunder could be heard and Ruth suddenly

remembered the rain which had fallen during the visit to the cemetery with Maria. She looked round for her but Maria was not to be seen. The door was completely filled by Sir George and Peter standing side by side.

'I'm writing a letter to London about you two,' Sir George said. 'Going by the next East Indiaman. I'm sure you'll be a great asset to the Company if you take your brother's place as Member of Parliament, Mark. Someone like you who knows this country well.'

'Ruth and I will have to sort out my brother's estate first, Sir George,' Mark replied.

Sir George looked hard at Ruth. 'I'm sure your wife will be a pillar of strength to you. You're a lucky young man.'

'I know, Sir George.'

A bell rang, followed by a loud shout in Portuguese. Ruth heard Fernando say, 'That is bell for visitors ashore, please.'

Sir George held out his hand to Mark, 'Good luck, lad. A safe journey to you.'

'Thank you, Sir George.'

'And you too, Ruth.' He took her by the shoulder, kissed her on both cheeks, said, 'Very affecting,' and hurried away.

Peter shook Mark's hand and then kissed Ruth on the cheek to wish her luck. Fernando came next saying, 'God go with you, Ruth my dear,' as he kissed both her cheeks.

When Maria followed her husband into the cabin, Ruth could see tears in her eyes. Maria held Mark tight, said 'Take care of my daughter Ruth for me, Mark' and burst into tears. Ruth could see tears still streaming down Maria's face as she looked into her eyes. She lifted up one of her garlands and slipped one end of it over Maria's shoulders so that the two of them were encircled. 'I am sorry, Ruth. I did not mean to cry.'

'I will always be grateful to you and Fernando.' She kissed Maria as a second bell rang, followed by a louder and more urgent shout.

'I must go,' Maria replied.

Ruth slipped the garland off her own shoulders, leaving Maria with the circle of flowers. 'Take it to Claire for me!' she cried as Maria hurried away. Ruth held her arms out to Sushi who was standing in the doorway, holding John in her arms. Mark took his son from Sushi who hesitated for a second before taking Lakshmi from Pushpa.

'You not let me say goodbye to my grandson, Captain Sahib.' John gave a cry of alarm as Sushi started to walk along the passageway. Her voice gradually receded as Ruth heard Sushi say, 'You follow me, please, Captain Sahib. I say goodbye to John properly. He will be good boy for grandmother. Not cry any more. I not cry when I say goodbye.' Mark followed her along the passage, carrying his son in his arms. Ruth looked across the cabin to see Pushpa standing alone in the doorway. They looked at each other for three or four seconds before Pushpa stepped into the cabin.

'Mother told me she did not want to say goodbye,' Ruth began quietly.

'I know,' Pushpa replied in Marathi. 'She has told me to do it for her. Mother wanted you to remember her as I am now. She did not want you to think of her as an old woman with thin, grey hair, a long, flat bosom and a crinkled face.' Pushpa lowered her eyes momentarily to look at Ruth's firm breasts showing through her wet dress. Ruth's eyes looked down in the same way a second or two later. She chuckled gently as she lifted her head to look back at Pushpa's smiling face. Lifting the one remaining garland in both her hands, she put one side of it over Pushpa's shoulders, enclosing the two girls in a circle of flowers.

'We are both women with good bodies,' Ruth said softly and reassuringly. 'I will always remember you as you are now, sister.'

Pushpa carefully gathered up Ruth's long, fair, curly hair. She eased the yellow hair over her own right shoulder, letting it fall down the back of her sari. Ruth reached out her right hand, picked up Pushpa's waist-length, black, shiny hair and brought it forward over her own right shoulder to hang down the back of her gown. 'My memories of you will never fade, Ruth,' Pushpa whispered gently, hesitating for a second over the name.

The ringing of the ship's bell became more insistent with louder shouts from the crew. 'It is time to say goodbye, sister,' Ruth said.

'I know, sister,' Pushpa replied.

As the girls continued looking into each other's eyes, Ruth saw the expression on the younger woman's face change to the look of fierce determination she had seen so often on the face of Sushi. Pushpa's eyes were bright with triumph as she pulled Ruth towards her. The memory of how Sushi had first kissed her on that dusty road to Damon came flooding back to Ruth. She clung to Pushpa's soft, warm, living body almost as if she hoped their long embrace would blot out the memory of her sister Claire, lying alone in her cold, wet, grave. Their lips came together while they still held each other tight, breathlessly looking into the other woman's eyes.

'You must tell Mother we are both proud to be true sisters now,' Ruth told Pushpa, looking into those soft, brown eyes so near her own.

Pushpa lifted her right hand slightly and began to stroke Ruth's hair. 'I will tell her today,' she replied. 'Mother was very angry with me. She will know I gave special love to her daughter Ruth. She did not need to push us sisters together this time.'

A wave of affection for Pushpa swept over Ruth. 'I love you, sister,' she said. 'I will never forget you.'

'I do love you, Ruth. I will always love you.' Pushpa kissed Ruth gently on the cheek and then looked into her eyes with an expression of loving tenderness. They gathered each other into a soft embrace, their lips coming together in a soft, lingering kiss. Their arms twined around each other, so that they could feel the closeness of each other's body through the damp clothes.

They were interrupted by the sight of Fernando standing stock-still in the doorway. There was a look of surprise on his face.

'We're coming now, Fernando,' Ruth told him.

He turned, and the two young women squeezed through the doorway together and followed him down the passage. They kept their arms round each other's waist to prevent the single garland of flowers being broken.

'I am so happy for us both, Ruth,' Pushpa said shyly. 'You and your husband go back to your husband's land in your own country. Des Raj and I go back to buy our own land in our village.'

'I am so happy for us too, Pushpa. But there will always be a part of my heart in Lalhulla. Take care of Mother for me.'

They giggled as they ascended the narrow stairway to the deck, side by side. When they reached the deck Ruth turned towards Pushpa and carefully lifted the garland from her own shoulders so that Pushpa had the whole circle of flowers on her. She saw that Sushi was holding John while Maria held Lakshmi. Heavy rain was still falling. 'Time to say goodbye to John now, Mother,' Ruth told her. Sushi spoke a few words in Marathi in a soft whisper and then covered John's face with kisses. She held him out to Mark and he went to his father's arms without protest. Ruth held her arms to Sushi but she turned away to take Lakshmi from Maria. As Maria was passing Lakshmi over, Sushi nudged Pushpa, causing her to slip and stumble on the wet deck. Ruth caught the other girl quickly and pulled her upright to prevent her falling. They both laughed at Sushi's transparency, and as Ruth looked over Pushpa's shoulder she could see Sushi looking at them with a broad smile on her face. The warm, heavy rain had completely soaked Ruth's thin, silk gown and Pushpa's cotton sari. As the two young women held each other tight, Ruth could feel Pushpa's breasts and thighs pressed against her own. 'Tell Mother I love her,' Ruth whispered.

Pushpa moved her head so that she was looking Ruth straight in the eyes. 'She told me to say she loved you, Ruth. And to show you how she loved you. As I love you, sister.'

'Tell Mother I am proud to have you as a sister, Pushpa,' Ruth replied softly. Pushpa kissed her for the last time.

# 21

## NOVEMBER 1666

Mark lowered his head to get some protection against the drizzle falling from the grey sky of the November afternoon. Even the borrowed horse seemed restive at being asked to battle against the rain and the strong north-easterly wind. Anne's husband, Benjamin Crawley, had tried to persuade Mark to stay at their farm for a few hours in the hope that the weather would clear. Perhaps I should have taken his advice, Mark thought ruefully as he was buffeted by yet another gust of wind. What a change from the weather during those long years in India! This moment of weakness passed, however, when he saw a milestone showing that he was only two miles from the village of Blackmoor. Although his horse had now slowed to a walk, Mark anticipated being inside Aireton Hall within half an hour. He wondered if Henry had made many changes to the estate. According to their mother, Henry had spent most of his time in London. Holding a position at Court, mixing with the fashionable set, and attending the House of Commons as the local Member of Parliament had absorbed almost all of Henry's energies. Mark thought how different this homecoming was, compared to his return from Sweden eight years before. Nine years of soldiering had involved serving three different masters and fighting in four campaigns but he had little to show for his time. Except Ruth, he thought to himself and even as the image of his wife came into his mind, he smiled. She was not only beautiful but also the mother of his son. His thoughts went back to that May morning over eight years before when as a naive, inexperienced, young man he had kissed the little orphan girl in the garden of the steward's lodge, even though their two families were natural enemies.

Providence had moved in a mysterious way to bring him, the youngest of the three brothers, back to Aireton Hall, accompanied, as his wife, by the same adopted ward of a Roundhead family. However difficult it might be for Ruth to be accepted by his mother, there could be no question that her son John would be master of Aireton Hall one day. He hoped that John would be a bridge between Ruth and Lady Catherine, especially as John was his mother's only grandchild. All these thoughts were going through his mind on his approach to Aireton Hall.

He looked at the gardens surrounding it. How different it had been when he and Ruth first met in the May so long ago. Mark spurred the horse into a trot and a minute later rode into the stable yard. He dismounted quickly and waited for a groom to appear. Nobody came in sight after a pause of several seconds. 'Groom!' he shouted loudly. Two men came slowly out of the stables without saying anything.

'Get this horse rubbed down, fed, and watered,' Mark commanded.

'You expected up at 'all?' asked the older groom.

'I'm Mark Fairbrother.'

The two grooms were galvanised into activity. The younger groom began removing the saddle as the older groom took the reins and said, 'I'll send Martin up t'all. Tell 'em you're 'ere, sir.'

'No need for that. You take good care of the horse. I have to return him tomorrow morning.'

'Leave 'im to us, sir, 'orse'll be fresh as paint in morning.'

When Mark walked across the grounds and up the steps in front of the house he thought that a little tightening up seemed to be needed. Just before he reached the front door Digby Foster opened it. He had obviously seen Mark's horse or heard the sound of its hooves.

'Sir Mark?' he asked half-questioningly. Mark grinned. 'Yes, Digby, It's me.'

'You are three inches taller than I remember you, sir. And sunburnt as well.'

'You've changed slightly, Digby. It's been a long time.'

'Indeed it has, sir.'

'We'll have plenty of time to chat about old times later. Now I want to see my mother and sister.'

'Is Mistress Ruth with you, sir?'

'She is Lady Ruth Fairbrother now.'

'Of course, Sir Mark. Accept my apologies. A stupid slip of the tongue.'

Mark laughed. 'You warned me against her, Digby. I'm glad I didn't take your advice. But you'll have a chance to judge for yourself soon. Now I really must go off to see my mother.'

'Shall I accompany you, sir?'

'No need. I want it to be a surprise.'

'Very well, sir. It is good to have you back again. For good this time. Let me take your coat and have it dried.'

Mark handed the steward his wet riding cloak and hat. He went through the ante-room and opened the door of the living room. 'Hullo, Mother. Hullo, Elizabeth,' he said as he saw the two of them sitting near the fire.

His mother's hand went to her mouth and she looked quite pale. 'Oh, Mark. I didn't know you were home.' She got up and embraced him, kissing both his cheeks. She started to sob quietly. 'I am so happy. Seeing you is so unexpected. The last news we have is your letter from London.'

'We only stayed a day and night there. Then we came straight up to Yorkshire. Ruth's eldest sister and her husband lost everything in the fire of London two months ago. They're sailing to America any day now. They may have already gone.'

'I'm sorry. That fire was a great disaster. Are you alone?' Lady Fairbrother asked.

'Yes. Ruth is staying with her sister Anne. You remember her husband, Benjamin Crawley, who has a farm near Great Hampendown. About nine miles from here.'

'Will we see her soon?' Elizabeth asked eagerly.

'Yes, Elizabeth.' Mark went across and kissed her on the forehead. 'And you'll be able to see little John as well.'

'How is John?' his mother asked.

'He's a beautiful boy. Not quite two yet but quick and clever, just like Ruth.'

'She always was a lovely girl,' Elizabeth said wistfully. 'And you two were such a handsome couple.'

'Is Ruth well? When will we see her and her son?' Lady Fairbrother asked.

'Our son, Mother,' Mark corrected gently. 'There is no question about his paternity.'

'Of course not, Mark. Ruth and I have not always seen eye to eye but there have never been any doubts about her chastity.'

'You two are very much alike you know, Mother. She is stubborn, impulsive, and proud.' Mark turned his head slightly so that he was not looking at his mother. 'Ruth is a passionate woman. She feels things very deeply.'

Lady Fairbrother was silent for a few seconds before replying. 'I must admit I thought you had made a mistake. Still now that Henry's dead, perhaps it was all for the best. But Ruth is the only person who has ever had the gall to order me out of my own house. Perhaps if you had returned with Henry that wouldn't have happened. With you here, Ruth wouldn't have wanted to leave Aireton Hall.'

'That's fate. But remember our son is now your only link with immortality, Mother.'

'I know, Mark. And I'm grateful to Ruth for that.' She scrutinised her son carefully before continuing. 'I thought she was only after rank and position. I wanted you to marry a woman of fortune. If you had married my brother's daughter Sarah, Uncle George would have given you a handsome dowry. She still hasn't married. Although you have come into your father's estate, Henry left us with a lot of debts. The net income from our property now is only eight hundred pounds a year.'

'I'm sorry, Mother. That's not important to me. There have been times when eight hundred pounds would have seemed a fortune to me. I owe my life to Ruth. Every day I live is a debt of honour I can never repay. We spent our wedding night together with the city of Surat burning around us. Not knowing if we would live to see another sunset if the Maratha army decided to attack the English factory next morning. My life hung by a thread when Ruth chose to become my wife. She risked her life to save mine and my only possessions were the clothes I stood up in.'

'Ruth never said anything about this in the letters she wrote to me.' Elizabeth interrupted.

'Of course she didn't. Ruth wouldn't want to worry you or Mother. She's intelligent and resourceful. Brave as well. When John was born she hardly uttered a sound. And not afraid to work. She helped her foster-father run his farm. During our time in India she managed my house for me. She's literate, educated, and can handle household accounts.' Mark's speech became more breathless as he continued. 'Ruth will make a wonderful mistress of Aireton Hall. Together we'll make it an inheritance for our children to be proud of.'

Lady Fairbrother came across and embraced her son again. 'I've been such a fool, Mark. A stubborn old fool. I always knew that girl was meant for you. But I wouldn't accept it. Instead I drove both of you to a far country.'

Mark kissed his mother. 'We can only do what we think is best at the time.' His voice became much gentler. 'Perhaps because the two of us have been through so much together, there's a special bond between us, and the love which Ruth and I have for each other is fiercer than if we had stayed at home. She has been alone so many times in her twenty-two years she is anxious not to be rejected again.'

'I don't follow you, Mark,' his mother replied.

'Ruth told me that she quarrelled with you the last time the two of you met. She said she told you she never wanted to see Aireton Hall again. Ruth wished me to ask you if she may come home.'

There were tears in his mother's eyes when she replied. 'She was a hot-headed young girl then. We all say things at the age of sixteen which would be better left unsaid. I'm the one who ought to ask forgiveness. I was old enough and experienced enough to know better. She has asked you to seek permission to come home because I told her she would never be mistress of Aireton Hall. I lost my temper and said I was the one who decided which people lived here, who left and who stayed. She was a frightened sixteen year old, being driven from her home after Henry threatened her. I should have held her in my arms and asked her to stay.'

'Ruth didn't tell me that you had said she would never be mistress of Aireton Hall. Or that you would decide who stayed here.'

'More credit to her. You are the master here now, Mark. Ruth is the mistress of Aireton Hall. Your wife will decide if Elizabeth and I stay or leave here. Tell her that when you return to Master Crawley's farm.'

'Oh, Mark.' Elizabeth cried out. 'I never thought of that. Do you think Ruth will be kind to us?'

'Stand up.' He put his arms round his diminutive sister and smiled. 'John's still got a long way to go before he catches up to Aunt Elizabeth. Promise not to spoil him.'

'I promise,' Elizabeth answered eagerly. 'Anything Ruth asks.'

Mark looked across at the slightly forlorn figure of his mother sitting in the chair by the fire. Her grey hair was streaked with white now and, for the first time, he noticed how old she seemed. He released his left arm from round Elizabeth's shoulders and beckoned across to his mother.

'You realise, Mother, don't you? You'll be John's only living grandparent?' Lady Fairbrother hurried across and buried her face in her son's shoulder. She started to cry.

'That's enough of that, Mother. My coat's wet enough already.'

'I'm sorry, Mark,' she sobbed. 'Why didn't you change?'

'No clothes,' he answered, succinctly.

Lady Fairbrother broke free. She rang the bell and waited

for the steward to appear. He must have noticed that she had been weeping but was too polite to make any comment.

'Can you get some clothes for Sir Mark, Master Foster?' she asked.

'I am sure we can find some, your ladyship, but they may not be an exact fit.' Digby Foster turned to Mark. 'I have taken the liberty of asking the farm manager to come across to the house, sir. Whenever you are ready, he and I await your instructions.'

'Thank you, Digby. I'll be glad to see both of you when I get out of these wet clothes.' Mark looked at his mother and sister. 'I would like to go round the house and estate after I've changed and before it gets dark. Please excuse me now, Mother. There'll be time to talk over the evening meal.'

'When will we see Ruth and your son?' his sister asked.

'I'll stay overnight, Elizabeth. Leave here early and bring Ruth and John back in time for the midday meal.'

'Do you wish any special arrangements to be made for their arrival, sir?' Digby Foster asked.

'I'll ask the coachman to follow when I leave tomorrow. The rest I can leave in your capable hands. Come on now, Digby, or I will catch pneumonia.'

\* \* \* \* \*

The servants must have made a special effort, Mark thought, as he sat down with his mother and sister to their evening meal. Although it was difficult to be sure in the soft candle light all the furniture in the dining room seemed to have been polished to a high gloss. The silver candlesticks and cutlery reflected the light from the oil lamps placed round the sides of the room as well as from the burning candles. He noticed that Digby had brought out the finest crockery, cutlery, and glasses for his benefit. Mark thought this was a little premature and that he must remind the steward to make the same effort on the following night.

The two girls who brought in the food from the kitchen looked at him in a way which was both coy and wary. The wariness was similar to that which he had seen when inspecting the farm and the rest of the estate in the afternoon. After the food was served and Digby Foster had poured out the table wine the servants withdrew.

'Tell me if I'm wrong, Mother,' Mark began. 'I get the impression that neither the estate servants nor the house servants are overjoyed to see me. Apart from Digby Foster, possibly. Am I imagining this?'

His mother waited a few seconds before replying. 'I don't want to speak ill of the dead but Henry was a harsh master. I know many of the servants used to compare him unfavourably with the Trents. It will be easier for you when Ruth arrives. She was one of the daughters of the house until she was sixteen. Ruth was very popular with the servants when the Trents were here. Some of the servants still ask for news of her. She'll find it easy to take her place as mistress of Aireton Hall.'

'I know that. But why should the servants be wary of me?'

'Because you're a Fairbrother, my son. None of the servants remember your father, except Master Foster. Henry drove everyone very hard. He spent most of his time in London. Needed money badly. When he was in Yorkshire he used to make himself unpopular with tenants and servants alike. Tried to get as much as possible out of them and give as little as possible in return. Spent the money on the mistresses he kept in London. When he sat on the bench as a local magistrate, Henry gave severe sentences. He was especially hard on quakers and other non-conformists who didn't attend services at the parish church. You'll have to give the people here time to adjust.'

'I see.'

'It hasn't been easy for me in the last six years; running the estate in Henry's absence, squeezing what I could out of it to meet his constant demands for money. It's going to be better now that you and Ruth are here to take up the reins again.' She hesitated briefly. 'Henry told me neither your wife nor your son would be welcome here.'

'I didn't realise it had been so difficult for you, Mother.'

Lady Fairbrother paused for a few seconds before continuing. 'You're aware that Henry was the local Member of Parliament?'

'Yes, I knew that,' Mark answered.

'He held the identical seat as your grandfather. They were members for the same constituency. The present member is our attorney. I'm sure the seat could be yours for the asking if you wanted it.'

Mark laughed softly. 'I have no ambition to follow in Henry's footsteps. I want to be a country gentleman. Like father and Edmund.'

'How does your wife feel?'

'Ruth and I have done enough travelling. We both want to stay here for the rest of our lives.'

'Please let me stay with you,' Elizabeth asked earnestly.

'You know what I told you this afternoon.' Mark gave a wicked grin. 'If you promise you won't spoil John, Ruth will let you stay.'

'I won't, I won't. I mean I will promise. I will.'

'Please!' her mother exclaimed. 'Let's relax until Ruth arrives.'

'Why don't you tell me what has happened to you in the last eight years?' Mark asked. 'After all, I've only had half a dozen letters in all that time.' The rest of the meal was taken up with his mother and Elizabeth telling him how they had moved back into Aireton Hall after the restoration of the monarchy.

The independent preacher had been ejected from the parish church and the old Anglican incumbent restored. From time to time they heard rumblings of discontent. During the three or four years after the restoration a few dissenters and old supporters of the Commonwealth were rounded up and executed. The most serious outbreak had been at the end of

1663, three years previously, when a couple of hundred armed malcontents had collected at Farnley, south-west of Leeds. There was unrest at present in the district because of high taxation resulting from the unpopular war against the Dutch.

'We still have a few Commonwealth sympathisers around,' Lady Fairbrother continued. 'I'm sure it will help to settle the district down when you become a justice of the peace. People round here will be pleased because they know that your wife was a ward of Colonel Trent. Many of the farmers, and especially their labourers, thought highly of him. They still remember him as the Cromwellian governor for the area.'

'Time enough for that, Mother, when we settle in.' After a brief pause, Mark asked. 'What was life like here during the plague?'

'The people round here were very fortunate. We had no cases in the village among the workers on our farm or servants in the house,' his mother replied. She sighed. 'Henry was a fool. He stayed in London until June, two months after the outbreak of the plague and then came back to Yorkshire. Henry was like a caged lion here. He had become fat and looked much older than his thirty-three years. Try as he might, he was unsuccessful in his attempts to seduce the servant girls in the Hall, even when he dismissed six of them. The servant girls will have no need to worry about their virtue in future with a Puritan as their mistress again.' Lady Fairbrother smiled. 'Especially when their master is so obviously in love with the mistress of the Hall.'

'But how did Henry catch the plague?' Mark asked.

'Well, in August he gave up his attempts at seduction in order to return to his three mistresses in London. When he arrived there, he found two of them had died of plague. lie wrote to me at the beginning of September to say he had decided to face up to his responsibilities and that he was going to visit Uncle George to ask for the hand of his cousin Sophie. Twenty-four hours after he arrived at Uncle George's estate he went down with the plague.'

'I'm very sorry, Mother.'

'I'm over it now.' Lady Fairbrother looked intently at her son. 'Perhaps it was Providence. You'll make a better master of Aireton Hall than Henry. You still look so young and handsome.' Her voice trembled a little. 'So like your father. Ruth must have taken good care of you in the last three years. It says somewhere in the Book of Proverbs that the worth of a capable wife is far beyond any jewels.' She pulled out her handkerchief and started to blow her nose vigorously. At that moment the two servant girls followed Digby Foster into the room and began clearing away.

'Shall I bring in the port and brandy, Sir Mark?' the steward asked.

'No, Digby. I just like a glass or two of wine with meals. Keep the port and brandy for guests. I acquired quite a taste for tea while in India.'

'Very well, sir.'

'I'll go into the drawing room now, with the ladies.'

'Before you go, sir,' Digby Foster said. 'I assume you'll be sleeping in the master bedroom overnight.'

Mark reflected for a moment or two. 'Is anyone using the room Lady Ruth slept in when she was here before?'

His mother looked at Mark curiously but the steward's face was impassive as he asked, 'The old nursery, sir?'

'That's right. I'd like to sleep in there tonight.'

'In the nursery, sir?' The steward's face was expressionless but his voice expressed surprise.

'Yes, Digby. Lady Ruth and I will occupy the master bedroom tomorrow night.'

'As you wish, Sir Mark. I will make all the arrangements.'

He stood aside to allow the Fairbrother family to go into the drawing room. When the three of them were seated Mark asked, 'Do you think I'm foolish, mother?'

'Foolish? In what way, son?'

'In wanting to sleep in the bed Ruth slept in when she was a girl.'

'Foolish? Maybe.' His mother smiled. 'I'm nearly fifty-five but I haven't forgotten what it was like to be young and hot-blooded.' She leant forward. Her voice became earnest. 'Don't become like me or Henry. Don't start being cynical about love, Mark.'

Her son nodded. 'I remember I once read a poem about a girdle. It was written by Edmund Waller. I used to think it rather foolish. It began:

*'That which her slender waist confined*
*Shall now my joyful temples bind.'*

I forget how the rest of it goes but I know it finishes,

*'Give me but what this ribbon bound,*
*Take all the rest the sun goes round.'*

I didn't understand what the poet meant until I married Ruth.' There was silence for a few moments.

'It's strange to hear you talk about young Ruth as Lady Ruth.' Elizabeth said.

'She's a grown woman now. And the mother of my son.'

'You promised you were going to talk to us about your time abroad.' Elizabeth continued. 'Let us know how you met Ruth in India. Henry told us one of the East India Company directors said Ruth had been given a silver medal by them.' They listened intently as he told them about his return to Sweden just before the renewal of the Baltic War, his second campaign in Denmark, and his return to Holland after peace was made between the warring countries. Both he and his brother had been short of money and Henry had suggested that he should enrol in the army of the Mogul Emperor, where European mercenaries were well paid. He had sailed for India before General Monck invited Charles II to return to England and did not hear of the restoration until five months later. By that time he had already enlisted in the Imperial Army and was sent to the north-western province of the Empire to help put down a Pathan uprising in Peshawar. After the revolt ended, his regiment moved first to Delhi and then to Agra. When the Emperor found out that the governor of Surat had transferred most of the garrison away but kept their pay, the governor was executed and Mark's regiment was sent to Surat as reinforcements. This was just before the Maratha attack on the town at the beginning of January 1664. He had been captured along with a number of other Imperial troops. When the attempt on Shivaji's life failed, there were widespread demands for retribution. He and others were brought before Shivaji for punishment and he was about to be executed. His life was saved when Ruth pleaded for him, risking her life to save his.

'It must have been awful,' Elizabeth said.

'Ruth was told she would have to marry me there and then if my life was to be spared. She didn't hesitate even though I had behaved badly towards her in the past. I must admit I hesitated. She was dressed in native clothes. I didn't recognise her. Sir George Oxindon, the English President appointed by the East India Company, was on a peace mission to the Maratha headquarters and Ruth had accompanied him as his interpreter. That was why she was given a medal. For her bravery at that time.'

'What happened then?' his mother asked.

'Ruth whispered in my ear. She told me who she was. I couldn't believe it. Couldn't take it in. Shivaji agreed to release me if I promised not to rejoin the Mogul army and to get married that day. He and his men all thought it a great joke. There I was, with just the clothes I stood up in. I couldn't go back to the Imperial Army to collect my clothes, my possessions or my arrears of pay because they would have said I was a deserter. Shivaji and his troops had a good laugh when they thought I was being forced to marry, on that day, a native girl I'd never seen before. They made me give my word.'

'I think that's a dreadful thing to do,' Elizabeth said. 'I wonder what I would have said if they'd forced me to marry,' she mused softly.

'It's better than being dead,' Mark remarked drily. 'Sir George took us back to the English factory. There was a native woman with us as well. She'd befriended Ruth when Ruth was alone and penniless. The English chaplain was ill and Ruth persuaded Sir George to conduct the form of marriage for us, which was legal during the Commonwealth. You know where you declare in the presence of God and before witnesses that you take someone as your wedded wife. It wouldn't have been legal, of course, but Ruth told me not to worry. We had both given our word to Shivaji and she thought we ought to go through with it. As it happened, we didn't need to take up Sir George's offer. One of the Maratha officers took us to a French Capuchin missionary who blessed our union.'

'But neither of you are Catholics!' Elizabeth exclaimed.

'Quite so. That's why we asked the English chaplain to marry us. So that we would be married according to English law.'

Elizabeth looked perplexed. 'The letter Ruth wrote to me said that you were married on the eighth of February. But you said the attack on the town took place at the beginning of January.'

'That's correct. We had to wait until the English chaplain was well again.'

'Ooh, Mark!' Elizabeth said. She looked vaguely shocked. 'That means you and Ruth weren't legally married all that time. And she's such a Puritan, too. So concerned about her honour when Henry was here.'

'Don't be such a fool, girl!' her mother interrupted sharply. 'If Mark and Ruth had their union blessed by a priest that's good enough for me. They were husband and wife in the eyes of God.'

'But even so, Mother,' Elizabeth replied. 'They could have waited for the chaplain to get well again.'

Mark looked away and stared into the fire. 'Ruth was not concerned with legal formalities, Elizabeth. It was my life she had saved and she wanted to be with me. I knew I would have to take my turn guarding the factory next morning. Sir George offered to let me go but I couldn't leave Ruth behind in there.

We expected another Maratha attack and there were only twenty of us against a Maratha army who could bring four thousand troops into action. All the time the Mogul gunners were firing from the fort on to the town. There were fires everywhere. To tell you the truth, I don't think Ruth would really have cared if we hadn't found a priest that night. She just wanted to stay with me.'

'That's a terrible thing to say about her!' Elizabeth exclaimed in a shocked voice.

'Be quiet, Elizabeth, if you can only talk nonsense,' her mother said brusquely. 'Ruth behaved exactly as I would have expected her to behave. Like a true Cavalier lady. Staying at the side of her man when he was in danger. I would have done the same thing in similar circumstances. It is lucky for most women that they are not tested in that way.'

Lady Fairbrother moved across to behind the chair where her son was sitting. She placed her hands on his shoulders, bent her head over Mark's right shoulder, and kissed him on the right cheek.

'I am very proud to have Ruth as a daughter-in-law, Mark,' she said softly. Her voice wavered as she whispered, 'My only daughter-in-law.'

Mark moved his arm across his chest and took his mother's left hand in his right hand.

\* \* \* \* \*

Digby Foster had dried all of Mark's clothes by next morning. He came quietly into the nursery to place them on a chair beside the dressing table. Mark sat up in the canopied bed which used to belong to Ruth and said, 'Good morning, Digby.'

'Good morning, Sir Mark. I hope you were comfortable.'

'Yes. I had an excellent night.'

The steward's eyes flickered over the bed where his master had slept. It was just big enough for a man of Sir Mark's height. He used to wonder why Mistress Ruth stubbornly insisted on keeping the four-poster bed which was really too big for her.

Now the girl he had always regarded as an interloper was coming back as his master's wife and her son would probably occupy this nursery. His train of thought was broken as he heard Mark speaking again. 'I won't wait to have breakfast with Lady Catherine and Mistress Elizabeth. Send one of the servants to the stables to tell the grooms to have my horse ready. I'll be off as soon as I have some bread and honey with a pot of coffee, Digby.'

'Yes, sir. We are all looking forward to seeing your son. And Lady Fairbrother as well, sir.'

'Of course, Digby. I'm sure my wife is impatient to return home. Now I must hurry and get dressed.'

'I'll order coffee for you, sir,' the steward said as he left. 'And I'll ask the coachman to follow you to Master Crawley's farm.'

\* \* \* \* \*

Twenty minutes later Mark was standing in the stable yard giving orders to the coachman and head groom. Although the winter air was cold, it was crisp and sunny, so different from the weather of the day before. After Mark mounted the horse he had borrowed from Benjamin Crawley, the head groom and coachman took their leave of him. He was left alone with a young stable boy who was holding the horse's head.

'How old are you, lad?' he asked.

'Twelve, Sir Mark,' the boy replied.

'And what's your name?'

'Martin, sir.'

'How long have you worked at Aireton Hall?'

'Nigh on four years, sir.'

'Are you happy here?'

The boy waited a second or two before answering. 'Well enough, sir. Considering many folks 'ere can't get work.' He paused and looked warily at Mark as if wondering if he should go on. 'Sir 'enry always shouted about us servants being lazy. Said we wanted to go back to days of Old Nod and Tumbledown Dick.'

'And do you, Martin?'

'Oh no, sir. I pray for King Charles in church every Sunday.'

'Good.'

The boy still held the horse's head as though reluctant to let go. 'Sir 'enry was always on about 'is father and 'is brother being killed. Fighting against wicked parley ment men.'

'You're too young to remember those times. Thank God they're over now.'

The boy looked up cautiously. ''ead groom said you married to Round'ead lady, sir. One of Colonel Trent's daughters. 'e was governor of district.'

Mark laughed. 'He told you the truth, Martin. You'll have a chance to see my wife and son this afternoon. Work hard, lad and you'll be head groom yourself one day. Or perhaps you'll have a farm of your own.'

The boy released the bridle and stood back smiling. 'Good luck, Sir Mark.'

'Thank you, Martin.' Mark dug his heels into the horse's side and trotted through the archway out of the stable yard. He rode towards the gate leading to the road and thought that one of his servants would be on his side. Mark's horse was fresh and there was no wind and rain to fight against. The horse broke into a canter and overtook Mark's coach which was going in the same direction.

Mark had seldom been in such high spirits and he waved his hat to the coachman as he passed. He was going to bring his wife and son home. The nine miles between Aireton Hall and Benjamin Crawley's farm seemed to fly by. Around an hour after leaving home he brought the horse to a stop in Benjamin's farmyard. Mark dismounted, led the horse into the stables and started taking the saddle off.

Benjamin Crawley followed him through the stable door and said, 'Thought you might be back early. That's why I haven't been out to the fields yet. Leave rubbing down the horse. I'll get one of my men to do that.' The two shook hands.

'Thanks, Benjamin,' Mark replied. 'Everything all right?'

'You've only been away a night. What could have gone wrong?' He laughed. 'You're as bad as Ruth.'

Mark finished removing the harness, put the horse in its stall and the two men left the stable together. Benjamin saw one of his men in a nearby field. 'Come and rub 'Thunder' down,' he called, 'and see if he needs some water.' The man shouted an acknowledgement and Mark followed his host towards the farmhouse.

'You're a lucky man, you know, Mark.' Benjamin said.

'In what way?'

'Having Ruth, I mean. Don't misunderstand me. I'm not complaining about Anne. She's a good wife and mother. But from time to time yesterday evening Ruth kept wandering about the farmhouse, calling your name, "Mark, Mark".'

Mark could not make up his mind whether to laugh or be embarrassed. Benjamin waited for a reply but none came. 'She's very much in love with you,' he continued.

'Yes. I know. I realise how lucky I am.'

Benjamin winked and then grinned as they approached the door of the farmhouse.

'She doesn't have to know I told you.'

He opened the door and called, 'Anne, Mark's here.'

Anne and Ruth appeared together in the doorway of the living room. 'Hullo, Anne,' Mark said as he kissed her on the cheek.

'Where are John and the girls?' Benjamin asked, moving past Anne. 'Somewhere around,' she answered, going back into the living room with her husband, leaving Ruth and Mark alone together.

Ruth looked across at Mark but neither spoke. She could feel the intensity of his eyes on her. It was as though she could melt in front of him. He had looked at her like that before he had returned to Sweden eight years ago and again on that dreadful but wonderful night in Surat when they had become husband and wife. At last she could bear it no longer. She ran into his arms saying, 'Mark, darling, it seemed you were away so long.' His only answer was to put his arms around her shoulders and gently kiss her. She put her arms around his waist and pressed her lips on his. The pressure of their lips became more intense and she pulled her body against his, pushing her breasts against his chest and her thighs against his. Although only a few seconds passed it seemed an eternity of time before Mark lifted his head to release his mouth from hers.

'Steady, sweetheart,' he whispered huskily in her ear. 'We're in Anne's house now and I've only been away one night.'

Ruth kissed the side of Mark's neck. She continued to hold her husband tight as she whispered, 'It seemed such a long time. It's the first night we've been apart since we married. Promise you'll never leave me, darling.'

'Of course I promise.' He kissed her once more and then gently took hold of Ruth's arms saying, 'The coach will be here soon. And the children will be bursting in any minute.

Ruth laughed. 'Wait till I get you home,' she threatened. 'Come on. Let's go and get John ready.'

They went hand in hand into the living room. Anne and Benjamin had discreetly withdrawn to the children's room where the floor was covered with toys. Mark peered round the door and his son came running towards him. He picked John up and kissed him.

'Mark tells me that the coach will be here soon, Anne. We'd better get John ready,' Ruth said. 'Would it be a lot of trouble if we left some of our luggage here and sent a cart to pick it up tomorrow?'

'No, of course not. Would you like Benjamin to send somebody across with it today?'

'You've both done more than enough already,' Ruth answered. 'It's been lovely to see you and all your family but I'm impatient to get home. Our cart will collect our bags tomorrow.'

'I'm sure you'll be very happy. I remember Aireton Hall very well. Strange to think of one of the Trent girls going back there to live. As Lady Fairbrother.'

Anne's six year old daughter Hannah caught hold of her mother's skirt and asked, 'Is Auntie Ruth taking John away? Sarah and I want to play with him.'

'John has to go to his own home now,' Anne replied. 'He's going to stay in the big house where your mummy used to live.'

'Why can't we go with him?' Hannah demanded.

'Your home is here, darling,' her mother answered, in a slightly exasperated tone. Hannah started to cry and was soon followed by three year old Sarah and then by John. Ruth picked up her son to comfort him as Benjamin looked enquiringly at Mark.

'Come here, Hannah. Come here, Sarah,' Mark called and knelt on the floor. As the weeping children came towards him he said, 'If you stop crying Mummy and Daddy will bring you across to see Auntie Ruth and Cousin John on Sunday. And if you're good, they'll bring you again on John's birthday in two weeks time. And when the spring comes you can play in the gardens and by the ponds. If you're very good, perhaps Mummy will let you stay for a little while, but only if you're good.'

'Thank you, Uncle Mark,' Hannah replied.

'Well dry your eyes now and let John get ready to go. You'll see him soon.' Mark raised himself slowly from the floor.

'That's very thoughtful of you, Mark,' Anne said. 'Thank you very much. Frances and her family will probably have sailed for America by now. Benjamin hasn't any living relatives which means that John will be my daughters' only cousin in England and Ruth their only aunt.'

'Don't forget Uncle Mark,' he replied, in a mock indignant tone. 'Anyway I have an ulterior motive. I want Benjamin to come across with them. Get him to give his advice on making the estate farm more profitable. Ruth worked on your father's farm but I know nothing about farming.'

'I'll be glad to help, Mark. Any time you want advice let me know.' Benjamin was secretly pleased at Mark's suggestion. The arrogant Sir Henry Fairbrother had made it very clear to him that former Cromwellians were unwelcome in his district. Benjamin had been told that there was no possibility of his ever being considered for a position as a local magistrate or even as a member of the Parochial Church Council, especially when he was married to a daughter of the district's former military governor. Oddly enough, Benjamin recalled, Sir Henry became even more offensive to him and his wife after they heard the news of Sir Henry's brother marrying Anne's foster-sister. It was, therefore, with a certain amount of trepidation that he learned from Anne that Mark Fairbrother was returning to England to inherit Sir Henry's estate and would like to spend two or three days with them.

In the event, he had been pleasantly surprised. A few tears had been shed by both his wife and Ruth when they met, especially when they talked about their mother and two nephews who had died of plague and their sister Claire who had died in India. Mark seemed devoted to Ruth and obviously worshipped John. There was some mystery about their meeting in India and subsequent marriage which he had never quite been able to fathom out. Mark seemed much more interested in discovering all he could about the care and breeding of stock, rotation of crops, and crop yields. Although Benjamin knew that possession of the Aireton Hall estate made Mark the largest landowner in the area, and even the estate farm was three times the size of his, Mark always listened to him carefully on the subject of farming. Now that their two wives had children of their own, the eight years difference in ages did not seem as important as it had to the two girls when he had married Anne ten years before.

Ruth and Anne hurried the three children into the living room, leaving the two men alone together.

'I'm sorry we have to go off like this, Benjamin,' Mark said. 'You know how it is. My mother and sister are anxious to see our new offspring. Anyway, you'll be glad to get back to normal.'

'Happy to have you here, Mark. All of you. We'll miss you.' Benjamin looked thoughtful and then asked, 'I suppose I'll have to call you Sir Mark when I come to Aireton Hall.'

Mark laughed. 'Good heavens, no, Benjamin. You're part of the family. Anne wouldn't even think of calling her sister Lady Ruth. Don't give it another thought. Come on, let's join the ladies. That's the coach I can hear.'

Ruth sat subdued and quietly tense at the beginning of the journey back to Aireton Hall. Soon after the coach started, she asked Mark how his mother and sister felt about their marriage.

'I don't really mind how they feel. But, in fact, they are very pleased now.'

'What do they think about my coming back here?' she asked anxiously.

'Stop worrying, dearest. They are both looking forward to seeing you and little John.'

At the sound of his name, their son seized his father's ear to attract attention. He was only pacified when his father started to talk to him again, pointing out the trees, cattle, and fields they were passing. Two or three minutes passed before Ruth asked, 'Will your mother and sister stay at the Hall?'

Mark laughed. He transferred John to Ruth's lap. Then he placed his arm around his wife's right shoulder and took her left hand in his. 'My mother is a clever woman.' He kissed Ruth lightly on the forehead above her left eye. 'Almost as clever as you. She said you would decide if they stayed at Aireton Hall. My mother knows I would always take your advice and never take a decision which might distress you. She told me you were the mistress there now.'

'Oh, Mark. I know why your mother used to resent me so much. It's not just that I fell in love with you,' Ruth smiled up at her husband, 'without her sanction. It's that she'd been forced out of her house for eight years to live in that steward's lodge.

And I was a trespasser to her. A representative of a regime which had expelled her from her home. I am sure that's why Master Foster was never more than polite to me.'

'Don't take it all so seriously, sweetheart. That's all in the past now. You're my wife now.'

'Yes, Mark. But I could never drive Elizabeth and your mother from their home. Not twice in their lifetime.'

John became restive at this point and had to be comforted by his mother. Mark took his arm from Ruth's shoulder and released her left hand.

'That's the trouble with being a family man,' he said. 'Just when I wanted to be romantic, too.'

Ruth laughed for the first time since the start of the journey.

'Don't be so impatient, darling. We've got our whole life before us.'

'That's not what you were saying an hour ago.'

'Mark! If you say things like that in front of your mother, you'll have me blushing.'

They pressed their foreheads together and chuckled, much to the puzzlement of their young son.

* * * * *

When the coach approached the entrance of the grounds of Aireton Hall, Mark saw a horse and rider on the driveway. The rider turned and rode off at a hard gallop as the coach turned into the entrance and Mark recognised him as Martin, the young groom he had spoken to earlier. The coachman slowed his horse down as soon as he saw the groom gallop away. It was obviously arranged to allow time for everyone to turn out to greet him. Both Mark and Ruth fell silent as they entered the grounds and their mood communicated itself to John, who was still for the first time since they had left the Crawleys' farm. It seemed almost an age before the coach drew up at the end of the drive, in front of the steps leading to Aireton Hall. A groom ran forward to steady the horses and the coachman climbed down from his box to open the door so that Mark could leave.

Ruth picked John up and moved to the open door of the coach. She could see a group of about fifteen estate workers standing to the left of the steps with a similar number of house servants ranged on the right hand. Ruth glanced up to the terrace at the top of the steps and saw Digby Foster standing there. Her eye was caught by Lady Fairbrother standing at the front entrance of Aireton Hall but Elizabeth did not seem to be visible. Ruth felt like a general reviewing an army as she stood in the coach doorway. Mark took John from her, placed his son on the ground and held her hand as she came down the steps. Ruth sensed that the servants did not appear particularly friendly and instinctively took Mark's left arm. She was rather surprised when he made no attempt to walk up the steps towards the house. After waiting three or four seconds, Mark held up his right arm in a beckoning gesture and called out, 'Gather round, everybody.' The groups of servants moved towards them and John turned to clutch his mother's skirt, alarmed by the press of people coming forward. 'A few of you saw me yesterday. Some of you will remember my wife from the time she used to live here with the rest of Colonel Trent's family. We are both very happy to be back.' Mark paused for a few seconds. 'I know one or two of you may feel you were harshly treated by my brother. I can promise those days are behind us now.'

He took Ruth's hand from his arm and picked up John, holding his son shoulder-high in front of him. 'Take a good look, everybody. This boy is our son, John. He is the new master here. Half Cavalier, half Roundhead. My wife and I will hold this land in trust for him. We'll work alongside all of you. To make sure our son can have an inheritance he will be proud of. At peace with all our neighbours.' He handed his son back to Ruth who snuggled John into her arms.

'Now if you'll make way for us, my wife wants to take our son to meet his grandmother.'

There was a buzz of conversation among the servants. Several of the women gave admiring looks in John's direction. Ruth and her husband started to walk forward together, with Ruth carrying John. They had just reached the first step when someone in the crowd called out, 'Three cheers for Sir Mark. Hip, hip, hooray.'

There was a ragged, half-hearted cheer in reply. Mark and Ruth turned round and when the second 'Hip, hip, hooray,' was called, Mark noticed that Martin was the one leading the cheers. His face broke into a smile and the second cheer was firmer and more resonant. The third cheer was even louder and more prolonged.

Mark held his hand up. 'Thank you, everyone. But we really must take the new master to see his grandmother.' He turned and began walking up the steps. Just before Ruth turned to follow him she heard a few cries of 'Good luck, Lady Fairbrother,' from the crowd milling around.

She smiled, said, 'Thank you,' and turned to climb the steps after her husband. Mark stopped after he had climbed three or four steps to allow her to catch up.

'You were magnificent, darling,' she whispered. 'There's no substitute for sincerity.'

They reached the terrace at the top of the steps and Digby Foster stepped forward to greet them.

'Good day, Master Foster,' Ruth said.

'Good day, your ladyship,' he replied. 'Good to see you back in Aireton Hall.'

'It's good to be back. And with my son this time.'

'Perhaps after you have seen Lady Fairbrother, madam, we can discuss the domestic arrangements.' He shot a quick glance at Mark. 'And where your son will sleep tonight.'

'Of course, Digby. Time enough for that later.' Ruth smiled. 'I have kept John and his grandmother apart too long already.'

She put John on the ground and held him with her left hand, placing her right hand on Mark's arm. She looked towards the front entrance where Mark's mother was still standing thirty feet away. The three of them began walking towards her.

* * * * *

Mark's mother studied Ruth's appearance as they approached. Elizabeth was quite right in saying that she remembered her as a lovely girl. The adolescent's body had filled out, she had put on a couple of inches of height and was now a beautiful woman. It was no wonder that Mark was head over heels in love with her. But Ruth was not a woman of fashion, Lady Fairbrother thought. She had been born a tenant farmer's daughter and still looked like one. Ruth was wearing a plain, light grey bodice with a dark grey skirt. On top of this, she wore an open, black velvet jacket, with a dark blue scarf loosely folded over her head. Mark's mother's eye was caught by the flash of winter sunlight reflected from the plain gold ring on Ruth's left hand. She also saw that Ruth was wearing a slim silver bracelet on her right wrist but could see no further evidence of other jewelry. As the three of them came closer, she saw that Ruth was wearing a plain, black, bead necklace, which had been partly concealed by the black velvet jacket. Lady Fairbrother was beginning to feel a trifle overdressed with her own rich silk gown, large white lace cuffs and collar, the rings on her fingers, the pearl necklace around her neck, and the heavy jewelry on her wrists and in her hair. A momentary feeling of annoyance flashed through her mind because Ruth was not frivolous like other women. This was quickly replaced by a feeling of guilt as she watched the sturdy little boy walking slowly towards her. He was tall for his age and well proportioned. He looked so like young Mark in the picture of the family group painted all those years ago. Her mind went back to the day in the long gallery when she had really looked at Ruth for the first time. There's fine, sturdy stock there, she thought, which will stand the Fairbrothers in good stead for generations to come. She wondered if Mark's son would have looked so healthy if he had married Sophie Usher as she had planned. Perhaps there was too much in-breeding among the landed gentry, she thought. Ruth's fresh, young blood would invigorate the Fairbrother line far more than Sophie's blood would have done.

The closer the three of them approached her, the more diffident Mark appeared to become. When Ruth was about ten feet from the entrance she smiled at her mother-in-law and called out, 'Hello, Mother. Come and meet your grandson.'

Lady Fairbrother hurried forward and Ruth released her husband's arm and her son's hand. 'Welcome back, Ruth,' her mother-in-law said as the two women embraced and kissed each other on the cheek. 'Hullo, John,' she said, looking down at her grandson.

John clung to his mother's skirt, looking at his grandmother out of the corner of his eye. Ruth picked up her son and held him so that he and her mother-in-law were almost nose to nose. 'Meet your grandmother, John. She's daddy's mummy.'

'You my mummy.'

'I know that, darling. I will always be your mummy. But grandmother is daddy's mummy. You must love her like daddy does.'

John looked suspiciously from his mother to his grandmother and back again. 'He has seen so many new people in the past few days.' Ruth explained with a chuckle. 'Frances and her family. Anne, her husband Benjamin, and their two little girls. These relationships must seem confusing for someone who is not quite two.'

'May I hold him, Ruth?' her mother-in-law asked.

'Yes, of course, mother,' she replied and put her son in his grandmother's arms. For about five seconds grandson and grandmother solemnly looked at each other without moving. Suddenly, Lady Fairbrother clutched John towards her and covered his face with kisses. He started to cry.

'Let me take him,' Mark said. 'You'll have to give him a little time.' She made no reply except to hand her grandson over and to turn her face away. Lady Fairbrother's move had not been quite quick enough to prevent Ruth seeing that her eyes were moist. John was still clinging to his father and the crying had diminished to a muted sob. Ruth took her mother-in-law by the arm and started to walk her towards the entrance.

'Come inside, Mother,' she said. 'You'll get a chill, standing outside like this.'

They were followed by Mark carrying his son, with Digby Foster coming behind. As they went into the ante-room Digby called out, 'May I take your coat, your ladyship?'

'But I haven't,' Lady Fairbrother replied and then started to laugh, 'Of course, there are two of us now. We'll have to come to some arrangement with you, Master Foster.'

He looked a trifle embarrassed as he answered, 'Yes, my lady.' Digby Foster waited until Ruth had placed her velvet jacket in his arms and then said, 'Thank you, Lady Fairbrother.' He looked at Mark who was still holding John and asked, 'May I have your cloak, sir?'

'Yes, Digby,' Mark replied.

He stood John down and handed his cloak to the steward.

'Where's Elizabeth?' Ruth asked.

'In the drawing room,' her mother-in-law replied.

'Look after John for me, please, Mother. I must see her.'

She went running across to the drawing room door and opened it to see Mark's sister sitting by the fire.

'Elizabeth,' she cried as she ran towards her.

'Ruth,' the other girl called out as she stood up. The two of them embraced.

'Why are you trembling?' Ruth asked her. 'Why didn't you come outside to meet us?'

'Oh, Ruth, Ruth, please,' her sister-in-law answered in a half-sob. She pressed her head against Ruth's breasts.

'What's the matter? Tell me.' Ruth continued to comfort her and when there was no reply she said, 'You may be Mark's little sister but you're older than I am.'

'Oh, please, Ruth. Please let me stay.' Elizabeth begged.

John came through the door before Ruth could answer.

One hand was held by his grandmother and the other held by his father.

'Come across to meet Aunt Elizabeth, John.'

Lady Fairbrother helped her grandson and stood him about four feet from his aunt. John stared hard at Elizabeth for several seconds but neither of them made a move towards each other.

'You'll have to do better than that, Elizabeth. I want your help in bringing up our children. And I want mother to watch her grandchildren grow.'

Lady Fairbrother's eyes slid quickly over Ruth's stomach.

'Children?' she asked enquiringly.

'Yes, Mother. I am with child.'

The two women put their arms around each other's shoulders. Her mother-in-law's cheek was pressed against her own. After five seconds or so Ruth became aware that her face was wet from Lady Fairbrother's tears. She made no attempt to disturb her. 'If you have a girl,' her mother-in-law said in a soft, gentle voice, 'I hope my granddaughter will be like you, Ruth. Welcome home, daughter. Welcome home.' Lady Fairbrother relinquished her hold at last, reached for a handkerchief and blew her nose vigourously. A brief time later Elizabeth realised the full significance of her mother's remark. She came across and put her arm around Ruth's waist.

'Does that mean we're sisters? Really sisters? Like you and Claire? Sisters at last?' she said.

Ruth put her arm around Elizabeth's shoulder, kissed her on the forehead, looked down at her eager face and replied, 'Yes, Elizabeth. Like me and Claire.'

'Sorry to break up this happy reunion,' Mark said ironically, although he was secretly pleased at the turn of events.

'Did you know about this, Mark? About Ruth, I mean?' his mother asked.

'Yes, Mother. But we thought it best if she told you herself. Can you and Elizabeth look after John? I want to take Ruth up to the long gallery for two or three minutes.'

'Of course. We'll be delighted to take care of your son.'

Lady Fairbrother smiled first at her son and then at her daughter-in-law. 'You two don't have to hurry back.' She held her arms out wide and John slowly advanced towards her.

'Sorry, big sister,' Ruth said, lifting her arm from Elizabeth's shoulder. 'I have to go now.'

She and her husband looked round when they reached the door to see John still regarding his grandmother suspiciously.

'Come on,' Mark said, taking his wife's hand and pulling her outside towards the stairs, 'if we stop now, he'll never let us go.'

Memories came flooding back to them as they went upstairs and through the door into the long gallery. So much had happened since that day eight and a half years ago when Mark had handed Ruth the posy of lily of the valley flowers and they had been at a loss to know what to say to each other. Halfway down the gallery they stopped in front of the painting of Adam and Eve which Mark's father had brought back from Europe.

'Remember how embarrassed I felt,' Mark said, 'the last time I was here with you? The day before I left for Sweden.'

Ruth felt suddenly shy in front of her husband. When she had looked at the painting previously she had been a young girl, who had not known a man. Now she was a woman with the man she loved standing beside her.

'I was embarrassed because I'd never seen a naked woman,' Mark continued. 'And didn't until I'd married you.'

'Let's hope the two of us can make your dream come true, darling.'

Mark moved away slowly and the two of them walked towards the room which used to be Colonel Trent's office. He opened the door and stood back to allow his wife to enter the room first. As Ruth looked round she saw that the furniture was virtually unchanged from her foster-father's time. It was obvious that the room had been swept and the furniture dusted from time to time but it did not appear to have been used recently. Mark moved round behind Colonel Trent's writing cabinet and grinned at her.

'I remember this room well, sweetheart,' he said.

His expression became more serious as he bent his head forward and removed the shoulder belt to which his sword was attached.

'This is the hook on which Colonel Trent used to hang his sword,' he continued. 'I'm a farmer now. This is where I'm going to hang up my sword. For good. Let's hope it won't be needed again in our lifetimes or in our children's lifetimes.'

'I love you, dearest,' Ruth said. She ran forward, put her arms around his waist and kissed him.